Variations on the Canon

Eastman Studies in Music

Ralph P. Locke, Senior Editor
Eastman School of Music

Additional Titles in Music Criticism

A complete list of titles in the Eastman studies in Music Series,
in order of publication, may be found at the end of this book.

Variations on the Canon

*Essays on Music from Bach to Boulez
in Honor of Charles Rosen on
His Eightieth Birthday*

EDITED BY ROBERT CURRY,
DAVID GABLE, AND ROBERT L. MARSHALL

UNIVERSITY OF ROCHESTER PRESS

First published 2008

University of Rochester Press
668 Mt. Hope Avenue, Rochester, NY 14620, USA
www.urpress.com
and Boydell & Brewer Limited
PO Box 9, Woodbridge, Suffolk IP12 3DF, UK
www.boydellandbrewer.com

ISBN-13: 978-1-58046-285-3
ISBN-10: 1-58046-285-8

ISSN: 1071-9989

Library of Congress Cataloging-in-Publication Data

Variations on the canon : essays on music from Bach to Boulez in honor
of Charles Rosen on his eightieth birthday / edited by Robert Curry,
David Gable, and Robert L. Marshall.
    p. cm. — (Eastman studies in music, ISSN 1071–9989 ; v. 58)
  Includes bibliographical references, discography, and index.
  ISBN 978-1-58046-285-3 (hardcover : alk. paper) 1. Music—History
and criticism. 2. Rosen, Charles, 1927– I. Curry, Robert, 1952 Sept.
26– II. Gable, David, 1955– III. Marshall, Robert Lewis.
  ML55.R636V37 2008
  780.9—dc22
                            2008014153

A catalogue record for this title is available from the British Library.

This publication is printed on acid-free paper.
Printed in the United States of America.

Contents

Three Tributes

Appendices

Acknowledgments

The editors wish to express their appreciation to the following individuals and institutions for their interest, advice, and support. Early on, Professor Ralph Locke of the Eastman School of Music and senior editor of the series Eastman Studies in Music expressed his enthusiasm for this project, and, as it evolved, demonstrated his energetic advocacy for it. In particular, he was altogether supportive of our conception of the volume as an undisguised offering of tribute—in a word, a *Festschrift*—to one of the profoundest musical spirits of our time. Professor Locke was also sympathetic to our wish to concentrate the contributions on the central repertory of the Western tradition of the past three hundred years, the repertory that has always been the focus of Rosen's career as a concert pianist, writer, and critic. We have also benefited substantially from the helpful suggestions of Suzanne Guiod, editorial director of the University of Rochester Press, of Katie Hurley, the Press's managing editor, and of Tracey Engel, the production editor.

Henri Zerner, Professor of the History of Art and Architecture at Harvard University, a longtime friend and collaborator of Charles Rosen's, offered wise counsel on the diplomatic way of breaking the news of this little conspiracy to the honoree.

The accuracy, efficiency, and the resourcefulness of Matthew Cron, the musical typographer for this volume, in preparing—under enormous pressure of time—musical examples of often staggering complexity, have been nothing short of breathtaking. His achievement contributes mightily to the attractiveness, and the value, of the book.

The challenge of preparing the discography and bibliography of Charles Rosen's prodigious output of recordings and writings required turning repeatedly for advice and information to a number of his admirers, whose deep knowledge of the arcana of "Roseniana" proved invaluable: his former students Kevin Byrnes, Robert Hatten, and Tina Muxfeldt, along with Donald Manildi, of the International Piano Archive at Maryland (IPAM), and Maynard Solomon.

The following institutions have generously granted permission to reproduce materials from their collections: the Wienbibliothek im Rathaus, Vienna (an excerpt from the autograph score of Haydn's Piano Sonata in E-flat Major, Hob. XVI:49); the National Széchényi Library, Budapest (an excerpt from the autograph score of Haydn's String Quartet in G Major, Op. 77, no. 1, Hob. III:81);

the Lila Acheson Wallace Library of the Juilliard School, New York City, for kind permission to reproduce two complete pages from the autograph score of Beethoven's four-hand version of the *Grosse Fuge*, Op. 134; and the Arnold Schönberg Center, Vienna, Lawrence Schoenberg, and Belmont Music Publishers for permission to reproduce two autograph sketches by Arnold Schoenberg related to the March from the Serenade, Op. 24, and an excerpt from the published score of *Pierrot lunaire.*

We are also grateful to G. Henle Publishers, Munich, for permission to reproduce a page from the critical edition (*JHW*) of Haydn's String Quartet in F Minor, Op. 20, no. 5, Hob. III:35; to Breitkopf & Härtel, Wiesbaden, for their kind permission to include material from Beethoven's *Vestas Feuer*, published in *Beethoven Supplemente zur Gesamtausgabe*, XIII; to Universal-Edition, London, for permission to publish an excerpt from the score of Karlheinz Stockhausen's *Punkte*; and Edition Wilhelm Hansen, AS, Copenhagen, for allowing us to publish excerpts from Arnold Schoenberg's Serenade, Op. 24.

Finally, we wish to express our gratitude to Kevin and Susan Byrnes; to Clark Atlanta University, Atlanta, Georgia; and to the University of California, Los Angeles, for their generous support of this enterprise.

Robert Curry
David Gable
Robert L. Marshall

Introduction

Possessing "une culture vraiment intimidante," as Pierre Boulez remarks in a tribute included in this volume, the pianist and man of letters Charles Rosen is perhaps the single most influential writer on music of the past half century. Rosen's repertoire ranges from Bach to Boulez, and his immersion in this repertoire as a pianist informs his writing, contributing to its unique strengths. Rosen's abiding concerns include the definition of style and the nature of canon formation. He has written widely admired books on the Classical style, sonata form, Beethoven's piano sonatas, the Romantic generation, Romanticism and realism in nineteenth-century painting, and Schoenberg—as well as contributing a steady stream of influential essays on art, music, poetry, and criticism to the *New York Review of Books*.

Inspired in its liveliness and variety of critical approaches by Charles Rosen's work, the present volume features a selection from the best of recent research on canonical composers by some of the world's most eminent musical scholars. Contributors address such issues as style and compositional technique, genre, influence and modeling, and reception history; develop insights afforded by close examination of compositional sketches or literary *Nachlass*; and consider what language and metaphors might most meaningfully convey insights into music. However diverse their modes of inquiry, the contributors are animated by a desire to shed new light on the works of those composers posterity has deemed canonical.

Four contributors address aspects of fugal technique. Responding to suggestive remarks from Rosen on the expressive power inherent in Bach's use of various contrapuntal devices, Joseph Kerman detects an ambivalence toward the fugal project in some of Bach's late fugues, drawing examples from the second book of the *Well-Tempered Clavier* and the *Art of Fugue*. As in Rosen's discussions of the piano repertory, David Schulenberg's contribution marries observations about fingering in Bach's music to form, demonstrating how Bach's musical ideas derive from technical ones, showing how rudimentary keyboard figurations become articulatory devices in some of Bach's fugues. Exploring an observation of Rosen's, Richard Kramer delves into the deeper psychologies that lie behind Mozart's recourse to fugal technique at a remarkable juncture in the C-Major Quintet, K. 515. Robert Winter discusses the recently discovered autograph of Beethoven's four-hand piano arrangement of the *Grosse Fuge*.

Three contributors explore music for the piano, Robert Marshall examining the effect of piano sonority on large-scale structure in the piano sonatas of Beethoven's early and middle periods. Taking as his point of departure Rosen's performance of Chopin's Nocturne, Op. 37, no. 2, Jeffrey Kallberg examines the *scherzando* nocturne, explaining both why this subgenre was so short lived and its relationship to the later nocturnes. Robert Morgan explores the unusual "modular" form characteristic of certain of Chopin's piano works, forms that reveal something about the changing state of tonality at the time.

Taking their cues from Rosen, Julian Rushton and William Kinderman examine the role played by modeling—in Schubert's C-Minor *Quartettsatz* and Beethoven's early Piano Quintet, Op. 16, respectively. László Somfai reveals the extent to which Haydn's style has been misunderstood as a result of our imperfect grasp of the idiosyncratic expression and phrasing marks characteristic of Haydn's autographs. Lewis Lockwood and Philip Gossett examine unfinished or unrealized operas by Beethoven and Verdi respectively, shedding light on the evolution of their working methods in conveying a sense of what might have been.

Rosen's interest in the modernist traditions is reflected in the work of two contributors. Walter Frisch offers a critical reappraisal of Schoenberg's Serenade, Op. 24, in the same vein as Rosen's considerations of the role played by Romantic irony in nineteenth-century German music, examining the layers of cultural and musical meaning in a work more often cited as a historical milestone than appreciated for its multifaceted, often surprisingly playful qualities. Taking a cue from Rosen's insights into Boulez's conceptions of musical space, David Gable places the novel use of time and space characteristic of Boulez and Stockhausen within the context of French modernist culture in general as exemplified by impressionist painting, with its emphasis on the momentary impression.

The remaining contributors focus on criticism, James Webster demonstrating the extent to which Rosen's conception of Haydn is founded on "absolute-musical" principles, shedding light on Rosen's "modernist" approach to style in general. Responding to Rosen's essay on Adorno, Leo Treitler explores Adorno's language and rhetoric, underscoring Rosen's perception that Adorno's admirers tend to extol the worst features of his work, defending his sometimes breathtaking music criticism. In Rosen's case, *le style, c'est l'homme,* and Scott Burnham offers an exegesis of Rosen's style, noting the marriage of style and substance characteristic of Rosen's writing. Finally, Rosen himself offers a meditation on criticism and its language by way of a critique of Michel Montaigne.

Eloquent testimony to Rosen, the musician, is provided by brief tributes from Pierre Boulez, Elliott Carter, and Sir Charles Mackerras.

Part One

Johann Sebastian Bach

Chapter One

Fugue and Its Discontents

Joseph Kerman

Charles tells this story, I think: as Rossini and Meyerbeer are watching the cortège go by at Halévy's funeral, with Meyerbeer's funeral march, Rossini says sadly, "How much better if you had died and Halévy had written the funeral march." Rather than another analysis of another Bach fugue by the present writer, the world would be better off with a reprint of Charles Rosen's 1997 review of *Bach and Patterns of Invention* by Laurence Dreyfus.[1] This long review does more than set down and acknowledge Dreyfus's accomplishment in a remarkably comprehensive way, given the space that would have been available. It is also one of those reviews in which the writer takes the opportunity to move on from the book at hand and develop serious ideas of his own. Rosen makes points in the piece that I haven't seen made anywhere else, or made better. I quote liberally in reference to just one such point:

> The expressive power of Bach's music has several sources. . . . Most important of all, perhaps, is his understanding of emotional possibilities inherent in counterpoint—that is, in the way one voice can imitate another, in the dramatic effects that can be drawn from a melody inverted or played against itself, and also from the subtle ways the harmonic implications of a motif can be radically altered when it is played with another motif of different character.

Picking up on this later in his review, Rosen writes that in Bach's time

> Bach's extraordinary craft had been generally recognized internationally by professionals: the expressive force of this craft had been perceived only dimly. The virtuosity of his constructions literally obscured their affective power. . . . Bach had transformed and magnified the latent expressive capacities of the most esoteric achievements of the ancient contrapuntal art. . . .

But for later generations,

> Recognitions of his achievement now became official. It was, however, only the educational keyboard works of the final three decades of his life that were the basis at first for

the new evaluation. At last the extraordinary beauty of these works was perceived as well as the tremendous skill. . . . In this sense it is not the Romantic movement that salvaged the work of Bach, but his work that helped form Romantic aesthetics, as musicians who wanted to assert the independent dignity, and justify the complexity, of their art gradually realized through Europe that his work could be a model and an inspiration.

Thinking only of the educational keyboard works of a single decade of Bach's life—the last, from around 1740—one can imagine the effect on Mozart, Beethoven, Brahms, Bartók and Shostakovich of the fugues in D major and B major, F-sharp minor and B-flat minor and so many others from Book 2 of *The Well-Tempered Clavier*. One thinks of the serene and spirited *contrapuncti* of *The Art of Fugue*.

And yet: the same group of late Bach fugues includes certain prominent works that cannot be called serene or spirited, or "expressive" in any of the ways Charles Rosen means in his review of *Bach and the Patterns of Invention*. They convey another message—not of craft transformed into expressive power but of a reaction against the entire project. These are reflexive, ambivalent pieces, fugues about fugality, fugues about the fragility of fugality. They are all different, but however different, each of them registers to my ear a moment of discontent, when the composer drew back if not from fugue itself, from the comprehensive program he had established to house twenty-four and fourteen fugues (as well as preludes and canons). We have been comfortable for some time with Bach the progressive; perhaps it's time to get to know Bach the postmodernist, Bach in his postmodern moods.

Contrapunctus 11 from *The Art of Fugue* is one of the most famous, most daunting, and longest of Bach's keyboard fugues. Flowing eighth-note motion with a strong chromatic cast enters early on and soon dominates the surface. Rosen never lets us forget that educational fugues are always keyboard fugues, and here the tactile imperatives of the performer—the virtuoso—play out against composerly calculations. Carolyn Abbate's terms *gnostic* and *drastic* are already becoming overused in discussions of musicology, but they light up something important about this music: you can analyze the triple-counterpoint constructions, approve or disapprove of the melodic inversions, calibrate the enhancements Contrapunctus 11 makes over Contrapunctus 8, and weigh the cultural significance of the reception as long as you please, but listen to this fugue or (try to) play it, and manic keyboard energy overcomes the counterpoint. The flowing motion takes on a life of its own, a tsunami or an outpouring of volcanic agglomerate far outpacing its origins within a triple-counterpoint "invention," as Dreyfus would call it. While of course the counterpoint is there—for the gnostic or the knowing—in experiential, drastic terms the continuous chromatic eighth-note motion hypnotizes and lays waste. This piece was surely the model for the *terribilità* of Beethoven's *Grosse Fuge*. Alternatively, Contrapunctus 11 was already Bach's *Grosse Fuge*.

Of course Contrapunctus 11 does not stand alone but as one element in a unique, endlessly discussed and unfathomable cycle. Originally it capped the cycle, the last word on the art of fugue and at the same time its devastation. Later Bach conceived of another, less devastating conclusion and imposed a new order on the fugues. By separating Contrapunctus 11 from Contrapunctus 8, the new order has the effect of isolating it, leaving it with a stronger claim to individual integrity—like the *Grosse Fuge*, the Andante cantabile of Tchaikovsky's Quartet in D Major, Op. 11, and other such sturdy torsos. In any case, Bach here exploits the tension between virtuosity and "the most esoteric achievements of the ancient contrapuntal art" in a way that Burke would soon be calling sublime. We can hear a wonderful, lingering echo of brilliant early works such as the Prelude and Fugue in A Minor for Organ, BWV 543, where the counterpoint literally stops before the end, giving way to scales and passagework.

Within the cycle, Contrapunctus 11 offers an overheated answer to Contrapunctus 8 (an extreme if not atypical instance of Bachian hubris). A somewhat similar model and answer find place within a single composition, the Fugue in A-flat Major from Book 2 of *The Well-Tempered Clavier*. As is well known, Bach began by laying out with next to no alteration an innocuous early Fughetta in F Major, BWV 901/2. He then transposed it, elided the final cadence, and kept going with more entries and episodes—piling up flats and double flats and extra voices, more than doubling its length, and involving a brilliant cadenza on the Neapolitan prior to a final transfixed entry of the original subject-countersubject pair. In a striking analysis of this work, the semiotician Raymond Monelle sets up a dialogue between its two halves according to codes of signification employed more or less routinely when the piece begins.[2] He sees the diatonic subject referring to "the world of the trio sonata, connected with courts and drawing rooms, with rationalism and enlightenment, with the spurious stability of hierarchic society, with sophisticated badinage," while the countersubject is chromatic and ecclesiastical, the familiar topos of lament. In the second half of the piece, the tropes are spelled out and made more emphatic, until they are contrasted with increasingly disruptive expressive force; in the last bars the bland fugue subject is "put in thrall to a terrific chromatic system of immense grandeur and pathos."

Can we not also see the second half of the piece as an exposure of the puniness of the original invention? Late Bach performs an ungenerous critique of early Bach. Monelle wants us to see it as a deconstruction. The disruption cuts hard across the aesthetic of fugue.

Another familiar case of reworking a model—in a very different way—is the Fugue in C-sharp Major from *The Well-Tempered Clavier*, Book 2. David Ledbetter traces its evolution in detail from an early Fughetta in C Major, BWV 872a, by way of an interim version, in his recent comprehensive book on the *Well-Tempered*.[3] Whether you know the model or not, what catches attention at once about the final fugue is the slight subject—which I take to be eight notes long—

and the way even this subject disintegrates before our very ears. The last full subject entry comes (in inversion) before the midpoint (mm. 15–16). Not for this fugue the grand final entry of the Fugue in A Flat. Indeed, the model fughetta itself loses the subject before its midpoint; all it retains is the *incipit* G B G | C. In the *Well-Tempered* fugue, too, after Bach has *reinforced* the subject in the first part of the little piece he *curtails* it (in effect, drops it) in the second half, supplying instead a medley of four-note incipits—G♯ B♯ G♯ | C♯ *recto*, inverted, transposed, in augmentation and in diminution. If in the Fugue in A Flat he turned his back on an early fugue contemptuously, he does so here with good humor. Much more genially than in Contrapunctus 11, again keyboard virtuosity takes over:

> The pratfall near the end of the work, its most hyperbolical gesture, brings total negations of counterpoint and fugue (mm. 31–32). Scales rush down while counterpoint (the last appearance of the *incipit* figure) scrambles to safety on the dominant. It is as close as Bach ever came to a glissando. . . . The last bars with their octave C♯s luxuriate in finger physicality.[4]

The Fugue in F-sharp Major from Book 2 of *The Well-Tempered Clavier* does not figure on most people's list of favorite Bach fugues, and the reason may be, again, its ambivalence regarding the genre, expressed less flamboyantly than in the works discussed above, but expressed in many ways:

- *The incipit.* This fugue begins by repeating—by hiccupping—the cadence of its prelude, trilled E♯ to F♯, 7 to 1, in the treble voice. This is a curious effect, described as "witty and felicitous" by David Ledbetter;[5] or maybe petulant, as though the composer were unwilling to keep going after finishing the prelude; or maybe contemptuous, saying that for this composer anything at all, no matter how trivial, can function as a fugue subject (see example 1.1).
- *Cadences.* After its *incipit,* which is a melodic cadence, the paradoxical subject serves as a kind of wry compensation for the absence of any full cadences—any cadence with bass support—throughout the entire composition, eighty-four measures in all. The cadences come mostly after four-measure phrases (again, Ledbetter comments on this). I am reminded of the C-Minor Fugue of Book 1, though that supposedly paradigmatic work does have one central cadence, on the dominant. The effect in the F-sharp Major Fugue is not only restless but somehow disquieting, especially in view of the high complexity of some of the material to come.
- *The subject.* Beginning on the leading tone, the subject begins away from the traditional tonic or dominant pitch, an anomaly emphasized by the trill. Such anomalies are rare in Bach. The trill is echoed by the countersubject (m. 7). In later subject entries, the trill is occasionally spelled out

Example 1.1. J. S. Bach, Prelude and Fugue in F-sharp Major, BWV 882. Prelude, mm. 72–75; fugue, mm. 1–15.

in a rather odd, slowed-down way, as at measures 20 and 70; the latter entry, where the texture thins to allow the left hand to imitate the slowed-down spelling in the right hand (m. 72), is even odder. Tovey writes that the bass in measure 70 "captures the initial trill of the subject above it and mocks its written-out slower version (m. 72) before settling down to the culmination of its own devices."[6]

In measures 1–2 the subject moves by a quasi-sequence to the flat seventh degree—a contradiction of the anomaly, or a confirmation? The music tilts to the subdominant. Something like dominant modulation is needed to get the subject back to the tonic, another feature that contributes to this fugue's restlessness throughout. The flat seventh degree belongs to the minor mode—if not the Mixolyian—not the major, and in fact almost the whole of the subject can be construed in the minor (except for the end on major 3). Compare measures 41–45, where what Laurence Dreyfus is pleased to call MODESWITCH happens (drawing a gentle rebuke from Rosen) and the subject appears in D-sharp minor.

- *The main countersubject.* I do not know another Bach fugue that builds its countersubject so elaborately from the material of its subject: a counter-intuitive if virtuosic idea. Example 1.1 shows the subject analyzed into motifs and other fragments: motifs a, d, and e reappear in the countersubject; by treating both motifs a and e sequentially, Bach encourages us to hear them as retrogrades. Fragment c, the passage in running eighth notes, turns up in the first episode, both *recto* and in inversion, and b will put in an appearance in due time. Again, by trilling B♯ in measure 7 Bach seems to relate the tail of the countersubject, A♯ B♯ C♯ (marked α), to the *incipit* of the subject, E♯ F♯ (a). Figure α grows in importance after it returns as the tenor voice at the beginning of the first episode (mm. 12–14).[7]

Over the course of this fugue the subject begins on the following keys:

	I	V	I	I	V	I	vi	IV	I	V	I
Measures	1	5	9	21	33	37	41	53	65	71	77

A second countersubject is introduced for the exposition's third entry (mm. 8–12); it dissipates before reappearing to articulate the big returns to the tonic starting at measures 64–65. The melodic and rhythmic profile of this new countersubject may be distinct enough to serve this function, given some help from the performer.

- *Two pairs of episodes.* Dreyfus, Tovey, and others have observed that when Bach devises an invention in three-part invertible counterpoint, he seldom uses all six possible inversions. Episode 1 of this fugue with its recurrence as episode 3 furnishes an exception (mm. 12–20, 44–50). The very rich—"very mature," says Roger Bullivant[8]—counterpoint Soprano Tenor Bass (mm. 13–14, 19–20) inverts as Soprano Bass Tenor (49–50), T S B (51–52), T B S (15–16, 45–46), B S T (17–18), and B T S (47–48).

Though a few small adjustments are needed, this is certainly something of a *tour de force*. But if Tovey admired it, one would never guess from his dry, almost sour commentary: "Episode 1 and Episode 3 together exhaust the six permutations of the triple counterpoint." Tovey may have been put off by the extreme imbalance between this pair of episodes and the other pair, episodes 2 and 4 (mm. 24–33, 56–64), where Bach employs a facile trio style that is not only simple but simplistic. The sequential repetition of motifs d and e goes on for too long. In measures 79–84 a terser version of this episode, sequencing up instead of down, brings the fugue to a registral climax on high B just before the end; and by this time the maddening long line of four-measure phrases—seventeen in all—has at last been expanded to six measures. The final cadence, E♯-F♯, is not trilled.

• *A late countersubject.* Like some other items in Book 2 of *The Well-Tempered Clavier*, the Fugue in F-sharp Major makes oblique reference to its opposite number in Book 1. In both fugues, at some point after the subject and an original countersubject have been duly displayed, Bach introduces a new countersubject, providing the fugue with fresh energies. In the Book 1 fugue—included, by the way, in Charles Rosen's elegant anthology *Bach: The Fugue* in the Oxford Keyboard Classics series, 1975—this comes at a point soon after the opening exposition (m. 12). In the Book 2 fugue, it comes somewhat later—after six subject entries (m. 41, about halfway through the piece). This new countersubject appears three times; it ends with a canonic echo of yet another fragment of the subject, marked b in example 1.1.

There are no belated countersubjects of this sort in any of the other forty-eight fugues, unless I have missed something. (The procedure differs from that in double and triple fugues, where sections are clearly articulated.) In each F-sharp-major fugue, the new countersubject runs in continuous sixteenths or eighths—motion that has been anticipated in prior episodes—and covers a large interval, in Book 1 an octave and in Book 2 an eleventh. As counterpoint, the latter seems to be working too hard; the belated countersubject is performative, as Tovey must have meant to say when he spoke of it "settling down to the culmination of its own devices": a final twelve-measure rush of flowing eighth notes in the bass (with a couple of broken chords included for good measure.) The upper parts, he adds, "though full of life, must be carefully restrained from becoming hard or thin."[9] Still the piece ends *con brio*.

This is a lot of small print about a small piece of music. Bach's educational keyboard fugues were intended to be studied closely, as well as played with brio. The ever-present tension between gnostic and drastic may be creative, or it may be not. The reflexivity of the Book 2 F-sharp-major fugue *vis-à-vis* its prelude, the

Book 1 fugue, and fugue as genre; the anomalous subject and countersubject; the seamlessness, the restlessness, the ostentatious contrapuntal skill set against throwaway simplicity; the countersubject with the interval of an eleventh; and yes, the nagging gavotte rhythm in four-measure phrases: all this spells a kind of exasperation with fugue, at least to my ear. The artificial key of F-sharp major itself feels uncomfortable. The piece registers continuously the generic discontent that manifests itself occasionally in certain more forthright fugues, mentioned above, of the same period.

This is also a period in which Bach wrote untroubled fugues, his noblest. He also wrote brilliant, lighthearted, dancelike fugues—also untroubled, of course. For examples, turn back a little way in Book 2 to the Fugues in F Minor and F Major. The Fugue in F-sharp Major begins lightheartedly enough, but the subject spells trouble, and afterward the piece clams up (I have said nothing about its schematic structure) and seems less to enjoy its counterpoint than to harp on it. How different this is from the Fugue in F Major—and how different is the response of a critic such as Tovey, who grows positively ebullient with the latter fugue as opposed to being tight-lipped with the F-sharp Major. Predictably, my take on these pieces falls in line with Tovey's. To be sure, I haven't heard the Prelude and Fugue in F-sharp Major played by Charles.

Notes

1. "The Great Inventor," *New York Review of Books*, October 9, 1996; Laurence Dreyfus, *Bach and the Patterns of Invention* (Cambridge, MA: Harvard University Press, 1996).

2. Raymond Monelle, *The Sense of Music: Semiotic Essays* (Princeton: Princeton University Press, 2000), 197–206.

3. David Ledbetter, *Bach's Well-Tempered Clavier: The 48 Preludes and Fugues* (New Haven and London: Yale University Press, 2002), 249–51, 335–41. Ledbetter gives all the early versions, taken from the *Neue Bach-Ausgabe*, ser. V, vol. 6, 2, ed. Alfred Dürr (Kassel: Bärenreiter, 1995); see pp. 352, 358.

4. Joseph Kerman, "Salience and Serendipity," in *Remembering Oliver Strunk, Teacher and Scholar*, ed. Christina Huemer and Pierluigi Petrobelli (New York: Pendragon, 2005), 50.

5. Ledbetter, *Bach's Well-Tempered Clavier*, 292.

6. Donald Francis Tovey, "Commentary," in *J. S. Bach: The Well-Tempered Clavier*, ed. Richard Jones (London: Associated Board of the Royal Schools of Music, 1994), 2:179.

7. Any analysis must be subjective; Riemann, who is at his windiest discussing this fugue, derives the soprano figure at measures 14–15, in episode 1, from the end of the subject, a very gnostic derivation: Hugo Riemann, *Analysis of J. S. Bach's Wohltemperiertes Clavier (48 Preludes and Fugues)*, trans. J. S. Shedlock (London, Augener, 1890), 2: 177. Czaczkes sees the bass in the same bars as a retrograde of the subject *incipit*: Ludwig Czaczkes, *Analyse des Wohltemperierten Klaviers: Form und*

Aufbau der Fuge bei Bach (Vienna: Österreichischer Bundesverlag, 1965), 2: 139. What is more audible, I think, is the upward thrust of figure α in episodes 1 and 3 and also, in decorated form, in episodes 2 and 4.

8. Roger Bullivant, *Fugue* (London: Hutchinson, 1971), 106.

9. See note 6.

Chapter Two

Fugues, Form, and Fingering

Sonata Style in Bach's Preludes and Fugues

David Schulenberg

The conception of sonata form as expounded by Charles Rosen has proved enormously useful for understanding music of the later eighteenth and nineteenth centuries.[1] In this view, a sonata movement is a dramatization of fundamental tonal and motivic processes; to analyze sonata form is to uncover the expressive aspirations of a composer, even of an age. Neither a single formal structure nor a simple principle or device, Classical sonata form is central to the personal styles of Haydn, Mozart, and Beethoven. Hence it is almost a contradiction in terms to speak of the same form in music of other composers, particularly an earlier one such as Bach, whose preludes and fugues are in some ways the antithesis of a Classical sonata movement.

Still, many commentators have found elements of sonata form in Bach's music. Ten preludes in Book 2 of *The Well-Tempered Clavier* (*WTC*2) contain a central double bar; in some of these preludes the second half incorporates a distinct recapitulation section.[2] By the time Bach completed *WTC*2 around 1740, sonata form was being employed routinely by younger composers, including his son Carl Philipp Emanuel. But Sebastian's preludes differ from most contemporary sonata movements in their contrapuntal texture and their avoidance of verbatim recapitulation; his fugues bear even fewer outward resemblances to Classical sonata form, not least in their through-composed designs and elided phrasing. Yet even Bach's fugues may dramatize a tonal design—modulation away from and back to the tonic, articulated by thematic entries—in ways that anticipate Classical sonata movements. How substantial are those features shared with Classical sonata form, and what expressive aspirations might they embody?

Among the features *not* shared is a consistent division into exposition, development, and recapitulation sections, and the subdivision of the exposition and recapitulation into first and second thematic or tonal areas. Even the D-Major Prelude of *WTC*2 , the most sonatalike movement in the *WTC* , lacks a distinctly articulated "second theme." The passage after the double bar, although modulating more remotely than the outer divisions, is not so different from the latter that it could be called a development. Each of the three main divisions, as in countless sonata movements by Bach's younger contemporaries, differs from those of a Classical sonata movement by comprising, in essence, single opening and closing phrases that frame a series of modulating sequences. Yet the design is essentially bipartite, the first half moving to the dominant, the second being subdivided to produce an overall tonal plan (I–V–vi–I) corresponding to that of many Classical sonata movements. The final division opens with a strongly articulated return of opening material in the tonic, constituting the return (or "double return"). This final section restates much of the material of the first one, initially at its original (tonic) pitch level, then transposed from dominant to tonic.

These features of sonata form recur in innumerable lesser compositions by Bach's younger contemporaries, establishing formal symmetries that were no doubt pleasing in a rationalistic age that favored regular patterns—hence the use of rounded tonal designs and recapitulations, in pieces whose texture and material remain fairly homogeneous throughout. Classical sonata form, as Rosen has repeatedly shown, would retain the basic design but would substitute drama and continuous development for verbatim symmetry and homogeneity. Yet the D-Major Prelude of *WTC2* is already somewhat more dramatic and more "open" in its treatment of material than the typical sonata movement of the period. The return is prepared by a retransition passage that ends with a climactic scale descending through more than two octaves, from treble to bass. The return is far from literal; the original counterpoint is inverted (upper voices exchanged), and new counterpoint is added, starting in measure 43 (see example 2.1). Some matter returning

Example 2.1. J. S. Bach, Prelude in D Major, BWV 874/1, mm. 40–43.

later in the recapitulation is embellished melodically (from m. 52), reflecting the heightened level of energy that has prevailed since the retransition. These are perhaps small points, far from the "drama" of many a Classical work, yet they represent a divergence from the conventional sonata style of Bach's younger German contemporaries.[3]

A number of Bach's fugues, especially in *WTC1*, also follow an essentially bipartite design, with the center marked by a strongly articulated cadence to a foreign key (dominant or relative). Some of these fugues resemble less a sonata movement than a gigue, inasmuch as the second half opens by developing the subject through some new contrapuntal wrinkle, such as inversion or stretto.[4] Others, however, mimic sonata style in that the first division ends with a distinct closing phrase in the dominant that is eventually recapitulated in the tonic to end the piece.[5] One might think that the process of recapitulation would be antithetical to the through-composed nature of fugue, signifying either a failure of the imagination or a deliberate allusion to some other type of piece. Yet, outside the *WTC*, Bach's fugues frequently incorporate elements of da capo and ritornello form, pointing toward the Italian aria or concerto.[6] Within the *WTC*, Bach avoided the verbatim repetitions essential to these designs, no doubt deliberately. But large portions of certain fugues are nevertheless reprised, altered only by transposition or the exchange or addition of voices. For instance, in the C-sharp-Major Fugue of *WTC1*, most of the final section (mm. 42–53) is a recapitulation of the first (mm. 1–11).

Only two moments distinguish this particular recapitulation from the opening section: the insertion of half a measure (m. 48a) allows the latter half of the recapitulation to remain in the tonic, instead of modulating to the dominant; and a brief coda replaces the simple cadence that closed the first section (mm. 53b ff.). The first and more crucial of these alterations is as inconspicuous as possible, avoiding the palpable rewriting that can make a Classical recapitulation as dramatic as any development section. In this the piece conforms to the symmetrical, even geometric ethos favored not only in sonata movements but in the ubiquitous da capo aria during the first half of the eighteenth century. Bach wrote many such arias, yet he also uniquely cultivated the so-called modified da capo form, in which the first A section ends in a foreign key (usually the dominant), necessitating the reworking of the material in the second A section. The resemblance of this scheme to sonata form has been duly noted.[7] But although the second A section must therefore constitute a sonata-style recapitulation, in most cases the rewriting involves little more than in the C-sharp-Major Fugue. The prevailing ethos remains one of symmetry rather than drama.[8]

Still, Bach's use of modified da capo form already in his Weimar cantatas (by 1714) suggests conscious, and somewhat unconventional, thinking about the design of a lengthy composition as it unfolds in time.[9] The same holds for Bach's frequent use of *Einbau*, also beginning at Weimar, in which the ritornello of an aria or chorus is subsequently combined contrapuntally with one or more new vocal lines. Sometimes an entire movement, or at least its A section, consists essentially of restatements of the ritornello, alone or combined with other music, sometimes transposed, sometimes interrupted by episodes for the soloist.[10]

Both *Einbau* and modified da capo form are characteristically inventive instances of what Joel Lester has called "parallel structure," the design of a movement in several more or less analogous sections.[11] Fundamental to the trajectory of any such movement is whether successive sections are similar in size and level of activity, or whether on the other hand they grow in length and seriousness or intensity. Bach's reworking of material in the final division of the D-Major Prelude is an example of such intensification; Lester refers to the process as "heightening activity." But within a sonata movement such as the D-Major Prelude of *WTC2*, such heightening is a divergence from sonata style as it had evolved by 1740 or so; the Fugue in C Sharp from *WTC1* actually comes closer to what was at the time the prevailing aesthetic of sonata form.

Only a few other preludes in *WTC2* resemble the D-major in this respect. The F-minor intensifies the return at measure 56b through new counterpoint, concluding with a surprisingly emphatic variation of the original closing phrase.[12] The Prelude in B Flat, the longest of the sonata-form preludes, perhaps does something similar. Yet not even the presence of a fermata, followed by a potentially cadenzalike passage near the end (mm. 76ff.), raises the level of tension or energy in the final section much above that of the rest of the piece; unless one takes a very quick tempo or applies some vociferous dynamics, the overall impression is likely to be one of serene, untroubled symmetry. One piece from outside *WTC2* is remarkably similar in some respects: the Fantasia in C Minor, BWV 906/1, another sonata movement with hand-crossing passages in each half.[13] The C-Minor Fantasia operates on a more frenetic level of energy throughout, but like the D-Major Prelude it singles out the return as a particularly dramatic moment, surpassing the prelude by providing a unique instance in Bach's work of a return prepared by *chromatic* scales in contrary motion (example 2.2).[14]

Example 2.2. J. S. Bach, Fantasia in C Minor, BWV 906/1, mm. 33–34.

The return would become a critical moment in Classical sonata form, yet its dramatization is rare in earlier examples.[15] Thus it is striking to find instances of dramatized returns not only in Bach's sonata-style preludes but also in his fugues. Hardly ever does Bach use the type of extended dominant prolongation that Classical composers, especially Beethoven, would employ for this purpose. Not that Bach was unaware of the underlying technique—a number of relatively early virtuoso works contain extended dominant preparations for entries of the subject, as in the big A-Minor Fugue, BWV 944.[16]

More often Bach uses other devices to mark the return. The drama is never as intense as in a Classical work, yet within the relatively homogeneous material of a Baroque piece the sudden use of a new type of figuration can be a significant event. One favorite device is a descending scale, or scalar figuration, used either in the passage immediately preceding the return, as in the D-Major Prelude, or in counterpoint to the subject after the latter has re-entered. A particularly effective example occurs in the early Fugue in B Flat on a subject by Reinken.[17] The piece comprises three large expository sections that alternate with two lengthy episodes (at mm. 42 and 68). The last episode ends with scales descending through three octaves, passing through all three voices and providing a sort of halo around the subject as it reenters in stretto (see example 2.3). Naturally this is not the first time the subject has returned in the tonic.[18] But the new scale figuration, plunging down from the highest note in the piece, marks measure 81 as a crucial moment, the equivalent of a sonata-form return.

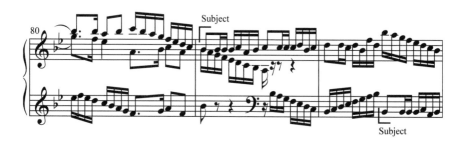

Example 2.3. J. S. Bach, Fugue in B-flat Major on a Subject by Reinken, BWV 954, mm. 80–82.

Comparable examples occur in the organ works. In the Fugue in G Minor, BWV 542/2, a scale of two and a half octaves serves as counterpoint against the subject at the opening of the final exposition (see example 2.4). This particular scale is perhaps not very impressive in context, for the piece has been permeated by idiomatic "zigzag" figuration since the initial statement of the subject.

Nevertheless, this is the only straightforward scale figuration in the piece; although it is confined to an inner voice its function to articulate the return seems clear. Much the same occurs in the five-part Fugue in C Minor, BWV 546/2. Here the last entry of the subject, in the tonic and in the pedals, is accompanied by a descending scalar figure that spans nearly two octaves in the tenor (mm. 140–41). The "Dorian" Fugue, BWV 538/2, Bach's most pervasive demonstration of stretto technique, goes somewhat further, concluding its final episode with scales in contrary motion (mm. 200–201).

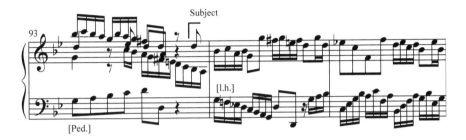

Example 2.4. J. S. Bach, Fugue in G Minor, BWV 542/2, mm. 93–95.

Scales may seem an obvious, if effective, sort of figuration to introduce at such points. But why scales, as opposed to some other type of figuration? We do not usually think of Bach as having been inspired musically by technical devices, as Chopin (or Schumann) was in his studies. Yet certain works, including the inventions and the duet movements from the Goldberg Variations, are clearly designed to exercise the fingers in particular patterns. Scales as such appear rarely—but the D-major organ *Praeludium*, BWV 532, opens with an unaccompanied scale in the pedals, perhaps a jab at those whose pedal technique was limited to playing long notes or zigzag passagework. And the little prelude known as the *Applicatio*, probably meant for the clavichord, is Bach's contribution to the repertoire of pedagogic pieces used for instruction in scale playing.[19]

A number of pieces by earlier composers, including works by the English virginalists, served the same purpose.[20] But the eighteenth century saw more systematic thinking about keyboard technique, especially scales, as is evident in C. P. E. Bach's prescriptions for fingerings in scales in all the major and minor keys. Emanuel Bach credited his father with having developed modern fingering at a time when many still played without using the thumb.[21] Although an exaggeration, this points to serious thought about technique, no less than about form; someone had to spend time at the keyboard working out all those fingerings, perhaps also practicing them and teaching them to pupils. It is unlikely that scales in Bach's keyboard works would have borne the concrete connotations that they might carry in vocal music or in older keyboard music.[22] But one reason for the use of scales at climactic moments might have been that they were becoming a critical element in keyboard technique; perhaps, too, they were beginning to acquire their modern popular significance as icons of capable musicianship, if not virtuosity.

The Well-Tempered Clavier is relatively restrained in style, perhaps because it was not intended for public performance. Except in the D-Major Prelude of *WTC2*, it is hard to find scales dramatizing returns, as in the C-Minor Fantasia or the Reinken Fugue in B Flat. But scales do appear as subtle climaxes elsewhere. For instance, in the D-Major Fugue of *WTC2*, the subject ends with a little descending figure; in the episodes this becomes a five-note descending scale fragment (m. 7), expanding into a two-octave descending scale in the bass as the culmination of a series of increasingly lively stretto passages (mm. 38–40). Something comparable occurs in the E-Major Fugue of *WTC2*, which concludes by extending a similar motive from the subject into a complete descending scale (in the process alluding to several chorale melodies).

But these examples have nothing to do with the Classical sonata technique of dramatizing a crucial formal articulation, which in general reflects an aesthetic fundamentally different from Bach's. If Bach sometimes does happen on devices that we associate with the Viennese Classical style, this merely indicates the breadth of his imagination, which was not limited to the conventions of the day. Haydn, Mozart, and Beethoven would, by the same token, be capable of rediscovering things that Bach had used, without necessarily copying from him. In the fugal finale of Beethoven's "Hammerklavier" Sonata, the six-note descending motive in the subject is eventually extended to more than an octave, in counterpoint that accompanies the last, strettolike return of the subject (example 2.5).

The idea culminates in a grand scale covering more than three octaves, leading into the work's closing phrase (mm. 386–88).[23] Such scales need not have been imitations of example 2.3 or 2.4 above, if only because they are a natural development of each movement's own motivic processes. Yet in each case the scales serve much the same function, to dramatize a critical formal articulation. This technique, although part of the Classical style, is hardly unique to it. In recognizing the presence of sonata-style drama in Bach, as well as in Beethoven, one is grateful for the way it has been so eloquently brought to our attention in the writings of Charles Rosen.

Example 2.5. Beethoven, Sonata in B-flat Major (*Hammerklavier*), Op. 106, mvt. 4, mm. 349–56.

Notes

1. See Charles Rosen, *Sonata Forms*, rev. ed. (New York: Norton, 1988), and Rosen, *The Classical Style*, expanded ed. (New York: Norton, 1997).

2. As observed by Robert L. Marshall, *The Music of Johann Sebastian Bach: The Sources, the Style, the Significance* (New York: Schirmer Books, 1989), 200. Central double bars occur in the preludes in C minor, D major, D-sharp minor, E major, E minor, F minor, G major, G-sharp minor, A minor, and B-flat major of *WTC2* (also in the Prelude in B minor of *WTC1*). In some preludes (e.g., those in C minor, E major, and A minor) the two halves are roughly equal in length, and there is no clear formal subdivision after the double bar to mark the beginning of a recapitulatory section. But the same is true of Classical movements that can be recognized as sonata forms.

3. At least as realized in the works of younger composers in northern Germany, such as Johann Joachim Quantz and C. P. E. Bach.

4. Inversion: Fugue in B Major; stretto: Fugue in C Major (both in *WTC1*).

5. As in the two fugues in B-flat major (*WTC1* and *WTC2*).

6. As in the large virtuoso fugues for solo violin and lute, the "Wedge" organ fugue, and the fugal preludes of the English Suites.

7. E.g., by Malcolm Boyd, *Bach*, 3rd ed. (Oxford: Oxford University Press, 2003), 144. Boyd commented that "the relevance of the Bachian modified da capo aria to the emerging sonata form is something still requiring investigation."

8. As in the popular aria "Ey! wie schmeckt der Coffee süße" from the "Coffee" Cantata, where the second A section, although a bit more extended than the first, does little to articulate its most emphatic new passage: an underlining of the word *süße* by means of a trill, a cross-relation, and a diminished chord (m. 137). Still, this "painful" treatment of the word "sweet" trumps a dissonant fermata on the same word that occurs earlier in both A sections; a Baroque metaphor for desire, it is consistent with the aria's satirical equation of caffeine craving with erotic longing.

9. Stephen A. Crist, "Aria Forms in the Vocal Works of J. S. Bach, 1714–24" (PhD diss., Brandeis University, 1988), 192, shows that modified da capo form became more common in Bach's vocal works of the Leipzig period (1723 and later).

10. As in the aria "Ein Fürst ist seines Landes Pan" from the "Hunt" Cantata, BWV 208, of (probably) 1713.

11. Joel Lester, "Heightening Levels of Activity and J. S. Bach's Parallel-Section Constructions," *Journal of the American Musicological Society* 54 (2001): 49–96.

12. Whether the passage at measure 56b really is a sonata-style return might be debated; the passage comes late in the form, and there is no clearly articulated subdivision of the second "half."

13. Marshall, 200, noting the similarity of the C-Minor Fantasia to the bipartite preludes of *WTC2*, raised the possibility that Bach had considered incorporating it in the latter work.

14. Could Mozart have had this passage in mind when he wrote the first movement of his A-minor piano sonata? No manuscripts survive from his orbit, but the C-Minor Fantasia was one of Bach's more frequently copied works.

15. I pointed out several instances in sonatas of C. P. E. Bach in my *Instrumental Music of Carl Philipp Emanuel Bach* (Ann Arbor: UMI Research Press, 1984), 65–67.

16. At measures 117 and 172. *WTC2* contains a restrained example of this device in the F-Minor Fugue, where a dominant prolongation begins with a pedal point and continues for another twelve measures (mm. 50–64).

17. Reinken's *Hortus musicus* was a set of pieces for two violins and continuo, published in 1687; Bach's sonatas BWV 965 and 966 are arrangements of further movements from this set.

18. The previous entry of the subject was also in the tonic (m. 67), but that entry functions like a premature reprise, leading without a break into the last episode.

19. BWV 994 is the first piece in the "Little Keyboard Book" for Wilhelm Friedemann Bach. It is an eight-measure bipartite prelude with a scale figure as its main theme; almost every note in the piece bears a fingering numeral.

20. For example, a prelude in G major by John Bull, full of scales and furnished with fingerings in several manuscripts (no. 121 in the edition by Thurston Dart, *Musica britannica*, vol. 19 [London: Stainer & Bell, 1963]).

21. Carl Philipp Emanuel Bach, *Versuch über die wahre Art das Clavier zu spielen*, vol. 1 (Berlin, 1753), chap. 1, para. 7.

22. In Cantata 12 of 1714, an ascending scale in the first violin part of an accompanied recitative provides a sort of cantus firmus as the voice expresses the idea of climbing to heaven (*das Reich Gottes*). Bach might have known Froberger's use of scales to symbolize the apotheosis of a dead Habsburg prince and a lutenist friend's fatal drunken fall down the stairs; these are represented by scales respectively ascending and descending in Froberger's *Lamento* for Ferdinand IV and the *Tombeau de Blancrocher*.

23. Descending scales also accompany the return of the subject in the quasi-fugal finale of Op. 10, no. 2, in F.

Part Two

Haydn and Mozart

Chapter Three

Notational Irregularities as Attributes of a New Style

The Case of Haydn's "Sun" Quartet in F Minor, Op. 20, no. 5

László Somfai

Musical notation is a most ambiguous way of recording musical intentions. As a form of "shorthand," it is, after all, rather good. Even centuries later musicians interested in recreating what composers intended to express to their own contemporaries can still make profitable use of it, despite not only changes in instruments but also wholly new social conditions—circumstances that have transformed once contemporary artworks into "period pieces" in the context of a later repertoire. But this shorthand can also be misleading for the modern musician interested in recreating "authenticity" of expression in ways unforeseen by the composer. Unless we are familiar with contemporary and local conventions, and with the idiosyncratic notational habits of the individual composer, essential indications in the written score can be dangerously misleading indeed. Basic symbols, especially performance indications, may have had a meaning different from what we are taught today.

The starting point for our discussion, of course, is the *Urtext* edition. It is hardly good news that critical scholarly editions, including the great-composer *neue Ausgaben* launched after World War II (several of them still unfinished), are already seriously outdated. The reasons for this are obvious. Since the 1950s the "philosophy" of scholarly editions that appear alongside good commercial editions—so-called practical *Urtext* editions—and individual performing scores based on a single source has changed radically. Yet editorial guidelines for an entire series cannot easily be substantially modified. Moreover, in producing the "impeccable" text of a scholarly edition the (defensive) attitude of the editor not infrequently takes priority over the interests of the performer. Add to this the fact that the editors of these volumes are not usually professional musicians but rather scholars—musicologists—leaders in their field, perhaps, but often with old-fashioned tastes.

It is no wonder that among the best performers the degree of respect for scholarly editions varies considerably from one player to the other. Although some pianists were willing to restudy Mozart's sonatas when they were finally published in the *Neue Mozart-Ausgabe* (and even to consult the facsimile edition of the recently discovered autograph score of the C-Minor Sonata, K. 475/457), others prefer a different *Urtext* edition. Some leading artists reject scholarly editions altogether—since such texts usually conflate different sources—preferring to trust a single original source (any contemporary source). They therefore work from a photocopy. My personal advice is to make use of the best *Urtext* edition(s)—but to use them critically: always be willing to discover new details in a composer's notation, and be just as willing to revise your convictions.

Musical notation, to repeat, is a shorthand system—especially with regard to performing instructions, by which I mean everything beyond pitch and basic rhythm. Needless to say, what makes great music memorable is not the bare pitches and rhythms themselves but the manner of their presentation and the expressive power of a musical statement.

We can begin our discussion by placing a short excerpt in Joseph Haydn's handwriting "under the magnifying glass" to show that, unless we are familiar with contemporary conventions as well as with the individual notational habits of a composer, we will not have much chance of properly understanding the actual "message" conveyed by the original expression marks. With this example—eight measures from the beginning of the E-flat major Adagio movement from Haydn's late String Quartet in G, Op. 77, no. 1, composed in 1799—I intend to demonstrate that

- Familiar symbols can be misleading.
- It is difficult (but important) to know which expression marks were new or innovative two hundred years ago.
- Even Haydn's own contemporaries neglected or misunderstood some of his expression marks.
- Present-day notation is not so well suited for conveying the composer's intentions as clearly as the composer's own.

I have already discussed this example in the commentary accompanying the 1972 facsimile edition of the autograph scores of the two String Quartets, Op. 77.[1] The passage was later discussed during a roundtable at the legendary 1975 Haydn Conference held in Washington, DC—a memorable meeting that included the spirited participation of Charles Rosen. Yet, from conversations with both colleagues and string quartet players today, I find that the significance of the case has not been properly understood (see example 3.1).[2]

Example 3.1. Haydn, String Quartet in G Major, Op. 77, no. 1, Hob. III:81, mvt. 2, mm. 1–8. Renderings of the articulation in early and modern sources. Autograph excerpt used by permission of the National Széchényi Library, Budapest (Library call number: Ms. Mus. I. 46B, fol. 7a).

As notated in Haydn's autograph score (ex. 3.1, top staff) there are two significant groups of signs in the violin 1 part: in measure 2 under the notes, and in measure 3 above the notes. In measure 2, the initial V-shaped sign (a *marcato* indication in current terminology) is followed by a decrescendo hairpin together with a staccato stroke. These indications are not to be understood as we would today, namely, as an accented a'♭ followed by a diminuendo and ending with a short d'. The d' would have been short in any case, owing to the conventions of the time governing an eighth note followed by rests. In Haydn's notation, a single stroke indicated an accent (but one weaker than *fz*)—here a short, but crisp, final note—in contrast to the typical eighteenth-century weak "sigh" (*Seufzer*) rendering of the end of a group of slurred notes. The V-shaped *marcato* was not generally used in Vienna. It is not found, for example, in Mozart's scores; Haydn, for his part, used it only in his later manuscripts—those written after his return from London. (He had only introduced the more common reclining, or horizontal, *marcato* sign, >, in the early 1790s, i.e., in scores written in and for London.) The V sign indicated a stronger *marcato*—one I prefer to call *marcatissimo*—and one that accordingly called, in the present instance, for a strong accent. Owing to its context, however, it also carried an additional instruction, namely, that the second measure was to be played with extra stress but within the prevailing *forte* dynamic. (The explicit *f* symbol in measure 1 is not typical of Haydn.) In other words, we may be sure that a player of Haydn's time understood that this notation called for an irregular bowing: the three slurred notes in measure 1 were to be played *forte* with an up-bow, whereas measure 2 was to begin with a down-bow.

The following eighth-note passage is even more of a novelty. We may assume that Haydn's notation, although unusual, was readily understood by the contemporary musician. Haydn obviously did not intend simultaneous staccato and legato performance. The staccato marking in this instance calls into play the third of the three contemporary meanings of strokes of this kind.[3] That is, the notes so marked should be played with equal strength; in other words, the prevailing eighteenth-century convention of alternating "good" (strong) and "bad" (weak) beats within the bar should be suspended here. The slur indicates the direction of the bow: it instructs the performer here to play the four short notes gently and in the same bow direction, specifically with an up-bow (since the sixteenth-note d' is an upbeat). In addition—and again unusually—the long slur arches up to the legato appoggiatura figure (b'♭ to a'♭), which is still to be played with an up-bow, so that we arrive at the strongest (*forzando*) accent of the theme on a down-bow.[4] In fact, what Haydn elaborated here with so much care was not at all typical of late-eighteenth-century style but rather pure *Zukunftsmusik* in its daring use of elements belonging to a future, "Romantic" style of string playing.

The corruption of this precisely notated passage had already begun during the composer's lifetime. Haydn's house copyist, Johann Elssler, copied a shorter slur above the strokes (example 3.1, second staff). The engraver of the

Viennese first edition omitted both the slur and the V-shaped *marcatissimo*—an unknown sign to him—and thereby made the markings in measures 2–3 and 6–7 uniform (example 3.1, third staff). If Haydn saw the proofs, he did not correct these important details. Twentieth-century scores have typically not only smoothed out the remainder but also, just as typically, introduced a serious misprint: changing the time signature from *alla breve* to **c** (see example 3.1, fourth staff). I could have predicted that the visual appearance of this section of the Adagio would be less striking in the critical edition printed in the *Joseph Haydn Werke* (as in example 3.1e) than it is in the autograph manuscript, since, in modern notational practice, the expression marks all have their proper placement within a hierarchy. When this volume of the *JHW* (edited by Horst Walter) appeared in 2003, I was pleased to note that this sensitive passage was essentially transcribed correctly: the markings in measure 2 diverge only in the cello line; the slurred strokes are restored—although they are placed under the notes of the first violin, rather than above them. All in all, the autograph is more "inspiring."

At this point the reader may be inclined to wonder whether the placement of a stroke above or below a note makes any real difference. In fact, there is a difference both in "semantic" meaning and in actual performance. To make a short digression: let us consider the opening of Haydn's famous "Genzinger" Sonata in E Flat, Hob. XVI:49. Contrary to the rules of modern musical orthography, the strokes in the autograph are placed above the staff—on the flag- or stem-side of each note rather than at the note-head (see example 3.2).

What is the meaning of this notation? Is the placement of the symbol on the "wrong" side of the note (from our point of view) an archaic indication of staccato? If it is, does it apply only to the notes in the right hand, or should an editor add strokes—in editorial brackets—in the left-hand part as well? And if so, should the strokes be added on the first beat only, or to the chord on the second beat as well? The modern scholar/editor would prefer not to add further strokes—in this case, properly so. Needless to say, the staccato strokes appear in the *JHW* edition at the note-head.

Bearing in mind that in Haydn's time a keyboardist played from sheet music placed on a music stand (players were not expected to have memorized a sonata), the strokes above the right-hand part, from the performer's point of view, visually suggested accentuation. For a sensitive musician who has seen the facsimile edition of the "Genzinger" Sonata such a graphic detail might well inspire an appropriate accent—a lovely "swing" in the performance.[5]

At this point I prefer not to join the debate (famous among Haydn interpreters) as to why the opening four-sixteenth groups—the articulation of which is crucial to determining the proper character and tempo—are not slurred in the autograph, whereas the same figure is slurred in measures 4 and 5. There is a four-note slur at the first appearance and a "two-plus-two" slur at the second. (The succession is meant perhaps to convey increasing excitement.) Did Haydn intend in this way to

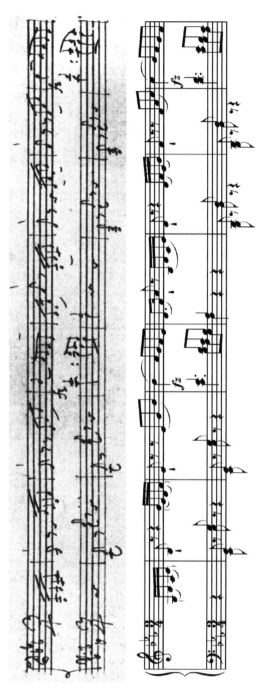

Example 3.2. Haydn, Piano Sonata in E-flat Major, Hob. XVI:49, mvt. 1, mm. 1–7. Readings of the autograph and modern critical edition. Autograph used by permission of the Wienbibliothek im Rathaus.

grant the performer a "free hand" with regard to the articulation of the beginning of the sonata—a freedom that the scholar/editor denies the player if the slurring of the passage is made unnecessarily uniform on the basis of secondary sources? Additional slurs such as those typically supplied in modern editions may be helpful in conservatory classes, where notes lacking articulation marks are often understood to be played non legato; but for the accomplished performer they are misleading. Additional editorial markings of this kind—in the present instance two-note or four-note slurs—can only make fine musicians, who care deeply about a composer's original notation suspicious indeed of a "scholarly" edition.[6]

We are finally ready to turn our attention to the opening theme of Haydn's "Sun" Quartet in F Minor, Op. 20, no. 5, Hob. III:35 (see example 3.3).

The basic character of this theme has traditionally been misconstrued and, just as traditionally, it has been played incorrectly. It is my contention that for the contemporary musician the tie-plus-slur notation that Haydn introduced in the violin 1 part, though rare, was readily comprehensible and was understood to signify an extremely intense legato: one making use of the entire length of the bow—and calling for a *forte*.[7] Such a rendition was certainly not the usual one at the time with which we are familiar; it was, rather, a forerunner of the "endless" legato—in the Romantic sense of the term.

In Haydn's autograph the tie and the beginning of the slur in the first measure of the violin 1 part clearly meet on the second f'. This is reproduced correctly in the *JHW* critical edition (see example 3.3). In earlier editions, however (the old Peters edition of the parts, the Eulenburg pocket score, and even the H. C. Robbins Landon–Reginald Barret-Ayres *Urtext* edition in the Doblinger series), the slur is shifted to the last three notes (see example 3.4).

For the player of a period instrument using a shorter and lighter bow, such slurring makes sense. But it is nonetheless an arbitrary—indeed a distorted—reading of the composer's notation. In fact, in measure 12 the autograph offers solid proof for my "theory" of uninterrupted bow change (see the passage marked A in example 3.3). If Haydn had intended a conventional legato here, he could have written a single slur for the whole measure. Instead, in three of the parts he consistently draws two legato slurs, which touch on the first eighth note of the third beat. The meaning of this notation must be this: one is to play this as a continuous legato but with two bow strokes—down-bow, up-bow—tied together in order to produce a more powerful singing tone and with a slight stress on the second half of the bar.

Other interpretations of the bowing implied by the notation of the opening violin theme are feasible. The first reading would be the typical rendition of a modern player aware that an additive tie-plus-slur notation was common in the eighteenth century. In modern editions this articulation is printed with the slur above the tie (see example 3.5a). This interpretation, however, is not correct. The second reading (example 3.5b) would seem at first to be more acceptable.

Example 3.3. Haydn, String Quartet in F Minor, Op. 20, no. 5, Hob. III:35, mvt. 1, mm. 1–19, as printed in the *JHW* critical edition ©1974 by G. Henle Verlag, Munich. Used by permission.

Example 3.4. Haydn, Op. 20, no. 5, mvt. 1, violin 1, mm. 1–3, as rendered in modern editions.

Example 3.5. Haydn, Op. 20, no. 5, mvt. 1, violin 1, mm. 1–2, alternative bowings.

But, as will be seen, this reading, too, is incorrect. I am convinced that a contemporary string player would have chosen the third reading (example 3.5c) and would have performed the phrase with a continuous motion while changing bow direction.

The notion that the additive tie-plus-slur notation was used exclusively in eighteenth-century string parts (see example 3.6a) and that the slur above the tie is its modern equivalent is simply not true (see example 3.6b). This second, "two-level," notation, although relatively rare, can be found in music of Bach's and Haydn's times. It appears, for example, in the autograph notation of the solo part of Bach's A-Minor Violin Concerto, BWV 1041, where it clearly calls for an up-bow stroke (example 3.6c). It also appears in several of Michael Haydn's carefully notated string parts. Example 3.6d is taken from his Symphony in B Flat, P 18 (1784), where the notation calls for a down-stroke with specified dynamics.

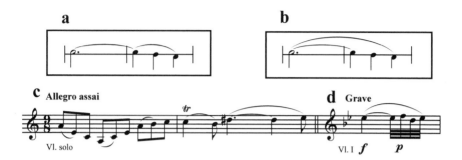

Example 3.6. a) Tie-plus-slur notation; b) slur-above-tie notation; c) J. S. Bach, Violin Concerto in A Minor, BWV 1041, mvt. 3, mm. 25–26; d) Michael Haydn, Symphony, P 18 (1784), mvt. 1, m. 1.

The existence of such instances suggests perhaps that—as with the beginning of the F-Minor String Quartet—every example of such additive tie-plus-slur notation found in string parts of Haydn's and Mozart's generation should normally be played with a change in bow direction.

The performance of the accompaniment of the opening theme of the F-Minor Quartet was less irregular: the three *portato* notes were "automatically" played with an up-bow, the following accented quarter with a down-bow (see example 3.3, passage C).[8] During the course of these four measures—and then repeatedly throughout the movement—the contemporary musician and listener would have experienced something surprising: instead of an eloquently articulated performance largely based on "short-bow" execution, a new and fascinating "singing" style had made its appearance—a style that we would describe today as "Romantic." I do not object to performers today aiming for an "eloquent" interpretation, one perhaps incorporating rhetorical features characteristic of Haydn's music. But in emphasizing the "speaking" element in Haydn, we may be underestimating the extent and significance of those elements of his style that Haydn had invented precisely in order to override the rhetoric-based, speechlike articulation and flow of a musical composition.

Innovation itself—the creation of something new in music—was most important to Haydn, and not only in those aspects where it was easily manifested, for example, in the realms of harmony and key relationships. (One thinks of the music of Schubert.) Clocklike accompaniment patterns (as encountered in many slow movements from his later works), or a recitativelike thematic contour compressed into a solid $\frac{3}{4}$ allegro rhythm (as in measures 67–84 of the *Allegro spiritoso* finale of the Quartet in E-flat Major, Op. 76, no. 6, Hob. III:80), or the attempt at an "endless" legato melody (in the F-Minor Quartet that is the subject of the present discussion) are all manifestations of Haydn's effort precisely to reduce the performer's inclination to shape a musical idea in the traditional manner, that is, as "speech."

It should be clear from the examples discussed here that in Haydn's time the purpose of performance indications added to the bare notes was often (perhaps usually) to advise the musician *not* to read the music according to the conventions but differently. The question for us then becomes: Precisely how can we reconstruct the conventions that informed the reading of a musical score in the past? Needless to say, the available information is fragmentary, and our understanding remains incomplete—despite sophisticated studies of contemporary treatises, the scrutiny of musicians' correspondence, the examination of old performing parts, and so on. The performance conventions of Haydn's time had already changed with the next generation. Moreover, they differed from genre to genre, from one geographic region to another, and under different working and social conditions. Yet notational innovations, such as those embodied in the violin theme of the F-Minor "Sun" Quartet, make it clear why we must continue to try to understand them.

Notes

1. László Somfai, ed. *Joseph Haydn: String Quartet in G, 1799, Hoboken III:81: Reprint of the Original Manuscript (National Széchényi Library, Budapest) with Commentaries* (Budapest: Editio Musica; Melville, NY: Belwin-Mills, 1972).

2. László Somfai, "String Quartets: Remarks and Discussion," in *Haydn Studies: Proceedings of the International Haydn Conference, Washington, D.C., 1975*, ed. Jens Peter Larsen, Howard Serwer, and James Webster (New York and London: Norton, 1981), 229–32.

3. The three meanings are: (1) short note(s); (2) accented single note, occasionally at the beginning or in the middle of a slurred group of notes; (3) equally accented notes in succession. For a detailed discussion, with examples from the scores of J. S. Bach, Joseph and Michael Haydn, and Mozart, see my study (available only in Hungarian) " 'Staccato vonás?' Kottakép és jelentése," [" 'Staccato Stroke?' Notation and Its Meaning"], *Magyar Zene* 41 (2003), 49–62.

4. The crescendo in measure 3, leading to the *fz*, was probably added in the proofs of Artaria's first edition of the parts. Haydn subsequently introduced it into his autograph score. Originally, as Elssler's copy proves, it was not there.

5. In addition to the facsimile-plus-*Urtext* reprint in the *Wiener Urtext* series, see the lavish edition *Joseph Haydn. Klaviersonate in Es-dur Hob. XVI:49. Vollständige Faksimile-Ausgabe im Originalformat*, ed. Otto Brusatti (Graz: Akademische Druck- und Verlagsanstalt, 1982).

6. One of the greatest performers of Haydn's piano music on modern instruments, András Schiff, follows the editor's advice in his recording of this work (*Joseph Haydn Piano Sonatas* [Teldec 0630-17141-2]). By his own account, he practiced "a lot" to be able to play two-note slurs clearly—and he did so perhaps unnecessarily!

7. In the autograph (and therefore in the *JHW* edition) there is no dynamic marking in measure 1; the *poco piano* in measure 5 is Haydn's own. The editorial suggestion [*p*] in measure 1 of the Doblinger *Urtext* score is erroneous.

8. See the first page of the score reproduced above (example 3.3). One detail must be commented on. In measures 10–11 the two violin parts have different articulations—a distressing conflict (see the marking D). The explanation for this is that the editor of the *JHW* edition has contaminated two versions. Haydn's original articulation appears in the earliest layer of the autograph score as reproduced in example 3.7a. He then corrected it—but only in the violin 1 part (example 3.7b). The form printed in the *JHW* edition (example 3.7c) is thus not only unusual but senseless.

Example 3.7. Haydn, Op. 20, no. 5, mvt. 1, violin 1, m. 10.

Chapter Four

The Fugal Moment

On a Few Bars in Mozart's Quintet in C Major, K. 515

Richard Kramer

"Although the C-major quintet is accepted as one of Mozart's greatest works, it is not generally recognized as perhaps the most daring of all," wrote Charles Rosen in a discussion that no one who has since thought about this work can ever put out of mind.[1] I want to pursue Rosen's claim with some observations about a few notes in the midst of the first movement of the work, where the daring, to my ears, is most deeply felt.

The passage that I have in mind is a famous one, but identifying the moment at which it begins—testimony no doubt to the seamless unfolding of thought and idea in this remarkable work—is no simple matter. At measure 170, the cello finally joins a cadencing in A minor that had begun a few bars earlier. Its deep E might at first suggest the incipit of another of those grand arpeggiations that have been setting new paragraphs in motion since the opening bars. Of course it is nothing of the kind, but rather the incipit of a fugal subject. Here, too, the identity of this subject at its inception and its close is intentionally complicated. The subject means to recall the expansive closing bars of the exposition, music of perfect equipoise, spun out over what seems an endless pedal on the new tonic, G major. The phrasing of this closing music is not quite so simple as it may seem. The whole note at measure 131, emphatically the final note of the structural cadence before the closing theme, has a Janus-like aspect to it, triggering this lavish epilogue of afterbeats. Here too, the whole note is ambivalent, for while the downbeat at measure 131 sets up the first of a series of four-bar metrical units, the new theme itself begins only at measure 132, suggesting a downbeat that cuts across the larger metrical background, oblivious of the whole note G that sets the passage in motion (see example 4.1).

Example 4.1. Mozart, String Quintet in C Major, K. 515, mvt. 1, mm. 129–35.

At the inception of the fugue subject, this whole note now seems to reexamine the ambivalence of its articulative function at measure 131. Its placement here, before the resolution of the big cadence in A minor, suggests its articulation as an upbeat, pointedly reversing its function as a powerful downbeat that establishes structural closure toward the end of a very long exposition. In the chemistry of fugue subjects, such matters of articulation are intensified, fixed in a state of rhetorical certitude. That's the case here. This E at measure 170 begins life in the larger narrative of the piece, at an extreme moment of crisis, but is then immobilized, so to speak, in the highly wrought intervallic casting of this fugue subject (see example 4.2).

What follows is no fugal exposition in even the loosest sense, but a complex passage that drives its entries relentlessly around the circle of fifths from A minor to F minor. The chromatic saturation of the passage puts us in mind of fugue, but somewhere in the belly of the thing, where the implications of the opening of the subject are played out. To put it more schematically, the music beginning at measure 170 in the cello and second violin sets off a canon, strictly enforced through the circle of fifths in all the voices: A minor, D minor, G minor, C minor, F minor. At measures 185–90 the subject is abbreviated, the canon reconfigured: cello and violin 1 paired against violin 2 and viola 1 (viola 2 has its own independent counterpoint), bringing the music to the edge of a dominant pedal at measure 193.

The creation of a fugal subject begins here, in the reconceiving of this whole note whose function is radically altered: the whole note at measure 131 is a tonic, the whole note at measure 170 a dominant, and this of course has everything to do with its syntactical relationship to the music that follows. The cool balance of the phrase at measure 131 is now subjected to radical metamorphosis, a compression of interval and prosody, and of diction. The whole-note *Kopfton* of the subject remakes itself, for in the closing music in the exposition, it is the tone of ultimate arrival, from which the rest of the exposition is mere, but exquisite, afterbeat. Its articulation in the fugue subject is consequently problematized. The E behaves as an upbeat, and yet the implicit performance of the thing is such that the player will need to breathe between the E and its continuation, suggesting of the fugue subject not that it comprises two "motives" in the conventional sense— motivic analysis, as it is conventionally practiced, would reject a naming of the E as a motive unto itself!—but rather, that it is consumed in the idea to signify and to reconcile, as subject, two disparate musics that stand on either side of a cadential divide. This E, then, is an intensely charged note whose performance is deeply engaged in the playing out of these contraries. The extremity of the music is only intensified in the counterpoints, whose dissonances strain at the edge of comprehensibility. The resolution of the dissonant B in the second violin is made coincident not with a tonic A minor, but with its subdominant, and in six-four position. The intervallic structure of the subject traffics in "difficult" intervals, finally in a diminished fourth followed by a stunning *downward* leap of a major ninth—except, of course, at its initial statement, where the bottom string of the cello constrains it to the closer octave: in retrospect, we must imagine hearing this B♭ an impossible octave lower—grating against a suspension in another voice.

What sets all this off? I return to the crux at measure 170 and its release in fugue. The music around this cadence, in its pitching of E in the highest register,

Example 4.2. Mozart, String Quintet in C Major, K. 515, mvt. 1, mm. 1–15, 150–81, and explanatory sketch of mm. 11–15.

Example 4.2. (continued)

will bring to mind what might be called the first crisis of the piece, at measure 15. It is here that the controlled decorum of the opening of the quintet is threatened. The E high in the first violin seems to catch the players by surprise. The incessant eighth notes in the inner voices give way to the pitches of a dominant ninth chord—the first truly chromatic notes in the piece—whose root, strongly implied, is A. In its place, the cello sounds a deep F, anticipating the resolution of the high E to D and ignoring the powerful appeal of the other voices to provide a missing root. The effect of this F is exceptional, clinching the linear configuration plotted out by the cello at the incipits of its three arpeggiations, at C, G, and E. The F, heard for a fleeting moment to initiate yet another such arpeggiation, upsets this neat patterning.

Everything happens at just this moment: an eruption of the chromatic (C♯ and B♭, suggesting—but only suggesting—trajectories along the sharp, dominant axis and the flat subdominant), conjoined with a rupture of the rhythmic engine (in a local, surface sense), where the throbbing stops and the first violin and cello touch one another for the first time. And then the bass disturbs, yet more violently, the larger rhythmic unfolding, or rather, reacts to the five-measure out-of-phase motion of the opening phrases. The F in the bass comes a half bar too soon, if we legitimize those chromatic inner voices with real harmonic, functional purpose. Kirnberger (for one) would have installed a deep A as a fundamental bass at this point, identifying the implicit root of the harmony; and of course a full bar too soon, in the playing out of *Fünftaktigkeit*. But then our deeper ear hears the F as just right, the upper voices as the ephemeral ones, four appoggiaturas to the true harmony, D minor in first inversion.

And it is precisely here that something in our inner, theorist's ear is triggered a mere instant before the actual downbeat. That is because the deep E in the bass, continuing to sound across those three bars of arpeggiation, is doubled at the extreme treble: doubled only for a barely audible instant, but doubled nonetheless, and thereby stakes a modest but compelling claim for rootness. The phrasing—the narrative—won't allow that claim to take root just yet. But then, the central crisis of the development is brought on precisely in response to this moment: again, the harmony unfolds around C major (see m. 164) and the first violin turns its figure to the high E. When it does, the throbbing stops once again, and E is isolated for three full measures, finally doubled deep in the bass, the root of a big dominant and the incipit of a chromatically bent fugue subject. The graphing in example 4.2 suggests how this goes.

The attack at the downbeat of measure 15 is highly charged. The opening bars of the development pick up precisely at its dissonant pitches—a diminished seventh with powerful implications of a dominant ninth on A. In a sense, the entire first part of the development might be understood as a coming round again to the "problem" of measure 15. The first violin reaches up to its high E at measure 168. The other instruments, as though recalling measure 15, again break off their chattering, endorsing the E as the root of a dominant seventh that is sustained for three chromatically infused bars and finally supported by the deep E in the cello whose deft placement is endowed as the first note of the fugue subject.

Fugue, a studied disquisition on a subject, takes on another layer of meaning—signifies, beyond the self-referential world internal to fugue—when it is staged as a scene in the unfolding of the larger drama of sonata. The subject of this disquisition, itself a transformation of theme, seems to bring its own consciousness of theme to some deeper place, as though in exploration of its recesses. A counterpoint of difficult intervals, a stretching of harmonic coherence to its limits, a saturation of texture: these are what fugue allows, and it is only in the dramaturgy of classical sonata that fugue takes on this role in the extreme, where the identity of fugue itself signifies an intensification of thematic consciousness: fugue as sign. This E, the defining note of the subject, contains within itself the heavily freighted E-ness that reaches back to measure 15, at a first hint of crisis.

The temptation to situate the quintet in a context, to identify its antecedents—its precursors, to think with Harold Bloom in the more aggressive language of influence and its anxieties—is only a response to the call to write it into a history. Rosen (p. 267) hears echoes of Haydn's String Quartet in C Major, Op. 33, no. 3: "the same mounting phrase in the cello, the same inner accompanying motion, the same placing of the first violin . . . Even Haydn's remarkable use of silence . . . is turned to account here." And yet the two openings are so manifestly different in concept as to suggest some other process of mind. The matter is complicated by the evident, transparent play on Haydn's radical opening bars in the String Quartet in C Major, K. 465, the last of the quartets that Mozart dedicated to this "caro Amico."[2] It is as though the fraught Adagio with which Mozart famously begins is a convoluted response to the problem of beginning itself. For it is clear that Haydn's opening sets loose a theoretical problem of a certain magnitude. The bare sixth is a dissonance, E posing as a root, C as an unprepared neighbor to B. And it is precisely this configuration to which the recapitulation addresses itself (see example 4.3). The opening of Mozart's Allegro is tame by comparison. But at the outset of the development, those opening bars are recast with a seventh, B♭ squarely in the bass, an echo (if not an allusion more convoluted in how it signifies) of this very moment in the Haydn quartet (see example 4.4).

In the quartet, the engagement with Haydn is intense. The quintet, it seems to me, spins in some other orbit. If Rosen is right to hear the "same mounting phrase in the cello," it might be worth a moment to ponder the ways in which Mozart's phrase seems determined to obliterate Haydn's, to put it out of mind. The syntax of Mozart's opening paragraph is contingent on the deep notes with which each arpeggio opens. Those notes themselves become thematic. And yet a vestige of Haydn's texture is felt here as well. It is as though the quintet, in

Example 4.3. Haydn, String Quartet in C Major, Op. 33, no. 3, Hob. III: 39, mvt. 1, analytical sketch.

these opening bars, forces a rehearing—but of what, exactly? Perhaps one might think that Mozart here reenacts the sense of an earlier, and difficult, engagement with Haydn's quartet: the quintet, then, is a response, on the grandest imaginable scale, to that earlier engagement. The symptoms of it can be sniffed out here and there, but in the end, the quintet breaks away.

Its expansive opening was not lost on Beethoven. Rosen (pp. 265–66) notes of the String Quintet, Op. 29, composed in 1801, that it possesses "a breadth and a tranquil expansiveness" that stand in contrast to the six quartets of Opus 18, evidence that Beethoven understood the "fundamental difference between quartet and quintet" manifest in even the earliest of Mozart's works in the genre. I want, however, to propose that K. 515 seems to have entered into Beethoven's consciousness during the composition of another work noted for its grand expanse: the Quartet in F Major, Op. 59, no. 1, written in 1806.[3] The famous opening paragraph of Beethoven's quartet, in increasingly anxious pursuit of a tonic cadence, is of course nothing like the opening of Mozart's quintet. In other respects, Beethoven's exposition seems to echo Mozart's: in the tonicizing of the dominant of the dominant, and in its brief but consequential closing theme. The timeless breadth of Mozart's twenty-one bars is compressed into a two-bar phrase, repeated twice in variant form before the close of the exposition is elided with the opening bars of the development: "*la prima parte solamente una volta*," Beethoven inscribed at the top of the autograph. Even here, one might think that Beethoven means a play on this moment in K. 515, where the F♮ in the viola at measure 147 leads the music seamlessly back to the tonic. At the repeat of the exposition, this same return to the tonic is interrupted by the deep

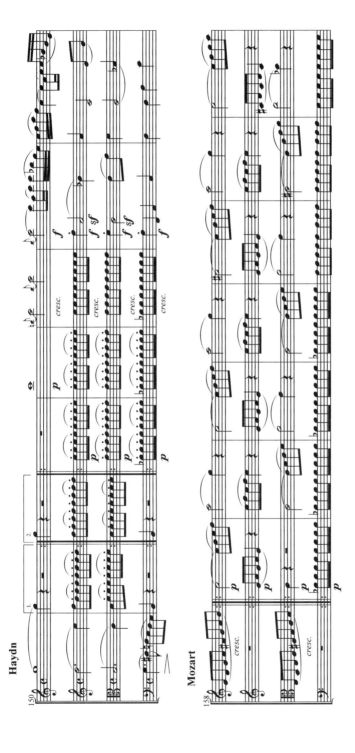

Example 4.4. Haydn, String Quartet in C Major, Op. 33, no. 3, Hob. III:39, mvt. 1; Mozart, String Quartet in C Major, K. 465, mvt. 1. Beginnings of the development sections.

C♯ in the cello. With Beethoven, it is the G♭ in the cello at measure 108 that interrupts the sense of a return to the tonic, for it is only at that moment that we can know that the exposition will not be repeated.

But it is to Beethoven's fugal moment that I want to turn (see example 4.5). It too happens at a crisis in the development, but one that differs in every respect from Mozart's. Here, the music settles comfortably—too comfortably, one might think—into D-flat major. At measure 169, the closing theme is invoked in the three lower strings, and the conversation continues for some fifteen bars, toward a cadence that promises closure on the deepest D♭ at measure 184. Closure, however, is thwarted: the cadence is interrupted by a dominant on B♭, setting in motion the first of two voices that together will formulate the "double subject" of a fugue. The subject in eighth notes is of course an elaboration of the opening motive as it appears at the tail end of the exposition, here in its varied form. The true subject—a counterpoint chiseled in suspended dissonance, expressive intervals, and rhythmic gesture—is yet more abstruse in its relationship to the music of the exposition. That, of course, is much to its point. We are meant to hear it as a kind of abstraction that pulls from its running counterpoint a thematic essence, and in so doing, establishes itself as the primary thematic substance of the fugue.

Coming at all this from Mozart's quintet, one might wish to hear in these two fugal moments a kind of colloquy in which the one work engages the other. Both draw on the final measures of the exposition in the formulation of a fugue subject. Then, Beethoven's abstruse subject seems to draw its sense of abstraction as much from Mozart's subject as from the thematic surface of its own quartet. (The subjects are shown in example 4.6.) Mozart's *Kopfton*, for all that I have suggested of its signifying presence, is missing. But a closer look at Beethoven's autograph score—actually, at a page which was finally stitched into oblivion with the rewriting of the fugue—is revealing in this connection. It shows Beethoven at work precisely here, as though in search of an opening, if not an actual *Kopfton*, that would at once illuminate its source in the music of the quartet and enshroud it in abstraction: again, fugue subject as intervallic abstraction and as signifier of some deeper inner engagement.[4] (This earlier layer is shown in example 4.7.)

To hear Beethoven's quartet as a text unencumbered by its ritual of creation ought to be enough for any of us. And yet the convoluted implications in the drafting of these difficult measures leave their mark, suggestive not only of a vigorous process muted in the finality of a final version, but of an engagement with antecedents. The figure of Mozart seems to come alive in these draftings, as though enmeshed in the signifying. That Beethoven even in 1806 continued to hear Mozart in his inner ear is plain enough from evidence that is both complex and plenteous.[5] In the end, Beethoven's quartet goes its own way. Its fugal moment, to which there is not the faintest allusion in the heroic celebrations of its coda, simply vanishes. Here the two works part company.

Example 4.5. Beethoven, String Quartet in F Major, Op. 59, no. 1, mvt. 1, mm. 180–94.

Example 4.6. Beethoven, String Quartet in F Major, Op. 59, no. 1, mvt. 1; and Mozart, String Quintet in C Major, K. 515, mvt. 1: fugue subjects compared.

Example 4.7. Beethoven, String Quartet in F Major, Op. 59, no. 1, earlier version of the principal fugue subject.

Coda

"The coda," Rosen (p. 273) writes of the Mozart, "is masterly: the closing theme, which in the exposition was a tonic pedal on G, starts once again as a pedal on G, becoming thereby a dominant pedal instead of a tonic." Here I would quibble. The moment is set up by a terrific cadencing that brings the music to a halt on the familiar diminished seventh in anticipation of the big six-four. But the six-four is delayed, and the diminished seventh echoes across a measure of rest. Above the pedal tone on G, the upper voices return to that fugal moment, the whole note G again placed as the incipit of the subject, now recast in C major. The entries unfold in a kind of unsystematic stretto: at the fourth entry, the first violin touches a high E♭, poignant and signifying. Sounding, as all this does, above a *dominant* pedal—more accurately, a protracted six-four before the dominant—the effect is of a cadenza that continues through to the close on the tonic at measure 353, where now the music echoes the closing section of the exposition, the cello finally moving to its deep open-string C for four bars and a quarter toward the very end. But it is the cadenza that sticks in the memory.[6] A prototype for cadenzas of this kind, as though a conversation among the voices, was described eloquently by Emanuel Bach. His topic was the extraordinary cadenza in F-sharp minor at the end of the Largo in the Fourth Sonata of the *Probestücke* published to accompany the first part of the *Versuch* in 1753.[7] Bach was writing about performance at a keyboard by a single player who must inhabit the voices embodied in the texture. In chamber music, the bodies perform. Mozart had himself composed other cadenzas of this kind, most notably at the close of the finale of the great Quintet for Piano and Winds, K. 452: "I myself consider it to be the best work I have yet composed," Mozart wrote of it.[8]

This astonishing confession tells us much about Mozart in April 1784. But in coming to terms with this music, the critic must do without the help of its author, who of course hears his work with a biased ear. For all that we would give to know what Mozart might have thought of K. 515 after its composition in April 1787, it is to Rosen's "perhaps the most daring of all" that we return. It sets us to imagine how such daring, at its extremity, might be figured, for with Mozart the ritual of creation, rarely exposed, remains inscrutable. That's the thing about Rosen, and about *The Classical Style* in particular. We are brought up to the edge of the imponderable. Rosen places us there, deftly and without the tedious exertions of conventional scholarship, and inspires us to work through for ourselves the insight that he is content to offer as an allusion, expressed with a brilliance and wit that manages always to capture the spirit of the thing. The laboring of the point he leaves to us.

Notes

1. Charles Rosen, *The Classical Style: Haydn, Mozart, Beethoven*, expanded ed. (New York: W. W. Norton, 1997), 268.

2. The dedication published with the Artaria print of 1785 is often reprinted and much discussed. Mark Evan Bonds, "The Sincerest Form of Flattery? Mozart's 'Haydn' Quartets and the Question of Influence," *Studi Musicali* 22 (1993): 365–409, reads the rhetorical strategies in the document. Maynard Solomon, *Mozart: A Life* (New York: HarperCollins, 1995), 315, argues that its "imagery seems to resonate with Mozart's very personal yearning for an ideal paternal/filial harmony, for a vigorous, creative, and accepting musical father." I want to suggest that its convoluted conceit may harbor a more complex strain in the relationship, that the identification of Haydn as "father" carries with it that obscure vulnerability that fathers must often endure in the aggression of their sons to supersede them.

3. In a conversation recorded in August 1826, Karl Holz turns the talk to string quintets. "Welches von den Mozart'schen halten Sie für das Schönste [which of those by Mozart do you take to be the most beautiful]?" asks Holz. To Beethoven's (unrecorded) response, Holz writes "Auch G moll [the G minor too]," from which it might be inferred that Beethoven replied "C dur [the C major]." Dagmar Beck, ed., with the assistance of Günter Brosche, *Ludwig van Beethovens Konversationshefte* (Leipzig: Deutscher Verlag für Musik, 1993), 1:130.

4. This matter is the topic of my "'*Das Organische der Fuge*': On the Autograph of Beethoven's Quartet in F Major, Opus 59 No. 1," in *The String Quartets of Haydn, Mozart, and Beethoven: Studies of the Autograph Manuscripts*, ed. Christoph Wolff (Cambridge, MA: Department of Music, Harvard University, distributed by Harvard University Press, 1980), 223–65.

5. See, for one, my "Cadenza Contra Text: Mozart in Beethoven's Hands," *19th Century Music* 15/2 (1991): 116–31. For a remarkable instance from the 1820s, see Bathia Churgin, "Beethoven and Mozart's Requiem: A New Connection," *Journal of Musicology* 5 (1987): 457–77.

6. The defining moment for any cadenza in Mozart is the fermata above the six-four. Here, the fermata is written out in the measure rest, ensuring the players no doubt as to where it ends. The six-four is written into the cadenza itself, a license that only deepens the engagement with the convention. Within the discussion of K. 515, Rosen writes a rich paragraph on the problem of length in sonata movements (pp.

269–70), noting the function of the cadenza in the concerto, but curiously refusing to note the appropriation of cadenza into such works as K. 515.

7. The passage is also discussed in "Cadenza Contra Text," 118–20.

8. "Ich selbst halte es für das beste was ich noch in meinem leben geschrieben habe." Letter of April 10, 1784; see *Mozart: Briefe und Aufzeichnungen*, ed. Wilhelm A. Bauer, Otto Erich Deutsch, Joseph Heinz Eibl, *Erweiterte Ausgabe*, ed. Ulrich Konrad (Kassel: Bärenreiter, Gemeinsame Ausgabe, 2005), 3:309; and Emily Anderson, *The Letters of Mozart and His Family* (New York: St. Martin's Press, 1966), 2: 873. I have slightly altered Anderson's translation.

Part Three

Beethoven

Chapter Five

A Tale of Two Quintets

Mozart's K. 452 and Beethoven's Opus 16

William Kinderman

In the repertoire of chamber music for piano with wind instruments, Mozart's Quintet, K. 452, and Beethoven's, Opus 16, occupy a special place. Each of these works stems from a time when its creator celebrated signal triumphs as a keyboard virtuoso. Mozart's quintet dates from the spring of 1784, when he was otherwise occupied with the great series of piano concertos beginning with K. 449 to 451, and this work was originally performed at Vienna in concerts alongside his concertos. Beethoven's quintet was evidently composed during his only extended concert tour, a journey in 1796 that took him from Vienna to Prague and Berlin. Both pieces employ oboe, clarinet, horn, and bassoon in addition to the keyboard. Although Beethoven also arranged his composition in a piano quartet version with strings, the quintet was originally written for piano and winds in a configuration identical to Mozart's K. 452.

There is evidence of Beethoven's awareness of Mozart's model when he wrote his Opus 16. Douglas Johnson has speculated that woodwind players at Prague might have given Beethoven the idea of composing such a work, possibly after a performance of Mozart's K. 452, and that Beethoven subsequently completed his quintet while in Berlin.[1] The evaluations of commentators have often been to Beethoven's disadvantage. John Warrack wrote, "In the direct line of descent from Mozart's piano and wind quintet is Beethoven's work for the same combination . . . an inferior work to its begetter."[2] Donald Francis Tovey's characterization has been particularly influential:

> In the quintet for pianoforte and wind instruments, Opus 16, Beethoven is, indeed, obviously setting himself in rivalry with Mozart's quintet for the same combination; but, if you want to realize the difference between the highest art of classical composition and the easygoing, safety-first product of a silver age, you cannot find a better illustration than these two works, and here it is Mozart who is the classic and Beethoven who is something less.[3]

The conspicuous similarities between the two works indeed go beyond the choice of instruments. Both quintets are in three movements and employ E-flat major as the tonic key, with the dominant B-flat major being the tonic key of the slow movement. The opening movements are in sonata form, the finales in a rondo design. Distinctive is the use in each piece of an extended slow introduction to the first movement. These parallels could scarcely have been accidental and indeed convey the impression of Beethoven "setting himself in rivalry with Mozart's quintet."[4] In other respects, however, Beethoven departs decisively from Mozart's model.

The comparison of Mozart's K. 452 and Beethoven's Opus 16 casts light on Beethoven's efforts during the 1790s to come to terms with Mozart's legacy. Surprisingly, Beethoven's quintet has received little close scholarly attention.[5] Lewis Lockwood, in his study "Beethoven before 1800: The Mozart Legacy," for instance, does not mention Beethoven's Opus 16 and its relationship to Mozart's K. 452.[6] In his more recent book *Beethoven: The Music and the Life*, Lockwood describes Beethoven's quintet as "one of the more developed [of] the lesser works, designed for popularity and little more." He implies that with Opus 16, as with the Clarinet Trio, Op. 11, "Beethoven did well to make his piece attractive to audiences and performers . . . but he was fully aware that instead of attempting a really serious work that could stand up to Mozart's he was trolling the surface for easy dividends."[7]

The quintet merits reevaluation in this context. Nigel Fortune once described the piece as having suffered from "otiose though perhaps understandable comparisons with Mozart's great work for the same forces in the same key."[8] Several distinguished writers have regarded Beethoven's Opus 16 as a lesser or even substandard piece, yet without providing much justification for this view. Maynard Solomon, for example, sidelined the quintet by relegating it to a "preparatory" category: "Beethoven's chamber music for winds, or for winds supported by strings or piano, did not survive the century that adored such combinations. In terms of Beethoven's further development, these works may be regarded as preparations for his long-delayed entry into symphonic music."[9]

However, even brief examination of recent concert schedules and record catalogues clearly shows that Beethoven's quintet quite easily "survived the century that adored such combinations." A more substantive basis for critique might be offered by Charles Rosen's glancing remark in his book *The Classical Style*, to the effect that "the Quintet for Piano and Winds may be called 'classicizing' rather than 'classic' in style, like the works of Hummel: they are reproductions of classical forms—Mozart's in particular—based upon the exterior models, the results of the classical impulse, and not upon the impulse itself."[10] Yet this assertion, too, raises more questions than it answers. To what extent did Beethoven seek to imitate Mozart's style and forms in composing this work? Can Lockwood be correct in asserting that Beethoven deliberately avoided "attempting a really serious work that could stand up to Mozart's"?

The imposing dimensions and originality of Beethoven's composition seem to belie such a claim.

The following essay reassesses the quintets through an examination of Mozart's and Beethoven's aesthetic goals and preoccupations. I will argue that their artistic aspirations were not identical, and in some respects even sharply divergent. The role of improvisation in Beethoven's creative process deserves attention in this regard. The ways in which Beethoven utilized preexisting compositional models are complex, and can be elucidated only partially through the study of sources and the circumstances of composition. In a study of "Influence: Plagiarism and Inspiration," Rosen observed that "when the study of sources is at its most interesting, it becomes indistinguishable from pure musical analysis."[11] In this context, we shall return to Tovey's much-echoed judgment that Mozart "is the classic" and Beethoven "something less."

Motivic Affinities and Beethoven's Techniques of Improvisation

The lofty evaluation of Mozart's quintet began with the composer himself. As noted above, the piece belongs to a crucial period in his production of piano concertos during the first months of 1784, following the trio of concertos, K. 449 to 451. This group of works marks the beginning of a superb period in Mozart's creativity, a phase that saw the composition of a dozen concertos from K. 449 to K. 503 that he wrote for his successful seasons as virtuoso performer before the Viennese public between 1784 and 1786. In their sharply defined, expressive characters, their richness of invention, and their formal innovations, these pieces constitute an extraordinary achievement and have become cornerstones of the concerto repertoire.[12] Mozart began to compile a personal catalogue of his compositions with precisely these works, entering the Concerto in E Flat, K. 449, on February 9, 1784.[13]

Immediately after composing K. 449–451, Mozart wrote his Quintet, K. 452, the Piano Concerto in G, K. 453, and the Violin Sonata in B Flat, K. 454, completing all six major compositions in just ten weeks. He entered the quintet into his catalogue on March 30, 1784, and performed the piece to enthusiastic acclaim in the Vienna Burgtheater on April 1. To his father, he proudly described K. 452 as "the best work I have ever composed."[14] It does not seem coincidental that the genesis of this composition was sandwiched between his impressive piano concertos and that it has concertolike features, such as the extended "Cadenza in tempo" for all five instruments beginning at measure 159 of the finale. The colorful sonorities, lively dialogue, and masterful balance in the handling of the wind instruments that characterize K. 452 also appear in the concertos written around the same time. An enhanced role for the winds in relation to the piano, which becomes a mainstay of Mozart's concerto style, is signaled by this remarkable quintet, his sole work for this particular combination of instruments.[15]

Distinctive features of the musical language of K. 452 are displayed at once in the slow introduction, marked Largo. Since this section particularly invites comparison with Beethoven's work, we shall examine it in some detail. The phrases heard at the outset of Mozart's introduction juxtapose the combined harmonic sonority of the winds and piano with a sensitive gestural interplay of individual voices. Hence the chords in the downbeats of measures 1–3 and 4–6 are *forte* and *tenuto* and are assigned to the full ensemble, whereas all of the other motives are marked *piano* and given to the piano or the winds (see example 5.1). At the same time, Mozart promotes a sense of dialogue by assigning the opening four-bar phrase mainly to the piano while granting prominence in the following phrase to the winds, with the oboe and then the clarinet taking up the figure in dotted rhythm first heard from the piano in measure 1. After having been played by the pianist in each of the first three measures, this motive in dotted rhythm migrates from one instrument to another before returning to the piano on a new pitch level in measure 7.

Of special importance is the ensuing upbeat motive of three slurred eighth notes, which appears in measures 1–3 and 5–8. This motive is typically harmonized in three or four voices but emphasizes a stepwise descending line. After the diminished-seventh chord at the beginning of measure 7, the piano echoes the oboe's highest tone, D♭, from that sonority, and carries the line downward as D♭–C–B♭–A. This four-note descending motive is heard twice in measure 8, played *dolce* in the wind instruments. An expansion of this *dolce* phrase in the horn leads to a cadence in E-flat major at the outset of measure 10.

Beginning in measure 10, Mozart modifies this descending motive so that it unfolds in sixteenth notes instead of quarter notes and passes through a falling seventh instead of a fourth. Heard in the bassoon, the motive moves by step through the seventh from G to A♭; in the ensuing statement in the horn, the figure begins on A♭ and leads downward to B♭. Mozart arranges the ensuing chain of motives so that these entries sustain an ascending linear pattern passing through an octave. Consequently, the descending figure in octaves in the piano in measures 13–14 reattains the pitch level of the falling seventh G–A♭, corresponding to the original statement in the bassoon in measure 10. Meanwhile, another motive in dotted rhythm appears in measures 12–14. The arrival of a pedal point on the dominant B♭ beginning in measure 15 signals the last section of the introduction.

Turning now to Beethoven, let us consider what motivic features his Opus 16 and Mozart's K. 452 share. The question might be posed as follows: what concrete features of Mozart's musical language did Beethoven retain in shaping his own quintet? It is relevant in this context to take into account the surviving reports from contemporary observers about the way Beethoven improvised at

Example 5.1. Mozart, Quintet for Piano and Wind Instruments in E-flat Major, K. 452, mvt. 1, mm. 1–14.

Example 5.1. (continued)

the keyboard. His ability to improvise was extraordinary and was much commented on by his contemporaries. Indeed, some critics charged that Beethoven's approach to musical composition was harmed by its closeness to improvisation. In 1815, the critic August Wendt found it unfortunate that most

Example 5.1. (continued)

of Beethoven's sonatas and symphonies were spoiled by the formlessness of the fantasy.[16] Similar responses were common, and Beethoven's own propensity for injecting a sense of improvisation into established musical genres is reflected in pieces such as his two Piano Sonatas, Op. 27, each of which he described as "sonata quasi fantasia." It is noteworthy too that during his long years as a piano virtuoso, Beethoven was disinclined to play his published works and preferred to extemporize. His student Ferdinand Ries reported that when they made preparations for a tour together, he was to have played Beethoven's concertos and other finished compositions, whereas Beethoven "wanted only to conduct and improvise."[17]

Eyewitness reports of Beethoven's improvisations stress his capacity for developing much out of little, seeing the world in a grain of sand by making some accidental scrap of musical material into the springboard for an astoundingly imaginative musical discourse. The composer Johann Schenk described the unforgettable impression of a free fantasy more than a half hour in length that Beethoven played in 1792.[18] A report in the *Allgemeine musikalische Zeitung* from April 1799 emphasized that he "shows himself to the greatest advantage in improvisation, and here, indeed, it is most extraordinary with what lightness and yet firmness in the succession of ideas Beethoven not only varies a theme given him on the spur of the moment by figuration . . . but really develops it."[19]

Another such account stems from 1800, when Beethoven was matched with the flamboyant virtuoso pianist Daniel Steibelt in a competitive keyboard encounter. According to Ries, Steibelt responded to a performance of Beethoven's Clarinet Trio, Op. 11, with polite condescension, offering in turn a showy improvisation on a popular operatic theme—the same tune chosen by Beethoven for the variations forming the finale of his trio. Beethoven retaliated by seizing the cello part of a quintet by Steibelt: after placing it upside down on the music stand, he poked out a theme with one finger from its opening bars. Offended, Steibelt walked out during Beethoven's ensuing brilliant improvisation and refused any further association with him.[20]

Beethoven's ability to transform any materials on hand into artistic coinage is illustrated in yet another story from his student Carl Czerny. Czerny reported that around 1809 the composer Ignaz Pleyel came to Vienna with his latest string quartet, which was performed at the home of Beethoven's patron Prince Lobkowitz. Beethoven was in attendance and was urged to perform at the piano. Rather typically, he was hesitant to play and became irritated, and then suddenly grabbed one of the parts from Pleyel's quartet—the second violin part—and began to improvise. Czerny relates that "Never had one heard something so ingenious, so captivating, so brilliant from him; but in the middle of his fantasy one could still hear plainly a banal run drawn from the violin part. . . . He had built his entire beautiful improvisation upon this figure."[21] In this case, as surely in many others, the improvised music also left its mark on one of Beethoven's major compositions from the time, his String Quartet in E-flat Major, Op. 74.[22]

The last of these reports thus makes explicit a characteristic aspect of Beethoven's improvisation practice: he would often seize on a particular audible motivic configuration—such as Pleyel's "banal run"—that could become the springboard for his own musical ideas and elaborations. Such evidence indicates that his practice in extemporized playing displayed the same kind of motivic concentration as occurs in his completed works. As has long been observed, Beethoven's finished pieces often display a tight motivic integration, a quality by no means confined to single movements. The famous upbeat motive of repeated notes in the Fifth Symphony is a paradigmatic example of this pervasive feature of Beethoven's compositional style.

This brings us back to Beethoven's Quintet, Op. 16, in relation to its presumed model, Mozart's K. 452. As we have seen, the slow introduction of Mozart's quintet emphasizes a descending scalar pattern—the stepwise falling motive first heard outlining the seventh G to A♭ heard in the bassoon in measure 10. In view of the prominence of this motive of a stepwise falling seventh near the outset of K. 452, it is striking that the opening motive in the main *Allegro, ma non troppo* section of the massive first movement of Beethoven's Opus 16 also outlines a stepwise fall through a seventh G to A♭ (see example 5. 2).

Following the upbeat figure B♭ to G, the high G is placed on a downbeat, supported by tonic harmony. The four-measure antecedent phrase that unfolds from this gesture outlines the descending seventh, closing on dominant harmony. Although the consequent phrase in measures 5–8 of the *Allegro, ma non troppo* reaches A♭, and unfolds over more than an octave, it comes to rest on B♭, so that the overall shape of the gesture retains the contour of a descending seventh, A♭ to B♭. Within the entire opening theme of sixteen bars, measures 10–14 isolate and emphasize the motivic idea of a falling step; the descending scale in measures 15–16 is articulated as a series of two-note figures.

We should note the striking ways in which Beethoven alters the motive in the opening theme of his *Allegro, ma non troppo*. Mozart's figure had appeared in steady sixteenth notes in a lower register, and it was then repeated in a series of sequences. In Beethoven's work, the motive appears in 3/4 time rather than in duple meter, as in K. 452, and it receives a much more distinctive melodic and rhythmic profile in a higher register. The highest pitch, G; the E♭ a major third lower; and the lowest tone, A♭, are each emphasized through the use of notes of longer duration, ornaments, or note repetition. By setting off his four-bar phrases with silences in measures 4 and 8, Beethoven presents the motive as a more characteristic entity. It will indeed assume an enhanced role in the unfolding musical discourse.

The descending motivic pattern can be heard throughout Beethoven's *Allegro, ma non troppo*, and not only when the opening subject is restated and developed. The *dolce* phrases at the beginning of the second subject and at the outset of the closing theme also partake of this gestural shape. The four-bar unit at the head of the second theme, played legato, outlines a falling stepwise pattern beginning on F and reaching A, a sixth lower; the five-bar phrase that introduces the cadential theme descends through the fifth, F to B♭, while uti-

Example 5.2. Beethoven, Quintet for Piano and Wind Instruments in E-flat Major, Op. 16, mvt. 1, mm. 1–20.

Example 5.3. Beethoven, Quintet for Piano and Wind Instruments in E-flat Major, Op. 16, mvt. 1: a) mm. 66–69; b) mm. 119–23.

lizing a variant of the sigh-figures that had been prominent in the opening subject (see example 5.3a and b). Particularly resourceful is Beethoven's compression of the closing theme into a two-bar unit in triplets. In turn this unit is reinterpreted as a falling staccato figuration in the piano, leading to the end of the exposition.

Our examination of the first movements of the two quintets has already indicated that the motivic figure based on a descending scale, and specifically the falling seventh G–A♭, assumes more prominence in Beethoven's work than in Mozart's.[23] Although this figure is conspicuous in Mozart's slow introduction, it is merely a localized musical element in K. 452.[24] By contrast, the same motive pervades the principal themes of Beethoven's entire first movement, and its importance is by no means confined to the opening *Allegro, ma non troppo* of Opus 16. The second movement, marked *Andante cantabile*, is a kind of slow movement rondo form with episodes, assuming the pattern ABA¹CA² coda. The main theme, which is varied and decorated each time it recurs, again displays the descending scalar contour so familiar from the first movement. The opening phrases of this *dolce* theme seem to reshape the *dolce* phrase at the head of the second subject of the opening *Allegro* (see example 5.4).

Andante cantabile

Example 5.4. Beethoven, Quintet for Piano and Wind Instruments in E-flat Major, Op. 16, mvt. 2, mm. 1–4.

Beethoven's sensitive reinterpretation of these phrases in his variations and coda ensures that the stepwise descending melodic contour remains prominent. This is nowhere more so than in the coda, with its falling scale in octaves played *fortissimo* in triplets in the piano over a dominant pedal point (m. 103). In the last moments of this *Andante cantabile*, the descending scalar motion is heard yet again in the piano. Falling thirds sink with a *decrescendo* through a three-octave descent into the bass, leading to the cadence of the movement in *pianissimo*.

In Beethoven's closing rondo, on the other hand, a melodic relation to Mozart's quintet is not in evidence. Instead, another of Mozart's finale themes becomes his model—the opening subject of the rondo finale of the Piano Concerto in E-flat Major, K. 482, from 1785. The main rondo theme of K. 482 is based on a swinging, hunting-type theme in $\frac{6}{8}$ meter. The two-bar phrases of this theme outline a rising contour, so that the upward shift from B♭ to E♭ reaches in G in measure 2; a sequence of this phrase moving from B♭ through F reaches A♭ in measure 4 (example 5.5). The overall melodic peak is reached in the third phrase, which passes from B♭ through G to the B♭ an octave higher, before the final two-bar unit brings a balancing melodic descent to a tonic cadence.

Like Mozart in K. 482, Beethoven initially gives the rondo Allegro theme in the finale of Opus 16 to the pianist; the swinging, hunting quality in 6/8 meter is retained from K. 482. Moreover, the opening pair of two-bar phrases of this theme outlines the same basic ascending pattern from B♭ through E♭ to G, and then from F to A♭. Significantly, the third two-bar phrase departs from its model, as Beethoven intensifies the ascent to reach C, a melodic peak underscored by a crescendo and a shift to subdominant harmony (example 5.6). Beethoven composed his main theme as a kind of variation on the rondo theme of Mozart's K. 482, but the model is effectively transformed, and the rest of the movement displays little contact with Mozart's work.

Example 5.5. Mozart, Piano Concerto in E-flat Major, K. 482, mvt. 3, mm. 1–8.

Example 5.6. Beethoven, Quintet for Piano and Wind Instruments in E-flat Major, Op. 16, mvt. 3, mm. 1–8.

Our comparison of Mozart's K. 452 and Beethoven's Opus 16 has uncovered motivic and thematic affinities that both confirm and limit the kinship between these compositions. As in his improvisatory practice, Beethoven seized on some specific structural features of Mozart's music while developing these aspects in ways that extend far beyond his models. At the same time, in the forms and proportions employed in his quintet, Beethoven departs substantially from Mozart, and his thematic model for the rondo theme in Opus 16 is taken from a different Mozartean work, K. 482. In particular, Beethoven's extensive development of the descending motive first heard in the bassoon in measure 10 of Mozart's K. 452 provokes reflection. Mozart's motivic idea is extensively developed and transformed in the different musical environment of Beethoven's Opus 16. Was he merely "trolling the surface for easy dividends" here? This situation calls for an interpretative approach that gives more recognition to the challenging and original features of Beethoven's energetic early style.

"*Odensprünge*": A Reevaluation of Beethoven's Opus 16

A reassessment of Beethoven's quintet can fruitfully engage with the early reception history and compositional genesis of the work. A review in 1803 described it as "a new quintet by Beethoven, brilliant, serious, full of deep expression and character, but sometimes too bold, with occasional rips in the framework [*Odensprünge*], in accordance with the inclination of this composer."[25] A key term that the reviewer uses is *Odensprünge*, meaning digressions or artistic leaps, flights of fancy related here to the theory of the literary ode. Reinhold Brinkmann has linked this notion of *Odensprung* to the "rip of the century" (*Riß des Jahrhunderts*), connecting it to Romantic currents and specifically to the formal experiments that would characterize Beethoven's "Rasumovsky" Quartets and subsequent works. Brinkmann observes in this context that the term *Odensprung* relates to "pathbreaking conceptions in chamber music and piano music, changes in formal function in sections and movements, and particularly to the discontinuities of later works, with their richly divergent semantic and structural aspects poised between fugue, homophonic sonata design, and instrumental recitative, as well as to changes in tempo and texture, breaks in narrative continuity, expressive contrasts, and to tensions between form and subjectivity, aspects that Adorno sought to recognize as definitive for Beethoven's late works."[26]

This perspective thus differs greatly from the dismissal of Beethoven's quintet as not a "serious work that could stand up to Mozart's." We can gain a richer sense of context from Beethoven's musical manuscripts and what is known of the origins of the quintet. Douglas Johnson has claimed on the basis of study of the manuscripts that "the Grave introduction to the first movement was in fact a late addition, or at least . . . did not reach mature form until after the remainder of the quintet had been worked out at length."[27] This insight makes good sense in light of the motivic affinities we have discussed. For unlike the main body of the first movement, the Grave introduction does not show a relationship to Mozart's quintet. Instead it displays an obvious parallel to the main theme of the finale, with its independent Mozartean source, K. 482. The first notes of the unison fanfare idea that opens the Grave—B♭–E♭ (repeated)–G–E♭—correspond to the beginning of the hunting-style theme of the finale. Most probably, Beethoven shaped the theme at the outset of the Grave introduction as a variant of the main subject of the finale, thereby casting connecting threads across the work as a whole. The evocation of a character suggestive of the hunt is especially appropriate here in light of the presence of the woodwind instruments, and particularly the horn.

Each of the movements of Opus 16 moves beyond Mozartean models, even when these are evoked, as in the first movement and the rondo. Instead of the compact development section of the first movement of Mozart's K. 452, Beethoven writes a spacious, wide-ranging development that modulates initially to C minor, a key that was emphasized in the slow introduction. A reprise of the opening theme follows in the subdominant, A-flat major, a gesture that proves to function as a false recapitulation. Beethoven balances the development with a long coda, in which the winds stress the head motive of the original theme, with its stepwise fall to the tonic E♭, heard under a high trill in the piano, before emphatic chords bring the movement to a powerful close.

The increasingly elaborate variations of the main theme in the *Andante cantabile* owe nothing to Mozart and foreshadow Beethoven's practice in many of his later slow movements, from the "Andante favori," WoO 57, to the slow movements of the late sonatas and quartets. The transitions to each return of the main theme are delicately handled, and the exquisite use of the winds echoing the piano in some later passages foreshadows the antiphonal effects between strings and winds in the *Adagio molto e cantabile* in the Ninth Symphony. This touching slow movement provides a fitting center of gravity to the work as a whole.

Nowhere in Opus 16 does the notion of an *Odensprung*, or creative flight of fancy overturning a preexisting framework, seem so appropriate as in the concluding rondo, marked *Allegro, ma non troppo*. As we have seen, Beethoven both draws here on a particular Mozartean model—the rondo theme from K. 482—and transforms it, especially through his use of the accented subdominant chord in measure 6, which is the climax of his theme. Beethoven's propensity for reinterpreting his thematic material is much in evidence in this movement. It contributes to the comic character of the music, which assumes a more robust character than Mozart's lighthearted wit and revelry. To be sure, Mozart's finale incorporates unexpected developments. At measure 150 of his rondo, Mozart brilliantly overturns our expectation of a symmetrical, resolving passage as we enter an astonishingly new expressive path including the "Cadenza in tempo." The central episode of Beethoven's rondo, on the other hand, is full of mock bluster: all the instruments first hammer out the head of the rondo theme in the minor. Then this motive is tossed about among the winds while the piano embroiders the harmonies with rapid virtuosic passagework. This whole minor-mode episode culminates in a showdown between the pianist playing double octaves *fortissimo*, and the ensemble of winds in harmony. But an ensuing transitional *decrescendo*, featuring a long descending scale to a soft landing on the familiar rondo theme, dissipates the commotion, confirming Beethoven's humorous intent.

This mischievous dimension also surfaces in a colorful report about Beethoven's own performance of the quintet. Ferdinand Ries related an occasion when Beethoven performed the piece with Friedrich Ramm as oboe soloist. Ries wrote that "In the last Allegro there are several holds [or pauses] before the theme is resumed. At one of these Beethoven suddenly began to improvise, took the Rondo for a theme and entertained himself and the others for a considerable time, but not the other players. They were displeased and Ramm even very angry. It was really very comical to see them, momentarily expecting the performance to be resumed, put their instruments to their mouths, only to put them down again. At length Beethoven was satisfied and dropped into the Rondo. The whole company was transported with delight."[28]

The "sore" note of the main theme—the high C first heard in the piano in measure 6—creates a large-scale tension that is intensified as the rondo subject is repeated and varied throughout the movement.[29] Beethoven's strategy is to bring this tension to a head in the final stages while reserving an active role for the pianist as soloist within the ensemble. Therefore the last full statement of the theme consists of antiphonal statements between the winds and piano, beginning at the upbeat to measure 227. The winds blast the opening phrase *fortissimo* in measures 227–28, answered by the pianist in *forte* in measures 229–30. Then the winds venture their statement of the crucial phrase, including the *crescendo* to high C, in measures 230–32 (see example 5.7).

At this juncture, Beethoven has the listener precisely where he wants him, in a state of suspense and uncertainty, surely not unlike the situation that so irritated Friedrich Ramm in 1804. For long moments, the pianist seeks alternatives to the familiar course of the rondo theme. The repeated Cs are carried upward to D♭, and from D♭ back to C; another attempt tries the rising third from C to E♭, with the harmonic ambiguity expressed through a diminished-seventh sonority in the winds and the left hand of the pianist. All of this is heard as a *decrescendo*, apparently in full retreat from reliable structures and formulaic patterns. Nevertheless, the goal of the mysterious *decrescendo* reached in measure 240 is none other than a $^6_4$ chord of the E-flat major tonic, the structural springboard to a cadence. The next, and last, version of the

Example 5.7. Beethoven, Quintet for Piano and Wind Instruments in E-flat Major, Op. 16, mvt. 3, mm. 221–57.

Example 5.7. (continued)

Example 5.7. (continued)

Example 5.7. (continued)

main motive in the piano is played softly on the dominant, B♭, leading into a long trill, heard over still-subdued gestures in the winds. Then, all at once, the accumulated tension is released in a delightfully surprising *fortissimo* close, with rapid scales across the keyboard leading into an emphatic motivic assertion suggestive of a hunting-type signal, a gesture reminiscent of the beginning of the entire work.

In this rondo, and the quintet as a whole, we encounter a situation in which resemblances to Mozart have been diminished in a thorough process of transformation. Beethoven undoubtedly found Mozart's music inspirational, but despite the parallels between these compositions, the differences weigh more heavily than the similarities. Tovey clearly overstated the imitative aspects of Beethoven's work, and our analysis does not support his view of Beethoven's quintet as an "easygoing, safety-first product." More to the point is Charles Rosen's insight about the elusive aspects of artistic influence, as expressed in his claim that "the most important form of influence is that which provokes the most original and most personal work."[30] In this context, Beethoven's quintet has been often misunderstood and underestimated. Hermann Abert's more balanced assessment of Mozart's K. 452 and Beethoven's Opus 16, that "both works truly mirror the qualities of their creators and stand artistically on the same level,"[31] has much to recommend it.

Notes

1. "Music for Prague and Berlin: Beethoven's Concert Tour of 1796," in *Beethoven, Performers, and Critics: The International Beethoven Congress, Detroit, 1977*, ed. Robert Winter and Bruce Carr (Detroit: Wayne State University Press, 1980), 35. Beethoven's sketches for Opus 16 are found exclusively on paper that he obtained during his tour.

2. Thomas K. Scherman and Louis Biancolli, eds., *The Beethoven Companion* (New York: Doubleday, 1972), 156.

3. *Beethoven* (London: Oxford University Press, 1945), 88.

4. In his book *Mozart, His Character, His Work*, translated by Arthur Mendel and Nathan Broder (New York: Oxford University Press, 1945), 265, Alfred Einstein writes that "Beethoven . . . considered it worth while to try to surpass this work [K. 452] in his Piano Quintet, Opus 16, although he did not succeed in doing so."

5. The most detailed study is Hartmut Krones, "Quintett Es-Dur für Klavier und Bläser Op. 16 (zusammen mit der Bearbeitung für Klavierquartett)," in Albrecht Riethmüller, Carl Dahlhaus, and Alexander L. Ringer, eds., *Beethoven: Interpretationen seiner Werke* (Laaber: Laaber Verlag, 1994), 1:121–28.

6. "Beethoven before 1800: The Mozart Legacy," *Beethoven Forum* 3 (1994): 39–52.

7. *Beethoven: The Music and The Life* (New York: Norton, 2003), 108.

8. "The Chamber Music with Piano," in Denis Arnold and Nigel Fortune, eds., *The Beethoven Reader* (New York: Norton, 1971), 208. One is inclined to reject Fortune's suggestion about Beethoven's Opus 16 that "a detailed comparison sheds no light on his work" (208).

9. *Beethoven* (New York: Schirmer, 1977), 102. This statement is deleted, however, from the second, revised edition of Solomon's book (New York: Schirmer, 1998).

10. *The Classical Style: Haydn, Mozart, Beethoven*, expanded ed. (New York: Norton, 1997), 381.

11. "Influence: Plagiarism and Inspiration," *19th Century Music* 4 (1980), 100.

12. A recent discussion of these works is offered in my book *Mozart's Piano Music* (New York: Oxford University Press, 2006), 156–212.

13. This catalogue has been published in facsimile as *Mozart—Eigenhändiges Werkverzeichnis Faksimile*, intro. and ed. Albi Rosenthal and Alan Tyson, British Library, Stefan Zweig MS 63 (Kassel: Bärenreiter, 1991).

14. Letter of April 10, 1784. See Emily Anderson, trans., *The Letters of Mozart and His Family* (London: Macmillan, 1985), 873.

15. In 1783 Mozart made a sketch for a quintet for piano, oboe, clarinet, basset horn, and bassoon, a work he never completed. See the entry for K. 452a in Ulrich Konrad, *Mozarts Schaffensweise* (Göttingen: Vandenhoeck & Ruprecht, 1992), 163–64.

16. Wendt's critique appeared in the *Allgemeine musikalische Zeitung* and is cited by Elaine Sisman in "After the Heroic Style: *Fantasia* and the 'Characteristic' Sonatas of 1809," *Beethoven Forum* 6 (1998), 96.

17. *Thayer's Life of Beethoven*, ed. Elliot Forbes (hereafter Thayer-Forbes) (Princeton, NJ: Princeton University Press, 1964), 367.

18. Hermann Deiters and Hugo Riemann, eds., *Ludwig van Beethovens Leben von Alexander Wheelock Thayer* (Leipzig: Breitkopf & Härtel, 1917), 1:355.

19. Thayer-Forbes, 205; and Theodor von Frimmel, "Der Klavierspieler Beethoven," in Frimmel, *Beethoven–Studien* (Munich and Leipzig: Georg Müller, 1906), 2:243–44.

20. Thayer-Forbes, 257.

21. Walter Kolneder, ed., *Erinnerungen aus meinem Leben* (Strassburg and Baden-Baden, 1968), 45.

22. Hartmut Krones has identified the "banal run" in the "Rondeau" Finale of Pleyel's G-Major Quartet, Op. 8, no. 2, and discovers its transformation in the trio of Beethoven's Quartet in E-flat Major, Op. 74, from 1809. See Krones, "Streichquartett Es-Dur op. 74," in Albrecht Riethmüller, Carl Dahlhaus, and Alexander Ringer, eds., *Beethoven: Interpretationen seiner Werke* (Laaber: Laaber Verlag, 1994), 1:587.

23. In view of these motivic similarities, as well as the general parallels between Mozart's K. 452 and Beethoven's Opus 16 in their overall structure and key schemes, it is hard to maintain skepticism about Beethoven's knowledge of Mozart's work, such as is expressed by Barry Cooper in his study *Beethoven* (New York: Oxford University Press, 2000), 66–67.

24. There is a suggestion of descending linear motion through G–F–E♭–D in measures 21–22, at the beginning of the *Allegro moderato* in K. 452, but these motivic relations are present only to a very limited extent in Mozart's quintet.

25. "[E]in neues Quintett von Beethoven, genialisch, ernst, voll tiefen Sinnes und Characters, nur dann und wann zu grell, hier und da O d e n s p r ü n g e, nach der Manier dieses Componisten," in Hermann Deiters and Hugo Riemann, eds., *Ludwig van Beethovens Leben von Alexander Wheelock Thayer* (Leipzig: Breitkopf & Härtel, 1922), 2:380. Although the work under discussion is not explicitly identified, it seems clearly to be Op. 16, which had been published in March 1801.

26. "Wirkungen Beethovens in der Kammermusik," in Sieghard Brandenburg and Helmut Loos, eds., *Beiträge zu Beethovens Kammermusik. Symposion Bonn 1984* (Munich: Henle, 1987), 100–101.

27. "Beethoven's Early Sketches in the 'Fischhof Miscellany': Berlin Autograph 28" (PhD diss., University of California, Berkeley, 1978), 614. A few sketches for the first movement and more extended sketches and drafts for the second and third movements are transcribed in Joseph Kerman, ed., *Ludwig van Beethoven. Autograph Miscellany from circa 1786 to 1799. British Museum Additional Manuscript 29801, ff. 39–162 (The 'Kafka Sketchbook')* (London: British Museum, 1970), 2: 39–42.

28. Thayer-Forbes, 350. Actually, there is only one fermata before a return of the main theme, in measure 75, and this is likely the place where Beethoven chose to extend the rondo through spontaneous improvisation.

29. This is a compositional strategy that Beethoven employed brilliantly in other works, such as the rondo finale of the Piano Concerto in C Minor, Op. 37, in which the high "sore" note of the main theme—A♭—is subject to reinterpretation. For a more detailed discussion, see my study *Beethoven* (New York: Oxford University Press, 1995), 68–72.

30. "Influence: Plagiarism and Inspiration," 88.

31. Hermann Abert, *W. A. Mozart, herausgegeben als fünfte, vollständig neu bearbeitete und erweiterte Ausgabe von Otto Jahns Mozart* (Leipzig: Breitkopf & Härtel, 1921), 2:189. An English translation of Abert's book containing a somewhat different rendering of this passage has been made available as Hermann Abert, *W. A. Mozart,* trans. Stewart Spencer, ed. Cliff Eisen (New Haven: Yale University Press, 2007), 862. In addition to its dedication to Charles Rosen, this essay is written for my friend Carles Riera, clarinetist and basset horn player, with whom I have enjoyed performing these delightful works.

Chapter Six

Vestas Feuer

Beethoven on the Path to Leonore

Lewis Lockwood

Clinging all his life to an improbable dream of operatic success, Beethoven achieved it only once, with *Fidelio* in 1814—the third version of the opera he had originally written as *Leonore* in 1805 and revised in 1806.[1] All his other dramatic projects remained mirages, though some were vivid, since he was never able to develop any of the operatic subjects that he sought independently or those that were urged on him by his friends and acquaintances. His letters and conversation books contain various references to operatic ideas, some of them matched by brief musical jottings in his sketchbooks.[2] But aside from *Leonore* the only operatic scene that he ever actually set to music in essentially complete form was the first scene of Emanuel Schikaneder's *Vestas Feuer*, written in late 1803 before he gave up the project and began work on *Leonore*.[3]

How should we understand Beethoven's lifelong hope of writing operas, only once fulfilled? It is a commonplace that his only finished work centers on a faithful and courageous wife who saves her imprisoned husband. This idealistic theme fit well with Beethoven's high moral standard for operatic plots and, on the personal side, his obsessive fantasy, equally unfulfilled, of what an ideal woman might do for him if he could achieve a lasting relationship.

But opera was uncomfortable terrain for him, and he knew it. Immersed in his work and career, in later years increasingly deaf, sick, isolated, and eccentric, he always understood that instrumental music was his natural habitat, the domain in which he was free to develop his creative powers to the fullest. He could write effective vocal music, both secular and sacred, solo and choral, to keep his hand in or to satisfy occasional commissions, but he was never able to put his highest artistry into lieder until he came to write the song cycle *An die ferne Geliebte* in 1815, nor into sacred music until the monumental *Missa solemnis* in 1819–23. As for stage music, he could compose overtures and sometimes incidental music for spoken dramas, such as *Coriolanus, Egmont, King Stephen,* and

The Ruins of Athens, for these projects enabled him to elaborate his dramatic imagination without becoming entangled in the constraints of opera. In a related genre, his early *Ritterballet* in Bonn was a minor effort, and his *Prometheus* of 1800–1801 for the ballet master Salvatore Viganò was a colorful orchestral experiment that he never repeated. There is credibility in the claim that he disdained the stereotyped plots and characters of much traditional opera. Contemporaries report his saying that, despite his reverence for Mozart, he would never have composed a *Don Giovanni* or *Così fan tutte*. Such feelings resonate with his deep-seated idealism, his growing sense of having a call to greatness not only as a composer but as an artist dedicated to Enlightenment and libertarian ideals in an age disillusioned by the failure of the French Revolution to live up to its ideals and to produce much besides despotism and war. He writes to Prince Galitzin to say that "my most ardent wish is that my art may find favor with the noblest and most highly educated men; unfortunately, and in a manner none too gentle one is dragged down from the heaven of art into what is earthy."[4] By "earthy" Beethoven meant daily life and everything pertaining to life's necessities, including money. Opera certainly qualified for this rubric, the more so since Beethoven knew that operatic success was a high road to financial security, a nagging concern all his life.

Thus far the generally accepted view. But my argument is that he had a more nuanced lifetime romance with opera than is generally thought, and that the world of opera was more important for his artistic development than we could possibly judge from the very thin ratio of fantasies to results. In a larger sense, operatic thinking and many of his unfinished—in some cases, hardly begun—operatic ideas found their way into his instrumental music. His exposure to opera during his early years in Bonn, where he was an orchestral musician, resulted principally in his many sets of variations on operatic tunes.[5] This exposure continued during his years as a composer and listener in Vienna. Later, operatic elements appear in his instrumental music in the form of recitatives, ariosos, and aria types, including the Cavatina of the String Quartet, Op. 130. Although this is not the place for a close look at the many operatic projects he considered setting over his lifetime, I want to look at his approach to opera during the earlier phase of his career as embodied in the first scene of Schikaneder's *Vestas Feuer*.

In 1803 Emanuel Schikaneder (1751–1812) had passed the peak of his notorious career as a theater entrepreneur, singer, actor, and librettist, and was forever reaping the glory of having been Mozart's librettist for *The Magic Flute* as well as the original Papageno.[6] Yet even now, twelve years after Mozart's death, Schikaneder was still fully active in the theater. Living by his wits and ingenuity, he had become the director of the large new Theater an der Wien that had opened in June 1801. The building was equipped with machinery that would dazzle audiences with Schikaneder's beloved exotic stage effects. The property also included a four-story house with offices and apartments for Schikaneder and members of his company. Early in 1803 Schikaneder offered Beethoven one of these apartments, obviously to promote his collaboration. Beethoven took it rent free as part of an apparent agreement to write an opera for the new house, no doubt with the expectation of sharing in the proceeds. It was not a bad move for Beethoven, who also got his brother Carl, his business manager, into another apartment in the same building and promptly used the theater for a concert of his own music in early April 1803.[7] Beethoven seems to have lived in this theater apartment from April 1803 to about May 1804, leaving only in the summer months to go out of town to Baden and Oberdöbling.[8]

His correspondence and the "Eroica" sketchbook, which he used that year, confirm that for most of the year Beethoven paid no attention to Schikaneder's libretto or any other opera, and he did not even have the text of *Vestas Feuer* in hand before late October. Instead, he was wholly engaged on a much more important project, his Third Symphony. At first he called this symphony *Bonaparte*, but he ripped up the dedication to the newly crowned Napoleon in December 1804. The work was labeled *Eroica* only when it was published in 1806.[9] Meanwhile, in November 1803, as he reported in a letter, he finally started work on the first scene of *Vestas Feuer*.[10]

Schikaneder's farces and popular stage works had long appealed to the coarsest tastes of the public, but now he was looking for more serious theatrical pieces that would keep up with current trends. These included a libretto on Alexander the Great that he had evidently offered to Beethoven in 1801, when the theater opened, but which Beethoven ignored; it was set instead by Franz Teyber. New postrevolutionary French operas, especially by Cherubini, began to sweep Vienna in these years, and Schikaneder himself rushed to put on Cherubini's *Der Wasserträger (Les deux journées)* in 1802, in competition with Baron Braun, a rival entrepreneur who ran the Kärntnertortheater at the time.

Sometime early in 1803 Schikaneder cranked out the libretto of *Vestas Feuer*, a "grand heroic opera" based on a subject from ancient Rome. Beethoven worked on *Vestas Feuer* for about two months before dropping it abruptly in favor of the much more congenial and politically relevant *Léonore* by Bouilly, which had been set earlier by Gaveaux and Paer. In a letter of January 4, 1804 he called *Leonore* "an old French libretto [which] I have quickly had . . . adapted and am now beginning to work on."[11] Besides the Third Symphony he had the "Waldstein" Sonata in progress during the fall of 1803, along with some lesser compositions. We see from his letters and from the position of the *Vestas Feuer* sketches in the "Eroica" sketchbook that he got down to work on the opera only in early November. But by late December he was fed up with Schikaneder and the whole project, as he wrote to Friedrich Rochlitz in January 1804:

> However fortunate I should have counted myself to be allowed to compose the music for this text [of yours] [i.e., an unnamed libretto that Rochlitz had sent him], yet it

would have been quite impossible to do this now. If the subject had not been connected with magic, your libretto might have extricated me from a most embarrassing situation. For I have finally broken with Schikaneder, whose kingdom has been entirely eclipsed by the light of the clever and thoughtful French operas. Meanwhile he has held me back for fully six months, and I have let myself be deceived simply because, since he is undeniably good at creating stage effects, I hoped that he would produce something more clever than usual. How wrong I was. I hoped at least that he would have the verses and the contents of the libretto corrected and improved by someone else, but in vain. For it was impossible to persuade this arrogant fellow to do this. Well, I have given up my arrangement with him, although I had composed several numbers. Just picture to yourself a Roman subject (of which I had been told neither the scheme nor anything else whatever) and language and verses such as could come out of the mouths of our Viennese women apple-vendors.[12]

If Beethoven found Schikaneder's stubbornness over textual changes impossible to bear and his faith in exotic stage effects outmoded, it's not difficult to imagine his wondering how Mozart could have put up with Schikaneder as a librettist and actor–stage manager. Beethoven might also have considered that, if he did collaborate with Schikaneder, his contemporaries and posterity would forever compare him as such directly with Mozart—above all in opera, the one field in which he knew Mozart reigned supreme and in which Beethoven was unlikely to prosper, let alone rival him. At all events, he found good reasons to extricate himself, as he said to Rochlitz, from this potential mode of comparison with Mozart and *The Magic Flute*, a work he loved and that he knew like the back of his hand.[13] Beethoven had been living with the spirit of Mozart all his life. His early teacher, Christian Gottlob Neefe, had publicly declared that his young pupil in Bonn had the makings of a "second Mozart." Beethoven's patron in Bonn, the Elector Max Franz, had deeply admired Mozart and had tried to bring him to the Rhineland. When this did not happen, Beethoven at sixteen had been sent to Vienna in 1787 to visit Mozart and possibly become his pupil; the visit had been cut short when news of his mother's illness forced his return. When he finally left Bonn to move to Vienna in November 1792, less than a year after Mozart's death, his patrons envisioned him as Mozart's true successor. His friend Count Waldstein wrote in Beethoven's farewell album the much-quoted remark that by studying with Haydn, Beethoven would be the recipient of the genius of the dead Mozart and would be granted the "spirit of Mozart" from the hands of Haydn. In 1803–4, moreover, Beethoven's problems with Schikaneder were emerging during the later phases of his monumental labor on the *Eroica*, the powerful new symphony that was launching him into a new artistic phase, and that more than any other single work embodied his decisive break with the Mozart-Haydn legacy on which he had essentially built his earlier style.

It's interesting that in his letter to Rochlitz, Beethoven condemned the language and verse forms of the libretto, thus displaying a degree of critical acumen about operatic language with which he has not been generally credited. If we look at what he actually did with Schikaneder's material for the opening scene of the opera, we can gain a new sense of why he abandoned this project but also, on the positive side, what he might have learned from it about operatic technique.

The plot of *Vestas Feuer* ("The Vestal Flame") centers on the Temple of Vesta, a shrine in ancient Rome that had been built to contain the sacred fire believed to have been brought from Troy by Aeneas. It was dedicated to Vesta, goddess of the household and hearth, and its six virgin handmaidens were sworn to keep the eternal flame burning lest a great calamity should follow. The basic subject is related to that of *La Vestale*, famously set by Spontini in 1807 to a text by Etienne de Jouy, and a work that Beethoven admired. Other Vesta libretti had been set by various Italian composers in the later eighteenth century, and as late as the 1840s it was still employed by Pavesi, Pacini, and Mercadante.[14]

Schikaneder presents four main characters:

Porus, a noble Roman	Baritone
Volivia, his daughter	Soprano
Sartagones, Volivia's lover	Tenor
Malo, a slave of Porus	Tenor

There are at least ten other minor figures in the plot, but they hardly matter to us, since Beethoven never got beyond the first scene, in which only the four principals appear. The plot, in simple terms, centers on the heroine Volivia and her lover Sartagones, "a noble Roman," whose father is Porus's sworn enemy.[15] Intrigues are hatched by the jealous slave Malo and by other characters led by Romenius, a Roman official. Romenius also loves Volivia and, for her, has abandoned his former lover, Sericia. Romenius manages to banish both Porus and Sartagones from Rome. Volivia seeks refuge from Romenius's advances by becoming a priestess in the Temple of Vesta, thus giving Romenius and his soldiers a reason to destroy the temple—whereupon the sacred flame is extinguished. After various episodes, including the reappearance of Porus and Sartagones, Romenius has Malo drowned in the Tiber but is himself stabbed by his jealous lover, Sericia. When all the evildoers are dead, the sacred flame miraculously reignites itself, the Vestal Virgins rejoice, and Volivia is reunited with Sartagones and Porus amid general rejoicing. The terrific scenic effects include a moment when the moon and stars turn blood red, a sword and comet appear in the sky, and the Tiber turns red below them.

The first scene, like the rest, is written in the verse forms typical of German Singspiel. As the curtain rises, the stage setting is:

a charming garden of cypress trees, with a waterfall in the middle, which flows into a stream on the right side of the stage. On the left is a cemetery . . . [and] the morning sun glows through the trees.

Malo has been spying on the lovers, Volivia and Sartagones, and he rushes on to tell Porus he has seen them together, presumably all night since it is now morning. Porus is furious, because he hates Sartagones, and declares he will disown his daughter:

Ha, verflucht sei diese Stunde,	Ah! accursed be this hour,
wenn die Tochter sich vergisst!—	when my daughter forgets herself—
Komm! Sie hör aus meinem Munde	Come! let her hear from my lips,
dass verstossen sie nun ist.	That now she is disowned.

Porus and Malo hide as the lovers appear. Now Sartagones and Volivia swear to love each other, but she anxiously begs Sartagones to ask her father's blessing, assuring him that Porus is good hearted. Porus suddenly emerges and confronts Sartagones, evoking their ancient family feud. Volivia pleads, but Porus is adamant. Then Sartagones draws his sword, asking "Will she not be mine?" Porus refuses, whereupon Sartagones points the sword at his own breast. But Porus, whose anger turns in a flash to sympathy, strikes the sword at once from Sartagones's hand, singing with Volivia, "Halt ein!" (arousing memories of similar scenes, including that in which Papageno puts the noose around his own neck and then is saved from suicide by the Three Boys).

Now Porus immediately turns magnanimous, in the manner of Sarastro, declaring, "Since you love her so much, I will bestow her upon you" and affirms his friendship for Sartagones. Malo, upset by all this, leaves the stage, whereupon the three main characters—the father and the two lovers—close the first scene in a joyful trio of mutual affection. The trio opens with Volivia and Sartagones singing

Nie war ich so froh wie heute!	Never was I so happy as I am today,
Niemals fühlt ich diese Freude" (etc.).	Never did I feel such joy.

To which Porus adds:

Gute Götter, blickt herab,	Oh Gods, look down
segnet ihre reinen Triebe	bless their pure desires,
ewig treu sei eure Liebe,	May their love be ever true,
ewig treu bis in der Grab.	Ever true unto the grave.

This is the trio from which Beethoven borrowed directly for Leonore and Florestan's reunion duet on the text "O namenlose Freude."

Beethoven sets up the scene as follows:

Section 1 G minor, [Allegro], 4/4, mm. 1–60
Orchestral introduction (mm. 1–19)
Dialogue of Malo and Porus (mm. 29–60), closing on V/E-flat with fermata

Section 2 E-flat major, [Andante], 6/8, mm. 61–99
Dialogue of Volivia and Sartagones, closing in E-flat major plus brief transition
Section 3 C minor, with subsidiary harmonic motions; 4/4, mm. 100–145
Accompanied dialogue recitative: confrontation of Sartagones and Porus, ending in their reconciliation
Section 4 G major, [Allegro], 4/4, mm. 146–275
Final trio: Volivia and Sartagones declare their happiness; Porus blesses them.

Seemingly undaunted by Schikaneder's scenic language, Beethoven follows Mozart by setting up a multisectional operatic *Introduzione*, though he does not label it as such. Mozart's last three operas—*Don Giovanni, Così fan tutte*, and *Die Zauberflöte*—all have such "Introductions," each one expressly designated. Each Introduzione frames the opening of its opera in a miniplay that has a specific dramatic and musical shape and its own rounded harmonic plan. With each Introduzione Mozart sets up and anticipates the expanded harmonic system of the entire opera.

Beethoven's first scene has the kind of tonal unity that he found in Mozart's "Introductions." His key centers move, section by section, down through thirds from G minor to E-flat major to C minor (with modulatory motions). He then returns to the tonic, G, now in major mode, which is appropriate for the happy ending of the first scene. This scheme is the exact harmonic retrograde of the "Introduction" that opens *Die Zauberflöte*. That "Introduction" moves, section by section, upward in thirds from C minor (Tamino's encounter with the serpent) to E-flat major (the three Ladies) to G major (the 6/8 Allegretto as the Ladies decide to leave) and finally C major (smitten with the handsome and unconscious Tamino, the Ladies say farewell to him).

Beethoven's first segment, in G minor, begins with some modest dramatic tension as Malo rushes on, accompanied by pianissimo running figures, each measure starting with a dissonant appoggiatura. The dialogue of Malo and Porus sets Schikaneder's threadbare language effectively enough (see example 6.1).[16]

In segment 2, for the two lovers, Beethoven shifts to an E-flat-major 6/8 interlude of quiet expressivity, apparently an Andante (no tempi are marked in the autograph, but Andante makes sense), The character of the section recalls some other early Beethoven 6/8 movements, such as the E-major slow movement of the Piano Trio, Op. 1, no. 2, though without its strong melodic sweep (example 6.2):

Not far in the background is the E-flat-major 6/8 duet of Pamina and Papageno, "Bei Männern, welche Liebe fühlen," which Beethoven had used for a set of cello and piano variations, WoO 46. In that work he had simplified Mozart's metrical scheme by starting on a simple upbeat to measure 1 rather than, as Mozart does, with the upbeat in the middle of the first measure. There is even a partial hint here of the 6/8 *Andante sostenuto* quartet in *Leonore*, "Mir ist so wunderbar," though without the quartet's spellbound concentration.

Example 6.1. Beethoven, *Vestas Feuer*, scene 1, mm. 1–18. Willy Hess, ed., *Ludwig van Beethoven: Supplemente zur Gesamtausgabe*, XIII. Wiesbaden: Breitkopf und Härtel, ©1970. Used by kind permission.

But the novelty in the first scene is certainly Section 3, which may be Beethoven's only example of real operatic dialogue in *recitativo accompagnato*, in the traditional sense—that is, in which Beethoven imitates Mozart's assimilation of that tradition into German opera. It is true that this was not Beethoven's first experiment altogether with *recitativo accompagnato*. He had used it in his solo aria "Ah, perfido," Op. 65, of 1796, a scene from Metastasio's *Achille in Sciro*, with

etc.

Example 6.1. (continued)

modified text.[17] And he had included solo recitatives in his early cantatas, that for Emperor Joseph II and that for Leopold II, both from 1790. Further, *Christus am Ölberge*, Op. 85, the first version of which was written in March 1803, about eight months before *Vestas Feuer*, also has several accompanied recitatives for Jesus and one for the Seraph, plus a short one in dialogue for Jesus and Peter, just preceding their climactic trio with the Seraph that opens the last part of the oratorio. But the short dialogue in *Christus* is at best a very partial parallel to the recitative duet in *Vestas Feuer*; its twenty-five measures hardly compare in length or modulatory range with the forty-six measures of the scene for Sartagones and Porus (example 6.3).

In this dialogue section the point is to advance the action swiftly. There is a modest dramatic climax when Sartagones draws his sword and threatens suicide if he cannot have Volivia, followed by Porus's benevolent change of heart. All of this is barely credible, unashamedly naive in expression and in pacing. Still, Beethoven does all he can to fortify the dramatic moment, above all Porus's sudden reversal, a modest *peripateia* typical of operatic scenes of this type. Consider this high point (examples 6.4a and b):

Example 6.2. *Vestas Feuer,* opening of E-flat-major duet, Sartagones and Volivia.

The musical material of the Trio in section 4, the closing segment, is on a much higher level than all that has preceded it. The rolling two-note arpeggiated figures run throughout, effectively sustaining the long lyric lines, and Porus furnishes a solid bass to the soprano-tenor pair above (example 6.5).

Example 6.2. (continued)

As the big ensemble winds toward its close (mm. 196–202), Porus adds a slight chromatic motion to the bass line on the word "Grab" as he exhorts the lovers to love one another "unto the grave." Winton Dean once pointed out that the declamation of the opening line, "Nie war ich so froh wie heute" is actually better than that which Beethoven was forced to use for Leonore and Florestan,

Example 6.3. Accompanied recitative: Porus, Sartagones, Volivia, mm. 99–110.

who sing "O namenlose Freude!" In the 1806 *Leonore* he adds an upbeat quarter-note for "O" then continues as before; but for the full phrase "O namenlose Freude," he has to repeat the first two syllables of the second word to fit the music, making it "O namen- namenlose Freude."[18] When he rewrote the duet

etc.

Example 6.3. (continued)

for the 1814 version, he allowed Leonore and Florestan to move forward in separate utterances, she leading, he answering.

Giving up on Schikaneder's feeble libretto after two months, Beethoven turned gratefully to a drama that offered characters and actions he could take seriously: Leonore, Florestan, Pizarro, and his underling Rocco, along with the profoundly moving chorus of suffering prisoners, confined in Pizarro's dungeons, who yearn for the light that symbolizes freedom. At the end appears the

Example 6.4. Accompanied recitative: Porus, Sartagones, Volivia, Malo:
a) mm. 114–23; b) mm. 134–45.

benevolent minister, Don Fernando, who resolves all troubles. All these individuals, bearers of meanings far beyond operatic plots and intrigues, embody
authentic human issues in ways that permitted Beethoven to integrate operatic
conventions into his moral vision.

Yet *Vestas Feuer* shows Beethoven advancing his knowledge of operatic technique for the first time. We see him carefully fashioning an opening scene on
the Mozartean model, devoting himself to it with his usual concentration and
creative seriousness, determined to give it his best despite the triviality of the

Example 6.4. (continued)

text. This score and its sketches (the latter still unpublished) show him working to rescue something of value from Schikaneder's libretto. More than a few moments in the score—Malo's running feet, the hero and heroine's quiet pledge of love, Sartagones' confrontation with Porus, and finally, the swiftly moving, well-knit Trio—show the mature Beethoven endeavoring to make something

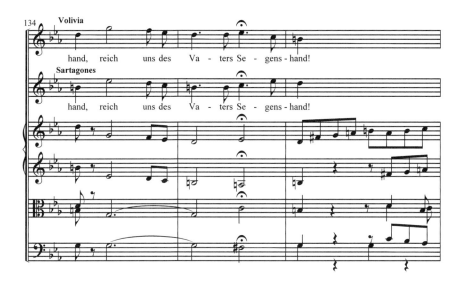

Example 6.4. (continued)

emotionally and musically effective from the materials he had to work with. However modest its place in Beethoven's larger development, *Vestas Feuer* is valuable for what it reveals: Beethoven, in a crucial year of his artistic life, striving to master operatic technique, poised between one of his greatest models, *The Magic Flute*, and his own first complete opera soon to come.

Example 6.4. (continued)

Example 6.5. Accompanied recitative, end, and trio: Volivia, Sartagones, Porus, mm. 146–63.

Example 6.5. (continued)

etc.

Example 6.5. (continued)

Notes

1. For a survey of recent *Leonore/Fidelio* scholarship, see H. Lühning and W. Steinbeck, *Von der Leonore bis zum Fidelio* (Frankfurt am Main: Peter Lang, 2000).

2. On Beethoven's approach to opera, see Winton Dean, "Beethoven and Opera," in *The Beethoven Reader*, ed. D. Arnold and N. Fortune (New York: Norton, 1971), 331–86. For a survey of approximately fifty operatic projects that Beethoven considered at various times, and helpful plot summaries, see Rudolf Pecman, *Beethovens Opernpläne*, translated into German from the original Czech (Brno: Univerzita J. E. Purkyne, 1981).

3. Willy Hess published *Vestas Feuer* twice: in a separate edition issued in 1953 by Bruckner-Verlag (Wiesbaden) and again in 1957 by Alkor Edition (Kassel); and in Hess's *Beethoven: Supplemente zur Gesamtausgabe* (Wiesbaden: Breitkopf & Härtel, 1970), 13:143–68. See No. 115 in Hess's *Verzeichnis der nicht in der Gesamtausgabe Veröffentlichten Werke . . . Beethovens* (Wiesbaden, 1957). Clayton Westerman's edition is *Vestas Feuer* (New York: G. Schirmer, 1983). The source for all these editions is a full manuscript orchestral score for the work, in the Bibliothek der Gesellschaft der Musikfreunde in Vienna, that was to include all parts for voices and strings plus pairs of flutes, oboes, clarinets, bassoons, and horns. After sketching the work in his current sketchbook (later Landsberg 6) Beethoven completed the vocal parts and basic orchestral content of scene 1 in his score, leaving only the wind and brass parts to be added. As Hess puts it, "[T]he entire redaction of the score shows remarkably few corrections." See Hess's critical notes for *Vestas Feuer. Supplemente,* 13: XXXVIII.

4. For Beethoven's approach to opera, besides Dean's article "Beethoven and Opera" in *The Beethoven Reader*, see Maynard Solomon, *Beethoven*, 2nd rev. ed. (New

York: Schirmer Books, 1998), 237, 256, 268–69, 347, 350; and Lewis Lockwood, *Beethoven: The Music and the Life* (New York: Norton, 2003), especially pp. 252–61. For the letter to Galitzin, one of Beethoven's most important and revealing letters, see *Beethoven Briefe*, No. 2003; for this letter I prefer the translation by J. S. Shedlock, *The Letters of Beethoven* (London: J. M. Dent, 1926), No. 404, here slightly modified. On Beethoven's aesthetic ideals, see Maynard Solomon, "Reason and Imagination: Beethoven's Aesthetic Evolution," in *Historical Musicology: Sources, Methods, Interpretations*, ed. Stephen Crist and Roberta Marvin (Rochester: University of Rochester Press, 2004), 188–203; reprinted in Solomon, *Late Beethoven* (Berkeley, CA: University of California Press), 92–101.

5. On this aspect of Beethoven's early variation sets based on operatic themes, see Stephen Moore Whiting, "To the 'New Manner' Born: A Study of Beethoven's Early Variations" (PhD diss., University of Illinois at Urbana-Champaign, 1991), and Elaine Sisman, *Haydn and the Classical Variation* (Cambridge, MA: Harvard University Press, 1993). Beethoven's early variations are based on tunes from operas by Righini, Dittersdorf, Mozart, Grétry, Paisiello, Salieri, Winter, and Süssmayr.

6. On Schikaneder see, most recently, Kurt Honolka, *Papageno: Emanuel Schikaneder, Man of the Theater in Mozart's Time*, translated by Jane M. Wilde from the original German edition of 1984 (Portland: Amadeus Press, 1990); Max Kammermeyer, *Emanuel Schikaneder und seine Zeit* (Grafenau, 1992); and Günter Meinhold, *Zauberflöte und Zauberflöte-Rezeption* (Frankfurt am Main: Peter Lang, 2001). For a pithy overview of Schikaneder's relations with Beethoven, see Peter Clive, *Beethoven and His World* (Oxford: Oxford University Press, 2001), 308–9.

7. At this concert he premiered his Third Piano Concerto, Second Symphony, and *Christus am Ölberge*.

8. On Beethoven's many apartments in Vienna and his summer residences out of town, see Kurt Smolle, *Wohnstätten Ludwig van Beethovens von 1792 bis zum seinem Tod* (Munich: G. Henle Verlag, 1970).

9. For an introductory overview of the "Eroica" sketchbook (MS Landsberg 6, Deutsche Staatsbibliothek, Berlin—now in Kraków) see D. Johnson, A. Tyson, and R. Winter, *The Beethoven Sketchbooks: History, Reconstruction, Inventory* (Berkeley: University of California Press, 1985), 137–45, and earlier literature cited there.

10. *Briefe*, No. 165, ca. October 22, 1803, Ferdinand Ries to Simrock in Bonn: "Beethoven will soon receive the subject of his opera"; No. 169, November 2, 1803 (Beethoven to Alexander Macco in Prague): "I am just now beginning work on my opera, and that may last until its performance next Easter."

11. *Briefe*, No. 176, Beethoven to Rochlitz in Leipzig.

12. *Briefe*, No. 176. The translation here slightly modifies that of Anderson, No. 87a.

13. On Beethoven's admiration for *The Magic Flute* and his use of material from it not only as source for two sets of variations (WoO 46 and Opus 66) but in other ways, see my *Beethoven: The Music and the Life*, 100, 242, 253 (on Seyfried's testimony that Beethoven revered the opera), 256, 316, 446, 523, n. 11.

14. See Harold Rosenthal and John Warrack, *The Concise Oxford Dictionary of Opera*, 2nd ed. (Oxford: Oxford University Press, 1979), 527.

15. For the full text of the libretto, see Willy Hess, "'Vestas Feuer' von Emanuel Schikaneder," *Beethoven-Jahrbuch* 3 (1957–58): 63–110. For one of several published plot summaries, see G. Biamonti, *Catalogo Cronologico et Tematico delle opere di Beethoven* (Turin: ILTE, 1968), 435–36.

16. In the following musical examples, missing rests, slurs, and similar markings have been supplied.

17. That the text of "Ah, perfido" is not taken entirely from Metastasio, at least in the aria section, is indicated by Giovanni Biamonti, *Catalogo cronologico e tematico dell opere di Beethoven* (Torino: ILTE, 1968), 117.

18. Dean, "Beethoven and Opera," 354–55.

Chapter Seven

Sonority and Structure

Observations on Beethoven's Early and Middle-Period Piano Compositions

Robert L. Marshall

By the time Beethoven was thirty years old he was already an accomplished composer. By then he had completed, among other things: a symphony, two piano concertos, two cello sonatas, four piano trios, three violin sonatas, and no fewer than a dozen piano sonatas. Most of these are major works, obviously revealing, along with Beethoven's characteristic boldness of invention and unprecedented power of expression, a thorough—and thoroughly original—mastery of the well-established formal and tonal principles governing large-scale instrumental form.[1]

What is striking about this tabulation is the preponderance of compositions for or with the piano. This is not at all surprising, of course, since by 1800 Beethoven was also one of the most successful pianists of his time. Moreover, he had been performing, and composing, piano music for more than half his life—for almost twenty of his thirty years, in fact, if one is willing to count the juvenilia produced by the eleven-year-old in the year 1782. His first extraordinary piano composition, however, was written at about the age of twenty. It confirms that by 1790, i.e., two years before he had left Bonn for Vienna in order to begin the "serious" study of composition with Joseph Haydn, Beethoven had completely mastered the art of writing effectively and idiomatically for the keyboard.

The "Righini" Variations, WoO 65

The composition is the set of Twenty-Four Variations on the Arietta "Venni amore" by Vicenzo Righini, WoO 65.[2] The variations display a thoroughgoing familiarity with and command of the most brilliant keyboard virtuosity, featuring

Example 7.1. Beethoven, 24 Variations on the Arietta "Venni amore" by Vincenzo Righini ("Righini" Variations), WoO 65, a. Theme.

such sensational difficulties as parallel legato chromatic thirds for both hands and rapid octave passages (see example 7.1).

It is well known that Muzio Clementi and others had been writing dazzling passagework and other feats of keyboard legerdemain by the early 1780s. Evidence is abundant that Beethoven was familiar with, and influenced by them.[3] But it is important to realize that such passagework is really not any more specifically idiomatic for the piano than other rapid scales and arpeggios. They could just as well, and just as effectively, have been played on the harpsichord. In fact, until

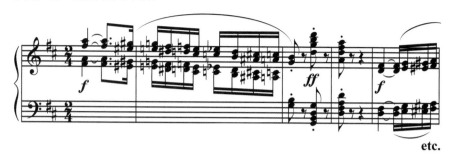

etc.

Example 7.1b. "Righini" Variations, variation 9: Legato, chromatic thirds.

etc.

Example 7.1c. "Righini" Variations, variation 13: Octaves.

about 1784, Clementi, the celebrated "father of the pianoforte," is known to have played his solo recitals exclusively on the harpsichord.[4] This means that virtually all of Clementi's early sonata publications, including the brilliant virtuoso vehicles found as early as his Op. 2 Sonatas of 1779–80, with their famous passages in thirds, sixths, and octaves and their extravagant running figurations, were evidently conceived for (at least, they were performed in public by the composer on) the harpsichord. As Leon Plantinga points out, these sonatas call for "a sparkle and clarity impossible to achieve with [the] early square piano" available at the time in England.[5]

On a different and more significant level, however, the technique of the young Beethoven's "Righini" Variations was original indeed, especially in those variations in which the composer was more interested in exploring the coloristic resources of his instrument than in testing the dexterity of his fingers. Here one can observe Beethoven exploiting the properties of the different registers and textures of the pianoforte and, more important, assessing their compositional potential. In Variation 14, for example, every four measures bring a systematic alternation of register, tempo, and even meter: the tune in the first, third, fifth, and seventh phrases is located in the warm tenor-baritone range,

Example 7.2. Beethoven, "Righini" Variations, variation 14.

accompanied by a crisp staccato walking pattern set in the lowest available register of the keyboard. The even-numbered phrases, in contrast—all marked *adagio* and in $\frac{3}{8}$ meter—are set more traditionally as a treble melody with chordal accompaniment in the bass (see example 7.2).

Similarly, in Variation 4, the melody in the first strain is placed in the middle voice—the tenor—to the accompaniment of a succession of trills in various registers above it. In the second strain, the conceit is developed: the tune (or its fragment) is placed alternately above or below the chain of trills (see example 7.3).

In Variation 20, the contrast of registers is humorous and explicitly playful. (The variation is marked *scherzando, sempre piano*). The main point of this variation, it seems, is to evoke an imaginary woodwind ensemble featuring (at first) a dialogue of sorts between, say, a pair of horns or bassoons and a solo flute. But

Example 7.3. Beethoven, "Righini" Variations, variation 4.

as the duos and solos are shifted about from one register to another, any analogy with real woodwind instruments becomes increasingly tenuous. Surely no woodwind instrument of the time, for example, could negotiate the chromatic run to the low A at the end (see example 7.4).

Finally, with Variation 24, the composition ends not with a flourish but with a notable denouement (see example 7.5).

Example 7.4. Beethoven, "Righini" Variations, variation 20.

This is an extended *calando* (so marked), in which a rapid and conventionally pianistic accompaniment pattern in the treble, consisting of an isolated melody tone plus pseudo-trill or mordent figure (evidently derived from one of the mannerisms—the "trill (or tremolo) with sparks"—of the Mannheim symphonists)[6] embellishes horn-call-like harmonizations of the tune below. The trill figure is gradually and systematically brought to rest. The tune itself is gradually fragmented and rhythmically dilated, ultimately "atomized." Considered pianistically, an exercise in the performance of a rapid ornamental figure has been transformed into a study in touch and tone. Considered compositionally, ornamental decorations have been given thematic significance as the "trill with sparks" is rhythmically augmented and thereby invested with expressive power.

It would be interesting to know, too, how many keyboard works of the time ended with anything like the ethereal four-part chord (marked *pianissimo*) found here: consisting of a sustained open fifth at the bottom of the keyboard, joined after four measures at a distance of almost three octaves by the remaining notes of the tonic chord. This is not just a final chord: it is a memorable, poignant, "Romantic," sonority. In his book on Beethoven's piano sonatas, Charles Rosen observes in connection with the "Tempest" Sonata in D Minor, Op. 31, no. 2: "It is astonishing how often Beethoven, compared to his contemporaries and predecessors, preferred a delicately soft ending to an emphatic final chord. These soft endings, however, are not modest, but more pretentious than the standard closures. They prolong the atmosphere beyond the final

Example 7.5. Beethoven, "Righini" Variations, variation 24, conclusion.

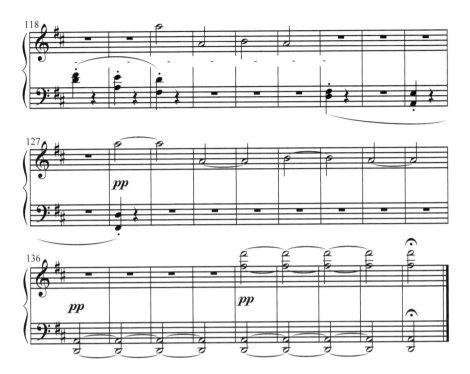

Example 7.5. (continued)

chords."[7] The "Righini" Variations reveal how surprisingly early Beethoven's tonal imagination had begun to outstrip that of his contemporaries.

With this precocious work, then, Beethoven has amply demonstrated his command of what we may call the "Clementi style" or, more generally, the "virtuoso style" of keyboard writing and, at the same time, transcended it. In the course of the "Righini" Variations the young Beethoven has already managed to expand the limits of, and in the process, has begun to redefine and revitalize, the variation form. Specifically, by systematically employing contrasts of register, sonority, and textural density as techniques of variation the way earlier composers used ornamentation and embellishment, he has taken substantial steps toward the creation of a new genre: the "character" variations.[8] Finally, Beethoven's exploitation of instrumental resources in this composition constitutes an early stage in what would be a life-long concern with the nature of tonal space—i.e., the (gradually expanding) pitch gamut—and its potential value in constructing convincing large-scale musical forms in his keyboard music and in other instrumental genres as well.[9]

Example 7.6. Beethoven, Piano Sonata in C Major, Op. 2, no. 3. a. mvt. 1, mm. 1–4.

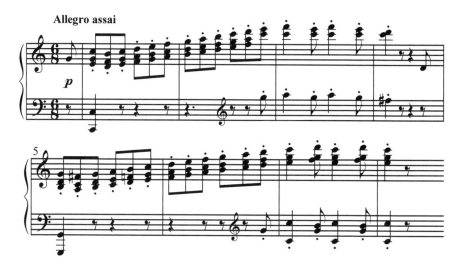

Example 7.6b. mvt. 4, mm. 1–8.

Beethoven would continue to indulge unabashedly in the "virtuoso style" of keyboard writing in his later compositions, but only occasionally. A well-known example is the C-Major Sonata, Op. 2, no. 3, which is permeated throughout with Clementian effects: doubled thirds, leaping octaves, broken chords and arpeggios of all kinds. The opening themes of the outer movements—the first with its stylized quasi-trill in thirds, the finale with its rapid scales of six-three chords—are programmatic for the entire work (see example 7.6).

In a sense, with this third (and last) of his very first published collection of piano sonatas Beethoven had begun to bid farewell to the flashy aesthetic of virtuosity for its own sake. In fact, it seems that Beethoven gradually developed a distaste—perhaps approaching moral disapproval—for "empty" (i.e., compositionally unmotivated) virtuosity, similar to his well-known aversion to what he considered the objectionable morals inherent in Mozart's comic operas.[10] This stance may in part explain why Beethoven wrote relatively few concertos. Needless to say, the composer's evidently negative, or at least ambivalent, attitude toward virtuoso display by no means precluded the inevitability that Beethoven's future piano compositions were to be increasingly demanding and difficult—both musically and technically.

Many striking effects in Beethoven's piano music clearly reflect his desire to imitate the sound of other instruments.[11] The "Righini" Variations presented several such instances, and it is easy to think of countless similar examples in Beethoven's later piano compositions. (Hans von Bülow was famously inspired to label these allusions as they went by in his edition of the "Waldstein" and "Appassionata" Sonatas.) Producing sound effects of this kind has been a crucial factor, of course, in the development of keyboard technique from at least the time of Domenico Scarlatti to that of Franz Liszt. (One need only think of the former's guitar imitations and the latter's Paganini etudes.) But it is doubtful that Beethoven's pianistic imagination and the far-reaching stylistic and formal innovations flowing from it were primarily inspired by the desire to imitate this or that particular instrument. Rather, the new piano style probably evolved in an effort to emulate the developments that had taken place a generation earlier—in the 1760s, seventies and eighties—in the realm of orchestration as a whole.

A plausible case can be made that the orchestra was a crucial element in the formulation of the new "Classical" style. The increased use of woodwind instruments both individually and in blended sonorities (thanks to the introduction of the clarinet on the one hand and on the other, the abandonment of the high *clarino* tessitura of brass instruments) and then the redefinition of the function of the winds (from melodic to primarily harmonic reinforcement), led in time, among other things, to the elimination of the keyboard continuo.

Mozart, of course, had already discovered how effectively the piano could be combined with a skillfully scored ensemble of winds. In his Quintet for Piano and Winds, K. 452, as well as in his concertos of the mid-1780s, he brilliantly exploited the possibilities of these combinations. Given that Mozart was the supreme master of the dramatic confrontation and combination of opposing forces, it is not surprising that his greatest works for piano are not his solo sonatas but his concertos. Beethoven, for his part, not only greatly admired Mozart's K. 452 Quintet but closely modeled his own Quintet for Piano and Winds, Op. 16, after it—or, more precisely, allowed himself to be provoked and stimulated by it.[12] It is symptomatic, too, that the young Beethoven, besides producing numerous sets of piano variations, was also composing woodwind pieces for various combinations, notably the Octet, Op. 103, and the Rondino for Wind Octet, WoO 25, both dating from about 1792.

Beethoven, however, unlike Mozart, was intrigued not so much by the combination of piano and wind instruments as he was by the prospect of capturing as far as possible on the piano itself something like the characteristic richness and variety of tone color, and, perhaps most of all, the ability to sustain—or subtly shift and transform—harmonies and sonorities that are a hallmark of the woodwind ensemble. In short, as a composer of piano music, Beethoven was mainly interested in enabling the instrument to function ever more effectively as a fully autonomous vehicle of modern musical expression. To achieve this end, it was continually necessary to expand the resources available to it. This ambition led, perhaps inevitably, to (in the words of William S. Newman) a "lifelong dissatisfaction with the piano as an instrument."[13] As Beethoven put it himself, in a remark to his friend Karl Holz after the completion of the Sonata, Op. 111, "[The piano] is and remains an inadequate instrument."[14] Before that time, however, and unlike Mozart, he devoted his main energies as a piano composer to the solo sonata.

The Middle-Period Piano Style

Ferruccio Busoni once suggested that "most of Beethoven's piano compositions sound like transcriptions of orchestral works."[15] Nowhere is Beethoven's "orchestral" understanding of the piano more apparent than in the works of his middle period. As much as they embody a breathtakingly grand and expansive conception of instrumental form, these compositions cultivate tone color and sonority as essential, formative, compositional elements.[16] (One of the most valuable benefits of the recent interest in early pianos is that it encourages us to consider the ways in which timbre, register, articulation, and the exploitation of tone color were concerns of fundamental significance to Beethoven.)

Exactly which compositions properly belong to Beethoven's "middle" period is by no means self-evident in this repertoire, for Beethoven composed piano music almost continuously for a decade beginning in the mid-1790s. The Opus 2 Sonatas were largely composed in 1794–95; the three Sonatas, Opus 10 between 1796 and 1798, the "Pathétique," Op. 13, in 1798–99; and the four Sonatas, Opp. 26, 27, and 28 in 1800–1801. The three Op. 31 Sonatas followed in 1802; the "Waldstein," Op. 53, in 1803–4; the "Appassionata," Op. 57, in 1804–5. Only then is there any appreciable break in the production—one that lasted about four years. The Sonatas, Opp. 78, 79, and the "Les Adieux," Op. 81a, were composed in the years 1809–10. The next three Sonatas, Opp. 90, 101, and 106, began to appear after a gap of another four years but were composed over a longer span (from 1814 to 1818). The final Sonatas, Opp. 109, 110, and 111, were again produced in a cluster in the years 1820–22.

It has become fashionable to regard the Sonatas of Opus 26, 27, and 28, and those of Opus 31 as forming a group of "experimental" or "transitional" works on the way to, rather than fully belonging to, the "middle" period. It can also be argued, with some plausibility, that the Sonatas, Opp. 78, 79, and 81a have more in common with those that followed than with those that preceded them. By the strictest criteria, then, only three sonatas qualify unambiguously as middle-period works: the "Waldstein," Op. 53; the F-Major Sonata, Op. 54; and the "Appassionata," Op. 57. (For Lockwood "the principal second-period piano sonatas are the 'Waldstein,' the 'Appassionata,' and the '[Les Adieux],' Op. 81a.")[17]

As Charles Rosen has pointed out in this connection,

> There is no line that can be drawn between the first and second periods, and if there is a clear break in the continuity of his work around the beginning of what is called the third period, the works that contain many of the characteristic new developments belong just before the break as well as after it. When the division into three periods is retained, it should be clear that it is a fiction for the purposes of analysis, a convenience for understanding, and not a biographical reality. The steady development discernible in Beethoven's career is as important as its discontinuities even if these are easier to describe.[18]

Mindful of Rosen's sobering warning, it nonetheless seems helpful for the present purpose to suggest that there is a sufficiently dramatic change in style and in the approach to the piano—beginning with the Sonatas, Opp. 26 and 27, on the one hand, and again, after the composition of the "Les Adieux" Sonata—to regard Beethoven's "middle period" as bounded by the decade from 1800 to 1810.[19] That is, it includes thirteen sonatas that fall rather clearly into four groups: the four Sonatas, Opp. 26, 27, and 28 (composed 1800–1801); the three Sonatas, Op. 31 (composed 1802); the "Waldstein," the Opus 54, and the "Appassionata" (composed between 1803 and 1805); and, to conclude the series, the three Sonatas, Opp. 78, 79, and 81a (composed in 1809–10).

Opening Themes

Nowhere did Beethoven demonstrate so vividly the degree to which his imagination at this time was inspired—and that is the best word for it—by the unique qualities of his medium as in the formulation of his opening themes. The opening themes of virtually every one of the piano sonatas of the middle period do more than present a striking melodic and/or rhythmic idea: they establish, with remarkable economy—within at most a few seconds—an "atmosphere" that captures at once the character of the entire movement, if not indeed of the entire work. Beethoven achieves this to a great extent by creating what may be called a "characteristic sonority."

First, Beethoven often elicits the "characteristic sonority" by setting the thematic idea in a relatively unusual (and hence unusually colorful) register. This is typically the warm middle or lower register of the instrument—the tenor and baritone ranges. Second, he largely avoids the conventional differentiation between melody and accompaniment whereby the melody sounds relatively high in the tre-

Example 7.7. Beethoven, Piano Sonata in C Major ("Waldstein"), Op. 53, mvt. 1, mm. 1–7.

ble, in the right hand, supported by a discreet, left-hand "Alberti"-type accompaniment in the bass some two octaves below. In fact, at this time Beethoven evidently preferred not to conceive of his opening themes as "melodies plus accompaniment" at all. The melody or theme may "happen" to be, seemingly by chance, the uppermost note of a succession of chords. Often (and characteristically enough) it is a reiteration of the same chord involving no change of harmony, perhaps not even involving a change of chord position. The opening theme of the "Waldstein" Sonata, Op. 53, provides a vivid example (see example 7.7).

The sonority that opens the Sonata in E Flat, Op. 31, no. 3, consists of little more than an evocative, almost static, tonal color, a *Ding an sich*—freed (at first, at any rate) of its contextual harmonic meaning as a secondary seventh chord (see example 7.8).

What is especially remarkable about this sonority (which is intentionally not described here as a dissonance) is that it sounds, if anything, less dissonant (i.e., less unstable) than the six-four chord to which it eventually "resolves."[20] A single chord, then—a "characteristic sonority"—owing to its distinctive placement and disposition, could now serve Beethoven as a viable motivic entity. The "Gestalt" and the memorability of such a theme are secured by registral placement, spacing, and rhythmic profile.

This coloristic approach to thematic invention is different from Beethoven's earlier practice of avoiding the traditional melody-plus-accompaniment

Example 7.8. Beethoven, Piano Sonata in E-flat Major, Op. 31, no. 3, mvt. 1, mm. 1–8.

Example 7.9. Beethoven, Piano Sonata in F Minor, Op. 2, no. 1, mvt. 1, mm. 1–4.

disposition, a practice that often entailed dispensing with a harmonic accompaniment altogether. Themes such as the unaccompanied, rapidly ascending "rocket" theme at the beginning of the Sonata in F Minor, Op. 2, no. 1 (or its converse, the theme at the beginning of the Sonata in A Major, Op. 2, no. 2, which consists of an unharmonized descending theme presented in octaves) were part of a longstanding Classical-period tradition of piano sonatas written in "orchestral" style (see example 7.9).

Mozart composed a number of sonatas of this type throughout his career. They typically begin with fanfarelike themes presented in bare octaves.

Example 7.10. Mozart sonatas with unharmonized "fanfare" beginnings. a. Piano Sonata in D Major, K. 284, mvt. 1, mm. 1–4.

Example 7.10b. Piano Sonata in C Major, K. 309, mvt. 1, mm. 1–2.

Example 7.10c. Piano Sonata in C Minor, K. 457, mvt. 1, mm. 1–11.

Example 7.10d. Piano Sonata in B-flat Major, K. 570, mvt. 1, mm. 1–4.

Example 7.10e. Piano Sonata in D Major, K. 576, mvt. 1, mm. 1–8.

Examples are his Sonatas in D, K. 284; in C, K. 309; in C Minor, K. 457, in B Flat, K. 570 (whose beginning is more suggestive of a string quartet, perhaps, than of a symphony), and in D, K. 576 (see example 7.10).

The Sonata in C Minor, K. 457, in fact, clearly was a model for Beethoven's "Pathétique" Sonata. The allegro themes of both sonatas—like the opening of Beethoven's Opus 2, no. 1—are allusions to the Mannheim "rocket." Beethoven, however, offers an original, *Sturm-und-Drang*-inspired, chromatically enriched distortion of the rocket theme, adding to it an agitated tremolo pedal point in the bass—a favorite device of Clementi's (example 7. 11).[21]

As the openings of the Sonatas, Op. 27, no. 2; Op. 31, no. 2; and Op. 57 make clear, the characteristic sonority, in its characteristic register (or registers) is often presented not in the form of a solid chord but as an arpeggio. Once again, traditional notions of melody and accompaniment do not apply. The opening

Example 7.11. Beethoven, Piano Sonata in C Minor ("Pathétique") Op. 13, mvt. 1, mm. 11–19.

arpeggios of the "Moonlight" Sonata are, if anything, more thematic, and memorable, than the monotone melody that eventually enters (see example 7.12).

The "Appassionata" is another sonata that begins with no "accompaniment" at all but with the unfolding of a tonic arpeggio in the tenor register, doubled two octaves below. The essence of the thematic idea here—its originality, and surely its inspiration—is obviously to be found in the extraordinary registration (the range, the spacing, the doubling), not in the contour or the particular pitches (see example 7.13).

Incidentally, just as Mozart's C-Minor Sonata, K. 457, was a model for Beethoven's "Pathétique," it may be that the Fantasia in C Minor, K. 475, influenced Beethoven's approach to register and sonority in the "Appassionata" Sonata. Specifically, Mozart's presentation of the opening theme in multiple octaves in the lower registers, alternating with woodwindlike cadential punctuations in the upper register—followed by its immediate repetition in an unexpected key—anticipates the opening of Opus 57 (see example 7.14).[22]

Example 7.12. Beethoven, Piano Sonata in C-sharp Minor ("Moonlight"), Op. 27, no. 2, mvt. 1, mm. 1–9.

Even in the more traditionally melodious opening of the Sonata in A Flat, Op. 26 (which is the theme of a set of variations), the melody is not simply presented above a subordinate accompaniment in the conventional manner. Rather, it is presented in octaves between the low-lying soprano and the tenor, with the notes of the accompaniment interspersed. The thematic interest can also alternate between the strands of the texture, as in the dialogue between the right-hand chords and the bass melody at the beginning of Opus 27, no. 1, or even between the reiterated pedal point and the side-slipping harmonies above it at the beginning of Opus 28 (see example 7.15).

It is hardly necessary to point out that every one of these themes—that is, every one of these sonatas—begins softly, marked *piano* or *pianissimo*. Both the low dynamic levels and the low registers imply inevitable growth and expansion.

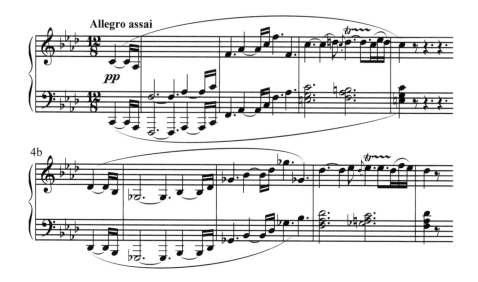

Example 7.13. Beethoven, Piano Sonata in F Minor ("Appassionata") Op. 57, mvt.1, mm. 1–8.

Example 7.14. Mozart, Fantasia in C Minor, K. 475, mm. 1–6.

Example 7.15a. Sonata openings with unusual melody-accompaniment dispositions. a. Piano Sonata in A-flat Major, Op. 26, mvt. 1, mm. 1–4.

Example 7.15b. Piano Sonata in E-flat Major, Op. 27, no. 1, mvt .1, mm. 1–9.

Example 7.15c. Piano Sonata in D Major, Op. 28, mvt. 1, mm. 1–10.

Every one of these thematic ideas takes full advantage of the peculiar timbral resources of the piano, especially the piano of Beethoven's day. It is clear that Beethoven assumed that a piano had clarity of tone, as well as crispness and incisiveness of attack and response in the low register. But although the themes are all idiomatic in that respect, they are by no means all equally pianistic in terms of style. Some indeed draw on traditional keyboard patterns. The constant arpeggios of the first movement of Opus 27, no. 2 have something in common with the opening prelude of Bach's *Well-Tempered Clavier,* and the opening arpeggio of Opus 31, no. 2 is a keyboard cliché borrowed from operatic recitative via C. P. E. Bach. Other thematic ideas seem to have been inspired by (or at least are intended to suggest) other media: these are the orchestral associations referred to earlier. The opening of the E-flat Sonata, Op. 27, no. 1, with its cellolike interjections every measure, suggests possibly a string quartet. Perhaps more abstractly, so does even the opening of the "Waldstein," with its repeated *spiccato* chords. The opening of the Sonata in D, Op. 28 (see example 7.15c), however, and even that of Opus 31, no. 3 (see example 7.8), are rather reminiscent of woodwind writing; and there is, of course, the deliberate evocation of horns at the beginning of the "Les Adieux" Sonata. Finally, the opening of Opus 57 (see example 7.13), with its sense of vastness suggested by the extraordinarily empty spacing combined with the melodic expansiveness of the idea itself, is as evocative as a Romantic orchestral tone poem. The ultimate destiny of this vast space, of course, is to be filled in with shattering explosions of full-fisted fortissimo chords stretching to both extremes of the keyboard, another altogether unforgettable and "characteristically" Beethovenian sonority.

The "characteristic sonority," then, that informs virtually every one of Beethoven's middle-period piano sonatas is a compound of register, texture, spacing, harmonic complexion, and dynamic level. It also entails subtle phrasing and articulation—a dimension that can be understood to include pedaling as well. Beethoven's instructions in these respects can be breathtaking in their precision and differentiation. With respect to articulation, the theme of the E-flat Sonata, Op. 27, no. 1, is again instructive. The right-hand chords are variously marked *portamento, legato,* with accent, or without any marking at all. The intervening bass melody is marked either completely *legato,* completely *staccato,* or again deliberately without marking (see example 7.15b). (In contemplating this bass line one is not surprised at all to recall that Beethoven practically single-handedly invented the Classical cello sonata.)

As for the pedal—more specifically, the damper mechanism—we need only consider the famous (or infamous) instruction in the first movement of the "Moonlight" Sonata, apparently commanding that the entire movement be performed with the damper off: *si deve suonare tutto questo pezzo delicatissimamente e senzo sordini* (see example 7.12).[23] However we may understand the degree of absoluteness implied by this prescription, there can be little question that Beethoven was calling for a "pedaling" that would produce a substantial amount of overlap, even blurring, of the changes of harmony. Nor can there be much question that the resulting "impressionistic," "shimmering" effect not only constitutes a most "characteristic" sonority, indeed, but is in fact the essential point of the entire movement. Moreover, it is quintessentially "pianistic" both in conception and in effect.

Sonority and Structure

Sonority also has substantial structural and formal functions in the middle-period piano sonatas. The discoveries Beethoven made at the time that he composed the "Righini" Variations, and that he cultivated ever since, came to full fruition at this time. Consider, once again, the opening of Opus 31, no. 3. After the principal theme is stated in its entirety, and in its integrity, it is—in accordance with conventional eighteenth-century propriety—about to be repeated. The repetition is not a literal one, however; nor is the theme simply repeated an octave higher, as we are led to expect. Nor is it a "varied repetition" in the usual sense, that is, embellished with diminutions. Rather, the theme is broken into fragments of different lengths (some one measure long, some two measures), and these fragments are shifted about from register to register (see example 7.16).

The registrally distorted repetition of the theme then precipitates the pattern for the motivic development of the material, as the individual thematic components just isolated by the octave shifts are subsequently subjected to typically Beethovenian manipulation.

Example 7.16. Beethoven, Piano Sonata in E-flat Major, Op. 31, no. 3, mvt. 1, mm. 9–16.

Another, more celebrated, instance of varied repetition by means of sonority occurs at the beginning of the "Waldstein" Sonata. The counterstatement of the theme is not only raised an octave: the characteristic *spiccato* (see example 7.7) has been transformed into a tremolo (see example 7.17).

Beethoven, it seems, is attempting to find a pianistic analogy for a stringed instrument's vibrato—or perhaps for the clavichord's *Bebung*. But he does so not for an expressive but rather a compositional objective: that of "developing" the motivic idea initially represented by the *spiccato/staccato* repetition. The articulated, pulsating eighth-note rhythm has evolved (or dissolved) into the softly humming, vibrating tremolo. The "meaning" of the theme has changed accordingly.[24]

It is worth observing, incidentally, that in both Opus 53 and Opus 57 the counterstatement of the opening idea consists of a repetition beginning on an unexpected, chromatically (i.e., literally coloristically) altered scale degree. In the "Waldstein" the opening theme is repeated a whole tone down from C, beginning on the lowered seventh degree, B♭ (see example 7.7); in the "Appassionata" the repetition is up a half tone, from F to the flat second degree, G♭ (see example 7.13). In both instances, the motion is stepwise to the nearest pitch foreign to the tonic scale.[25] The contemporaneous G-Major Piano Concerto, Op. 58, also calls for a disconcerting repetition of the opening theme in an unexpected key.

The "Waldstein" Sonata can serve, finally, as a paradigm for the structural use of register on a large scale.[26] The sonata opens with the pulsating theme in the

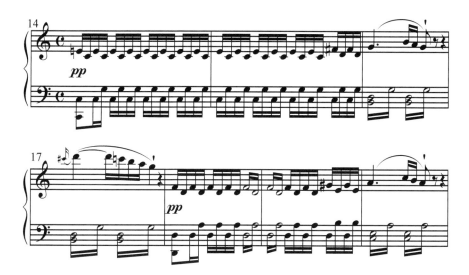

Example 7.17. Beethoven, Piano Sonata in C Major ("Waldstein"), Op. 53, mvt. 1, mm.14–20.

lowest register answered by a brief flicker of light at the opposite end of the key-board. The two extremes of register then sound simultaneously (mm. 9–11), creating a gaping tonal space that will inevitably have to be filled in (and even-tually is). The process begins in the transition (mm. 14–34): first, rather tenta-tively, with scales and arpeggio figuration in sixteenth notes (mm. 23–30), then more deliberately with striding broken octave in eighth notes (mm. 31–34). It is finally consolidated with the arrival, in the mediant, of the block chords of the second theme. If the opening, vibrating, theme is suggestive of low strings, then the smooth and closely spaced chordal second, theme is equally evocative of woodwind writing (see example 7.18).

Discussing the "Waldstein," Charles Rosen remarks: "In no other work . . . was Beethoven as inventive with sonority. The variety of sound effects and tech-nical display in the *Prestissimo* is astonishing: octave *glissandi*, trills that are almost forty bars long, a double trill, trills played with the thumb and second finger and the melody with the fourth and fifth, and fifteen bars of heavily pedaled pure C major at the end. Never again in his career did the composer try to find so many tone colours and technical inventions for the pianist in one work. This is set out in the first page of the first movement, when the pulsating opening is recon-ceived as a measured tremolo."[27]

As Busoni had suggested, Beethoven's ambition as a composer for the piano was to treat the instrument as a self-sufficient microcosm of the contemporary

Example 7.18. Op. 53, mvt. 1, mm. 14–42.

Example 7.18. (continued)

orchestra. This project no doubt contributed to his lifelong frustration with the instrument. The instrument makers of the time may have approached the piano as the successor to the harpsichord and clavichord—and, in a technical sense, that is true. But Beethoven himself may have regarded the piano, with its greater (if still limited) sustaining power and dynamic range, and its coloristic resources, instead as a potential successor to the organ and, moreover, capable of producing graduated dynamics.[28] Johann Sebastian Bach's most grandiose keyboard works, after all, are for the organ. And Beethoven's musical imagination had a predisposition for the grandiose. Yet, with the exception of a juvenile two-part student fugue (WoO 31) composed at the age of thirteen, Beethoven never wrote anything at all exclusively for the organ. It was obviously essential for him to have the dynamic gradation and the flexibility of attack and touch unavailable on the organ.

For Beethoven, perhaps more than for any other composer before him, the piano offered not only a complete gamut of pitches efficiently capable of sounding one or many at a time, fast or slow, high or low. It was also a kaleidoscope of tone colors. Each register had its own color and character. Its chordal sonorities were capable of producing a remarkably wide range of different effects, depending on their density, spacing, volume, duration, and manner of attack. In sum, Beethoven was powerfully drawn to the raw materials of this medium. And at no time in his career was this truer than during his so-called middle period. Thereafter, his growing deafness (which had forced him to end his public career as a pianist after a particularly disastrous Akademie in December 1808), along with his compositional evolution, irreversibly altered his attitude toward the piano.

Beethoven continued to test the resources and limits of the piano in his later years. As Lewis Lockwood comments, in reference to the last three piano sonatas: "Beethoven's pianistic imagination is stamped on every page of these three sonatas. . . . Undreamed-of sonorities and multivariate figuration patterns . . . [exploit] both keyboard and pedals in ways that went beyond even his most innovative earlier keyboard works. We find arpeggiated, cadenza-like passages through several octaves; rapid parallel thirds and sixths, delicate figurations, use of *una corda* pedal effects; and sustained trills in extreme registers against continuing melodic and contrapuntal lines in other parts. In each case these pianistic effects were grounded in the structural marrow of the individual movement and of the work as a whole."[29]

Nonetheless, a hallmark of Beethoven's late piano music is precisely that it is frequently nonidiomatic, often approaching "anti-piano" music. Above all, the pervasive contrapuntal writing in this repertoire attests to an abstract rather than a coloristic conception of musical texture, one much less "orchestral" or even pianistic in its inspiration and aspiration. If the attitude of the Beethoven of the middle-period piano sonatas toward his medium was to exploit it, that of the late Beethoven, it would seem, was often enough not to defy it, but to transcend it.[30]

Notes

1. In the words of Lewis Lockwood, "If Beethoven's career had ended in 1801, ten years after Mozart's death, he would still be regarded as the most important

composer of his time." Lockwood, *Beethoven: the Music and the Life* (New York: Norton, 2003), 174.

2. The "Righini" Variations exist in two editions. The first, considered lost until quite recently, was published in 1791 (according to an advertisement in the *Wiener Zeitung* of August 13, 1791); the second edition was published by Johann Traeg in Vienna in 1802. The two versions are essentially identical. See Sieghard Brandenburg and Martin Staehelin, "Die 'erste Fassung' von Beethovens Righini-Variationen," in *Festschrift Albi Rosenthal*, ed. Rudolf Elvers (Tutzing: Hans Schneider, 1984), 43–66.

3. A comprehensive, systematic survey of the pianistic techniques of Beethoven, along with those of his predecessors and contemporaries, appears in Andreas Rücker, *Beethovens Klaviersatz: Technik und Stilistik* (Frankfurt am Main: Peter Lang, 2002), III:191–231. Among the pianists Rücker cites (apart from Clementi), to whom Beethoven was indebted, are Daniel Steibelt (1765–1823), for his atmospheric tremolo and sophisticated pedal effects; Johann Baptist Cramer (1771–1858), along with Clementi, for refined legato playing; and Abbé Georg Joseph Vogler (1749–1814), for such devices as octave glissandi and advanced permanent and multiple trill techniques.

4. See Leon Plantinga, *Clementi: His Life and Music* (New York: Oxford University Press, 1977), 286–91.

5. Plantinga, *Clementi*, 289.

6. See the foreword to Hugo Riemann, ed., *Sinfonien der pfalzbayerischen Schule (Mannheimer Symphoniker)*, *Denkmäler der Tonkunst in Bayern* (Leipzig: Breitkopf & Hartel, 1906), 7/2:xv–xix.

7. Charles Rosen, *Beethoven's Piano Sonatas: A Short Companion* (New Haven: Yale University Press, 2002), 173.

8. See Robert U. Nelson, *The Technique of Variation* (Berkeley and Los Angeles: University of California Press, 1962), especially chap. 5.

9. In discussing the first movement of the String Quartet in F, Op. 59, no. 1, Lewis Lockwood observes: "In the whole movement Beethoven will explore and dramatize the use of register. . . . The whole opening paragraphh . . . builds gradually from its octave-wide opening melody . . . to its first four-octave climax, anticipating the far-flung organization of the whole movement around the preparation of registral climaxes, their postponement, and their eventual arrival. . . . This registral strategy resembles that of the 'Eroica' first movement." See Lockwood, *Beethoven*, 318–19. As the "Righini" Variations show, Beethoven's experiments along these lines, too, began much earlier and were continued throughout his keyboard works, especially the sonatas of the last decade of the eighteenth and first decade of the nineteenth centuries.

10. According to Maynard Solomon, Beethoven "found fault with Mozart's librettos (*Don Giovanni* being too 'scandalous' a subject)." Solomon, *Beethoven*, 2nd rev. ed. (New York: Schirmer Books, 1998), 256.

11. Beethoven himself was presumably the first to observe, or acknowledge, this. In a sketch for a keyboard piece from 1793/94, Beethoven writes: "hier muß der Effect von Hörnern hervorgebracht werden." See Douglas Johnson, *Beethoven's Early Sketches in the "Fischhof Miscellany" Berlin Autograph 28* (Ann Arbor: UMI Research Press, 1977), 1:400, 442.

12. For the most recent, and most substantial, comparative analysis of the two works see William Kinderman, "A Tale of Two Quintets: Mozart's K. 452 and Beethoven's Op. 16," this volume, chapter 5, pp. 55–77.

13. William S. Newman, "Beethoven's Pianos Versus His Piano Ideals," *Journal of the American Musicological Society* 23 (1970): 497.

14. See Solomon, *Beethoven*, 391.

15. Ferruccio Busoni, *Sketch of a New Esthetic of Music*, trans. Theodore Baker (New York, 1911; reprinted in *Three Classics in the Aesthetic of Music* [New York: Dover Publications, 1962], 86.

16. According to Lewis Lockwood, the Variations in E Flat, Op. 35 (which Lockwood dubs the "Prometheus" Variations), composed in 1802, "[point] the way to the orchestra-like keyboard writing of his middle period and his later piano writing, including that of the later piano concertos." Lockwood, *Beethoven*, 141.

17. Lockwood, *Beethoven*, 202.

18. Rosen, *The Classical Style*, 389.

19. As Rosen has pointed out, "Opus 26 marks a significant progress in Beethoven's efforts to give an unmistakable individuality to each new work, as if he were not simply writing a new sonata but redefining the genre each time." Rosen, *Beethoven's Piano Sonatas*, 150.

20. In *The Classical Style*, Charles Rosen points out that in the opening of the G-Major Piano Concerto, measure 27, a root-position tonic triad, owing to the treatment of its harmonic environment, effectively "resolves" to a dominant. *The Classical Style*, 387–88.

21. Clementi's Sonata in C, Op. 30 (1794), was evidently another direct influence on Beethoven's "Pathétique." In addition to the bass octave tremolo, the right-hand theme of the first movement has some resemblance to Beethoven's. See Rücker, *Beethovens Klaviersatz*, V:8.

22. It is conceivable that Mozart's use of the Fantasia as a preface to the C-Minor Sonata gave Beethoven the idea of prefacing the Allegro section of the "Pathétique" Sonata with a slow introduction beginning in the tenor-bass register and featuring diminished-seventh sonorities.

23. Beethoven did not have access to a piano with a damper pedal until he received an Erard grand from the manufacturer in the autumn of 1803. It had an immediate impact, which is evident in the extensive pedal markings in the final movement of the contemporaneous "Waldstein" Sonata.

24. Rosen remarks that "the transformation of a musical idea by touch, dynamics and phrasing had never been seen before Beethoven on such a scale or with such concentrated intensity. Nor was it ever seen again. This is one of the reasons the sonatas remain so fascinating to play." *Beethoven's Piano Sonatas*, 42.

25. One can speculate as to whether Beethoven conceived of these transposed repetitions on chromatically altered steps as modal inflections (to the Mixolydian seventh in the case of the "Waldstein" Sonata, to the Phrygian second in the case of the "Appassionata"). The argument for doing so is considerably stronger in the case of the "Appassionata." Since the "Waldstein" has a modulating theme moving from the tonic to the dominant, beginning its repetition on the lowered seventh insures its conclusion on the subdominant where it can, and does, become part of a large I–IV–V cadential plan in the tonic.

26. See Lewis Lockwood's related comments on the roughly contemporary Opus 59, no. 1 in note 9 above.

27. Rosen, *Beethoven's Piano Sonatas*, 188. Andreas Rücker points out that octave glissandi and permanent trills with decorated cantus—as in Opus 53; movement 3, measures 485–514—were a specialty of Abbé Vogler's. Beethoven got to know

Vogler's keyboard works in 1803, that is, just before composing Opus 53, and presumably met him personally in Vienna in September/October 1803. (Rücker, *Beethovens Klaviersatz*, III:225.) He also reminds us that octave glissandi were easier to play on Beethoven's pianos owing to their narrower keys (Rücker, V:145).

28. According to Rücker, Beethoven was the first to use graduated dynamics systematically in his keyboard music, taking advantage of technical advances in keyboard construction. Rücker, V:86.

29. Lockwood, *Beethoven*, 385.

30. The author wishes to thank Lewis Lockwood and Mark Kroll for their helpful suggestions.

Chapter Eight

Recomposing the Grosse Fuge

Beethoven and Opus 134

Robert Winter

Overture

A long-time colleague, who has had the privilege of knowing Charles Rosen as well as I, recalled an occasion some years ago when they were together and the subject of Beethoven's four-hand arrangement of the *Grosse Fuge*, Op. 134, came up. Rosen, without pausing to catch a breath, burst out: "But ____, you know that it's unplayable!"

Since the artist rendering this judgment plays Beethoven's "Hammerklavier" Sonata, Liszt's *Reminiscences on Don Juan*, Boulez's Third Sonata, and Carter's *Night Fantasies* with equal aplomb, you are obligated to take the charge seriously. General support for Rosen's position comes from the utter rarity of Opus 134 on four-hand programs. Ask your music-loving friends how often they have heard it, either live or on disk, and you will witness a great deal of head scratching.[1] Is there any explanation? This is a story still largely untold.

For more than 175 years, Beethoven's *Grosse Fuge*, Op. 133, intended as the original finale to the 1825 String Quartet in B-flat Major, Op. 130, has stood at the pinnacle of classical counterpoint—rugged, unflinching, take-no-prisoners counterpoint, to be sure, but grand counterpoint nonetheless. Eighteen minutes in duration (exceeding by more than double, for example, the impressive fugues that close the Gloria and Credo of the *Missa solemnis*, Op. 123), it remains the most encyclopedic treatment not only of fugue but of thematic development since Bach.

The general outlines of the story of Beethoven's friends intervening with their misgivings about the appropriateness of Opus 133 as a finale to Opus 130 are well known. What is more elusive is why Beethoven eventually acceded to their wishes (especially those of his publisher, Matthias Artaria), for his late works show little regard for the conventions of either composition or performance, and equally little regard for their public reception. Even more mysterious is why Beethoven would have agreed to the proposition of a four-hand piano arrangement when he had in fact never made or sanctioned the keyboard arrangement of one bar of his string quartets.[2]

Thayer-Forbes presents the standard English-language account:

> The doubts about the effectiveness of the fugue felt by Beethoven's friends found an echo in the opinions of the critics. Matthias Artaria, the publisher, who seems in this year to have entered the circle of the composer's intimate associates, presented the matter to him in a practicable light. He had purchased the publishing rights of the Quartet, and after the performance he went to Beethoven with the suggestion that he write a new finale and that the fugue be published as an independent piece, for which he would remunerate him separately. Beethoven listened to the protests unwillingly, but, "Vowing he would ne'er consent, consented" and also requested the pianist Anton Halm, who had played the B-flat Trio [the "Archduke," Op. 97] at the concert of March 21 to make the four-hand pianoforte arrangement for which there had already been inquiries at Artaria's shop. Halm accepted the commission and made the arrangement, with which Beethoven was not satisfied: "You have divided the parts too much between the *prim* and *second*," he remarked to Halm, referring to a device which the arranger had adopted to avoid crossing of hands—giving passages to the right hand which should logically have been given to the left, the effect being the same to the ear but not to the eye. Nevertheless, Halm presented a claim for 40 florins to Artaria for the work, and was paid. Beethoven then made an arrangement and sent it to Artaria.

The matter might be considered settled there, but more negotiations remained. Beethoven sent his arrangement to Karl Artaria via Holz,

> to whom he sent a note beginning with the salutation "Best Wood of Christ" [a pun on "Holz," meaning "wood"] in which he asked Holz to give the arrangement to Artaria, hoping that he would accept it and give Beethoven 12 ducats for the work.[3] He concludes: "However, Herr M. knows anyhow that we gladly and often are at his service without payment and shall be—but the present service which I rendered him is too menial not to have to insist on compensation—Appointing you now Executor in this matter, I beg of you, honorable Sir, to receive everything."
> To this Artaria demurred and asked Beethoven for Halm's manuscript. Beethoven sent it via Holz with instructions to get back his own arrangement in return for it. At the same time he told Artaria that while he did not ask that Artaria publish his work, he was under no obligation to him; he might have it for the twelve ducats. Artaria reconciled himself to this matter and paid Beethoven his fee on September 5. The arrangement which Artaria announced on May 10, 1827, as Op. 134 (the original score being advertised at the same time as Op. 133) was Beethoven's.[4]

According to this account, Halm was clearly guilty of the most rudimentary errors—errors that he should have known how to avoid. His failure to do so forced Beethoven to right Halm's obvious mistakes. Since Halm's arrangement has not survived, nothing exists to contradict this version.

The German language Thayer-Deiters has more on Opus 134. There we find an even stronger condemnation of Halm's efforts: "Weiter erzählt Holz, dass Artaria die Fuge im Klavierauszug als Op. 132 [sic!] als eigenes Werk herausgeben wolle.—"Den Halmschen kann er im Feuer vergulden lassen" [Further explained Holz that (Matthias) Artaria wished to publish the fugue in a separate piano edition—the version by (Anton) Halm can be gilded with fire (i.e. incinerated).][5]

The fuller account in Thayer-Deiters adds important and clarifying details to Thayer-Forbes. First we have the letter that Halm wrote Beethoven to accompany the delivery of his arrangement:

Hochgeehrtester Herr v. Beethoven,
Ich habe Ihre Fuge, welche zu übersenden die Ehre habe, mit möglichstem Fleisse, und aller Sorgfalt beendigt. Ich staunte bei jedem Takte, über Ihre Macht der Harmonie und dessen Fluss sowohl, als auch über die bis zur Erschöpfung angewendeten Kunstfiguren und deren Bearbeitung! Was meine Umarbeitung betrifft, war es leider nicht möglich, dass die Suges [Sujets] immer in ihrer Gestalt geblieben, sondern öfters zerissen werden mussten.

Übrigens ist sie so brilliant, gut spielbar, und wie ich hoffe noch verständlich genug, dass Ihr höchstes Meisterwerk für das anerkannt werde, was es ist. Ich werde bis längstens 1/4 auf 4 Morgen Nachmittag mit Ueberbringung Ihres Manuscripts so frey seyn, über meine Bearbeitung Ihre gütige Meinung einzuholen. Unterdessen bin ich mit der höchsten Achtung
Ihr
Ergebster
Anton Halm[6]

Wien den 24ten April 826

[Most honored Mr. Beethoven,
I have completed your fugue, which I have the honor of sending to you, with the greatest industry and all care. I was astonished at every bar, with the power of your harmony and its flow, as well as the artistic motifs, which are worked out so exhaustively. As far as my arrangement goes, it was unfortunately not possible to maintain the subjects in their original form; rather, they frequently had to be torn apart.

Otherwise the fugue is so brilliant, very playable, and, I hope, sufficiently understandable that your supreme masterpiece will be recognized for what it is. I will bring your manuscript at the latest by 3:45 tomorrow afternoon hoping to receive your good opinion of my arrangement. Meanwhile I remain with the highest regard
your
most devoted
Anton Halm

Vienna the 24th April, 1826]

The letter makes clear that Halm was simultaneously aware of the stunning originality of Beethoven's achievement and of what he absolutely felt forced to do in
order to achieve playability for both performers. He says nothing about hands
or crossing of hands but states simply that "the subjects frequently had to be torn
apart." Halm's very mention of this conundrum to Beethoven suggests just how
acutely aware he was of the rarity of his procedure.

In addition to the letter, Thayer-Deiters elicited from Halm the following
statement:

> Während dieser Zwischenzeit ersuchte mich B. eine Fuge, die als letztes Stück von
> diesem Quartett componiert war und einmal öffentlich gespielt wurde und später
> wegblieb, zu 4 Händen fürs P.F. zu arrangieren.—Nachdem dieses Arrangement
> fertig war, brachte ich dasselbe zum B. . . . —Er sah es durch und äusserte sich: "Sie
> haben nur diese Stimmen zu viel zertheilt in prim und Second." Nähmlich ich
> hatte das Spiel zu erleichtern gesucht, indem ich das Überspringen der Hände ver-
> meiden wollte, und deswegen mehreres in die rechte Hand gegeben, was die Linke
> spielen sollte. Freylich war der Effect ganz derselbe, aber nicht für das Auge.
> Beethoven hat die Fuge deshalb selbst arrangirt und so wurde sie herausgegeben.

> [During the interim Beethoven requested of me that I arrange for piano four-
> hands a fugue that had been composed as the last movement of this quartet [Op.
> 130] and which had been played one time in public but [whose finale] was later
> omitted. After the arrangement was finished I brought it to Beethoven. . . . —He
> looked through it and opined: "Too frequently you have divided these voices
> between *primo* and *secondo*." That is, in order to simplify the playing, in which I had
> wanted to avoid the crossing of hands, and therefore giving more to the right
> hand that the left should have played. To be sure the effect was exactly the same,
> just not for the eyes. Beethoven consequently arranged the fugue himself and thus
> was it published.]

This largely parallel account to Thayer-Forbes reinforces that what Halm meant
by "simplification" was the consistent tactic he apparently adopted to avoid hand
crossings (by definition a "complication") between *primo* and *secondo*. In practice
it must have worked like this: say, for example, that the second violin line crossed
over the viola line in Opus 133.[7] At the point of overlap, Halm's arrangement
would switch the second violin line to the viola line, and vice versa. As soon as
the overlap ended, he would switch both back. According to Halm, this occurred
"frequently."

How did Halm reach the decision to proceed in this manner? Clearly his first
priority was to preserve the absolute pitch integrity of Beethoven's fugue. He did
not feel that he had permission to indulge in octave transpositions or, God for-
bid, outright changes of pitch. After all, he had been asked to arrange (i.e.,
essentially to transcribe), not to recompose. His reasoning can certainly be
defended. The notes would all sound at exactly the same place on the same

instrument, so what difference would it make if some of them were not attached to the same voice? If the reports are accurate, it would not be difficult to reconstruct a hypothetical version of Halm's arrangement. Could a skilled four-hand team that was aware of every part crossing convey the essence of Beethoven's counterpoint? Apparently the composer did not think so.

Beethoven's initial confidence in Halm seems scarcely misplaced. In his *Beethoven-Handbuch*, Theodor Frimmel describes Halm as "Musiker, Tonsetzer, Klavierspieler" [musician, composer, pianist].[8] Born in Untersteiermarkt in 1789, Halm, as a "very young man" (even "before his military service") had already played the Piano Trio in C Minor, Op. 1, no. 3 and the Piano Concerto in C, Op. 15. By 1811 he was concertizing successfully in Graz. Moving to Vienna around 1815, within a year Halm had received Beethoven's blessing to dedicate his Piano Sonata in C Minor, Op. 15 to the master. Even after Beethoven's rejection of Halm's arrangement of Opus 134, the two composer-pianists remained on cordial terms until Beethoven's death less than a year later. Halm was no rank amateur whose lack of requisite training led to uninformed decisions. Why was he unable to please Beethoven? There has to be a better explanation, and it requires looking at four-hand music in a new light.

Music for Four Hands

We can get closer to the conventions that Halm would have been familiar with by looking first at the etiquette of four-hand writing in the Vienna of Mozart and Beethoven. If Charles Burney's Four Duets of 1777 were the first four-hand pieces to be published, then within just a few years four-hand music had reached, and become the rage in, Vienna, a musical capital enamored of the piano.[9] Unlike violin or vocal duets (the two other favored Viennese pastimes), four-hand playing afforded a physical proximity, even intimacy, between the two players. In most passages four-hand partners could feel their arms press against one another. They might brush flanks, even if through thick layers of petticoats. They could catch one another's odor and get a sense of how the partner moved. Best of all, the entire interaction occurred under the guise of respectability. At a time when the Ländler was evolving into the waltz, "touch dancing" and four-hand playing were on the cutting edge of social change (evoking heated opposition as well).[10]

Published four-hand music came in two flavors—original works and arrangements of other media, most often orchestral. The weighting of the mix varied from composer to composer. As far as we know, Haydn composed nothing original for this medium. There was no demand at Esterházy, and when he landed in England the piano trio was already the rage. That did not prevent publishers from issuing half of his symphonies and several of his string quartets in four-hand arrangements. On the other hand, one of Mozart's earliest compositions

(K. 19d) was a four-hand sonata. With sister Nannerl readily available, he penned two more sonatas (K. 381 [123a] and 358 [186c]) in Salzburg. Between August 1786 and May 1787—five years after moving to Vienna—he composed two more sonatas (K. 497 and 521) and a set of variations (K. 501), as well as writing most of the first two movements of another (K. 357 [497a], thereby raising four-hand music from an amateur pastime to a serious genre. In this rich harvest of works there is not a single example of hand or part crossing between the two players. Perhaps to compensate, Mozart consciously provides both players with solo passages that permit the *primo* to play low and the *secondo* to play high. This transgression of normal range might result in the players pressing against one another but would not materially interfere with their execution of the music.

Against this backdrop, the young Beethoven who moved to Vienna in 1792 expressed only mild interest in the four-hand genre. Over his first eleven years in Vienna he published two sets of variations (WoO 67, WoO 74), an easy sonata (Op. 6), and a set of three marches (Op. 45). Of this meager output, only the first (the *Variations on a Theme of Count Waldstein*, WoO 67, probably composed around the time of Beethoven's move) and the last (Three Marches, Op. 45, 1803) betray any compositional or technical ambition. Following Mozart's lead, Beethoven engages in no part or hand crossings, observing the musical and social conventions of four-hand playing. By the time Artaria broached the idea of a four-hand arrangement of the *Grosse Fuge*, Beethoven had not composed in the medium for twenty-three years.

Unlike Haydn or Mozart, Beethoven actually selected the four-hand arrangers of some of his orchestral music. Two of the best-known instances are the arrangement of the *Fidelio* Overture, Op. 72b, by Ignaz Moscheles and the *Leonore* Overture No. 3 by Carl Czerny.[11] Because of the noncontrapuntal nature of these works, there are only the occasional near misses, as when the seventh of a dominant seventh in the *secondo* is placed right below the root in the *primo*. Four-hand arrangements of most of Beethoven's major orchestral works were often published at the same time as the symphonic parts. An example is S. A. Steiner's nearly simultaneous publication of the multiple versions of the Seventh Symphony.[12] As was traditional, the four-hand version, though technically demanding, contains no part crossings.

We know little about Beethoven's first-hand familiarity with the music of Schubert. Throughout Beethoven's last decade, Schubert infused the amateur four-hand medium with a series of startlingly original works that quickly outgrew the drawing room.[13] But even Schubert rarely transgressed the hand-crossing ban. To be sure, he ran the *primo* and *secondo* nearer to one another than previous composers, inviting closer physical contact. Even more provocatively, he privileged voice leading that would periodically land the right hand of the *secondo* and the left hand of the *primo* on the same note. This could be even more thrilling than crossing hands, for actual contact was unavoidable. During the first few run-throughs, players would be unprepared for just when or where the contact might occur.

In addition to a single instance of hand crossing (m. 85), the *Fantasie in F minore*, D. 940 (composed the year after Beethoven's death), contains six same-note conflicts in measures 83–84 and 514–16. Each collision—of which the composer must have been acutely aware—could have been avoided by altering the natural line in the *secondo*, but Schubert declined to do so. Equally relevant from the perspective of Opus 134 is what Schubert did in the slight ninety-six-bar four-hand fugue that also dates from 1828. The genre evoked considerable conservatism from the composer. All voices maintain a respectful distance from each other. Most telling, Schubert crafted a subject with the minimalist range of a perfect fourth, almost guaranteeing the avoidance of collisions or crossings. Yet Beethoven seems to have been much more aware of (or interested in) Schubert's *Lieder* than in his four-hand music. No evidence survives that suggests Beethoven ever saw (he could not have heard) any of Schubert's mature four-hand works.

Beethoven's Quartets and Fugues

Although we have no such original works from Beethoven, fugue was an increasing preoccupation of his last decade, including the late piano sonatas. The most ambitious of these, the finale of the Sonata in B-flat Major, Op. 106, never exceeds three voices but contains the kind of thematic (subject) transformations with which we are familiar from Opus 133. Ironically, it contains a single hand crossing (mm. 15–16), placed dramatically at the first statement of the subject. The left hand then takes the careening sixteenths for the next nine bars, allowing the second entry in the higher right hand. From then on the voices appear in clear layers, distributed cleanly between the hands. Indeed, Beethoven does not even cross voices *within* the hands.

The less athletic, more lyrical fugue that concludes the Sonata in A-flat Major, Op. 110, differs only slightly. Nowhere is a hand crossing even faintly indicated. However, in seven bars (mm. 45–47, 88, 91, 161–62) the upper voice descends briefly below the middle voice. In each case it is difficult to imagine most listeners following the voice leading. Yet Beethoven was careful to notate the stem directions precisely. The execution is uncomplicated.

If we look at the totality of this survey, we find few ambiguities. The culture of four-hand music—Beethoven's music included—precluded hand crossings. Voices could cross in only the rarest of circumstances. This applies to voices assigned to the same player as well as voices between players. Hence, when Beethoven selected Halm to make the arrangement of Opus 133, he could not have realistically expected Halm to be conversant with anything but the well-established, admittedly conservative tradition that had been firmly in place for almost half a century.

The *Grosse Fuge* in Context

When the American pianist Harold Bauer came to prepare one of the rare editions (for G. Schirmer) of Opus 134 in the 1920s, he remarked in the *New York Times* that "the quartet score fails to correspond exactly with the parts, and the piano version (arranged by Beethoven himself) corresponds with neither."[14] Though this is an accurate assessment, even Bauer probably did not grasp the full extent of the discrepancies.

What did Halm face as he first stared at his assignment? An answer requires an assessment of the extent to which part crossings occur in Opus 133—a subject about which none of the various incarnations of Thayer or even the analytical literature have anything to say. As a frame of reference it is useful to recall that when Beethoven arranged the G-Major Sonata, Op. 14, no. 2, for string quartet he migrated from an instrument where part crossings were basically forbidden to a family of instruments where part crossings were routine and posed no problems. Beethoven's use of part crossings in his string quartets is worthy of its own study, but it takes only a modest examination to see that they were part of his quartet idiom from Opus 18 on.

The genre in Western music in which voice crossings are far and away the most prevalent is the string quartet. (Vocal quartets run a distant second; string quintets and sextets have fewer crossings because their part writing tends toward the symphonic.) Beginning in the 1780s, the string quartet's popularity increased not only because of the speaking quality and smooth gradations within the string family, but also because of the freedom with which one could treat voice leading. There was no inhibition about crossing parts because there were no physical (or aural) consequences. It was not simply that you could do so, but that voices could be moved around freely in a quadraphonic field.

It is no surprise that the string quartet was among the last media to be arranged for piano, four hands. The firm of C. F. Peters began to publish the Beethoven quartets only at mid-century, and only as part of a series of *"Duos, Trios, Quartette, Quintette, Sextette, Septet, Concerte u. Symphonien von L. van Beethoven. Für Pianoforte zu 4 Händen."*[15] For the same reasons that afflicted Opus 134 (and none of these arrangers proved as adept at Beethoven), very few four-hand aficionados will confess to string quartets as their passion.

The reverse process is immensely more problematic: When you take a work where part crossings are a customary part of the texture and then try to shoehorn it onto an instrument where part crossings are disallowed, you are faced with considerable obstacles. It seems more than likely that Beethoven seriously underestimated the magnitude of the task he assigned to Halm.

The only way to quantify the declared issue of hand crossings, of course, is to tabulate them measure by measure. The operative question is: How many times in the 741 measures of Opus 133 do the second violin and viola parts cross each other, precipitating the kind of voice-swapping fix to which Beethoven seems to have objected so strenuously? Even after you have examined the score bar by bar, the results are a surprise: 158 measures—almost 20 percent of the total—contain such conflicts.

The 158 bars between second violin and viola do not exhaust the crossings. Another 154 occur between the first and second violin, sixty-two between viola and cello, and even three between first violin and viola. Altogether, this adds up to 377 total crossings—almost half the bars of the entire fugue.

Even among Beethoven's quartets, this turns out to be extreme. For example, the 121 bars of the opening fugue of the C-sharp-Minor Quartet, Op. 131 (the movement that immediately followed the *Grosse Fuge*), contains only twelve bars with part crossing—fewer than one quarter the percentage of the *Grosse Fuge*. Messrs. Ulrich and Wittman, the Peters arrangers, made quick work of these problems, doing exactly that to which Beethoven apparently objected. Voice leading gives way universally to expediency.

To discover the primary reason that part crossings in the *Grosse Fuge* were exceptionally plentiful, we have only to look at its two subjects. The subject of Opus 131 spans a perfect fourth. In Opus 133 the first subject expands gradually to an octave; the second is even more dramatic. With its propulsive leaps of a tenth and twelfth, it flies across multiple registers with abandon.

Did Halm fully grasp the magnitude of the challenge that faced him? Probably as little as Beethoven understood how unworkable Halm's assignment was. By measure 70, Halm would have encountered a dozen hand crossings between the players and more than two dozen part crossings in the *primo*. He would surely have sensed that he was on new terrain. Halm, a reputable, professional musician in his time, would have been aware of the long-standing taboo against part crossings in four-hand music. But he would have been entirely unprepared for the avalanche of crossings requiring the attention of any arranger of the *Grosse Fuge*. Without fully realizing it, Beethoven placed Halm in a no-win situation that—even without his original manuscript—has left him looking like a bumbling amateur.

Although Beethoven clearly found fault with Halm's arrangement, he would also have come to the realization only the composer could carry it out. (This may support the rumor that, subsequent to Halm, Beethoven briefly considered Carl Czerny, though quickly ruled him out.) Formerly the only source for Beethoven's Opus 134 was the first edition published in 1827 by Matthias Artaria.[16] This is the edition published from Beethoven's manuscript, and by all appearances it was prepared with great care. Until 2006, the only way to determine what Beethoven had in fact done was via the Artaria edition—itself the only source for the sole modern edition published in 1966 by Henle. The recent resurfacing of Beethoven's autograph for Opus 134 will have little effect on any new edition but affords us a unique opportunity to discern in at least some instances just what the process was.[17]

Table 8.1. Schema for the *Grosse Fuge*

OVERTURA [Allegro]	Subject 1 in several guises (mm. 2–25 [4–27])
FUGA [*Allegro*]	
A Section	Subjects 1 and 2 (mm. 26–158 [28–160])
B Section [*Meno mosso e moderato*]	Subject 1 (mm. 159–232 [161–234])
C Section [*Allegro molto e con brio*]	Subject 1 (mm. 233–72 [235–74])
D Section [A-flat Fugue]	Subject 1 (mm. 273–452 [275–454])
	Subject 2, Subject 1 (mm. 453–92 [455–94])
E Section [*Meno mosso e moderato*]	(mm. 493–532 [495–534])
C′ Section	Subject 1 (mm. 533–656 [535–658])
[*Allegro molto e con brio*]	
A Section reminiscence	Subject 2 (mm. 657–59 [659–61])
B Section reminiscence	Subject 1 (mm. 660–62 [662–64])
Coda [*Allegro molto e con brio*]	Subject 1, Subject 2 (mm. 663–741 [665–743])

Recomposing Opus 133

The notion that Beethoven's recomposing of Opus 133 involved only the elimination of part crossings without surrendering contrapuntal integrity does not survive even the first bar. It was immediately clear to its composer that the sustained *forte* octaves across seven strings would create a puny sound when directly transposed to the fortepiano with its rapid tone decay. So Beethoven jacked the dynamic to *ff* and inserted two upbeat measures of wide-ranging, blood-curdling tremolos, thereby adding two bars to every corresponding bar in Opus 133 (see example 8.1).[18]

But what if, after the first four bars, we focus on representative examples of the very passages for which Halm was criticized—those where the crossing occurs between second violin and viola? How does Beethoven cope with something that, though of his own making, even he had never faced before? Given the value that Beethoven attached to contrapuntal integrity, we cannot expect him to have adopted Halm's method. Yet if he did not, he would be forced to resort to two compositional techniques not open to Halm: octave transposition and substitution of new pitches—i.e. recomposition. As benign as transposition may sound, within a contrapuntal texture it demands observing the rules of invertible counterpoint in order to succeed. Finally, what if Beethoven decided, in this most unconventional work, to abandon half a century of convention and retain most of the crossings as they were, leaving the intrepid performers to work them out?

Crossings Averted

1. Measures 20–21 [22–23]: Beethoven redistributes the pitches among the parts in the slow last beat of measure [22] and the first beat of measure

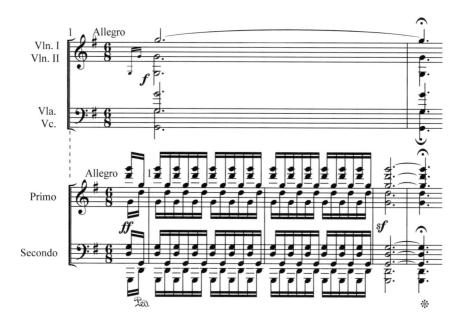

Example 8.1. Beethoven, *Grosse Fuge*, version for string quartet, Op. 133, mm. 1–2; *Grosse Fuge*, version for piano, four hands, Op. 134, mm. 1–4.

[23] so that there is no crossing. Though used only briefly, this is just the kind of strategy that Halm employed and Beethoven condemned.

2. Measure 48 [50]: Beethoven averts the crossing by raising up an octave the second through fifth eighth notes in the second violin.

3. Measures 53–54 [55–56]: On beats 3–4 of measure [55], Beethoven takes the viola down an octave, dipping below the second violin. On the last eighth note of measure [56], he turns an overlap of a sixth into a gap of an eleventh—far larger than a simple avoidance would have required. Incidentally, while toying with these bars, Beethoven changed the first note of the first violin in measure [56] from an e♮″ to an f″, removing the appoggiatura while upping the dissonance level. The autograph is unambiguous about the change.

4. Measures 66–73 [68–75]: A complex combination of selective transpositions and pitch changes averts three crossings in measures [68], [70], and [72], yet the overall changes go well beyond what is necessary, particularly the sixteen pitch substitutions that smooth out the second violin line (see example 8.2).

5. Measure 91 [93]: Beethoven avoids the crossing at the end of the first beat by lowering the viola part by an octave.

Example 8.2. Beethoven, Op. 133, mm. 66–73; Op. 134, mm. [68–75].

6. Measures 121–27 [123–29]: Although the issue is similar throughout this
   passage, Beethoven customizes the changes in virtually every measure: second
   violin up an octave (m. [123]); change of pitch in the viola on the downbeat
   (m. [124]); viola and cello down an octave (m. [125]); viola down an octave
   (mm. [126–27]); viola and cello down an octave (mm. [128–29]); eight

Example 8.2. (continued)

pitches altered in the second violin (m. [128]). It is an understatement to say that cleaning up this passage required the composer, not an arranger. In measure [129] the players will have to decide who plays the b♭ on beat 1 (see example 8.3).

Example 8.3. Beethoven, Op. 133, mm. 121–27; Op. 134, mm. [123–29].

Example 8.3. (continued)

Example 8.4. Beethoven, Op. 133, m. 155; Op. 134, m. [157].

7. Measure 145 [147]: Beethoven addresses the crossing on beats 2–3 by lowering the viola and cello by an octave and raising the last eighth note on the second beat of the second violin part by an octave, again smoothing out the line. In this way, rather than overlapping by a tenth, the parts come no closer than a tritone.

8. Measure 155 [157]: Beethoven dispatches an overlap of a sixth in a more dramatic fashion than required. He not only moves the second violin up an octave (by itself sufficient), but he also takes the viola and cello down an octave as well. Beethoven consistently spreads out the keyboard range so that the basic sound is more symphonic than chamberlike. Curiously, this includes eliminating the double stop in the second violin at the end of the bar (see example 8.4).

9. Measures 183–86 [185–88]: In this three-part passage from the B section (*Meno mosso e moderato*), Beethoven must compensate for the sizeable overlap of a tenth. As in the previous passage, he takes the second violin up an octave and the viola part down an octave. In so doing he eliminates the expressive upward leap of a tenth in the viola—the price to be paid for separating the hands. In essence, the two upper voices are inverted (see example 8.5).

10. Measures 209–13 [211–15] (see example 8.6): Beethoven may well have approached this passage by first noting the overlap in measure 212 [214]. He ends up with a more radical solution for the entire passage. The interior,

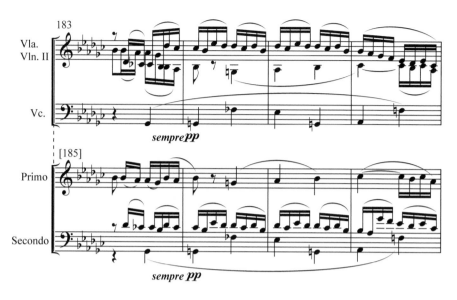

Example. 8.5. Beethoven, Op. 133, mm. 183–86; Op. 134, mm. [185–88].

sustained pedal point in the viola is relocated to the bass line, renewed as a series of eighth notes gently punctuated by rests. The subject elaboration in the cello moves up to the viola. The result is a more conventional sound, with a solidly grounded pedal. The viola and, especially, the second violin parts are extensively rewritten, largely to strengthen the motivic consistency. For example, in measure [211] of the second violin the penultimate pitch is changed from a b♭″ to a c♭‴. Along with the same consistency that precedes measure [211] (violin 2, m. [206], second beat; violin 1, m. [207], second beat, in inversion; second violin, m. [208], second beat; violin 2, m. [210], second beat), this suggests that Beethoven was making conscious *corrections*, or at least improvements, to Opus 133. Though the bars surrounding folio 15r/system 2/measure 3 in the Opus 134 autograph (see figure 8.1) are heavily corrected, the c♭‴ in measure [211] is crystal clear.

11. Measures 221–22 [223–24]: As he approaches the climax of the B section, Beethoven calls once again in Opus 133 on an interior pedal (here on the dominant) to push the two-bar *crescendo*. In Opus 134, he breaks the repeated-note pedal into an octave oscillation while moving both violin parts up an octave to avoid part crossing. The resulting c♭‴ is higher in pitch than any note in Opus 133, a situation repeated numerous times (mm. [116–17], [149] ff., [362–63], [401–2], [448–49], etc.) in Opus 134 and adding to its symphonic character.

Example 8.6. Beethoven, Op. 133, mm. 209–13; Op. 134 mm. [211–15].

12. Measures 236–37 [238–39]: A rare unison doubling between second violin and viola is easily handled by eliminating it from the viola part in Opus 134.

13. Measure 266 [268]: Beethoven avoids the part crossing of Opus 133 by swapping the second violin and viola parts and moving the new second violin part up an octave.

14. Measures 300–305 [302–7]: With a mix of moving the second violin up an octave and the viola down an octave, Beethoven dodges the part crossings in Opus 133. These solutions are never formulaic and could only have been carried out by their composer.

15. Measures 358–78 [360–80]: This remarkable passage employs strings of textural trills that set up the developmental combination of Subject 1 and Subject 2 at m. 414. Beethoven may have initially turned to this passage to address the liberal part crossings in measures 362 [364], 367–68 [369–70], 370–72 [372–74], and 375–78 [377–80]. This problem is complicated by the massive part crossings between the two violins in measures 359–62. The challenge is the extreme range in the second violin; in any given bar it can span a perfect twelfth as it explores the half steps of Subject 1. This produces repeated overlaps of an octave with the trill in the viola.

    As a solution Beethoven first takes the extraordinary step in measures [361–64] of raising the first violin by an octave and the second violin by two octaves—thereby clearing the viola but also inverting the counterpoint. Starting in measure [367], Beethoven embarks on an even more draconian strategy. After taking the viola down an octave he rewrites the second violin line completely; in twelve bars (mm. 365–76 [367–78]) he rewrites no fewer than fifty-two pitches (see example 8.7). What was perhaps the most jagged line in the entire fugue is shrunk to a range of less than an octave in each bar. He also removes the distinctive slurring/bow markings of Opus 133. What Beethoven does preserve is the half-step motive characteristic of Subject 1. The net effect is a smoother, more transparent, and less audacious-sounding texture.

16. Measures 384–98 [386–400] *passim*: In this gritty texture, Beethoven leaves the violins largely as they are while lowering by an octave the slow-moving viola and cello. This is one of the easiest fixes in Opus 134, though not the only one possible.

17. Measures 434–36 [436–38]: This instance had a simple solution—lower the two notes in the viola by an octave. But imagine for a moment that you are Anton Halm and do not feel you have clearance to transpose. What do you do other than what Halm presumably did?

18. Measures 475–84 [477–86] *passim*: Beethoven moves only those notes that would generate an overlap, thereby altering the shape and distribution of the affected lines.

19. Measures 502–9 [504–11] *passim*: In the E section (*Meno mosso e moderato*) Beethoven draws on all of the available techniques: lowering the viola line by an octave, selectively compressing it and the second violin to avoid clashes, and transposing the first violin up an octave. The result is a highly transparent and moving texture.

Example 8.7. Beethoven, Op. 133, mm. 365–76; Op. 134, mm. [367–78].

Example 8.7. (continued)

Before we praise Beethoven for his thorough devotion to convention, we need to examine a smaller second category: crossings that he left in place.

Crossings Retained

1. Measures 34–35 [36–37]: Beethoven's very first opportunity to deal with a crossing in a fast tempo occurs with the second entrance of the second subject (Subject 2). Although this situation is awkward for both players, he does nothing—presumably to establish the basic range for the double fugue. But immediately thereafter he avoids part crossings in the *primo* by transposing the variation on Subject 1 up either one or two octaves. This creates a line that feels new and now lies in the treble.

2. Measures 57–68 [59–70]: In this fresh set of Subject 1 and Subject 2 entries, Beethoven's recomposing becomes even more radical. First, he does nothing to avoid the part crossing (and generally close adjacencies) between the second violin and viola in measures 59–64. Instead, he focuses on the crossings in the *primo*. Not only does he raise the first violin part one or two octaves, he also smooths it into an alternately descending, then ascending sequence, replacing the jagged, asymmetrical line of Opus 133. In measures [61–63] alone, he alters ten pitches. Although we may argue that the ostensible purpose of these changes was to avoid crossings between the violins, they go far beyond what was necessary. Indeed, the avoidance could have been accomplished by octave transpositions alone (see example 8.8).

Part Crossings by the Same Player

Given the general conservatism Beethoven displays concerning part crossings between the second violin and viola, what did he do regarding less disruptive hand crossings (first and second violin; viola and cello) within the same player's part? Not surprisingly, these are concentrated in the *primo*.

1. Measures 35–46 [37–48]: Here Beethoven takes a more relaxed position. Although he uses octave transpositions to avoid most of the crossings between the first and second violins, he retains them in measure [37] (beat 4), measure [40] (beat 3), measure [43] (beat 2), measure [44] (beat 4), measure [45] (beat 1), and measure [48] (beats 2–4). Several of these overlaps nonetheless involve transposition; the composer was more interested in maximizing the acoustical space between voices.

2. Measures 57–68 [59–70]—The two violins in these twelve bars are saturated with overlappings. Through selective transpositions (producing inversions) and ten pitch changes, Beethoven eliminates all the overlaps

Example 8.8. Beethoven, Op. 133, mm 57–68, Op. 134, , mm [59–70].

Example 8.8. (continued)

in measures [59–63]. But with the prominent entrance of Subject 2 in measure [64], the overlaps are unquestionably intentional in spite of twenty-five pitch changes (including the replacement of notes with rests) designed to smooth out the second violin line (see example 8.8).

3. Measures 79–89 [81–91]: Although Beethoven makes a series of complex transpositions while altering several pitches, he retains virtually all of the part crossings.

4. Measures 309–12 [311–14]: Beethoven maintains the series of awkward trill-based crossings between the first and second violins exactly as they are in Opus 133.

5. Measures 358–66 [360–68]: In raising by an octave the first violin at the opening of the D section, Beethoven avoids both crossings.

6. Measures 573–80 [575–82]: In Opus 133, the viola and cello are inverted for all eight of these bars. Beethoven's solution in Opus 134 was as novel as it was unexpected. For the first four bars of the *secondo* he retains the crossings. In the fifth bar, however, he swaps the parts, thereby avoiding any crossings. Ironically, this is just the kind of part swapping that Beethoven purportedly found such fault with in Halm's arrangement.

Changes Independent of Part Crossings

What kinds of changes unrelated to part crossings did Beethoven make in Opus 134? The catalog is sizable. To start with, he treats the very first statement of Subject 1 (mm. 2–10 [4–12]) to octave doublings both above and below, suggesting a more symphonic cast than the quartet original. Other dramatic bass doublings occur in measures [52–59], [354], [455–62], [480–90], [504–8], [512], and the concluding bar [743].

In a related vein, perhaps the most transparent addition is the extension of the bass range to a full seventh below the lowest note of the cello (a D_1 appears in m. [57]). The assumption that Beethoven did this to avoid part crossings would be incorrect. Clearly he did it to inject, in essence, a double bass into the orchestral texture of the arrangement. It is inconceivable that Halm would have taken, or would have been expected to take, any such liberties.

Other changes are as simple as they are unexpected. For example, in measures [111–12] Beethoven assigns the second violin part for two beats to the *secondo*, just the tactic of practical convenience for which he reportedly criticized Halm. In another passage (mm. 38–39 [40–41]), Beethoven simply omits six eighth notes in the cello that straddle an entry of Subject 2 in the viola.

Finally, only Beethoven could have rewritten the string textures characterized by repeated chords—a sound Beethoven believed to be ill suited to the piano. In measures 161–64 [163–66], 177–80 [179–82], and 227–32 [229–34] of the B section, Beethoven freely moves noncontrapuntal voices around to create gentle rocking figures that downplay the percussiveness of the fortepiano.

The most compelling use of this technique occurs in the rush to the final cadence (mm. 716–25 [718–27]). The *secondo* is converted into a partly arpeggiated, partly rocking texture that facilitates the desired tempo of *Allegro con brio*. As the momentum grows, the *secondo* takes over the three lower parts, enabling Beethoven to make rare but effective use of doubling in the first violin (see example 8.9).

This incomplete but representative survey leaves open only one possible conclusion: Beethoven addressed each and every issue as an individual problem. We find no patterns, no stock solutions, no general rules that any arranger could possibly have implemented. Instead, Beethoven constantly weighed subtle issues of balance, clarity, thematic shape, range, register, and ease of execution. He provided almost as many solutions as there are measures in the work. No one but Beethoven could have made these hundreds of decisions.

It is clear that he felt compelled to observe in large measure the four-hand convention that forbade hand crossings between the players. It was no more because such crossings were impossible to negotiate than because social strictures in the Europe of his time governed issues of human interaction and sexual desire. Even so, Beethoven left several instances in Opus 134 where musical considerations overrode social convention. He felt far freer when it came to part crossings by the same player.

The Autograph

The recently discovered autograph is neither *Urschrift* nor *Reinschrift*.[19] Though heavily corrected in places, it could have served easily as the *Stichvorlage* for the Matthias Artaria edition of 1826—much as the autographs of Opus 110 (on the embattled side) and 111 (on the cleaner side) or several of the surviving autographs of the late quartets also functioned. It seems equally certain that for Opus 134, Beethoven made no separate sketches or score sketches of the kind we are now familiar with from the late quartets.[20]

Indeed, any analysis of the roughly three dozen pages in standard-format sketchbooks, a corresponding number of pages of pocket sketches, and the meager crop of fourteen score-sketch leaves for the *Grosse Fuge*, Op. 133, demonstrates clearly that these constitute only a small fraction of what the movement must have required. One could almost argue that in the eighty pages of the rediscovered autograph of Opus 134 we have our most complete commentary by Beethoven on Opus 133. We can assume that his only point of reference throughout the arrangement (more properly speaking, "recomposing") process was the now lost autograph for Opus 133.

The four-hand autograph shows that Beethoven was remarkably clear about many of the changes that he made. For example, although he experimented with the exact register of the tremolos in the revamped opening bars, he was res-

Example 8.9. Beethoven, Op. 133, mm. 716–25; Op. 134, mm. [718–27].

olute about the expansion from the start. In more instances he left a record of the struggle. Among the first bars (fol. 4v) to be subjected to the blade scraping so familiar from Beethoven's autographs are measures [64–65]; both bars are substantially rewritten. At folio 5v, containing measures [74–81], Beethoven replaces the lower system (mm. [78–81], whose second violin part is extensively rewritten) with a crude overlay attached with red wax that leaks all over both the verso and the opposing recto.

The autograph of folio 15r (see figure 8.1) illustrates how Beethoven sometimes entered a provisional solution before thinking it entirely through. Beginning with the second beat of measure [211] (see example 8.6) he liberally redistributes the parts. The *Vi=de* (Beethoven's characteristic method for making connections between passages) from the viola to the bottom staff below is almost comical. It has nothing to do with any arranging, but simply substitutes the bass clef expected by pianists for the unthinkingly written alto clef of the quartet version.

An even more dramatic set of corrections occurs on folio 22v (see figure 8.2, mm. [367–78]; see also example 8.7). In the first bar the second violin part is inserted on the first violin staff. Ten of the twelve bars in the second violin betray the blade scraping necessitated by the massive rewriting. The corrections in the viola and cello are partly a matter of downward transposition, partly a matter of sketching the problematic second violin part first on the cello line (compare mm. 368–71). What is perhaps most remarkable is that regardless of the density of the corrections, Beethoven's ultimate intentions remain perfectly visible.

Choosing the Instrument

The performance of Opus 134 is highly dependent on the instrument for which it was written. The original string version can carry off the jagged counterpoint and the liberal crossings, because blending is what the string family was bred to do. What may sound wild and audacious on the piano will sound considerably less menacing in a string quartet. This is, of course, why the achievements of late Beethoven as well as Béla Bartók in the string quartet are so impressive. Both composers developed original strategies for amplifying the prominence of individual voices within a contrapuntal texture. Yet, as both knew, the percussive quality of the piano could punch each voice out in a way that was alien to the slower attack time of a violin, viola, or cello. Beethoven's arrangement takes these characteristics very much into account. Indeed, in a sympathetic four-hand performance the counterpoint is clearer than in the original string version— aided, to be sure, by Beethoven's registral separation in Opus 134 of many of the lines in Opus 133.

Not surprisingly, there is another side. The piano's percussiveness may increase clarity but the instrument struggles to create the long, arching lines so integral to Opus 133 and so much more a natural part of a stringed instrument's delivery. Even in the most inspired, tightest performance, the pianists will always be struggling for a continuity that is more of an ideal than a reality.

Despite all of Beethoven's recomposing, Opus 134 remains the work in the four-hand repertoire that provides the greatest ensemble challenge. It still teems with overlappings and close adjacencies. Moreover, the persistent counterpoint leaves neither player an opportunity to simply lay back. My colleague Wu Han, who, with her partner Gilbert Kalish, has probably performed Opus 134 more often than any other recent duo (they performed it at the Juilliard dedication concert in 2005), commented to me that *after* they had already prepared and delivered a successful reading, she would want *five* full rehearsals to prepare for the next one. Few if any works in the four-hand repertoire make such demands.

One strategy that can be considered for rehearsal (or even performance) is to employ two pianos. Purists will quickly line up to protest any alteration of Beethoven's intentions. But anyone who is slavishly wedded to authenticity will need to procure themselves a perfectly restored Graf fortepiano from the 1820s to stake any claim of recreating the original sound.[21] Unlike Mozart (who wrote a sonata and a fugue for two Klaviers), Beethoven never made a foray in this direction. Mozart's contributions were essentially teaching pieces, and Beethoven taught as little as he could. My four-hand partner Gloria Cheng and I experimented with two pianos and discovered the usual tradeoffs. Two Steinway Ds allowed the individual voices more space in which to bloom. In fact, the sound field resembled much more closely that of a string quartet than did the closer quarters of a single instrument. At the same time, some of the intimacy of the four-hand version was lost. Provisional experimentation on a Kurzweil K-2500 (using the wide variety of synthesized instrumental colors available) also produced textures of considerable persuasiveness.

It is a testament to both the durability and the resilience of Beethoven's arrangement that it thrives in more than one environment—more so than those who first persuaded its composer to withdraw Opus 133 from Opus 130 could have imagined. Perhaps the most remarkable fact about Opus 134 is that Beethoven created it at all. Already ailing and with less than a year to live, he focused primarily on the completion of his last two quartets (Opp. 131 and 135). It is not clear for how long Opus 134 distracted Beethoven, but the task turned out to be more daunting—and a much more challenging compositional enterprise—than even he imagined.[22] If the result was a work that has perhaps intimidated four-hand players more than it has emboldened them, it is a tribute to the value that Beethoven placed on the *Grosse Fuge* itself. Opus 134 repays many times over the effort required to put together a compelling performance. At the very least, Anton Halm deserves complete exoneration, along with reinstatement of his once honorable reputation.

Figure 8.1. Beethoven, *Grosse Fuge*, version for piano, four hands, Op. 134. Autograph score, f. 15r, mm. 204–14. Used by the kind permission of the Lila Acheson Wallace Library of the Juilliard School, New York City.

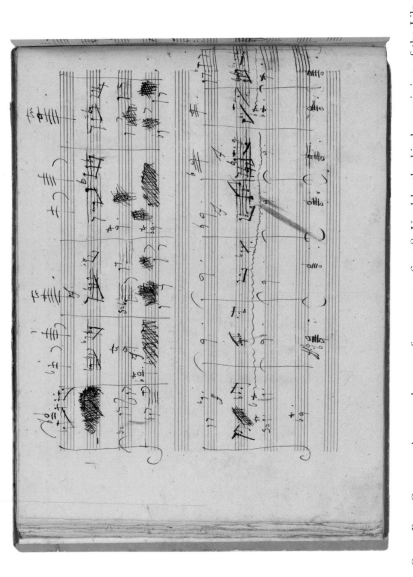

Figure 8.2. *Grosse Fuge*, Op. 134, Autograph score, f. 22v, mm. 367–78. Used by the kind permission of the Lila Acheson Wallace Library of the Juilliard School, New York City.

Notes

My thanks to Robert L. Marshall for spending the last night of his California vacation attending a concert at which Gloria Cheng and I performed Opus 134, and his subsequent encouragement for my pursuit of this topic. Thanks also to Jay Dillon of UCLA for his virtuosic reductions of parallel examples from Opus 133 and Opus 134.

1. Two recordings of Opus 134 are currently available through Amazon.com. The older is that made by Jörg Demus and Norman Shetler in the 1970 bicentennial year as part of the complete works of Beethoven for Deutsche Gramophon (now part of a multi-CD set). The newer is tacked on to a collection of lesser-known chamber music for strings on Aeon Records (B0007ST3R6). Both are in the mid-200,000s on the Amazon sales ranking.

2. There is, of course, one instance of the reverse: Beethoven took his Piano Sonata in E Major, Op. 14, no. 1, of 1798 and three years later arranged it for string quartet in the more congenial string key of F major. As he was to do later with Op. 134, he felt free to make compositional changes appropriate for the alternative medium.

3. This is the occasion for the canon "Da ist das Werk, sorgt für das Geld" ("Here is the work, give me the money"), WoO 197, which Holz was also given to deliver to Artaria.

4. Thayer-Forbes, *Thayer's Life of Beethoven* (Princeton, NJ: Princeton University Press), 975–76.

5. Thayer-Deiters, *Ludwig van Beethovens Leben* (Leipzig: Breitkopf & Härtel, 1923), 5:295.

6. Thayer-Deiters, *Ludwig van Beethovens Leben*, 5:298–99.

7. Here and in the discussion that follows, I refer to the lines in the four-hand piano arrangement by the voices in the original quartet version: first violin, second violin, viola, and cello. Beethoven largely preserves the integrity of these parts; when they deviate in the examples that follow, it is noted at the beginning of each system.

8. Theodor Frimmel, *Beethoven-Handbuch* (Leipzig: Breitkopf & Härtel, 1926), 1:192.

9. See the article "Piano duet" in *The New Grove*, par. 4.

10. Anyone who has ever played through Francis Poulenc's *Sonata for Piano Four Hands* (1918) will understand the manner in which a Frenchman at the end of World War I pokes merciless fun at Austro-German four-hand culture. Spoofs on Czerny-like figuration abound. But most tellingly, almost a dozen bars of the first movement require the primo player (gratuitous, except for the gag, which sometimes requires lunging) to play a loud four-note chord two octaves below the *secondo* part. Assuming that a man is playing *primo* and a woman *secondo*, a first reading of the sonata would run the very real risk of the *primo* inadvertently striking the woman in a forbidden zone. From the modest literature, the most important in this context is Richard Leppert's trenchant critique of Theodor Adorno's almost nostalgic views on the four-hand tradition in "'Four Hands, Three Hearts': A Commentary." *Cultural Critique* 60 (2005): 5–22.

11. Though without any evidentiary sources, on its Web site the Beethoven-Haus claims that Czerny was considered after Halm to make the Opus 134 arrangement, but was subsequently rejected.

12. The four-hand edition from 1812 carries Steiner's plate number C.D.A.S. 2566 (library of the author).

13. In "Piano four-hands: Schubert and the Performance of Gay Male Desire," *19th Century Music* 20 (1997): 149–76, Philip Brett argues convincingly that Schubert's primary expressions of homoerotic desire can be found in his late four-hand works. Brett is concerned primarily with subjective aspects, but whether one prefers homosexual or heterosexual desire, Schubert's use of register brings the *primo* and *secondo* into new proximity with each other. Beethoven was probably unaware of Schubert's four-hand edginess.

14. *New York Times*, October 6, 1929.

15. The two volumes carry the plate numbers 5407 and 5408, which can be only approximately dated to mid-century.

16. Plate number M.A. 878 (library of the author).

17. See stories in the *New York Times*: Daniel J. Wakin, "A Historic Discovery, in Beethoven's Own Hand," October 13, 2005; Jeremy Eichler, "String Quartet Fugue Gets the Four-Handed Treatment," November 18, 2005; Ben Sisario, "Arts, Briefly: Beethoven Score Sells for $1.95 Million," December 2, 2005. The autograph is now on permanent loan to the Juilliard School in New York City.

18. For this reason all measure numbers are given in the format of 50 [52], meaning measure 50 in Opus 133 and measure 52 in Opus 134. Even when measures appear as single numbers, this convention is preserved.

19. The autograph is numbered and circled in pencil in the upper right hand corner of each recto in a hand that is not Beethoven's.

20. The surviving sketches for Opus 133 are listed systematically, and the concept of score sketches is introduced, in Douglas Johnson, Alan Tyson, and Robert Winter, *The Beethoven Sketchbooks* (Berkeley: University of California Press, 1985). See especially pp. 306–17 (standard-format sketchbooks), 432–37 (pocket sketchbooks), and 478–81 (score sketches).

21. The first six-and-a-half-octave fortepianos were introduced in Vienna about 1816. Beethoven's Sonata in A Major, Op. 101, was written to take advantage of the new extension down to C_1. Although his hearing was compromised by 1816, Beethoven did not become clinically deaf until 1818. He certainly understood what Viennese instruments sounded like.

22. As the documents we have already presented suggest, the arrangement must have been made sometime between May and August of 1826. Greater precision is not possible.

Part Four

The Romantic Generation

Chapter Nine

Schubert, the Tarantella, and the Quartettsatz, D. 703

Julian Rushton

Recalling insights from Charles Rosen into reminiscences and connections between works by composers of different generations, I offer here some remarks on an intriguing musical figure that appears at a revelatory point in the first movement of Schubert's unfinished Quartet in C Minor, universally known as the *Quartettsatz*.

The movement stands alone within Schubert's output, not because it belongs to an incomplete project, but due to purely internal, musical factors. Not many of his first movements are in 6/8, and fewer still present so remarkable a deformation of sonata form (see table 9.1).[1] The movement conforms to type only in that the repeated exposition ends in the dominant, and the material presented in the dominant is recapitulated in the tonic, achieving the minimum requirement for resolution.[2] Even then, these sections are in the major mode, whereas conventionally they would be minor. The movement has a development and a recapitulation, but the latter is not identifiable by the tonic or the opening theme; instead it begins with the theme that followed the first modulation (m. 27), then in A♭, now in B♭ (m. 195) and E♭ (m. 199). The opening idea, in emphatic C minor, returns only at the very end.[3]

The *Quartettsatz* exemplifies an expressive trend common in, though not peculiar to, Schubert: the promise of a major-mode conclusion extinguished by ending in the minor. In this it foreshadows the first movement of "Death and the Maiden": both have three-key expositions and contrast a violent, minor-key opening to major-key lyricism; both revert to the minor with codas based on the opening bars. The first movement of "Death and the Maiden" is more orthodox in key structure, however, and its recapitulation begins with the opening motif, with the coda a further development. In contrast, the closing bars of the *Quartettsatz* are a recapitulation of the opening. It appears that in returning to the quartet medium in 1824, Schubert decided on a less daring venture than in 1820.

Table 9.1. Schubert, *Quartettsatz*, D. 703: Outline of the Form

	Measures	Key	Theme
Exposition	1–26	C minor	A
	27–60	A♭ major	B
	61–92	Modulates	C
	93–124	G major	D
	125–40	G major	Coda
Development	141–94	Development ends on V of G minor	
Recapitulation	195–228	B♭–E♭ major	B
	229–56	modulates	C
	257–88	C major	D
	289–304	C major	Coda
	305–15	C minor	A

After hinting at ♭VI (A♭) as his exposition goal, Schubert arrives instead at G major, a progression reversing the I– ♭II (Neapolitan) progression much emphasized near the opening. He finally reaches G through the augmented sixth on E♭ (mm. 83, 87), which in enharmonic spelling might have returned the music to A♭. At strategic points, Schubert uses a kind of motivic concentration as if to counterbalance his tonal waywardness, abrupt modulations, and extreme variations in mood: the transitions recover the ferocious opening but repeatedly yield to lyrical phrases, first in A♭, then in G. The opening motive is essentially a descending chromatic tetrachord (see example 9.1a).

On arriving in G, the opening motive is used in a lightly diatonicized form, emphasising the major, rather than the minor, sixth (viola at m. 93, cello at m. 99), in counterpoint to the violin melody (see example 9.1b). At measure 105, the first-violin figure seems to query, by its chromaticism, but also to confirm G major; this figure decorates the tetrachord with a more elegantly curving shape, marked by upper neighbor-notes and a descending third followed by an ascent (example 9.1c). It is then repeated an octave higher (m. 113).

Example 9.1a. Schubert, *Quartettsatz* in C Minor, D. 703, Opening.

Example 9.1b. Schubert, *Quartettsatz* in C Minor, D. 703, mm. 93–96.

Example 9.1c. Schubert, *Quartettsatz* in C Minor, D. 703, mm. 105–8.

This figure (example 9.1c) marks what Lockwood calls a "marvellous moment," one set in higher relief by Schubert's decision to cut some bars that further play on our expectation of a close in G minor.[4] The figure not only has a vital role within this curious form, but it also alludes, consciously or otherwise, to other music: it may be heard, almost literally, in works ranging from J. S. Bach and Mozart to William Walton (the "Tarantella" from *Façade*), although several instances are only half as long, covering only a minor third rather than the complete tetrachord (see example 9.2).[5] Schubert's placement of the figure, descending from tonic to dominant, could also be connected to the symbolic response to texts on mourning and death set by numerous composers in the tonal tradition; when such figures appear in instrumental music, as in Mozart's D-Minor Quartet, they tempt hermeneutic analysis.[6]

The figure has other associations than with death and mourning, and in the examples I have traced before Schubert, it starts from various points in the scale (see table 9.2).

The gigue from Bach's *Ouvertüre* (Orchestral Suite) in D, BWV 1068, exudes high spirits (see example 9.2a). This associates the figure with dance, and a fast

Example 9.2a. J. S. Bach, *Ouvertüre* No. 3 in D Major, BWV 1068, mm. 65–69.

Example 9.2b. J. S. Bach, *Well-Tempered Clavier*, Book 2, Prelude in A Major, BWV 888/1, mm. 17–19.

Example 9.2c. Mozart, *Don Giovanni*, "Batti, batti," mm. 68–73.

Example 9.2d. Mozart, String Quartet in B-flat Major ("Prussian") K. 589, mvt. 1, mm. 64–67.

Table 9.2. Notes on Example 9. 2

The motif from the *Quartettsatz*, first heard at measure 105 (269), appears in the following earlier works. That marked * includes only the model, not the sequence.

J. S. Bach (1): Gigue from the *Ouvertüre* (Orchestral Suite) No. 3 in D. Descent: dominant to supertonic (A to E).

Bach (2): Prelude in A Major, *The Well-Tempered Clavier*, Book 2 (BWV 888/1). The figure appears in the bass, which is atypical. Descent: tonic to dominant (A to E).

*Mozart (1): *Don Giovanni*, "Batti, batti," 6/8 section. Descent: tonic to submediant (F to D), with subdominant harmony, the flat seventh immediately neutralized.

Mozart (2): String Quartet in B Flat ("Prussian,") K. 589, mvt. 1. Descent: from supertonic to submediant degree (G to D, in F major); transposed in recapitulation.

dance at that. Schubert is unlikely to have known this; less unlikely is some knowledge of Bach's A-Major Prelude from the *Well-Tempered Clavier*, Book 2 (BWV 888/1), where the figure elaborates an already bubbling bass line (see example 9.2b). But the examples he surely knew are by Mozart. In "Batti, batti" (*Don Giovanni*) Zerlina is coaxing back her disaffected lover: the figure appears once, covering only a minor third, at "In contenti ed allegria notte e dí vogliam passar," but it stands out as the first chromatic element within the 6/8 section of the aria (example 9.2c). Zerlina alludes to the anticipated pleasures promised, and soon provided, at the dance in Don Giovanni's house (the Act I finale). The passage is echoed with some violence at a climactic moment in the waltz from Tchaikovsky's *Eugene Onegin* (during Onegin's flirtation with Olga that leads to the duel and Lensky's death).

In Mozart's second "Prussian" Quartet, K. 589 (see example 9.2d), the descending fourth links the sixth and third degrees of the scale (here F); in the recapitulation (mm. 201–3), it is characteristically split between two registers. (Schubert also states the motive in two registers.) The figure is supported by a segment of the circle of fifths, conveniently presented in the bass, and appears significantly in counterpoint to the main theme of the movement, as in the *Quartettsatz.*

These connections draw the *Quartettsatz* into patterns of reception and influence, and into the use of popular dance types in cultured instrumental music, Leonard G. Ratner's "speculative treatment . . . of dance rhythms as subjects for discourse."[7] As dances are assimilated, they get slower, and new, fast popular dances arise to take their place. The Ländler (Teitsch, or German dance, in *Don Giovanni*) may be the ancestor of the waltz, but it was implicitly slower by Schubert's time, in 3/4 rather than the 3/8 he uses in a small group of finales.[8] The gigue being anachronistic, nineteenth-century composers used the saltarello (Mendelssohn, "Italian" Symphony) and tarantella (piano works by Heller and Chopin); the latter has been associated with a group of highly characteristic Schubert finales, notably the Third Symphony, the D-Minor Quartet ("Death and the Maiden"), D. 810, the G-Major Quartet, D. 887, and the C-Minor Piano Sonata, D. 958. Tarantellas are obsessive, and their tendency to perpetual motion is more typical of finales than of first movements.[9] Significant precedents occur in two of Beethoven's Opus 31 sonatas. Rosen has shown how the finale of no. 1 formed the model for Schubert.[10] More pertinent here are the wonderful *moto perpetuo* finale of no. 2 in D Minor, and the finale of no. 3 in Eb, a tarantella in all but name; William Kinderman, indeed, compares it to D. 958.[11]

The *Quartettsatz,* of course, is no finale: Schubert began a slow movement, appropriately (in view of the first movement's early modulation) in Ab. And the *Quartettsatz* is—probably rightly—played more slowly than a tarantella, although it is marked *Allegro assai,* as is the G-Major Quartet finale.[12] Nevertheless the unusual meter and springing rhythms are certainly more readily related to the dance than to the singing Allegro or other first-movement types (heroic, tragic); the character of the music constantly suggests movement, often disturbed, irregular, twitching. The chromatic tetrachord, refreshed by its association with the tarantella-like curling figure and appearing near the end of the exposition and recapitulation, contributes to the intensification of activity typical of the lead-up to a cadence. The same could be said of the Bach gigue, and especially of the Mozart quartet. Schubert subverts cadential expectations in that by relocating the figure to the standard position for the mourning tetrachord, tonic to dominant, he brings it in with the reverse of Bach's or Mozart's high spirits: *ppp*, and repeated in the stratosphere. The figure (see example 9.1c) takes four bars to cover the tetrachord, twice as long as the simpler presentation at the opening (see example 9.1a). Thus Schubert singles out this motif as something special—indeed, spectral—within this remarkable movement.

The abrupt changes of mood in the *Quartettsatz* are typical of first movements rather than finales. But its mingling of major and minor, and the continual intrusion of variants of the descending tetrachord, contribute to an obsessive quality comparable to Schubert's tarantella finales. The tarantella is not strictly a dance of death but, in legend, a dance intended to escape death.[13] These Schubert finales may indeed induce a sense of uplift rather than of doom; for Charles Fisk, they are "a dance of death, though not a meek surrender to death, but a stoic and courageous confrontation," comparable to the self-discovery of *Winterreise*.[14] The *Quartettsatz*, however, is a true first movement in that it is more complex, less single minded. It sets out as if aiming at perpetual motion, presents its main idea in a completely different form, then almost immediately abandons it by turning to A♭ for the fully formed lyrical theme, which is rather longer than the opening (and eventually closing) period in C minor.

Oppositions of this kind continue throughout, but the intertextual element—the curling motive—may offer interpretive clues. At this point in the movement, lyricism is heavily qualified. The motive forms part of the G-major *Gesangsperiode*, but is itself a variation of the opening idea. Associated through Zerlina's aria with dance, but also a variant of an exogenous mourning *topos*, it may indicate some kind of dissension from tradition, and perhaps from society. We cannot know why the quartet was abandoned. The sentimental view—not necessarily wrong—is that Schubert may have felt unable to match the extraordinary power and originality of the first movement he had completed. Its formal properties mark it as special in the way the *Wanderer* Fantasy and the piano four-hands Fantasy in F Minor are special: in this case, a sonata movement deformed, or formed "quasi una fantasia," to adopt the generic apology of Beethoven's Opus 27. But string quartets are not supposed to begin with fantasias—at least not before the late works of Beethoven, composed after the *Quartettsatz*. If anything, Schubert anticipates the sonata deformations detected in Chopin's ballades: No. 1, for instance, with its refusal to relate the more lyrical theme to the tonic key.[15] Lockwood relates the opening of the *Quartettsatz* to Beethoven's Trio in C Minor, Op. 9, no. 3, where, however, a similar intensity of mood—anguished, defiant?—is evoked by the augmented second, later exploited in the C-sharp-Minor Quartet, rather than the descending chromatic tetrachord.[16] A closer model for Schubert, however, with early stress soon yielding, with similar overoptimism, to lyricism, is Beethoven's Quartet in F Minor, Op. 95—not the finale, also in a 6/8 too slow for a tarantella, but rather the first movement, whose abrupt opening proposition is displaced by lyrical material in D♭. The key relation (I–♭VI) is the same, and both quartets place considerable emphasis on the "Neapolitan" flat supertonic. Beethoven's development and recapitulation conform more to orthodox expectations of sonata form, but his movement also ends by returning emphatically to its incisive opening motive. With Opus 95 as a model rather than Opus 31, we can again observe how Schubert could respond to earlier music by venturing into new and highly personal forms of expression.

Schubert's movement is as dysphoric as any lament, but when lyricism is cast aside, its mood is angry rather than sorrowful—not least when the opening idea returns like a swarm of wasps to finish the movement off. At that point the explosive qualities I have associated with the tarantella return, although this movement lacks the terrifying control of the two great quartet finales. Can the extraordinary qualities of the *Quartettsatz* be related to events in Schubert's life? When he later planned his grand campaign of writing string quartets, then a great symphony, he was reviving from an illness whose ultimately fatal effects he probably understood. It is tempting to suggest that his massive finales, in the two quartets and the C-Minor Piano Sonata and in other meters, as in the "Great" C-Major Symphony, are musical dances not of death but of a vitality heroically resisting extinction.

When Schubert composed the *Quartettsatz*, he was not yet afflicted by the disease that eventually ended his life. But he may have been poisoned mentally, rather than physically. Walther Dürr and others identify 1819–20 as years of crisis—*Krisenjahre*—well before the disastrous illness of 1822–23.[17] The *Quartettsatz* was composed in December 1820; in November Therese Grob had married. We need look no further for a reason for Schubert to feel hurt, angry, and nostalgic by turns. Perhaps this first movement danced out the poison in his mind. That cannot explain why he never finished his C-Minor Quartet; nor does it fully account for the music's structural and expressive properties, nor for its intertextual relationship to Bach (perhaps) and Mozart (almost certainly). We are left to wonder why this powerful and compact utterance did not provide a model for later works. Perhaps a sense that the string quartet was becoming a public genre led to the broader canvas Schubert applied to similar expressive intensities in "Death and the Maiden."

Notes

1. On sonata deformation see, for instance, James Hepokoski, "Beethoven Reception: The Symphonic Tradition," in *The Cambridge History of Nineteenth-Century Music*, ed. J. Samson (Cambridge: Cambridge University Press, 2002). The section "Structural Deformation" appears on pp. 447–54.

2. See Charles Rosen, *Sonata Forms* (New York: Norton, 1980), 272–80.

3. For these reasons Martin Chusid calls the movement "bipartite" (binary): see "Schubert's Chamber Music," in *The Cambridge Companion to Schubert*, ed. Christopher H. Gibbs (Cambridge: Cambridge University Press, 1997), 178. A full discussion of the form of the *Quartettsatz*, with which I entirely concur, is in Lewis Lockwood,

"Schubert as Formal Architect," in *Historical Musicology: Sources, Methods, Interpretations*, ed. Stephen A. Crist and Roberta Montemorra Marvin (Rochester, NY: University of Rochester Press, 2004), 204–18.

4. Lockwood, "Schubert as Formal Architect," 207. The cut bars can also be seen in the *Neue Schubert-Ausgabe, Serie VI, Band* 5, ed. Werner Aderhold (Kassel: Bärenreiter, 1989), 203–4.

5. Closely related figures appear in Franz Krommer, *Sinfonia concertante* for violin, flute, and clarinet, mvt. 2; Friedrich Kuhlau, Overture *William Shakespeare*; Brahms, Horn Trio, Scherzo; Dohnányi, *Konzertstück* for cello and orchestra; Janáček, *Sinfonietta*, Finale.

6. Lockwood alludes to the *lamento* tradition—for example, "Dido's Lament," Bach's "Crucifixus"—but with qualifications ("Schubert as Formal Architect," 206). John Reed notes an earlier conventional instance in Schubert in *Schubert* (London: Dent, 1987), 6. See also Peter Williams, "Some Thoughts on Mozart's Use of the Chromatic Fourth," in *Perspectives on Mozart Performance*, ed. R. Larry Todd and Peter Williams (Cambridge: Cambridge University Press, 1991), 204–27, particularly 219.

7. Leonard G. Ratner, *Classic Music: Expression, Form, and Style* (New York: Schirmer Books, 1980), 17.

8. For instance the Piano Sonatas in A Minor, D. 537, and B Major, D. 575.

9. The finale of the Sonata in A Minor, D. 784, although in 3/4, could be related to the tarantella through its principal theme in triplets; but even if its lyricism is somewhat feverish, it lacks this obsessive quality.

10. The rondo finale of Schubert's second A-Major Sonata, D. 959. See Rosen, *The Classical Style*, 456–58.

11. William Kinderman, "Schubert's Piano Music," in *The Cambridge Companion to Schubert*, 161. On D. 958 see also Roy Howat, "Architecture as Drama in Late Schubert," in *Schubert Studies*, ed. Brian Newbould (Aldershot: Ashgate, 1998), 166–90; Charles Fisk, "Schubert Recollects Himself: The Piano Sonata in C Minor, D. 958," *Musical Quarterly* 84 (2000): 635–54.

12. The Third Symphony and D-Minor Quartet finales are marked *Presto*, the C-Minor Sonata merely *Allegro*.

13. The name may derive from Tarentum, rather than the poisonous tarantula. See Erich Schwand, "Tarantella," in *The New Grove Dictionary of Music and Musicians*, 2nd ed., ed. Stanley Sadie and John Tyrrell (London: Macmillan, 2001), 25:96–97. The traditional example cited includes the three-note upper-neighbor shape used in example 9.1c.

14. Fisk, "Schubert Recollects Himself," 650.

15. See Jim Samson, *Chopin: The Four Ballades* (Cambridge: Cambridge University Press, 1992), 45–68.

16. Lockwood, "Schubert as Formal Architect," 206.

17. *Schubert-Handbuch*, ed. W. Dürr and A. Krause (Kassel: Bärenreiter, and Stuttgart: Metzler, 1997). This includes a concise analysis of the *Quartettsatz*, pointing out its formal ambiguities (482–84). Chusid, however, offers 1818–23 as crisis years ("Schubert's Chamber Music," 178).

Chapter Ten

On the Scherzando *Nocturne*

Jeffrey Kallberg

Edginess infects even the best definitions of the nocturne. Consider as emblematic this description from the authoritative *New Grove*: "Nocturne: a piece suggesting night, usually quiet and meditative in character, but not invariably so."[1] The verb brims with ambiguity. (Suggesting how? To whom? Why state the matter so tentatively?). The substantive phrase redundantly hedges its claims ("*usually* quiet and meditative . . . *but not invariably* so" [my italics]).

Such squirrelly lexicographical practice rightly encapsulates the diversity of the genre it describes. Where once the history of the genre prior to Chopin strained to admit anyone other than John Field, now musicologists grasp the importance to Chopin's generation of the vocal nocturne, a vastly popular genre both before and after Field. The Irish composer in essence sought to craft "songs without words" in his nocturnes. Scholars recognize the continuing influence of the still older multimovement nocturne for diverse instrumental ensembles. Mozart's *Eine kleine Nachtmusik* is the most famous example of this kind of nocturne. And they recognize that other composers besides Field (including such figures as August Klengel, Ignaz Moscheles, and Henri Herz) articulated visions of the piano nocturne in the generation before Chopin. In short, it comprehends a broad range of meaning around the term *nocturne* before Chopin began to craft his attitudes toward the genre.[2]

This generic expansiveness tellingly frames the seemingly idiosyncratic aspects of Chopin's Nocturne in B Major, Op. 9, no. 3. This first of Chopin's three B-major nocturnes lies somewhat on the fringes of critical consciousness. It habitually garners citations for the chromaticism of its opening theme and the agitated acceleration of the tempo of its contrasting section—to be sure, both crucial aspects of the piece and crucial early instances of important features of Chopin's mature style. But few scholars note the distinctiveness of its principal tempo marking.[3] As table 10.1 shows, the *allegretto* direction in Opus 9, no. 3, represents the only instance in the nocturnes of a tempo falling outside the confines of larghetto, lento, and andante.

Table 10.1. Principal Tempi in the Chopin Nocturnes

Tempo	Work(s), by opus number
Larghetto	9/1, 15/2, 27/1
Lento	15/3, 32/2, 48/1, 62/2
Lento sostenuto	27/2, 55/2
Lento con gran espressione	Op. posth.
Andante	9/2, 55/1, 62/1, 72/1 (Fontana ed.)
Andante sostenuto	32/1, 37/1
Andante cantabile	15/1
Andantino	37/2, 48/2
Allegretto	9/3

And Chopin further differentiated the B-Major Nocturne by modifying the allegretto tempo with the expressive adverb *scherzando,* an indication he would never again use in the genre (see example 10.1). The two directions plainly contribute to the basic affect of the work, *scherzando* intensifying the allegretto or rendering it even more lightheartedly energetic. For convenience, we can refer to this basic affect as the "*scherzando* nocturne."

This term of expediency would certainly give our lexicographers pause. *Scherzando* implies jocularity or playfulness: what do these qualities have to do with the "usually quiet and meditative" nocturne? One cannot take refuge in the adverb *usually.* Any definition of the nocturne that conspicuously construes it as "quiet and meditative" would seem to exclude the possibility of a playful performance.

Of course, the fault lies with the definition and the anachronistic ways of thinking that it distills. Although Chopin used *scherzando* and allegretto only once in a nocturne, these terms appear commonly in nocturnes written by composers in the decades before and immediately after Chopin penned Opus 9, no. 3 (see tables 10.2–10.4).

Although I make no claims for the comprehensiveness of the data offered in these tables, I think that they do nonetheless demonstrate the ubiquity of the *scherzando* nocturne. The effect appears in every manner of piece called "Nocturne." Lively, playful tempi appear often in vocal nocturnes that date from the first decade of the nineteenth century (see the works by Blangini and Jadin in table 10.4). Similar effects occur in nocturnes that embrace qualities of the old multimovement genre (table 10.2, Moscheles), as well as in nocturnes that lack the widely spanned broken chords and plunging bass notes that produce the accompanimental "nocturne texture" popularized (but not invented) by Field (table 10.3, Klengel). Many more nocturnes featured the *scherzando* trope before Chopin published Opus 9, no. 3 than afterward. These later *scherzando*

Example 10.1. Chopin, Nocturne in B Major, Op. 9, no. 3, mm. 1–8.

Table 10.2. Nocturnes Marked Allegretto (Principal Tempo) and Featuring *Scherzando*

Composer	Work	Date	*Scherzando* Measures	Comments
Moscheles	Nocturne, Op. 71	1827	81	"Andantino quasi Allegretto"
Chopin	**Nocturne, Op. 9, no. 3**	**1830–31?**	**1, 31, 132**	**31, 132: "scherz."**
Kessler	Nocturne, Op. 29, no. 3	1833	45	"Allegretto E gustoso"
Wolff	*Nocturne en forme de Mazurke*	1841	46	"Allegretto cantabile"

nocturnes still command interest, though, since many of them came from the pens of composers who had particular reasons (personal or national) to be aware of Chopin's efforts in the genre (see in tables 10.2–10.4 the various nocturnes by Kessler, Wolff, Dobrzyński, and Gutmann).

Table 10.3. Nocturnes featuring *scherzando*

Composer	Work	Date	Scherzando Measures	Comments
Field	Nocturne no. 1 in E♭ major	1812	15	"Scherz."; marking only in Dalmas and Peters edition
Klengel	Nocturne, Op. 23, no. 6	1820	66	"scherz:"
Herz	*Nocturne caractéristique*, Op. 45, no. 3	1828	159	
Kessler	Nocturne, Op. 29, no. 2	1833	9, 84	
Field	Nocturne no. 16 in F major	1836	57	"scherzo"
Thalberg	Nocturne, Op. 28	1838	42	

Table 10.4. Nocturnes Marked Allegretto (Principal Tempo)

Composer	Work	Date	Comments
Blangini	*12 Notturni a due Voci*, Book 1, no. 2	1801	"Allegretto grazioso"
Blangini	*12 Notturni a due Voci*, Book 2, no. 1	1801	"Allegretto. con grazia"
Blangini	*12 Notturni a due Voci*, Book 2, no. 3	1801	"Allegretto. sostenuto"
Blangini	*12 Notturni a due Voci*, Book 2, no. 6	1801	
Jadin	*Huit Nocturnes à voix seule*, no. 6	1800–5	
Cramer	Nocturne for piano (violin and cello ad lib)	1811	
Field	Nocturne no. 3 in A♭ major	1812	"Un poco allegretto"
Szymanowska	*Le murmure*, Nocturne	1829	
Kessler	Nocturne, Op. 28, no. 2	1833	"Allegretto gustoso"
Bertini	Nocturne, Op. 87, no. 2	1832	"Allegretto agitato"
Dobrzyński	Nocturne, Op. 21, no. 3	1835	"Allegretto alla masovienna"
Döhler	Nocturne, Op. 25, no. 1	1838	"Andante quasi Allegretto"
Gutmann	Nocturne, Op. 8, no. 2	1847	"con tenerezza"

Chopin and his listeners recognized a more expressively capacious nocturne than do our modern lexicographers: the prevalence of the playful performing directions suggests that the *scherzando* nocturne constituted a notable subgenre in the early 1830s. The existence of this lighthearted type gains further credence when we consider some definitions of the vocal nocturne (and the closely related vocal romance) written before the time of Chopin's B-Major Nocturne. In 1825, François Henri Castil-Blaze described a genre that contributed to the graceful allure of a soirée: "The *nocturne* being made to add to the charms of a beautiful night, and not to disturb the tranquility of it, its character turns as much away from lively and loud gaiety as from sadness and the impetuous movement of grand passions."[4] In 1809, an anonymous reviewer of a collection of vocal romances portrayed the genre in even more telling terms: "*Galanterie* in the older, more sensitive sense is what the substance of the French romance chiefly amounts to; graceful language, light flowing verses, distinctive refrains, and above all a piquant, sententious or witty refrain—that is what the form particularly requires."[5] As I have noted elsewhere, these and other contemporary witnesses depicted a genre that supported structures of sociable communication.[6]

The term *scherzando* expediently allowed composers to signal affability. So suggested Gustav Schilling in his 1838 definition of "Scherz und Scherzhaft." Exploring the proper aesthetic nature of pieces or passages that used *scherzando*, he wrote: "It may not at all let the listener get to thinking or to serious feeling about the music; it should bring him to relaxation, cheer him up, delight him, thus it must keep him continuously in a mood in which the genuine provocation of laughter would be easy."[7] The avoidance of serious expression, the cultivation of an air of relaxation and cheerfulness—Schilling's description melds nicely with the atmosphere described by Castil-Blaze and the anonymous reviewer, an atmosphere, we may now also assert, customarily (if not uniquely) cultivated in all guises of the nocturne before 1830. Certainly all the works listed in tables 10.2–10.4, in various passages and in some cases in their entirety, convey the qualities of wit and sociability outlined by our contemporary witnesses.

The importance of the *scherzando* nocturne is thus twofold. First, and more generally, it confirms that in the years before Chopin wrote his first nocturne the promotion of conviviality lay at the heart of the genre. More poetic associations with such notions as visionary experience, longing, and supernatural mysteries had yet to coalesce around the nocturne. That such poetic associations gradually became more common after Chopin began to make his mark in the genre is, of course, no coincidence.

Second, and more particularly with respect to Chopin, knowing of the prior existence of the *scherzando* nocturne allows a more nuanced view of Chopin's approach to the genre in his first published set of nocturnes. Opus 9 forms Chopin's most heterogeneous collection of nocturnes. Viewed as a group, these nocturnes suggest a composer experimenting with different modes of articulating an identity within a genre. Should a nocturne frankly evoke a Fieldian limpidity of melody and relative restraint of expression (Op. 9, no. 2)? Should it try to push these Fieldian constraints toward a greater expressive range (Op. 9, no. 1)? Or should it embrace the kind of strong functional and expressive contrast (*scherzando* versus agitato, if you will) recently introduced into the genre by Henri Herz (Op. 9, no. 3)? The diversity of Chopin's compositional strategies mirrored the variety of the genre as a whole.

Example 10.2a. Chopin, Nocturne in B Major, Op. 9, no. 3, mm. 29–34.

It is also significant that this diversity reflected Chopin's transformational effect on the genre, the ability (in his mind and those of his listeners) to wrest control over preexistent genres and to make them into his own. Even in the details of his disposition of the *scherzando* indication in Opus 9, no. 3, Chopin distanced himself from the models of his predecessors (of which he surely knew, at least in part). Examining tables 10.2 and 10.3 again, we notice that only Chopin placed *scherzando* in the opening measure of his nocturne. Moreover, apart from Kessler in his Nocturne, Op. 29, no. 2 (see table 10.3), only Chopin repeated the direction (see examples 10.2a and 10.2b). As Mieczysław Tomaszewski observes, elsewhere in Chopin's music *scherzando* customarily appears once, typically attached to an internal phrase with dancelike characteristics, and then vanishes.[8]

What other composers invoked as a means of contrast (perhaps recalling the association of sociability with the idea of a "witty refrain," in the words of the anonymous 1809 reviewer) Chopin elevated into a governing mode of pianistic expression. He recognized the ability of *scherzando* to intensify the expressive effects implied by the allegretto tempo, and he determined to draw attention to this feature from the very start of his piece. The intensification tends to align the outer portions of this nocturne with the brilliant style, especially in moments such as measure 31, where Chopin adds a seemingly (though not actually) redundant *scherzando* in order to draw attention to a particularly sparkling ornamental decoration of the principal theme.[9] The critical tendency has been to

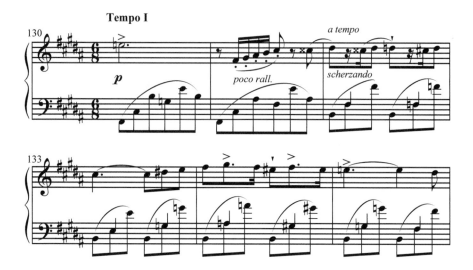

Example 10.2b. Chopin, Nocturne in B Major, Op. 9, no. 3, mm. 130–35.

assume that the brilliant style, though important to Chopin's early works generally, lay at the periphery of the apparently more lyrical domain of the nocturne,
but recognition of the *scherzando* subgenre suggests a need to reconsider this
viewpoint.

It is not quite right, though, to assert that *scherzando* governs the entire nocturne, for—to mention only the most patent exceptions—the *agitato* contrasting
section and the ethereal coda lead us far from the realm of the playful. In a
sense, Chopin gradually composes himself out of the *scherzando* trope. This
transformation already begins in the opening section with the plaintive ritornello on F-sharp major. This ritornello is first heard in measures 13–20, recurs
as many times as the beginning phrase of the principal theme in the opening
section, and indeed comes to stand in for this theme in the sprawling second
half of the opening section (example 10.3).

That the governing affect begins to shift toward something more *espressivo* may
be why Chopin felt the need to reassert *scherzando* in measure 31. The transforming process continues inexorably through the second half of the opening
section, into the *agitato*, and culminates in a delicate cadenza where (looking
backward from the perspective of Chopin's own later nocturnes) it seems as if
the composer settled on the nocturnal identity he had experimentally sought
elsewhere in the opus (see example 10.4).

What began playfully finishes dreamily. In a manner similar to his reshaping
of the raw materials of a ballroom dance into the evocation of an exotic landscape

Example 10.3. Chopin, Nocturne in B Major, Op. 9, no. 3, mm. 13–20.

that is the mazurka, Chopin thus at once elevates the *scherzando* trope and tries to erase it from the genre. The altered function of *scherzando* in Opus 9, no. 3 doubtless helped accelerate the decline in the popularity of the trope among other composers in the 1830s and 1840s.

Decline, however, does not translate to disappearance. Just as aural traces of the vocal nocturne endured in the piano genre, so too elements of the *scherzando* trope persisted after Chopin abandoned the explicit use of the terms *scherzando* and allegretto. The most intriguing of these echoes resonate in the two nocturnes that bear the tempo marking Andantino, namely the G Major, Op. 37, no. 2 and the F-sharp Minor, Op. 48, no. 2 (see table 10.1). Given the tendency of most pianists today to interpret andantino (or at least andantino attached to a nocturne) as a rather slow tempo, it might seem surprising to assert that hints of the *scherzando* trope survive in these two pieces. But evidence from Chopin's time suggests that, although uncertainty existed about just what

Example 10.4. Chopin, Nocturne in B Major, Op. 9, no. 3, mm. 154–57.

andantino should mean, many musicians construed it as something quite fast. Beethoven commented on the situation in an 1813 letter to his Edinburgh publisher George Thomson about expectations for the folk-song arrangements he would prepare for Thomson. Should Thomson wish a song arrangement to

Example 10.5. Chopin, Nocturne in G Major, Op. 37, no. 2, mm. 1–6.

carry the tempo andantino, Beethoven wrote, then he should specify whether he means andantino to be faster or slower than andante, "since this term, like many others in music is of such uncertain meaning that many times Andantino approaches Allegro and many other times is played almost like Adagio."[10] And in words that bear directly on the question of a possible relationship between allegretto and andantino nocturnes, Gustav Schilling's definition of andantino in his 1838 *Universal-Lexicon* explicitly associated the tempi for andantino and allegretto. After observing that the diminutive of "andante" should call for a tempo slightly slower than andante, Schilling noted that it was evident that not many people interpreted the term this way, and that "the tempo of andantino is often confused with that of allegretto, and taken much faster than that of the proper andante."[11] The tempo of Moscheles' 1827 Nocturne, Op. 71—*andantino quasi allegretto* (see table 10.2)—anticipates in a musical context what Schilling limned lexicographically. And Chopin himself used "andantino quasi allegretto" at the beginning of his *Krakowiak*, Op. 14.[12]

When played in more bracing tempos, the G-Major and F-sharp-Minor Nocturnes resonate audibly with the *scherzando* trope of Opus 9, no. 3. Consider first the G-Major Nocturne (example 10.5).[13]

We might already be inclined to hear connections between this nocturne and other works, given Jim Samson's smart analysis of its intertextual links with the

Example 10.6. Chopin, Nocturne in F-sharp Minor, Op. 48, no. 2, mm. 127–37.

Ballade, Op. 38 (especially with the *siciliano* opening theme of the ballade—by the way, another theme marked andantino).[14] At a livelier tempo, the suggestions of the *scherzando* trope sound most noticeably in the meanderingly descending conclusions of the three-bar phrases that animate the main theme, as well as in the surprising turns to new keys that are a defining feature of this nocturne. As in Opus 9, no. 3, what seems initially playful takes on a more serious cast, especially as the modulatory turns settle into predominantly minor, and more somber, terrain.

In the F-sharp-Minor Nocturne, we strain harder to hear the *scherzando* origins of some gestures. To my ear, the trope struggles to emerge through most of this work. Its cause certainly is not helped by the dragging tempos that most pianists adopt for the piece. Played more swiftly, the nocturne might evoke a hint of the *scherzando* idea in the restlessness of the long, circular phrases that define the principal theme. But this is a faint insinuation of the past. Only in one phrase does the *scherzando* signal come through more clearly, indeed tellingly, and this is in the final measures of the coda (example 10.6).

The sudden and stunning turn to the major mode makes internal sense as a resolution of the persistent A/A♯ ambiguity in the principal theme. But this internal sense of propriety gains even more force from the external history of the genre. The initial trills of this ending, with their resolutions by leap, lend an unexpected agility to this otherwise most serious of nocturnes, and through their very lightness recall the playful essence of the *scherzando* trope. The sense of goal-directed aptness that suffuses this ending thus stems from more than the resolution of ambiguities of pitch. In it we also perceive a magical unveiling of a governing trope hitherto more inferred in this nocturne than genuinely grasped. Although the reappearance of the *scherzando* reminds us at the end of the convivial past of the genre, it also underscores the emotional distance Chopin traveled in the nocturne since the early, lighthearted days of the B-Major Nocturne, Op. 9 no. 3.

Notes

A somewhat different version of the present essay will appear in the published proceedings of the December 2005 conference hosted by the Narodowy Instytut Fryderyka Chopina in Warsaw.

1. Maurice J. E. Brown and Kenneth L. Hamilton, "Nocturne," *The New Grove Dictionary of Music and Musicians*, 2nd ed., ed. S. Sadie and J. Tyrrell, 18:11 (London: Macmillan, 2001).

2. For support of these claims, see Jeffrey Kallberg, " 'Voice' and the Nocturne," in *Pianist, Scholar, Connoisseur: Essays in Honor of Jacob Lateiner*, ed. Bruce Brubaker and Jane Gottlieb (Hillsdale, NY: Pendragon Press, 2000), 1–46; and James Parakilas, " 'Nuit plus belle qu'un beau jour': Poetry, Song, and the Voice in the Piano Nocturne," in *The Age of Chopin: Interdisciplinary Inquiries*, ed. Halina Goldberg (Bloomington: Indiana University Press, 2004), 203–23.

3. Some of the more useful discussions of Op. 9, no. 3 include Raoul Koczalski, *Frédéric Chopin: Conseils d'interprétation*, ed. Jean-Jacques Eigeldinger (Paris: Buchet/Castel, 1998), 132–33; Vladimir Jankélévitch, *Le Nocturne: Fauré, Chopin et la Nuit, Satie et le Matin* (Paris: Albin Michel, 1957), 66; Tadeusz A. Zieliński, *Frédéric Chopin*, trans. Marie Bouvard, Laurence Dyèvere, Blaise de Obaldia, and Krystyna de Obaldia (Paris: Fayard, 1995), 272–75; and Mieczysław Tomaszewski, "Aspects de la réception poétique des Nocturnes de Chopin," in *La note bleue: Mélanges offerts au Professeur Jean-Jacques Eigeldinger*, ed. Jacqueline Waeber (Bern: Peter Lang, 2006), 84.

4. François Henri Castil-Blaze, *Dictionnaire de musique moderne*, 2nd ed. (Paris: Au Magasin de musique de la lyre moderne, 1825), 2:85.

5. Review of vocal romances by Charles Eisrich in *Allgemeine musikalische Zeitung*, 22 November 1809, cols. 121–22.

6. Kallberg, " 'Voice' and the Nocturne," 8.

7. "Er darf den Hörer gar nicht bis zum Denken oder ernsten Fühlen über die Musik kommen lassen; er soll ihm Erholung verschaffen, ihn aufheitern, ergötzen, muß ihn also auch stets in einer Stimmung erhalten, in welcher die wirkliche Erregung des Lachens leicht ware." Gustav Schilling, *Encyclopädie der gesammten musikalischen Wissenschaften, oder Universal-Lexicon der Tonkunst* (Stuttgart: Franz Heinrich Köhler, 1838; repr., Hildesheim: Georg Olms, 1974), 6:193.

8. Mieczysław Tomaszewski, *Chopin: Człowiek, Dzieło, Rezonans* (Poznań: Posiedlik-Raniowski i Spółka, 1999), 648–49.

9. For a fine discussion of the unconventional nature of Chopin's ornamental writing in this nocturne, see Charles Rosen, *The Romantic Generation* (Cambridge, MA: Harvard University Press, 1995), 402–3.

10. " . . . puisque ce terme comme beaucoup d'autres dans la musique est d'une signification si incertaine que mainte fois Andantino s'approche du Allegro et mainte autre est joué Presque comme Adagio"; letter of February 19, 1813 to George Thomson, in Beethoven, *The Letters of Beethoven*, ed. Emily Anderson (London: Macmillan, 1961), 1:406.

11. " . . . das Tempo des andantino oft mit dem des allegretto verwechselt und um vieles schneller genommen, als das des eigentlichen andante." Schilling, *Encyclopädie der gesammten musikalischen Wissenschaften*, 1:193.

12. The same tempo marking appears in Julian Fontana's copy of an earlier version of the Prelude in A-flat Major, Op. 28, no. 17; see Fryderyk Chopin, *Préludes Op. 28, Op. 45*, ed. Jean-Jacques Eigeldinger (London: Peters, 2003), 51.

13. It was Charles Rosen's fine, brisk recording of the G-Major Nocturne, included with the text of *The Romantic Generation*, that first inspired me to recognize that the *scherzando* trope extended beyond Op. 9, no. 3.

14. Jim Samson, "The 'Second Ballade': Text and Intertext," in *Muzyka w kontekście kultury: Studia dedykowane Profesorowi Mieczysławowi Tomaszewskiemu w osiemdziesieciolecie urodzin*, ed. Małgorzata Janicka-Słysz, Teresa Malecka, and Krzysztof Szwajgier (Kraków: Akademia Muzyczna, 2001), 55–65.

Chapter Eleven

Chopin's Modular Forms

Robert P. Morgan

In *The Romantic Generation*, closing the last of three chapters on Chopin, Charles Rosen remarks:

> That is the true paradox of Chopin: he is most original in his use of the most fundamental and traditional technique. That is what made him at the same time the most conservative and the most radical composer of his generation.[1]

Rosen is referring to Chopin's tendency to transform the traditional idea of musical "line" in order to "demonstrate the intimate relation between line and color in music."[2] But his characterization applies equally to many aspects of Chopin's work, including his conception of form. Near the end of his book, Rosen comments more generally on the Romantic view of such matters:

> In music, the most original minds of the 1830s were ill at ease with those Classical procedures conceived as valid for a large variety of forms, and which can therefore be projected in advance. . . . The aspects of their large forms which are conventional tend to be perfunctory—we can have few expectations of what directions the more original inventions in the large form will take because we have almost no precedents on which we can rely. It is true that the Romantic composer had models with which he worked, but he often tried successfully to make it seem as if the music had been created sui generis.[3]

For Rosen, Chopin obviously belonged with the "most original minds." and his comment points to a strange conjunction in the composer: a paradoxical ability to preserve Classical techniques while transforming them into something *sui generis*. In this paper I will explore one aspect of this paradox in relation to Chopin's "forms," a word I, along with many others, use to encompass essentially all aspects of the music: tonality, texture, rhythm, articulation, and the like. More specifically, I want to examine a number of compositions—among Chopin's most interesting and original—that retain the Classical notion of musical repetition yet reinterpret it in a "modular" fashion, producing significant departures from Classical practice.

One does not normally associate Chopin with modular thinking: that is, the use of fixed musical units repeated both at pitch and in transposition, with or without superficial alterations, and in different juxtapositions and combinations. The result, although perhaps normal sounding on the surface, produces an unusual effect that is significantly collage-like in character and thus markedly different from traditional practice. In Classical music, for example, paired phrases, if they are not simply marking time (as in segments of confirmation), are normally varied so that adjoining formal units, as in antecedent-consequent pairs, have a complementary relationship, the second phrase often completing something left unfinished by the first. In Chopin that distinction, even when partly in play, is often suppressed: what by Classical standards would be a complementary relationship becomes simply a repetitive, yet often developmental, one.

Chopin wrote a number of compositions in which modularity plays a significant role. Though he does not adopt the technique as consistently as did some predecessors, contemporaries, and followers (such as Schubert, Schumann, and Scriabin), he uses it in a characteristic manner, and with a skill that renders the music indeed *sui generis*. And even when modularity is not emphatic, it nevertheless often colors his work.

Modularity in the Mazurkas

Before undertaking three more extensive analyses, I want briefly to consider several shorter works drawn from the mazurkas in order to reveal how modular effects pervade even apparently traditional formal patterns in Chopin. The mazurkas offer an ideal repertoire for examining modularity, since, as dance forms, they are typified by traditional relationships and by frequent repetition. They thus provide a useful yardstick to measure the influence of modularity on traditional compositional thinking.

A good place to begin is with the middle section of the Mazurka in A Minor, Op. 68, no. 2, a sixteen-measure binary form in A major with each half repeated (mm. 29–44).[4] On the surface the music seems to be a more or less normal period. Each of the two main phrases has eight measures, the first ending on iii, the second on I. But there is a striking anomaly: the first measure not only repeats immediately, and again in measures 33 and 34, but more surprisingly, it recurs four times in the "contrasting" second phrase: measures 38, 40, 42, and 44. Remarkably, it is heard eight times in only sixteen measures (or, with repeats, sixteen times in thirty-two measures). Moreover, what was originally an opening gesture becomes purely a closing one in the second phrase, with significant consequences: the entire section not only begins with the A-major chord with melodic $C\sharp^5$, with which the oft-repeated measure opens, but returns to it over and over, finally ending on it. In addition, $C\sharp^5$ also appears as the top voice of the first phrase's cadential chord on iii (mm. 35–36). As a result, the whole antecedent-consequent period seems melodically anchored in a single place, even when it produces harmonic motion. The repeated measure seems to be "nonorganic": caught in collage-like juxtapositions.

A similar example is found in the Mazurka in E Minor, Op. 41, no. 1, in a sixteen-measure segment of the B section of its ABA form (mm. 17–32, repeated mm. 41–56). In this case, what is repeated within the phrase is not an isolated measure but an entire four-measure melodic subgroup that recurs four times (mm. 17–20, 21–24, 25–28, 29–32). In addition, a single, immobile melodic pitch dominates: D♯, the third of I in B major (the section's key) and the root of the iii chord on which each eight-measure subphrase cadences. Another case appears in the sixteen-measure C-major section of the Mazurka in G Major, Op. 67, no. 1, also in its middle section (mm. 29–44). Again, there are four repetitions of almost identical four-measure subgroups (the final two beats are altered to return to the original tonic). This is in itself modular; but particularly noteworthy is the assertive dominant chord, distinct in rhythm and texture from the rest, with which each subgroup begins. Indeed, despite its harmonic function as V, the chord is treated as the goal of both the preceding section and each but the last of the new four-measure subgroups, preserving formal ambiguity throughout the section. Following the final subphrase, subtly altered to lead to the return, the pun becomes explicit: the main material, in G major (m. 45, bringing back m. 5), begins with the same low G octaves as did the middle-section subphrases. (Only the dynamic is altered to help reorient us.) Once again the middle section is dominated by a single melodic pitch: each four-measure unit defines a circular motion from G^5 down to G^4, both supported by V of C.

Two simpler but equally instructive examples occur in the two contrasting sections of the Mazurka in F Major, Op. 68, no. 3, measures 17–24 and measures 33–44. The first consists of a repeated four-measure group, itself containing a repetition of the first two measures but with the last two beats varied to form a cadence. The second section, one of Chopin's signature Lydian passages, has only a single chord, a IV chord (or I in B♭), which is replaced by V of the original tonic on the last two beats.

The modularity of yet another contrasting section, the A-major phrase beginning at measure 9 of the posthumous Mazurka in D Major, stems not from literal repetitions of a fixed unit but from a quasi-sequential overlapping restatement of the first I–I subphrase (mm. 9–12), which now moves from I to V (mm. 12–15).[5] The modular quality is underscored by the varied recurrence of the idea heard in the first measure of the subphrase (m. 9) in measures 12 and 15, each time different yet, thanks to its apartness from the rest, instantly recognizable. Chopin exploits the first measure's ambiguity (might it be cadential?) in both of its "repeats," allowing it to be both ending and overlapping beginning. In the last measure of the second subphrase, it initiates a four-measure extension (mm. 15–18) that consists entirely of two versions of this measure. (The return to the original tonic at measure 19 stems simply from reinterpreting

A as V of D.) Because the second measure (m. 16) is virtually identical to measure 9, it even suggests the possibility that there will now be a full repetition of the previous seven-measure unit, thus making measure 15 purely a closing measure. But that does not happen: at measures 16 and 18 the chord is treated exclusively as a second measure, not a first.[6]

In this passage from the D-Major Mazurka, the second (overlapping) phrase at measures 12–15 sounds like a freely sequential repetition of the first; but that effect is merely simulated. Yet Chopin often does exploit stricter sequences to create modular effects. Although the sequence technique, of course, lends itself readily to traditional formal thinking, Chopin distinguishes his sequences by often treating them in a nonstandard manner. Phrases beginning with sequential and diatonically related pairs are, to be sure, sometimes "normalized" in his work by a third phrase (following Classical practice), as happens in the opening themes of Opus 6, no. 1; Opus 24, no. 4; Opus 41, no. 4; and Opus 59, no. 1, all in minor mode (F sharp, G, C sharp, and A). Each begins with a sequence up by minor third to III (the sequenced unit being two measures long in the first two, eight measures in the third, and four measures in the last), followed by a normally longer, contrasting unit (usually prepared by an alteration of the end of the preceding sequence) that carries the motion on to a uniquely marked V–i cadence.[7] Somewhat different is the opening subphrase of the Mazurka in B Major, Op. 56, no. 1, also two measures long but sequenced downward in *three* stages: first to I, then to natural VII, then to natural VI (mm. 1–2, 3–4, 5–6). The last overlaps with an extended fourth phrase (itself with several subphrases) that converts VI into an augmented sixth that eventually resolves V–I (mm. 6–22). (Overlapping, both structural and surface, always prominent in Chopin, is particularly notable in this final phrase.[8])

But Chopin's sequences are not always normalized. A favorite device is to construct antecedent-consequent phrases out of two symmetrically related subphrases, a practice very much at odds with the Classical one: the second phrase does not complete the antecedent but simply repeats it at another level. Examples open the Mazurkas in E Minor and C Minor, Op. 41, no. 1 and Op. 56, no. 3, both of which sequence the antecedent down a fourth. Does the antecedent arrive on iv and the consequent on i? Or does the antecedent arrive on i and the consequent on v? Since the phrases are identical (within transposition), the music offers little help. Thus the former holds in Opus 41, no. 1, the latter in Opus 56, no. 3. However, Chopin does aid the listener in both instances: by breaking the pattern at the end of Opus 41, no. 1, to allow for a unique (though modal) close on I; and by placing the cadential arrival on the third measure of the subgroup in Opus 56, no. 3, leaving an extra measure to convert the consequent's closing v into a true (major) V.[9]

The most striking example of a sequential period is the Mazurka in C Major, Op. 7, no. 5, which, except for a tonally ambiguous introduction, consists entirely of a single formal unit (itself a smaller antecedent-consequent period) and its (slightly varied) transposition up a fifth. Here the ambiguity (are the cadences on I and V or IV and I?) is fully exploited. First, both cadential measures continue on their second and third beats, producing an upbeat to the next phrase; and since the whole (except the introduction) is repeated, and since accompaniment and melodic motion remain essentially constant, there is an unbroken motion from antecedent to consequent to antecedent and so on. Chopin does not give himself, either tonally or rhythmically, anywhere to stop, something he acknowledges by marking the repeat "*senza fine.*"[10]

Of course, one can produce continuous circular periods without resorting to modularity, as Chopin does, for example, through overlapping in the Mazurkas in F-sharp Minor, Op. 6, no. 1 (mm. 1–16) and in G Minor and A Minor, Op. 67, nos. 2 and 4 (mm. 17–32 in both). As we might expect, however, the effect is less obtrusive. Closer to Opus 7, no. 5 is the opening period of the Mazurka in C Major, Op. 24, no. 2 (mm. 5–8), whose consequent, in A minor, sounds like a diatonic transposition down a third from C major (not strict, though the modification is negligible), leaving open whether the piece is in C major or A minor. Unlike in Opus 7, no. 5, however, the sequence, after repetition at pitch, gives way to a third phrase and its repeat (mm. 13–20), settling the matter for C. And after a contrasting segment, the mazurka ends with a return of measures 5–20 followed by a new version of the introduction that, though still somewhat ambiguous, ultimately affirms C.[11]

Nocturne in G Major, Op. 37, no. 2

For the first of the more extended analyses we turn to a somewhat longer piece, the Nocturne in G Major, Op. 37, no. 2, arguably Chopin's most consequential modular conception. It may seem relatively "normal" in form: five sections alternating ABA′B′A″ in rondo-like fashion. But this is deceptive, as the sections are constructed and relate to each other in remarkably innovative ways. I will focus mainly on the first A section and its two altered returns, which are the most complex and interesting from a modular perspective. The opening A consists entirely of repetitions and subtle variations of only two brief, very similar, one-measure modular units whose texture and rhythmic structure are rigorously preserved. Table 11.1 provides a formal diagram of the section. The two modular units, labeled "x" and "y," though only one measure each, always overlap with the opening of the next unit. For ease of reading, the modular units are ordered into five sections (the final overlapping measure is always included in the measure count for each group)—though, as we shall see, Chopin provides relatively little differentiation to articulate them as separate entities.

The first larger group, measures 1–7, is already significantly modular in composition. It has two balancing and overlapping subgroups, measures 1–4 and 4–7, the first moving from tonic to supertonic, the second returning from supertonic

Table 11.1. Chopin, Nocturne in G Major, Op. 37, no. 2: Diagram of the First A Section

Measures	1–7	7–13	13–21	21–26	26–27	(to 30)
Section	A					(B)
Module	xxyxxy	xxyxxy	xxxxyy	xxyy	xx	
Tonality	I–I	I–♭V	♭V–ii	ii–(VII)–	—	(IV)

to tonic. Both are strikingly regular, the first consisting of two almost identical x's in the tonic followed by one y, closely derived from x but moving to ii (m. 4). The second subgroup, overlapping with the arrival on ii, mirrors the first, beginning with two x's diatonically transposed to ii, followed again by y, altered so that it falls back to I. The whole is remarkably repetitive and undifferentiated: the accompaniment has the same rhythm and contour throughout; and although the right hand in y varies significantly, with contour inversion and continuous sixteenth-note motion (producing a continuous sixteenth-note stream from m. 2, beat 5 through m. 4, beat 1), it stems from the same basic fabric. True, there is some emphasis on the arrival at ii, thanks especially to the halt in melodic rhythm at measure 4, beat 1. Yet the textual layout remains essentially unaltered, and the cadence on ii transposes the same closing motive of the first two measures from E–D to F–E. By Classical standards the arrival is notably unmarked as a special event, with the overlapping continuing so that the second subgroup begins immediately, making y no longer than x.[12] The second subgroup, moreover, closely maintains the general melodic and harmonic pattern of the first, but falls back from ii to I instead of rising from I to ii. Again, the closing motive (now D–B) not only resembles the previous one but brings us back to the same note that we started from (b³; cf. m. 1, beat 5 and m. 7, beat 1).

This is fundamentally "non-Classical." Though one can find antecedent phrases moving from I to ii followed by consequents returning from ii to I, they are unusual and differently conceived. An example opens Mozart's Piano Sonata in D Major, K. 576. But the antecedent has two contrasting units, the second having not just more harmonic motion and rhythmic activity (as does the Chopin) but a new motivic and rhythmic impulse. And the pattern breaks at the cadence, setting it off as a unique event (even more so in the consequent). Chopin, however, almost completely suppresses such distinctive markers, preserving consistency in overall texture. The aggressively ongoing quality of the Mozart, strongly interrupted at measure 4 before completion at measure 8, is replaced by a seesaw effect. The first unit moves smoothly to ii, and the second answers with a downward version of the first, returning smoothly back to I. Whereas Mozart makes us feel that we have definitely gotten somewhere at measure 8, with measure 4 already clearly on the way, Chopin leaves us suspended, ending where we began. The midpoint, no longer an intermediate goal, is simultaneously a point of arrival for the initial motion and a point of departure for the return. This is underscored by the constant rhythm and texture, especially in the left hand, which seems oblivious of the unfolding form.

Although modularity is thus evident in measures 1–7, its extent becomes apparent only later. The two basic modular units continue uninterrupted in the second group (mm. 7–13), and, despite variation, are always unmistakable. The accompaniment remains rhythmically and textually consistent, while the right hand retains the rhythmic patterns and shapes of the melody. The second group nevertheless brings a new version of the opening module. It too begins with two x modules, but the first is now altered to rise a minor third (to B♭ major); and since the second repeats the first where the first ended, it moves on from B♭ to D♭ major (♭III of ♭III, or ♭V). Chopin subtly points toward the new harmonic goals, omitting the previous melodic upper neighbor to allow the line to rise directly to the cadential tonic. As in the first subgroup, the two x's are followed by y, which takes us up another step to ♭VI; and this is followed by the xxy succession of mm. 4–7, now returning to D♭, or ♭V. In brief, measures 7–13 mirror measures 1–7 exactly in form and content, except that the first two modular units are modulatory and sequential, not merely repetitive. As a consequence, the group ends a tritone higher than the original.

Module x again opens the third group, overlapping at measure 13, but now there are four x's instead of two, and they are altered to lead to a full cadence in A minor at measure 17. This is again followed by y, which like x appears not once but twice, and is altered so that it confirms A minor instead of modulating as before. And in the most significant rhythmic-textual change so far, these y's are extended to take up two full measures (mm. 17–18 and 19–20) before cadencing on A at measure 21, beat 1. The chords on A at measures 18, beat 1 and 20, beat 1 are thus not arrivals, but six-four chords that resolve through V to I. The six-four-to-five-three motion in measures 18 and 20 still accompanies a melodic figure derived from x. Indeed, the melody of measure 17 and measure 19 largely repeats, untransposed, that of module y in measure 3 (also headed toward A minor). Since the second halves of measures 16, 18 and 20 are all identical and all sound like part of x (which m. 16 in fact is), one might—depending on how much weight is accorded to rhythmic-textural vs. harmonic content—well analyze measures 17–18 and 19–20 as yx instead of a two-measure y.

The two extended cadential y's provide strong articulation for A minor, though again this is not highlighted through textual-rhythmic means. Moreover, A minor is left in the same manner as the arrivals on G and D♭ in measures 7 and 13, with another overlapping pair of x's, but now altered so that they descend by step, through G to F minor (mm. 21–22, 22–23). The arrival on F minor at first appears to receive as much emphasis as did the one on A, due to the transposed return of the extended y's from measures 17–20 in measures 23–26. But this time the second y is interrupted at measure 26, a measure before the cadence, by a dissolution leading toward the first contrasting section. The transition is also derived from x, though with a telling change: a sixteenth note is added on the downbeats of measures 26 and 27 to support the lack of harmonic arrival. The modular pattern fully breaks only when the music merges into the C major of the contrasting section, which happens as the new section begins (mm. 28–31).

In summary, the first section consists entirely of two one-measure units, altered to produce harmonic motion while the surface rhythmic-formal shape remains constant. Even the grouping of these units in the four main groups remains remarkably constant (all four begin with x and end with y, and the first two have identical combinations). The most important keys are G major and D♭ major (a tritone apart), followed by A minor, then F minor and E♭ minor. It is difficult to know what to make of these keys. It is as if the music, though almost constantly in harmonic motion, is confined to a limited set of discrete moves from a given starting point, a procedure reminiscent of chess: up and down by major second, up by minor third, and down by major third.[13] Similarly, the key of the contrasting section, C major, seems to be achieved almost by chance, as if the music arrived there inadvertently, without real preparation.

The two returns of A can be treated more briefly. The first begins by repeating the first subgroup, measures 1–7, but places everything except the final tonic arrival over a dominant pedal (mm. 69–75). When the pedal resolves at measure 75, the second modulatory group begins as before, moving up by minor thirds (cf. mm. 7–13); but then, after y, with the first half reaching E♭ minor (m. 78, as at m. 10), the entire modulatory subgroup reoccurs, starting from E♭ (mm. 78–81, beat 1). This carries the music up two more minor thirds to A major (so that it has moved twice by tritone, from G to D♭ in measures 75–77 and from E♭ to A in measures 78–80), and, after y, on to B minor (m. 81). This is followed by another dissolve, similar to the one in the first A, again leading to section B's return, which now begins on E major. The music of A′, though less tonally stable than A (there is only one tonic chord, appearing briefly at m. 75), is thus just as confined, both melodically and texturally.

A″ differs from the two preceding A sections in beginning on V of VI (m. 124) instead of the tonic. This enables Chopin to open with a transposed statement of the modulatory version of the first two x modules (as at mm. 7–9), their motion up by minor third now taking us back through E major (VI) to the tonic.[14] Overlapping with that arrival, the first group (mm. 1–7) returns complete, with the close on I at measure 130 corresponding to that at measure 7. The two modulatory x's then again appear, moving up by third to D♭ (mm. 130–32, exactly as in both previous A sections (mm. 7–9 and 75–77). But here, for the first time, the D♭ chord at measure 132 turns out to function as a lower neighbor to V. As the formal pattern breaks, two compressed, half-measure versions of the modulatory x pair (the only such compression in the nocturne) take us on through two additional thirds, to E and back to G, but with the rearrival on G temporarily aborted so that D♭ can reappear as C♯, bass of a vii[7] of V (m. 133) that resolves to I at measure 136. Once it reaches the tonic in measure 126, then, A″ remains consistently oriented toward G major, prolonging it through a complete cycle of minor thirds: G–B♭–D♭–E–G.

All three A sections thus consist of versions of only two modules, and all begin with complete statements of measures 1–7, the only stable group in the piece—though it is differentiated by a dominant pedal in A′ and a nontonic preface in A″. The latter results in the addition of a unique pair of modulatory x's as a preface to the final section, and near its end there are also two uniquely compressed modules. All three A sections, then, start from relative stability. Yet the stability of A′, thanks to the V pedal, is compromised by a loosened tonic opening (after which it then plunges off tonally more precipitously than before). In contrast, that of A″, despite the off-tonic opening, is underscored by a uniquely consistent tonic orientation.

A final word about the two B sections, which, measured against the ongoing character of the A sections, seem more tranquil. Yet despite their chordal texture; regular, nonoverlapping four-measure phrases; and considerably longer modules, making them seem more traditional in conception, they too are modular and in consistent tonal motion. The principal unit (mm. 29, beat 4 to 37, beat 3) has eight measures subdivided 4 + 4, the first part ending where it began, on C, but the second altered to end on E. Mimicking the A section, this unit then begins repeating sequentially on E (mm. 37, beat 4 to 45, beat 3), but is eventually altered to end on V^6 of F♯. A new four-measure module, also sequenced, takes us up two additional whole steps, to V^6 of A♭ (= G♯) and V^6 of B♭ (mm. 45, beat 4 to 53, beat 3). Derived from the previous module, it provides a transition to the repeat of the entire preceding segment, starting from B♭ (mm. 53, beat 4 to 69, beat 3). The last chord is altered to G $^6_4$, however, so that the A′ section returns with a dominant pedal (m. 69). B′ then exactly transposes B, beginning on E. The final chord, V of B (m. 124, beat 4, diatonically corresponding to V of G at the end of the first B section), overlaps with the two extra modulatory x's, whose downward-fifths progressions, F♯–B–E in the first (mirroring C–F–B♭ in mm. 7, beat 5 to 8, beat 1), neatly prepares the compressed progression in measure 132.

The key plans for the B sections—C–E–B♭–D in the first and E–G♯–D–F♯ in the second—are almost as puzzling as those of the first two A sections. In typical modular fashion, however, all the keys are drawn from one whole-tone scale, which is completed by the final F♯.

Fantasy in F Minor, Op. 49

Although the G-Major Nocturne is of medium length, the F-Minor Fantasy, Op. 49 (1841), one of Chopin's most important large-scale works, is also pervaded with modular construction. The Fantasy poses numerous problems, not least

Table 11.2. Chopin, Fantasy in F Minor, Op. 49: Formal Schema

Section:	Intro.	t1	A				t2	(A)		t3	B	t4	A'				t5	Coda
Module:			|m	n	o	p|		|m	n|		|x y x'|		|m	n	o	p|		
Tonality:	f		f	A♭	c	E♭		(c)	G♭		B		b♭	D♭	f	A♭		A♭
Measures:	1	43	68	77	93	109	143	155	164	180	199		223	235	244	260	276	310 320

because it begins and ends in different keys. As in the G-Major Nocturne, however, the unusual tonal structure derives directly from its modular conception. But whereas in the Nocturne the constantly shifting keys seem to swim in an ultimately static context, the Fantasy's equally shifting key progression traces a logical and dynamically conceived tonal plan.

Like the Nocturne, the Fantasy is, in Rosen's phrase, *sui generis*. Calling Classical conceptions into question, it consists of separate sections that are almost all in flux, in a complex whole whose elements are linked in tension. Individual formal units make little sense in isolation, acquiring definition only through reference to the larger process.

Table 11.2 provides a simplified formal schema. Four basic smaller modular units, designated m, n, o, and p, join to produce three closely related larger sections, A, {A}, and A'. The longest two, A and A' (seventy-six measures each), are identical within transposition (A' is a fifth lower than A), contain all four modules, and move consistently upward by thirds. Section {A}, however, is incomplete (hence the brackets), containing only modules m and n. It is also slightly altered at one point: measure 158 is changed—almost imperceptibly—so that it moves up a fifth rather than a third, after which the music then continues as before at the new level.

The three A sections together consume over half the piece (177 of 332 measures). The transition sections, labeled t, are all non-key-defining and based on similar materials (rising triplet figures, relatively sustained bass notes, upper-neighbor-note motive); and they are also marked by modularity: three completely, two less so. The strict ones, t2, t4, and t5, begin with very similar two-measure units, repeated three times in t2 and t4 (the last repeat down a minor second in t2) but only twice in t5. These three transitions are followed by closely related dissolutions. Four measures in t2 and t4 end with descending doubled octave leaps, expanded to six measures (plus fermatas) in t5 and reconfigured to lead to the Fantasy's coda (cf. mm. 143–55, 223–35, and 310–21). All three transitions interrupt the preceding segment's final cadences, and all end on the dominant of the following segment.

The two less strictly modular transitions provide moments of formal relaxation linked with rising-third motion. The first, t1, starts from the introduction's F minor and alternates minor and major thirds upward, first to a B♭ seventh chord—V⁷ of E♭ (mm. 50–53), then from E♭ to D♭, becoming an augmented sixth leading back to V of F and the first A section (mm. 64–67). In contrast, t3 moves up only one third, from E♭ minor to G♭ major, which becomes the dominant of the key of section B, the main contrasting unit (mm. 188–98).

Thus, all but 79 of the 332 total measures are modular (or in the case of t1 and t3, modularlike), and all are either consistently unstable or end up moving tonally. The only three nonrecurring, nonmodular sections are the introduction, section B and the coda. The first is a binary, marchlike section firmly anchored in F minor. Although its stability distinguishes it from most traditional introductions, it does anticipate both the rising thirds and the sequential motion of the modular segments. Section B, a lyrical ternary form in B major, is also tonally stable; and the coda, after a fragmentary reference to section B over V of A♭, is exclusively, and determinedly, tonic oriented. The introduction and the coda thus provide stable points of departure and closure for the developmental character typifying the main body, while Section B provides a quiet center (though at a tritone's distance from the starting tonic!).

The larger form is most easily grasped through the tonal relationships projected by the modular units, which are connected through an obviously constructed series of eight alternating minor and major thirds, starting from F and ending on A♭. They are projected exclusively by the three A sections: F minor–A♭ major–C minor–E♭ major in A, C minor (again)–G♭ major in {A}, and B♭ minor–D♭ major–F minor–A♭ major in A′. Section B's function, as an island of calm in this ocean of movement, is underlined by its position between the premature interruption of {A} by t3 and the subsequent return to A′ through t4. Though all keys in the plan are clearly defined, they are unequal in emphasis. The first module, m, is dominant oriented, beginning on V $^6_5$ of F minor and moving up by step in the bass through A♭ major to V's root (prolonged for four measures). Module n, however, appears without tonal preparation and is tonic oriented, with two repeating four-bar phrases that move down by thirds to D♭ (IV) followed by V. Yet these too give way (at m. 85) to eight measures of unstable transition (not indicated separately in table 11.2) leading to V of C minor and module o, which sequences up by third to E♭, also after four measures, eventually leading to a strong cadence on E♭. There, finally, module p brings forty-five measures of complete stability, contrasting sharply with the shorter and tonally shifting previous modules ending with a marchlike double period (beginning in m. 127) that recalls, despite differences in character and function, the opening march.

Module m in Section {A} uniquely begins back down a third, once again on C minor, but alters its progression so that it now ends a third higher, on V of E♭ rather than V of C, before moving on to G♭ (mm. 163–64), putting the rising thirds back on track. (This reorientation to V of E♭ allows Chopin to pass briefly through the dominants of the previous two keys in the cycle—C minor and E♭ major—before continuing to G♭ major.) G♭ major is followed, as was the modularly corresponding A♭ major in the first A section, by {A}'s internal transition, but here the transition converts G♭ into the dominant of B major, leading to section B. Following B, t4 takes us back to G♭, so that section B, viewed from the perspective of the third cycle, can be understood as prolonging its own enharmonically spelled dominant. A′ then continues the sequence from B♭ minor through D♭ and F minor to A♭, with module p, now in A♭, again capping the process with a more stable and extended tonal block.

The Fantasy's complex, nontraditional tonal process thus begins solidly in F minor, but with the introduction of modularity moves quickly by thirds up to E♭ in section A; {A} follows with G♭, and after section B's intervention, A′ continues the thirds from B♭ minor to A♭ major. (Except for the final A♭, this entire cycle is anticipated by t1, which immediately precedes it.)

In addition to its construction in thirds, one feature particularly stands out in this cycle: the ending is a minor third higher than the opening. Rosen has pointed out that in Romantic music, the relative major is often better thought of not as a different key, but as part of a minor-major tonic pair.[15] This applies well to portions of the Fantasy, especially to the way all three m modules in the A sections end on the dominant of the previous tonic before immediately shifting instead to the relative major. The relationships among rising thirds are so disposed, however, that in the two complete modular groups, A and A′, the last module rather than the second forms the principal tonal goal of the section. Thus modules m, n, and o all move on to—indeed almost seem to turn into—their successors, with module p alone acquiring real stability. Even p, however, does not reach a final cadence. The third progression always remains open, and this means that stability must ultimately be supplied by what precedes and follows the cycle: the introduction and coda.

Nevertheless, as was previously suggested, the two major-mode components of the A and A′ sections and the one of {A} do seem to form positive poles of an upward motion that swings toward them from the relative minor. The motion from major to minor, on the other hand, which occurs only three times, must each time be especially negotiated: from A♭ major to C minor and D♭ major to F minor through bridges provided by the internal transitions in Sections A and A′ (mm. 85–92 and 252–59); and from G♭ major to B♭ minor, preceding Section A′, through the insertion between them of t4 (m. 223). Indeed, the upward swing from minor to major is so characteristic of the piece that it is not difficult to see why Chopin felt an ending on F minor would have been contradictory. The A♭ major ending, on the other hand, remains true to the Fantasy's tonal nature; and significantly, it appears in conjunction with module p, the goal of both the A and A′ sections. This enables Chopin to retain traditional correspondences between thematic repetition and tonal return while treating them in a radically unprecedented manner (though there are perhaps certain analogies with Schubert's subdominant recapitulations). Moreover, despite the structural similarity of the two p modules, the final A♭ one, the ultimate goal of the entire process, is markedly differentiated from its E♭ predecessor: it is higher, louder, and marked *piu mosso.*

Table 11.3. Chopin, Fantasy in F Minor, Op. 49: Overall Pitch Relationships

	Section A	Section (A)	Section A′
Modular:	| f – A♭ – c – E♭ |	(c) – G♭ |	b♭ – D♭ – f – A♭ |
	↓	↓	↓
	↓	V	
Non-	↓	↓	↓
Modular:	| f |	| B |	| A♭ |
	Introduction	Contrasting	Coda

Table 11.4. Chopin, Fantasy in F Minor, Op. 49: Modular Keys

$$\downarrow$$

| G♭ | - | b♭ – Db | - | f – A♭ | - | c – E♭ | - | G♭ |

|- -|

Table 11.3 summarizes the overall pitch relationships.

All of the modular keys forming the rising-third sequence (that is, all those in the three A sections) are listed in the upper line, while all three nonmodular keys (those associated with the three nonmodular sections) appear in a lower one. In each case their relationship to the thirds sequence is indicated. The introduction and coda match the keys of the first and last modules, whereas the contrasting section provides a tonic resolution for the dominant, G♭ (enharmonically F♯). Note that the modular keys in the {A} section are unique: C minor repeats a level already traversed in Section A (and is thus placed in parentheses), and G♭ is the only modular key that functions as a dominant. (The transitional sections are not indicated in this table because they do not establish independent keys.)

Finally, table 11.4 shows that the modular keys, of which there are seven that are different, form a unified and quasi-symmetrical system.

The six keys of sections A and A′ have a purely symmetrical configuration, with the tonic F–A♭ pair at the center and the two additional minor-major pairs, C minor–E♭ major and B♭ minor–D♭ major, positioned a perfect fifth higher and lower. The remaining key, G♭ major (the only key that is dominant related within the overall scheme), is the system's opposite pole, and is the sole key in this system not paired with another third. It is located equally a minor third above E♭ major and a major third below B♭ minor, making the entire system diatonic and thus ultimately asymmetrical. The diatonic system formed, however, is not the four-flat one of F minor and A♭ major, but the five-flat one of B♭ minor and D♭

major. Here again, then, we see how unusual the larger tonal organization is.[16] Note that B major is omitted from the system: it is the one key in the Fantasy that does not appear within the modular-third progression, but relates to it only by perfect-fifth progression.

Ballade in F Minor, Op. 52

Another large-scale piece by Chopin, the F-Minor Ballade, though not so consistently modular as the F-Minor Fantasy, warrants consideration before we close. Not only does it have a significant modular component in its main theme, but this theme dominates the whole to an unusual extent and deeply influences the overall tonal and formal construction. One of Chopin's most genial creations, it appears frequently, taking up almost one-third of the piece's length. It consists of four closely related subunits:

An opening four-measure phrase in two halves, the first in the tonic, the second moving from tonic to relative major (m. 8, beat 4 to m. 12, beat 3);

A transposition of this phrase, the first half (in Ab major) exact, but the second ascending only a major second to Bb minor (m. 13, beat 1 to m. 16, beat 6);

A compressed, two-measure version of the second half alone, altered to remain in Bb minor, on whose dominant it closes (mm 17, beat 1 to 18, beat 4); and

An overlapping, final, four-measure phrase whose first half melodically repeats the original unit at pitch but harmonizes it as V of Bb, whereas the second half (resembling that of the second unit) ends with a full cadence on Bb minor (m. 18, beat 4 to m. 22, beat 3).

Two features of this theme, both stemming from its modular construction, are arresting: the tight motivic-formal interconnections and (especially) the precariousness of the resulting tonal balance. Regarding the latter, the first phrase begins solidly on i but then moves quickly to cadence on III, which the second phrase reveals to be only a temporary station on the way to iv. The third phrase goes to V of iv and introduces the fourth's striking pun: the return of the first unit at pitch but as V of iv, followed by a full cadence in iv. Is the theme's overall key then really Bb minor, and not F minor? F minor is supported by the introduction's C major (though it is not clear whether C is a V or a I), but that key gives way almost immediately; and the consistent emphasis on Bb throughout the final eight measures (of a fifteen-measure theme, only three of which are in F), along with the role of F as a dominant seventh participating in a sort of false "mini-recapitulation," clearly points toward iv. The accompaniment, typical of modular conceptions, remains texturally and rhythmically consistent, denying special emphasis to either arrival. This prevailing uncertainty justifies the brief, half-measure transition back to V of F minor following the end of the theme (m. 22, beat 4), itself beautifully prepared

Table 11.5 Chopin, Ballade in F Minor, Op. 52: Outline of the Larger Form

Form:	Intro.		Exposition			Dev. ·	Recapitulation			Coda
			Th.1		Th2		Intro. Th1	Th2		
			thı¹ thı²	insert thı³|						
Meas.	1		8 23 38	58	84	100	128 135	169		211–39

by two previous half-measure inserts at measure 8, beat 1 and measure 12, beat 4, prolonging C (V of F) and A♭. These inserts shift the phrases metrically, so that the phrase at measure 8, beat 4 opens on the upbeat, whereas the one at measure 13, beat 1 opens on the downbeat (yet another uncertainty); and both inserts complement the half-measure overlap at the beginning of the last phrase (m. 18, beat 4), as well as the half-measure retransition following that phrase, leading back to the tonic at measure 22, beat 4.

Table 11.5 shows the overall outlines of the larger form. Theme 1 occurs four times, always untransposed except for one added four-measure module that opens the recapitulation (discussed below). (One wonders if this constant tonic orientation doesn't reflect the fact that the theme contains its own tonal contrast.) The layout seems to resemble a sonata form. Yet Theme 1 is unevenly distributed in that form, occurring three times in the exposition (with an insert between the second and third appearance) and only once in the reprise. After the first statement, all break off following the final dominant of iv, eventually leading to Theme 2 in both exposition and reprise (after V/iv's prolongation in mm. 68–80 and 162–68): to the expected B♭ (IV—it is now major) in the former but deceptively to D♭—B♭ major's ♭III—in the latter.

Though the two statements of Theme 2 are structurally similar, they are not only in different keys but are also in many respects strongly differentiated. The first provides contrasting calm, with its texture, rhythm, *dolce* character, and regular form (aa′, 8 + 8) contrasting markedly with what precedes it. Despite the theme's typically Chopinesque surface freedoms (syncopations, unbalanced internal phrasing, and so on), its final cadence appears as expected (though overlapping with the following development, which thrusts the music quickly into G minor). In contrast, Theme 2's return complements what preceded it. Its left-hand accompaniment grows out of the previous dissolution, retaining the triplet rhythm that has been present for many measures, and the new accompaniment supplies a much more regular context against which the melodic freedoms are heard. Most significantly, the theme's second phrase does not end but is extended in the middle of the second half (from m. 181). And in lieu of the tonally unstable development that previously followed, this extension remains close to the tonic D♭ and eventually cadences there (m. 191), followed by a brief reinterpretation of D♭ as an augmented sixth resolving to a prolonged dominant (mm. 195–210), ushering in the coda on i.

Despite its obvious appeal, then, the sonata rubric is at least partly misleading. The character and treatment of the first theme (its lyrical, nondevelopmental, and variational nature) argue against it, as do the formal relationships among the sections. In its first appearances, for example, Theme 1 is extended by three statements plus a sizable insert and undergoes surface intensification. Its last repeat is followed by a brief dissolution over its final V/iv before arriving at the mysterious, four-measure B♭ preface at measure 80, beat 4 to measure 84, beat 1 (as a kind of buffer for Theme 2's marked contrast). In the reprise, however, Theme 1 is stated only once and undergoes much less intensification, whereas Theme 2 sounds as much like its extension as a separate unit (the "buffer" being eliminated), and leads logically, without abrupt interruption, to V and the coda.

Turning to the introduction and coda (mm. 1–7, 211–39), we find that both are more self-enclosed than the other sections. Yet the former's ambiguous C major provides an appropriately uncertain tonal preface for Theme 1. The explosive coda, determinedly rooted in the tonic, provides the only section consistently anchored in the tonic key.

Table 11.6 offers a more plausible alternative for the sonata-form interpretation: a binary structure in whose first half the unstable Theme 1 (A^1) is followed by a stable Theme 2 and overlapping development (B^1), with the first theme forming a sort of large-scale upbeat to the second. In the second half Theme 1 returns (shortened) and is again followed by Theme 2, but smoothed out so that the two now seem to form a complementary pair (A^2) that collectively provides an upbeat to the stable coda (B^2). The proportions of the four main sections are 76 + 51 in the first half and 76 + 29 in the second, the latter's compression resulting from the joining of the previous thematic pair into a single unit, A^2, and its restriction of the second part to a tonic extension (the coda).

Table 11.6 Chopin, Ballade in F Minor, Op. 52, as a Binary Design

		Section I		Section II	
Form:		A^1	B^1	A^2	B^2
	Intro.	Th1	Th2/Dev	Th1+2	Coda
Measure:	1	8	84	135	211
Tonality:	V	i-iv	IV—	i-VI-V	i

Although the introductory seven measures are absent from this binary graph, they do recur within it, growing out of the development's climax (mm. 125–34) and resolving it to A major, the first half's unexpected tonal goal. As a consequence, the introductory material appears more harmonically assertive than before, although it again cadences as a seemingly self-enclosed unit. (If the introduction is heard as beginning both halves, the binary proportions become more balanced: 84 + 43 and 83 + 29.) The bridge between Introduction and return is now partly provided by a *dolcissimo* arpeggio in measure 134. But more significant is the tentative, wrong-key start of the recapitulation, which seems to put itself together hesitantly, piece by piece. The return transforms the preceding A major into the dominant of D minor, where a reworked, formally intact but canonically projected version of Theme 1's first phrase begins, transposed so that it moves from vi to I instead of i to III. This takes us back to the tonic, whose arrival is brought out by the "normalization" of the texture (mm. 137–38). But Theme 1 then continues with another canonic statement of the first phrase, now in i (having been immediately converted to minor mode) as in the exposition, but again "resolving" texturally with the arrival on III. Chopin thus weakens the tonal moment of recapitulation by beginning in vi with texturally more tentative versions of the original phrase. The theme then continues as before, but with III again converted to minor mode. Not coincidentally, its permanent textural "normalization" occurs only when the second half of the third phrase (originally the second) arrives on iv (m. 143–45), eight measures after the thematic return has begun. This entire passage, with the theme emerging gradually from the mists in a manner perfectly conceived to underscore its modular design and attendant tonal ambiguity, forms one of music's most miraculous moments.[17]

Though the Ballade is not consistently modular, its principal thematic material is, and this modularity fundamentally influences the overall course of the piece. The theme's return, as we have seen, intensifies its modularity through the addition of a nontonic first phrase, which also plays down the tonic arrival as a significant event. But perhaps most telling is that, when the main theme returns in the binary's second half, it still ends on V/iv (now prolonged). The Db of Theme 2 follows directly from that chord's prolongation, making it sound like III/iv rather than VI/i. Only when Theme's 2's extension plus transition eventually converts that key into an augmented sixth is it finally heard as VI of F minor, a function that is then confirmed by the coda. The strong inclination toward the subdominant, inseparable from the theme's layout, is thus corrected only in the coda.

Conclusion

Chopin wrote many works in which modularity plays at least some role. Some, such as the F-sharp-Minor Nocturne, Op. 48, no. 2, have limited if well-defined modular features that influence the larger construction; others, such as the Barcarolle, Op. 60, give witness to a more muted application with less obvious ramifications for the total form. Even so, attention to modularity is in both cases useful for analysis. In this paper, however, I have argued for the significance of modularity by focusing primarily on three of Chopin's most consistently modular creations, each with an overall formal conception that is both original and analytically challenging. In these instances, at least, the pieces can be fully grasped only if their modularity is taken into consideration. Indeed, here the technique contributes significantly to explaining Rosen's "Chopin paradox": that he was at once "the most conservative and the most radical composer of his generation."

Notes

1. Charles Rosen, *The Romantic Generation* (Cambridge, MA: Harvard University Press, 1995), 471.

2. Ibid.

3. Rosen, 703.

4. All measure numbers, as well as other indications, refer to the Henle edition, edited by Ewald Zimmermann (Munich: G. Henle Verlag, 1975).

5. This piece appears as No. 2 in the *Anhang* of the Henle edition (p. 166). (It is No. 54 in the Paderewski edition; and to add to the confusion, a different version also appears as No. 54 of the Henle edition.)

6. Most of these examples have in common an intentional confusion of opening or closing functions, an ambiguity that obviously intrigued Chopin. An emphatic instance appears in the main theme of Opus 33, no. 1, an eight-measure phrase whose two opening measures are identical to the last two (though in this instance Chopin does not choose to exploit this formally). More consequential is the G-Minor Nocturne, Op. 15, no. 3, where the first measure of the opening four-measure sub-phrase of a theme apparently consisting of four subphrases returns unexpectedly as the second measure of the last of the four (m. 13, a number reflecting the fact that the first phrase overlaps with the second). This initiates a repetition of the entire first phrase three measures earlier than expected. Chopin exploits this ambiguity to produce four continuous, overlapping statements of the main theme (mm. 1–13, 13–25, 25–37, 37–50), with the end of the fourth finally altered to close on the minor dominant. One might be tempted to consider measure 13 as the end of a final six-measure subphrase beginning at measure 8; but nothing articulates this measure as an ending except the tonic chord itself, which, since it is undifferentiated textually and rhythmically, seems far too abrupt to fulfill that role—especially with the extended prolongation of III in measures 4–11.

7. The eight-measure sequential unit of Opus 41, no. 4, is itself modular, but by literal rather than sequential repetition. It is also melodically circular, moving between $C\sharp^5$ and $C\sharp^4$.

8. An excellent discussion of Chopin's overlapping appears in the chapter on the composer in William Rothstein, *Phrase Rhythm in Tonal Music* (New York: Schirmer Books, 1989).

9. In a fine treatment of tonal ambiguity in Chopin, Edward T. Cone remarks of Opus 41, no. 1's opening: "[W]e hear two cadences, the first in A minor and the second in E minor. Which is to be given precedence?" He refers to the question, however, mainly as "a tonal problem," not a formal one. Edward T. Cone, "Ambiguity and Reinterpretation in Chopin," *Chopin Studies* 2, ed. Jim Samson (Cambridge: Cambridge University Press, 1994), 142.

10. A more detailed discussion of this piece, from a related but different perspective, is found in my article "Symmetrical Form and Common-Practice Tonality," *Music Theory Spectrum 20* (1998): 45–47. It follows an extended section on the development of the sequential period, pp. 28–45.

11. The middle section of the Tarantella, Op. 43, is interesting in this connection. It is preceded by a transitional passage alternating dominant prolongations of F minor (mm. 68–71, 76–79) and A♭ major (mm. 72–75, 80–83), a tonal uncertainty that then reverberates through the entire middle section (mm. 84–99). The opening period, though constant in texture and rhythm, keeps shifting tonally. Is it in D♭ major (converting A♭ into a dominant) or in F minor? Chopin decides for F minor, but barely. After three statements of the period (the second and third separated by a middle segment), he moves back to A♭ without so much as a pause (m. 148–49). This is music truly in constant motion.

12. Rosen thus comments on "Chopin's rare use of a three-bar period" in *The Romantic Generation*, 273.

13. Note that the overall progression ultimately seems to negate the possibility of viewing the ♭V in A and A′ as ♭III of ♭III.

14. The return actually begins with F♯ in the bass; but it is treated as V of V/VI, leading first to E major (VI, m. 124) and then from there sequentially to the G-major tonic.

15. For example, *Romantic Generation*, 47.

16. Carl Schachter, a distinguished Schenkerian, has analyzed the fantasy from a more normative framework in "Chopin's Fantasy, op. 49: The Two-Key Scheme," in *Chopin Studies*, ed. Jim Samson (Cambridge: Cambridge University Press, 1988), 221–53. Though Schachter is aware that lack of formal closure, sudden shifts in tonal focus, and rising thirds keep the Fantasy "in a constant state of flux almost without parallel in the literature" (p. 251), he analyzes it according to Schenkerian principles, subordinating the rising-third structure to a more basic incomplete structural progression, vi–V–I, in A♭. The introduction's F minor supplies his vi, which resolves to E♭ (V) in module p of my first A section. After prolongation by a second vi–V progression in modules m, n, and o of my A′ (mm. 260–76), E♭ moves on to the final tonic in module p and the coda. Although he does acknowledge a more foreground occurrence of rising thirds, Schachter eliminates the progression entirely from his middleground and background levels, where they are absorbed without trace into his overall vi–V–I progression.

Since any analytical reading is selective, it can be said that Schachter focuses on one interesting aspect of the fantasy, the lingering trace of "normal" large-scale functional tonality. My analysis (and hearing), on the other hand, views that dimension as overwhelmed by the cycle of upward-striving thirds. It is also worth mentioning that Schachter's view requires some very strange claims regarding long-range prolongation, such as that V (E♭) is maintained from measure 109 to measure 176, and vi (F minor) from measure 235 to measure 260. Even more problematic, however, is the demotion of what seems to me the fantasy's most characteristic tonal motion to the status of a mere diversionary event. Instead of F minor as an all-important point of stable departure, for example, in Schachter's analysis it is only an upper neighbor, dependent on resolution to the dominant. The first A♭ region becomes only a contrapuntal event prolonging C major, the dominant of F. Similarly, Schachter's reading undermines the close correspondences between the expanded p areas in E♭ and A♭, beginning at measures 109 and 276. In a word, it substitutes for the work's remarkable instability a largely static arrangement: 275 measures of vi–V progression (repeated) followed by fifty-eight measures of closing tonic. Even my section A′, except for its final p module, becomes trapped within the repeated vi–V progression. Yet this section is not simply repetition: it reinitiates motion after section B's island of stability and takes us where we have not yet been.

17. The structural similarities between this modular moment in the ballade and the equally modular nontonic beginning of the third A section of the G-Major Nocturne are no doubt evident.

Part Five

Italian Opera

Chapter Twelve

The Hot and the Cold

Verdi Writes to Antonio Somma about Re Lear

Philip Gossett

It is difficult, even impossible, to demonstrate that something doesn't exist and never has existed. What if tomorrow we find an elusive source that has escaped detection? So it is with documentation pertaining to Giuseppe Verdi's *Re Lear*. Information about the libretto of the projected opera and correspondence concerning its creation has gradually emerged over the past century and now seems relatively complete. As early as 1843, Verdi mentioned the Shakespearean play as a possible operatic subject.[1] In 1845 he brought it to the attention of Francesco Maria Piave.[2] Toward the end of the decade (probably early in 1849), Verdi wrote *Re Lear* as the first item in a list of possible operatic subjects on a page of his *Copialettere*.[3] He worked seriously on the project in 1850, sending Salvadore Cammarano on February 28 a lengthy prose outline (*selva*) of a possible opera on *Lear*, in which he laid out the scenic structure as he envisioned it.[4] Cammarano gave the project some thought and drafted notes, but for Verdi other work with Piave intervened (*Stiffelio* and *Rigoletto*). When Cammarano and Verdi began to collaborate anew toward the end of 1850, they decided to pursue *Il trovatore* instead, leaving *Re Lear* for the future. The librettist's untimely death during the summer of 1852, while he and Verdi were preparing *Il trovatore*, blocked that avenue.

It was to Antonio Somma (1809–65) that Verdi then turned. A lawyer by profession, Somma was also a playwright, a journalist, and—from 1840 through 1847—the director of the Teatro Grande of Trieste. After settling in Venice in 1849, he became one of Verdi's close friends there, along with Antonio Gallo and Cesare Vigna. Since Somma was not enormously experienced as a librettist, Verdi gave him his usual advice to collaborators: keep it short, because "the public easily becomes bored" (*Carteggio Verdi—Somma* [henceforth *CVS*]4: May 22, 1853); avoid too many scene changes (*CVS* 6: June 29, 1853); and, most important, "I'll say nothing of the verses, which are always beautiful and worthy of you"—Verdi's standard concession to the self-esteem of his librettists—"but, with all the respect I feel for your talent, I will tell you that the form doesn't lend itself to music. No one loves novel forms more than I, but the novelty must be of the kind that can be set to music" (*CVS* 12: August 30, 1853).[5]

The correspondence concerning *Re Lear* falls into two principal chronological periods. In the first series of letters and drafts, generated between April 1853 and May 1854, Somma and Verdi worked on a first version of the libretto. The librettist sent a complete draft to the composer in four installments, beginning with the first scene on July 6, 1853, followed by the remainder of Act I shortly before August 30, Act II shortly before September 9, and Acts III and IV together on September 22. Verdi assembled these segments into a complete libretto, which survives in the collection at Sant'Agata and was published in facsimile by the Istituto nazionale di studi verdiani in 2002.[6] That publication also includes facsimiles of other libretto drafts and variants, along with transcriptions of these documents and some of the Verdi-Somma correspondence.

Verdi commented only briefly on these texts as Somma sent them, mostly insisting that they were too long (especially Acts I and II). By the time he had the entire libretto in hand, though, his plans had changed, and on October 15 he left for Paris to begin extended work with Eugène Scribe on *Les vêpres siciliennes*. Still, he found time to suggest modifications to Somma in November. (Only one of two letters has survived.) On December 4, Somma sent Verdi a package of variants, also published in facsimile in *Per il "Re Lear"* and transcribed in *CVS*. Verdi then proceeded to copy out the entire libretto, inserting the variants in their proper place, but making no other modifications.[7] This was a mechanical copy whose purpose was to facilitate Verdi's review of the libretto as amended. It was presumably accomplished before December 16, 1853 (*CVS* 25), for on that day, in a letter from Paris to Somma, Verdi made suggestions for modifying the conclusion of the Introduzione, in order to avoid a regular *stretta*. These were not unlike the changes he imposed on Cammarano at the end of Act I of *Luisa Miller*.[8] But these suggestions for the Introduzione of *Re Lear* are not reflected in Verdi's copy of the first version of the libretto as amended.

The correspondence now became less intense, although during the first five months of 1854, composer and librettist communicated several times, always in broad terms. That Verdi was not composing is clear from his letter of February 6 (*CVS* 27), in which he stated, "The changes in some verses or phrases that I might need are trivial, but I will only be able to tell you about them as I am writing the music." His other comments reinforce his assertion that the libretto is too long. Only on May 17 (*CVS* 31) does he clearly state that his work on *Vêpres* will not allow him to continue thinking about *Re Lear*, which "will be for another year."

In the second and final series of letters and drafts pertaining to *Re Lear*, generated between January 1855 and April 1856, Somma and Verdi worked on a second version of the libretto. Reacting to Verdi's insistent calls for cuts, Somma made a crucial decision: to remove almost entirely the story of the duke of

Gloucester and his two sons, leaving only a part for Edmund, whose villainy is necessary to advance the principal plot. In various letters Verdi accepted this change happily, but did point out some difficulties that resulted and suggested still other modifications that might be possible. Somma then sent Verdi the second version of the libretto in two installments, Acts I and II on March 21, 1855 and Acts III and IV on March 25. Verdi acknowledged receipt of the last shipment on April 5 (*CVS* 42), while still expressing reservations.

The next document in *CVS* was written almost a year later, a letter from Somma to Verdi of March 6, 1856 (*CVS* 43), with which Somma forwarded a further revised version of part of Act IV, but in her edition of the correspondence, Simonetta Ricciardi argues convincingly that the two must have met in Sant'Agata after Verdi's return from Paris in December 1855. The composer remained unhappy, as he wrote on April 7, 1856 (*CVS* 45):

> I am not sure whether the fourth act of *Re Lear* is acceptable as you recently sent it, and I am certain that it will be impossible to make the public swallow so many consecutive recitatives, especially in a fourth act. These are not demands of a composer: I would set to music even a newspaper or a letter, etc., but the public admits everything in the theater except boredom.

On this note Verdi's letters to Somma about *Re Lear* conclude. It was not merely that the Teatro San Carlo of Naples, from which Verdi had a commission to compose a new opera during the winter of 1857–58, was inadequate for *Re Lear*: he clearly felt that not even the second version of the libretto sent to him by Somma, with its variants, was redeemable. This setback did not sour him on Somma, with whom he promptly began to collaborate for the Neapolitan commission on what became—after a trying and complex history—*Un ballo in maschera*.

The fundamental question scholars have been asking for a long time is, Did Verdi ever prepare any music for *Re Lear*?[9] The Verdi family insists that there are *no* musical manuscripts of any kind pertaining to this opera at Sant'Agata, and there is no reason not to believe them.[10] There have been two suggestions about surviving music. The first pertains to a manuscript purporting to be autograph musical sketches for the opera in the collection of the New York Public Library.[11] Unfortunately, this manuscript shows absolutely no signs of having been written by Verdi. Indeed, the appearance is so different from Verdi's autographs in general that it is difficult to imagine how the presumption of its identification with Verdi arose. At no time during his life, for example, did Verdi ever make quarter rests as they are drawn in this manuscript. That these pages are related to *Re Lear* is nothing but wishful thinking.

More intriguing is the textual similarity between a solo for Cordelia in Somma's first libretto draft for *Re Lear* and the Romanza for Leonora in Act I of *La forza del destino*, a similarity that has long been noted.[12] The two texts are as follows[13]:

Re Lear	*La forza del destino*
Me pellegrina ed orfana	Me pellegrina ed orfana
Lunge dal ciel natio	Lungi dal patrio nido
Sospinge il fato mio.	Un fato inesorabile
	Sospinge a stranio lido . . .
Ai flutti inesorabili,	Colmo di triste immagini
Piena di sue memorie,	Da' suoi rimorsi affranto
Col mio dolor m'avvio!	È il cor di questa misera
	Dannato a eterno pianto. . . .
Non ho per te che lacrime	Ti lascio, ohimè, con lagrime
Dolce Inghilterra . . . e addio!	Dolce mia terra! . . . Addio!
Senza immortale angoscia	Per me non avrà termine
Non ti si lascia. . . . addio!	Sì gran dolor. . . . Addio!

There can be no doubt whatever that Verdi remembered this text from Somma's draft libretto for *Re Lear* and passed it on to Piave to use as the basis for Leonora's Cavatina in *La forza del destino* (where the piece is found in both the St. Petersburg version of 1862 and, without change, the Milan revision of 1869). Although the meter is *settenario* throughout in both versions, however, there are important differences in the structures of the texts. The *Re Lear* poetry involves two tercets and a final quatrain; the *Forza del destino* version is in three quatrains.

In any case, Verdi did not simply "remember" an earlier setting from *Re Lear* and plug it into *La forza del destino*. Investigation of the sketches for *Forza* makes it clear that Verdi earlier sketched the entire Cavatina with a very different melody, transcribed here for the first time (example 12.1)[14]:

Only after further layers of sketching, also preserved in the Sant'Agata manuscripts, did the composer enter a sketch very much like the music of the definitive version within his continuity draft for the entire opera. In short, the likelihood that Verdi was simply adapting music from an already drafted original seems minuscule, although the possibility (predicated on the nonexistence of a musical source for *Re Lear*) cannot be entirely dismissed. Notice, in fact, that the text Verdi set in this draft, although clearly using the quatrain structure of the *Forza* poetry, does have "lunge dal suol natio" instead of Piave's "lungi dal patrio nido." This would seem to indicate, however, nothing more than that Verdi did indeed remember Somma's beautiful verses.

There is another way to think about the problem, however. For a number of operas we have a larger group of sources, epistolary and musical. If we track closely what Verdi and his librettists write to each other and if we compare the music Verdi seems actually to be notating during the course of the correspondence, it is possible to differentiate two kinds of interactions, "cold" and "hot." In a "cold" interaction, Verdi comments to a librettist about dramaturgy, the development of characters, the quality and length of the verses, and the potential musical structure. During a "cold" interaction, there is no evidence whatever

Me pel - le - gri-na ed or - fa - na   lun - ge dal suol na-

-ti - o   un fa - to i-ne-so - ra - bi-le   so - spin - ge ad al - tro

li - do....   Col - mo di tri - ste im-ma - gi - ni   da' suoi ri-mor-si af-

Example 12.1. Verdi, *La forza del destino*, Romanza Leonora (N.2), early draft.

that the composer is actually setting down musical notation, although we cannot know what might have been going on in his head. In a "hot" interaction, on the other hand, Verdi refers to musical-poetic interactions that are developing as he sketches the music: he asks a librettist for specific modifications, and traces of his thought process are visible in the surviving musical manuscripts.

There are important examples of "cold" and "hot" interactions in most of the operas for which sketches have been made available by the Carrara-Verdi

Example 12.1. (continued)

Example 12.1. (continued)

family.[15] Since Verdi and Somma worked together not only on *Re Lear*, but also on *Un ballo in maschera* (which they actually completed and for which extensive sketches have been made available), it seems appropriate to draw some examples from that collaboration. Although I will concentrate here on the first scene of Act I, similar examples can be found throughout the score. This opera began life as *Gustavo III*, would later become *Una vendetta in dominò*, and was finally performed as *Un ballo in maschera*.[16]

Table 12.1 lays out the correspondence, in chronological order, as it pertains to the first scene of Act I (H = hypothetical; S = survives):

With respect to Act I, scene I, these are the most important stages:

1. Somma sends Verdi the first part on October 24 (adding small modifications on October 28); Verdi suggests changes on October 30; Somma sends some corrections on November 3 and the rest on November 5, but he also made a suggestion for a further change on November 10.
2. Somma sends Verdi the second part on October 28; Verdi suggests changes on about November 2; Somma sends the corrections on November 7.
3. Verdi asks for a specific change in the poetry at the end of the first scene on November 26; Somma sends the corrections on December 2.

Because Verdi's musical sketches survive, we can be relatively certain as to the date before which he could not have begun composing by examining the poetry he set to music and comparing it with the texts that flew back and forth between composer and librettist. Thus, it seems certain that Verdi did not begin sketching the first part of Act I, scene 1 until approximately November 10, *after* having received the modifications Somma sent on November 3 and November 5. In not a single place where Somma made revisions do we find the poetry the librettist had sent on October 24. Because there are also vast differences between the poetry Verdi used in his musical sketch for the remainder of Act I, scene 1 and the poetry Somma sent on October 28, we can similarly assume that he did not begin sketching this material until *after* having received the modifications Somma proposed on November 7.

The implication is clear: Verdi's original correspondence with Somma about this material is "cold." He receives the poetry, thinks about it dramaturgically, considers the language and structure, and then asks Somma to modify it. Only after receiving these modifications does the composer begin drafting music. Thus, since it apparently took about four days for a letter to be delivered, Verdi is unlikely to have begun sketching *Un ballo in maschera* until November 10 at the earliest. During this period he had many preoccupations, furthermore, some of them provoked by correspondence with the Teatro San Carlo in which it became clear to him that the text would need to be heavily modified.[17] He may therefore have proceeded rather slowly.

Table 12.1. Chronology of the Verdi-Somma Correspondence, October–December 1857, Regarding *Un ballo in maschera,* Act I, Scene 1

Date	CVS[a]	Content
ca. Oct. 20	184–85 (H)	Verdi sends Somma a prose treatment of the entire libretto.
Oct. 24	185–89 (S)	Somma acknowledges receipt; he sends poetry for the first half of Act I, scene 1 (through Ankastrom's solo, "Alla vita che t'arride")
Oct. 28	191–97 (S)	Somma—of his own accord—suggests modifications in the poetry sent on October 24 (which Verdi will enter into Somma's earlier manuscript) and then continues with the remainder of scene 1 and the first part of scene 2.
Oct. 30	197 (H)	Verdi suggests modifications in the poetry sent on October 24.
Nov. 1	198–205 (S)	Somma sends poetry for the remainder of Act I, scene 2.
ca. Nov. 2	(H)	Verdi suggests modifications in the poetry sent on October 28.[b]
Nov. 3	205–8 (S)	Somma acknowledges receipt of Verdi's letter of October 30. He sends Verdi a revised version of scene 1, but only through Gustavo's solo "La rivedrà, ma splendida"
Nov. 5	208–11 (S)	Somma sends Verdi a revised version of scene 1 from after Gustavo's solo through Ankastrom's solo "Alla vita che t'arride" (the poetry Somma had originally sent on October 24 and modified on October 28, and that Verdi had critiqued in his letter of October 30); he also sends poetry for the opening of Act II.
Nov. 6	212–13 (S)	Verdi suggests modifications in the poetry sent by Somma on November 1.
Nov. 7	213–14, 222–26 (S)	Somma has not yet received responses to his letters of November 1, November 3, or November 5. Here he sends Verdi a revised text for the remainder of scene 1 and the beginning of scene 2, in response to Verdi's letter of about November 2.[c]
Nov. 10	214–18 (S)	Somma acknowledges receipt of Verdi's letter of November 6. He asks Verdi to modify two verses in the second strophe of Ankastrom's solo (whose revised text he had sent on November 5) and to make other changes in the second scene of Act I. He sends Verdi the text of Act II, scene 2 (the duet for Gustavo and Amelia).

Table 12.1 (continued)

Date	*CVS*[a]	Content
Nov. 12	218–21[d] (S)	Somma sends Verdi a revised version of the remainder of Act I, scene 2 (the poetry Somma had originally sent on November 1 and that Verdi had critiqued in his letter of November 6).
Nov. 26	243–44 (S)	Verdi asks for a specific change in the poetry at the end of the first scene of Act I.
Dec. 2	246–47 (S)	Somma sends Verdi the poetry he requested in his letter of November 26.

[a]All documents cited are from *Carteggio Verdi-Somma* (*CVS*); page numbers are indicated in the table.
[b]Ricciardi does not mention this letter, but a close reading of the correspondence suggests that Verdi must have written to Somma on about November 2.
[c]Although Ricciardi says that this revised text is not extant, that is not true: it has been preserved (and printed) by mistake as part of Somma's letter of November 12 (see *CVS*, 222–26).
[d]As we saw above, the material printed in *CVS*, 222–26 actually pertains to Somma's letter of November 7.

Surviving documents make a few elements clear. The sketch for Act I, scene 1 is written on eight pages of thirty-staff manuscript paper, normally in systems of two or three staves, with an occasional blank staff.[18] As we have seen, Verdi probably did not begin sketching until November 10 at the earliest. When he arrived at the solo for Ankastrom ("Alla vita che t'arrendi"), on page 5 of these eight pages, he used the text Somma sent in his letter of November 10, which Verdi could not have received before November 14 at the earliest.[19]

We know *exactly* where he had arrived on November 26, when he wrote to Somma asking for a modification in the text. For the concluding section of Act I, scene 1, Somma had sent the following words on October 28:

> Gustavo: Ogni cura si doni al diletto
>   E s'accorra al fatidico tetto.
>   Per un dì si folleggi si scherzi—
>   Belzebù l'ha da fare con me.
> Oscar: E s'accorra: ma vegli il sospetto,
>   Sui perigli del sacro suo capo—
>   Che, che nasca laggiù, mi ci metto:
>   E mi pianto fra il diavolo e il re.

The librettist sent a much more extensive text on November 7, responding to Verdi's criticisms of about November 2, in a letter that does not seem to survive.

Gustavo:	Dunque signori aspettovi,
	Al tocco delle tre,
	Nell'antro dell'oracolo,
	Della gran maga al piè . . .
Tutti:	Nell'antro dell oracolo ecc.
Gustavo:	Ogni cura si doni al diletto
	E s'accorra al fatìdico tetto.
	Per un dì si folleggi si scherzi
	S'affratelli al suo popolo il re.
Duca[20]:	E s'accorra ma vegli il sospetto
	Sui perigli che fremono intorno
	Ma protegga il magnanimo petto
	Di chi nulla paventa per se.
Coro:	Scelga dunque ciascun la sua vìa
	E nell'ora segnata a quel sito
	Del suo prence, risponda all'invito
	Lo ricambi d'amore, di fé.
Oscar:	L'indovina ne dice di belle,
	E sta ben che l'interroghi anch'io.
	Sentirò se m'arridon le stelle:
	Qual presagio le dettan per me.
Congiurati:	Senza posa vegliamo all'intento
	E in silenzio s'afferri il momento.
	Anche là sotto gli archi fatati
	Può la tomba scavarglisi appiè!

In his sketch for this material (p. 8), Verdi did not enter a single word of the text, not because he did not have Somma's text in mind, but because he wanted important changes in it. He laid these out in a postscript to his letter to Somma of November 26:

Please excuse a bother for my sake. It would be helpful to me in the stretta of the Introduzione to transpose to the end of the scene the strophe:

Gust.	*Dumque Signori aspettovi . . .*
	...................................alle tre
	Nell'antro dell'oracolo
	Della gran maga al piè.
Tutti:	....
	.............................alle tre
	Nell'antro dell'oracolo
	Della gran maga al piè!

And it would be useful to me if you could find a *sdrucciolo*[21] instead of "al tocco" and allow me to say "alle tre." . . . Adjust it, further, so that everyone can repeat the entire strophe.

Verdi thus asks Somma to reverse the order of verses in the stretta (placing the stanzas of *settenari* after those of *decasillabi*) and to modify the internal structure. Somma responds to this request in his letter of December 2:

As for the stretta of the Introduzione, if I haven't misunderstood the postscript of your kind letter, this should work for the music:

Duca[22]:	*Dunque signori, aspettovi*
	Incognito *alle tre,*
	Nell'antro dell'oracolo,
	Della gran maga al piè.
Coro:	Tutti sarem di lancio
	E incogniti *alle tre*
	Nell'antro dell'oracolo
	Della gran maga al piè.

If you prefer, you might substitute for the first verse of this last strophe the following:

Tutti sarem di subito

Or else, changing the sense:

tutti sarem di voglia

But you choose.

Ultimately Verdi did indeed choose, and he needed to make important adjustments, since Somma's *sdrucciolo* was not quite what he had had in mind. At the moment in which he sketched this music, however, he was uncertain enough about how to present the text that he wrote out his entire draft without a single word. Example 12.2 presents the first half of the composition, an initial presentation of *decasillabi* and a first statement of the *settenari*.

Verdi's letter of November 26, requesting changes in this text, was certainly written as he drafted the music. That the passage is without text in the sketch does not mean that Verdi did not have a text in mind. It is clear from the text I have underlaid in the example that he knew exactly what he wanted.[23] On November 26, or immediately before, Verdi completed sketching Act I, scene 1 of his opera in precisely this fashion. There is other evidence that he turned immediately to Act I, scene 2, which would occupy him for the next ten days.

This is what I mean by a "hot" interchange. The composer is actually writing music and arrives at a place where the text provided by the librettist does not quite match the music he is imagining. In this example from *Gustavo III / Un ballo in maschera*, Verdi did not await new text, but instead drafted the passage

Example 12.2. Verdi, *Gustavo III/Un ballo in maschera*, Introduzione, stretta (N.2), draft.

Example 12.2. (continued)

without actually writing in the words. However, he did have a clear sense of how those words would finally emerge.

In the entire correspondence between Verdi and Somma about *Re Lear* there is not a single "hot" interchange. It is all "cold," dramaturgical, analytic, structural. Nowhere does the composer give even a hint that he is actually drafting music. After having received the entire draft of the libretto for Act I, Verdi writes Somma on August 30, 1853 (*CVS* 12):

> To make music you need stanzas for cantabili, stanzas for ensembles, stanzas for slow movements, quick movements, etc., and all of this alternating so that nothing seems cold and monotonous. Please let me examine your poetry.

And then the composer specifies why Somma's verses, however beautiful they might be, cannot be set to music. Considering the finale of the first act, for example, he is specific:

> The stanzas for the Fool are fine, but from the moment Nerilla enters I would no longer know what to do. Perhaps you meant to make a concerted piece with six stanzas of six verses each, but there is dialogue in those stanzas, hence the characters must respond to one another, and consequently the voices can't be united.

On October 15, 1853 (*CVS* 17), Verdi tells Somma:

> I have read and reread *King Lear* and I wanted to write to you, particularly about the second act, which more than the others needs modifications, but right now I wouldn't know which ones to tell you about. I will write to you from Paris . . .

And on November 7, 1853 (*CVS* 19), from Paris Verdi sends Somma a note so that he can be paid through Ricordi, and adds, "I haven't occupied myself with *Re Lear* yet, but I'll do it as soon as possible." But when he does write to him, on November 19 (*CVS* 22), it is with more requests for fundamental structural and poetic changes, and observations such as, "With this irregularity it is impossible that musical phrases won't limp along."

Instead of "hot" requests, Verdi's letters are filled with remarks saying what he might do *when* he begins drafting the score. So, on December 16, 1853 (*CVS* 25), he writes from Paris, "As I advance in the music I'll write you about everything that would, according to me, make [the opera] less effective." But, of course, that is precisely what he never does. Similarly, on February 6, 1854 (*CVS* 27), he states the fundamental principle of a "hot" interchange (as quoted above): "The changes in some verses or phrases that I might need are trivial, but I will only be able to tell you about them as I am writing the music [che mano in mano ch'io scriverò la musica]." By May 17, 1854 (*CVS* 31) he is so far behind on *Les vêpres siciliennes* that he tells Somma that *Re Lear* "will be for another year." The situation does not improve after Verdi's return to Italy in December 1855.

Somma massively recasts the opera, but Verdi still concentrates only on the larger issues of dramaturgy and poetic structure. And after having composed *Gustavo III* / *Un ballo in maschera*, he abandons all thought of Somma's libretto. Only on December 17, 1863 (*CVS* 101), the last letter in their correspondence, does he refer to it again, to say:

> I am not thinking at present about writing, and if later I should think about it, I have several poems in my briefcase, including your magnificent *Re Lear*.

Cold, cold, cold.

However much Verdi may have wanted to set Shakespeare's *King Lear* to music, his correspondence with Antonio Somma about the libretto of the opera does not offer the slightest reason to think he ever put pen to paper.

Notes

1. See Verdi's letter of June 6, 1843—to Count Alvise Mocenigo, an administrator of the Teatro La Fenice in Venice—printed in Giuseppe Morazzoni, *Lettere inedite di Giuseppe Verdi* (Milan: "La Scala e il Museo Teatrale"—Libreria Editrice, 1929), 17.

2. In his letter to Piave of November 24, 1845, printed in Franco Abbiati, *Giuseppe Verdi* (Milan: Ricordi, 1959), 1:591, he writes, "I am working on *Lear* and am studying it carefully, and I myself will bring a sketch from which you will prepare a fuller treatment for London." The date is derived from Evan Baker, "Lettere di Giuseppe Verdi a Francesco Maria Piave 1843–1865," in *Studi verdiani*, 4 (1986–87), 136–66 (at 142).

3. The list is reproduced as Table XI in *I copialettere di Giuseppe Verdi*, ed. Gaetano Cesari and Alessandro Luzio, with a preface by Michele Scherillo (Milan: Commissione esecutiva per le onoranze a Giuseppe Verdi nel primo centenario della nascita, 1913), facing p. 422. *Re Lear* is followed immediately by two other Shakespearean subjects, *Amleto* and *Tempesta*. In fifth place we find Victor Hugo's play *Le Roi s'amuse*, soon to become *Rigoletto*.

4. The most accurate transcription of this *selva* is found as letter 67 in *Carteggio Verdi-Cammarano (1843–1852)*, ed. Carlo Matteo Mossa (Parma: Istituto nazionale di studi verdiani, 2001), 166–70.

5. Most of the letters from Verdi to Somma were originally published in Alessandro Pascolato, *"Re Lear" e "Ballo in maschera": Lettere di Giuseppe Verdi ad Antonio Somma* (Città di Castello: S. Lapi, 1902). The entire correspondence is now available in *Carteggio Verdi-Somma*, ed. Simonetta Ricciardi (Parma: Istituto nazionale di studi verdiani, 2003). The original letters from Verdi to Somma are currently owned by Dr. Mario Valente of Los Angeles; the letters from Somma to Verdi are in the collection at the composer's home, Sant'Agata, together with all three complete drafts of the libretto. This paragraph and the next ones are derived from a review of *CVS* that I prepared for *Music & Letters* (2006).

6. *Per il "Re Lear,"* ed. Gabriella Carrara Verdi (Parma: Istituto nazionale di studi verdiani, 2002).

7. This copy is reproduced in facsimile and transcribed in *Per il "Re Lear,"* but does not appear in the *Carteggio Verdi-Somma.*

8. For a discussion of this point, as well as other correspondence between Verdi and Cammarano about *Luisa Miller,* see the introduction to the critical edition of *Luisa Miller,* ed. Jeffrey Kallberg, in *The Works of Giuseppe Verdi* (Chicago: University of Chicago Press, and Milan: Ricordi, 1991), ser. I, vol. 15, xvii–xix.

9. The most important analysis of the structure of the libretto—by Gary Schmidgall, in "Verdi's *King Lear* Project," *19th Century Music* 9 (1985): 83–101—treats the story as if Verdi did not write any music. But others have assumed the opposite, as we shall see.

10. Pierluigi Petrobelli, director of the Istituto nazionale di studi verdiani, who has personally examined the musical manuscripts at the Villa Verdi at Sant'Agata, confirms this.

11. The two pages are reproduced in William Weaver, *Verdi: A Documentary Study* (London: Thames & Hudson, 1977), plates 159–60. Weaver tentatively suggests that they are related to a possible baritone-soprano duet in *Re Lear.*

12. Piero Weiss, in "Verdi and the Fusion of Genres," *Journal of the American Musicological Society* 35 (1982): 138–56, writes: "he probably wrote some of the music" (150), which Weiss footnotes: "Leonora's first aria in *La forza del destino* is set to the text of Cordelia's first aria in Somma's libretto for *Re Lear;* despite Budden's argument (*Verdi,* 2: 450), I do not see why at least the first part of the music cannot have been composed for the original project." The reference is to Julian Budden, *The Operas of Verdi* (London: Oxford University Press, 1973–81), 3 vols.

13. The text for *Re Lear* in Somma's version is printed in *CVS,* 54. I have derived this transcription, which is essentially identical to Somma's text, from Verdi's own copy of the libretto. The relevant page in Verdi's hand is reproduced in *CVS,* facing page 64. Somma made small changes in this text in 1855 (see *CVS,* 139–40), where the third through sixth verses become "Preme il destino mio. / E a' flutti inesorabili / Piena di sue memorie / Fra miei dolor m'avvio!" and the last line becomes "Non ti si perde . . . addio!" The text from *La forza del destino* is derived from the original printed libretto for that opera, from St. Petersburg (1862).

14. I wish to thank the Carrara-Verdi family for their kindness and generosity in making this material available for work associated with the critical edition of *La forza del destino* and to Professor Pierluigi Petrobelli for his continuing efforts to further the research efforts of all Verdi scholars. This sketch is found in a group of diverse notations prepared by the composer during the summer of 1861, sketches that precede Verdi's continuity draft for the entire opera.

15. These include *Stiffelio, Rigoletto, La traviata, Aroldo, Un ballo in maschera,* and *La forza del destino.* In *Rigoletto,* a classical example of a "hot" interaction pertains to the sketching of the cabaletta of the Aria Duca (N. 8), "Possente Amor mi chiama." For a discussion of this point, see the introduction to the critical edition of *Rigoletto,* ed. by Martin Chusid, in *The Works of Giuseppe Verdi* (Chicago: University of Chicago Press, and Milan: Ricordi, 1983), ser. I, vol. 17, xviii.

16. For an overview of this history, see Philip Gossett, *Divas and Scholars: Performing Italian Opera* (Chicago: University of Chicago Press, 2006), 491–513.

17. So he informed Somma in a letter of November 14 (see *CVS,* 226–27). He wrote the same day to Vincenzo Torelli, the Neapolitan impresario. The letter to Torelli is misdated as October 14 in *Copialettere,* 563; for the correct date, see *CVS,*

226. As the composer told Torelli, "but now that the poet is hard at work, it is better to finish the drama, then we will think about changing the subject."

18. For a general consideration of Verdi's compositional process and his sketching, see Philip Gossett, "Der kompositorische Prozeß: Verdis Opernskizzen," in *Giuseppe Verdi und seine Zeit*, ed. Markus Engelhardt (Laaber: Laaber Verlag, 2001), 169–90.

19. On November 5, Somma sent these words: "E porìa dovunque sempre / Impedirne le ferite"; on November 10 Somma asked Verdi to substitute "E sarà dovunque sempre / Chiuso il varco alle ferite." Verdi set only these latter words.

20. At this point, "Duca" refers to the "Duca d'Ankastrom."

21. A *sdrucciolo* is a word that concludes with an accented syllable, followed by two unaccented syllables (- ∪ ∪), a dactyl in English metrics. "Al tocco," of course, is an unaccented syllable, followed by an accented syllable, and concluding with an unaccented one (∪ – ∪).

22. By now, King Gustavo had become the duke of Stettin, and Ankastrom's rank was reduced to that of a count.

23. I have included only text that is reasonably certain, not short repetitions of partial phrases. At the end, furthermore, the rhythm of the music and of the text do not quite match up as Verdi has sketched the melody. In the phrase for which Verdi asked Somma for changes, however, his draft fits perfectly with his request: I have rendered it as "sdrucciolo, sdrucciolo, sdrucciolo, alle tre."

Part Six

The Modernist Tradition

Chapter Thirteen

The Ironic German

Schoenberg and the Serenade, Op. 24

Walter Frisch

My title comes from a well-known book of 1958 by Erich Heller about Thomas Mann. For Heller, irony is a fundamental *Weltanschauung* and narrative strategy in all of Mann's fiction, from the early family tragedy of *Buddenbrooks* to the comic finale of *Felix Krull*. Heller defines irony in this context as "a calculated and artistically mastered incongruity between the meaning of the story told and the manner of telling it."[1] This is probably as good a basic description of literary or linguistic irony as one could find. And, *mutatis mutandis*, the irony that Heller and other scholars explore in Mann forms a far more significant dimension of the world of early German modernism—including music—than has generally been acknowledged.

There has been a fair amount of writing, including distinguished commentary by Charles Rosen, on how Austro-German music of the early Romantic period manifests irony of the varieties propounded and practiced by Friedrich Schlegel and Heinrich Heine.[2] What has been less studied is how in the decades following the next *Jahrhundertwende* in 1900, irony becomes a key compositional tactic for many composers working within essentially the same cultural milieu as Mann, including Mahler, Strauss, and Schoenberg. These and other composers achieve their mature compositional voices, and their status as modernists, in large part by evoking and treating ironically music from either the immediate past (Wagner) or the more remote past (Bach, Mozart, Beethoven). Our understanding of modernism has been hindered by too much commentary that views it as an ideology of rejection—as advocacy of the radical, the revolutionary, the progressive, the avant garde.

A consideration of historicizing irony can also encourage us to revisit what I believe is an exaggerated dividing point of World War I. Music histories take as a given that the years around 1920 marked a sharp break in European art music, when the intense, overheated styles of late romanticism, expressionism, and primitivism gave way to cooler, more brittle neoclassicism and *neue Sachlichkeit.* Of course, these latter terms were coined, or at least used, at the time to describe a genuine shift of aesthetic and compositional technique.[3] There are significant differences between Stravinsky's *Rite of Spring* and his Octet; between Strauss's *Elektra* and his *Intermezzo;* between Schoenberg's *Erwartung* and his Serenade, Op. 24; between Hindemith's *Mörder, Hoffnung der Frauen* and his *Kammermusiken.* And these differences surely have much to do with the cultural, political, and social changes that the war brought about. But throughout the works of these and other composers run important strands of continuity, such as irony, that have been obscured by the rhetoric of radical change.

Over thirty years ago, Rosen recognized aspects of commonality in this period. Without specifically identifying historicizing irony as a strategy, he associated the trio of works Schoenberg composed in the early 1920s—the Five Piano Pieces, Op. 23; the Serenade, Op. 24; and the Suite for Piano, Op. 25—with works written by his major contemporaries across the preceding decade: "The evocation of the elegant surface of the past was by 1923 as much a part of Schoenberg's music as of Strauss's (in *Ariadne auf Naxos*) or Stravinsky's (in *Pulcinella* and *L'histoire du soldat*). A high price was set on charm."[4] It is the goal of my essay to explore further what Rosen aptly identifies as the "elegant surface of the past" by looking more closely at Schoenberg's Serenade, one of the pivotal works of his own neoclassical, or *neue sachlich*, period. But before doing so, I want to go back before the supposed Great Divide, to 1912. This was something of a banner year for musical irony of the kind I am considering here, and it appears in the works of two composers generally understood (including by themselves) to be very different, Strauss and Schoenberg.

The first work is the Overture to Strauss's *Ariadne auf Naxos*, a work that Rosen alludes to. It is important to understand the context of the piece, because irony will always be dependent on the so-called horizon of expectations of the reader or listener. In its original form, *Ariadne auf Naxos* was an opera within a play; it was an entertainment viewed not only by us, the external audience, but by also the characters from Molière's *Le bourgeois gentilhomme*, which had been adapted by Hugo von Hofmannsthal.[5] This framing aspect already creates ironic "incongruity" and distance from the material.

The first part of Strauss's overture, scored for small orchestra (see example 13.1), is built from conventional two-measure units that are grouped on a higher level into traditional structures such as paired phrases (*aa'*, mm. 1–2) and antecedent-consequent (mm. 1–4; 5–8). The small- and large-scale harmonic goals are also traditional, such as the dominants in measures 2, 5, and 8. Yet local voice leading and resultant harmonies clash with the outward form. The melody begins by leaping down a major seventh, such that the G-minor harmony on the downbeat supports a dissonant E♭. In measure 2, the melody manages to be both lyrical and awkward, outlining a diminished triad that contains a prominent upward tritone leap (C–F♯). This triad is of course part of the

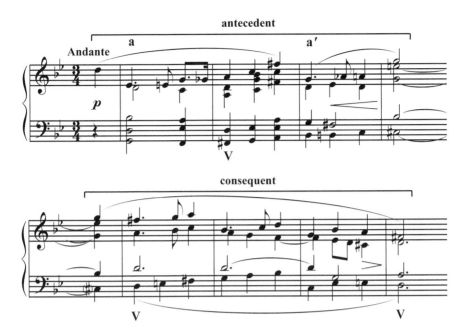

Example 13.1. Richard Strauss, *Ariadne auf Naxos*, Overture (1912).

dominant chord of G minor, which would be a normal harmonic goal for this measure, but which is distorted or diffused by the voice leading. The melodic phrase of measures 3–4 consists of a chromatic rise followed by a dissonant leap, again a seventh (A–G), and as such is like a compressed, transformed version of measures 1–2 (hence *aa'*).

Strauss's overture seems to me a good candidate for musical irony; in it we see a disjuncture between "form" and "content," or more precisely between the conventional melodic-harmonic gestures that are evoked and the way those gestures are distorted. To adapt a term from Gerard Genette, this is an overture "in the second degree."[6] The musicologist Stefan Kunze shrewdly observed that it has "the character of a quotation without being a quotation."[7] That is, Strauss evokes an idiom, a style, a genre without seeming to cite any specific work. Kunze's remarks resemble those made by Theodor Adorno about the first movement of Mahler's Fourth Symphony, another supremely ironic work of the time, which he said was "composed within quotation marks."[8]

In the same year as *Ariadne*, 1912, Schoenberg created the landmark work that tempered his expressionism with what he referred to a "light, ironic, satirical tone."[9] The irony of *Pierrot lunaire* is complex, but similar in spirit to that of Strauss and Mahler. The irony derives partly from Schoenberg's embedding

Example 13.2. Schoenberg, Serenade from *Pierrot lunaire* (1912). Used by permission of Belmont Music Publishers.

older forms and techniques (melodrama, barcarole, waltz, passacaglia, canon, ostinato, walking bass, tonal-sounding thirds and triads) in a sonic world of new tone colors, harmonies, and vocal practices.

The nineteenth number of *Pierrot*, "Serenade" (example 13. 2), is a clear precursor to Schoenberg's Opus 24, but also a worthy contemporary of Strauss's overture. As with Strauss, the outward gestures of Schoenberg's serenade—what Rudolf Stephan would call the *Aussenhalt*—are conventional and rub against, or are rubbed against by, the musical details.[10]

These conventional gestures include the meter, the initial four-bar phrase structure, and the basic contour of the piano part. To paraphrase Kunze again, this waltz has the character of a quotation without being one; or, with Genette, it is a waltz in the second degree. It may evoke any number of Viennese waltzes from Lanner through Lehár, but we would be hard pressed to find a specific model.

The opening interval in the cello is a major third, B♭–D, which is rendered almost unrecognizable or tonally nonfunctional by the high register of the cello and by the span of the tenth. Strauss similarly undermined conventional melodic shape with ungainly leaps. Some sense of B-flatness is reinforced by the bass of the piano in measure 2, which approaches the "tonic" from the "dominant" F. But here, as in the cello part of the preceding measure, the enormous span undermines any real cadential or tonal sense. And yet "Serenade" begins with a standard four-measure phrase that clearly moves toward a cadence on the downbeat of measure 4. The last three gestures have many of the earmarks of a progression to the tonic. The chords sounding on beats 3 and 4 of measure 3 each have respectively two of the pitches of IV (E♭, B♭) and V (F, A), in the key of B-flat. Of course, the progression is undermined by the note of resolution in the piano on the downbeat of measure 4, the low A♭, a pitch that has already been present through measure 3 in the G♯ sustained by the cello two octaves higher. Yet, as with Strauss, we experience a real tension between structure and materials, and we also have in the Serenade that special tone of detachment that is so characteristic of Mann, Mahler, and Strauss and that lies at the basis of modernist musical irony. For all their ideological and musical differences, Strauss and Schoenberg are not very far apart in 1912.

Ariadne auf Naxos was described by one of its creators, Hofmannsthal, as an "unrepeatable experiment," a phrase that could fit *Pierrot* as well. Schoenberg never created anything like it again. But he revisits its ironic tone and techniques in the works he composed between the summer of 1920 and the spring of 1923, notably the Five Piano Pieces, Op. 23; the Serenade, Op. 24; and the Suite, Op. 25. Table 13.1 gives a concise chronology of work on these three compositions, which evolved pretty much side by side.[11] This kind of parallel composing was relatively unusual in Schoenberg's career, at least over such a long span. But then this was not a normal period. It was the time when he was working out the serial technique; each of these works, opera 23, 24, and 25, was central to that development.

Schoenberg's Serenade has seven movements in the following disposition:

1. Marsch
2. Menuett [and Trio]
3. Variationen
4. Sonnett Nr. 217 von Petrarca
5. Tanzscene
6. Lied (ohne Worte)
7. Finale

Six of the movements are purely instrumental; the fourth movement is a setting for baritone of a German translation of a Petrarch sonnet. The finale is a recapitulation of the opening march. This plan, and Schoenberg's scoring for violin, viola, cello, clarinet, bass clarinet, mandolin, guitar, and male voice, make the Serenade at once unique and full of intertextual or intergeneric references. Schoenberg is evoking two different but related traditions of serenade—vocal and instrumental. The guitar and mandolin have a long iconographic and musical history as accompanimental instruments to vocal serenaders. Serenades of this type are also common within the Austro-German operatic and song tradition, of which Schoenberg saw himself as an heir. One thinks immediately, for example, of Don Giovanni's mandolin-accompanied "Deh, vieni alla finestra"

Table 13.1. Chronology of Schoenberg Opus 23, 24, 25

Date	Five Piano Pieces, Op. 23	Serenade, Op. 24	Suite for Piano, Op. 25
1920			
July 8	No. 2		
July 9	No. 1		
July 26	No. 4		
before July 27	No. 2		
August 3		Fragment (A); Variations	
August 6		Tanzscene; Fragment (B)	
1921			
before July 24			Row sketches
July 25			Prelude
before July 25			Row sketches
July 25			Intermezzo
July 26–29			Prelude
July 29		Marsch	
September 27–October 6		Marsch	
Oct. 8		Menuett and Trio	
October 19–22		Tanzscene	
1922			
October 8		Sonett	
1923			
February 6–9	No. 3		
February 10–13	No. 4		
February 13–17	No. 5		
February 19–23			Intermezzo
February 23–27			Gavotte
February 23–March 3			Musette, Menuett
February 26			Intermezzo
March 2–8			Gigue
March 11		Variationen	
March 16		Menuett	
March 16–29		Sonett	
March 19		Variationen	
March[?] 20		Menuett	
March 30		Lied (ohne Worte)	
March 30–April 7		Tanzscene	
April 10		Lied (ohne Worte)	
April 11–14		Finale	

Table 13.1. (continued)

Date	Five Piano Pieces, Op. 23	Serenade, Op. 24	Suite for Piano, Op. 25
April 16		Sonett	
April 18		Tanzscene	
April 19		Sonett	
April 23		Tanzscene	
April 27		Finale	

from scene 3 of Act II of *Don Giovanni*. Beckmesser's clumsy serenade of seduction in Act II of Wagner's *Die Meistersinger*, "Den Tag seh' ich erscheinen," is an obvious parody of Don Giovanni's. It is a serenade in the "second degree" in that it derives its effect in part from our familiarity with the Don's similar activity beneath the window of Donna Elvira. (Disguise and role playing also operate in these respective serenade scenes: Eva and Magdalena exchange clothing, as do Don Giovanni and Leporello.) The baritone in Schoenberg's fourth movement—it is clearly no coincidence that this voice type is the same as Mozart's and Wagner's—sings a different kind of serenade, to which I will return below.

Schoenberg's Opus 24 also makes self-conscious reference to the long, rich tradition of instrumental serenades that dates back to the eighteenth century and continued well into the early twentieth century, from Mozart through Brahms through Dvořák, Tchaikovsky, and Elgar. These serenades rarely include the strumming instruments common in the vocal type, but they often have a formal plan similar to Schoenberg's, beginning and ending with a march. The orchestral work that has perhaps the most immediate connection to Schoenberg's serenade is a single movement in one of the works he admired: the fourth movement of Mahler's Seventh Symphony, which is entitled *Nachtmusik* (German for "serenade") and includes both mandolin and guitar, the same instruments Schoenberg would use, here strikingly elevated into a symphonic context. With so many serenades in the generic background, or as part of what would today be called the generic "contract" between Schoenberg and his listeners in the 1920s, there is some truth to Bryan Simms's claim that if, as Adorno suggests, Stravinsky wrote "music about music," then Schoenberg's Serenade is "music about music about music."[12] In Genette's terms, the Serenade would be music in the "third" degree.

We can explore these aspects of Schoenberg's serenade more fully in the first movement, the March. Marches often open Mozart's serenades from the 1770s. They become less frequent in the orchestral serenades of the nineteenth century, though they of course become a basic topos in the symphonic works of

Mahler and Berg. Indeed, the idea of combining serenade and march in a single orchestral work probably has its greatest realization in the *Nachtmusik* movement from the Seventh mentioned above, whose steady $\frac{2}{4}$ meter and fanfarelike melodic figures in the woodwinds give it the quality of a sublimated march.

Chamber-music marches seem to come back into vogue around 1900. Max Reger's two serenades for flute, violin, and viola, Opp. 77a and 141a, both begin with marchlike movements in $\frac{2}{4}$ time. In 1918, Stravinsky filled his *L'histoire du soldat* with marches, including the opening "Soldier's March." Even more than Stravinsky's self-consciously neoclassical works of the 1920s, this one sets the stage for an ironizing treatment of the march topos. Schoenberg surely knew *L'histoire* when composing the Serenade, which seems to echo it at certain moments. Stravinsky would revisit the march in his *locus neoclassicus*, the Octet, completed in the same year as Schoenberg's Serenade, 1923. The Allegro portion of the opening movement, though not labeled as a march, clearly is one. It begins with a resolute theme in $\frac{2}{4}$, which then, after its fifth measure, begins to go metrically askew in Stravinskian fashion. If this is not an ironic march—a march about marches, or a march in the second or third degree—then I do not know what one would be.

Schoenberg could not have been familiar with the Octet when he was working on the Serenade. But we do know that he was feeling a sense of competition with "der kleine Modernsky" and other young neoclassicists. In the early 1920s, neoclassical chamber works by Austro-German composers were being played at important music festivals, including Donaueschingen, which began in 1921.[13] Audiences at the very first Donaueschingen festival heard a serenade for clarinet and string trio that had been composed by the nineteen-year-old Ernst Krenek.[14] It seems no coincidence that when the fifty-year-old Schoenberg was at last invited to the Donaueschingen Festival of 1924, the work that he brought was his Serenade, Op. 24, which was receiving its public premiere. Schoenberg was pleased by the favorable response the work received from the audience and most critics. He had successfully reinvented himself, at least for the time being, as a neoclassicist, if not a young, brash one.

The March is unique among the movements of the Serenade, and certainly unusual among Schoenberg's pieces, for having no notated modification of tempo at all. Schoenberg indicates no ritardandos or accelerandos. He notes that the movement is be played "throughout at a consistent march tempo," which he gives as ♩= 100 (see example 13.3). This marking makes for a relatively brisk march. If the movement were kept strictly at the notated tempo (which Schoenberg would not recommend), it would clock at about 3:49. No recordings complete it in that time, to the best of my knowledge. The closest would be Boulez's 1962 recording with the Ensemble Intercontemporain, which comes in at 4:08 and is also the best at keeping a steady tempo throughout.[15]

That steady tempo gives the March an almost mechanical feel and places it as far as can be imagined from the world of what has been called *Weltanschauungsmusik*, the large-scale, metaphysically striving music of the nineteenth and early twentieth centuries, to which Schoenberg had himself contributed in *Gurrelieder*.[16] Yet for all its regularity of tempo, Schoenberg's opening movement is in many ways hard to hear as a march. The opening viola solo is quirky, with a jumpy melodic-rhythmic pattern that is difficult to parse and places emphases off the main beats. Nor are the guitar chords in measure 1 a clear guide. They appear on the weak beats, for only a measure, then fall silent. The introductory passage dissolves in measures 7–8 into a rather indistinct buzz of triplet rhythms that sound more like shuffling than marching.

The arrival of the main theme at measure 9 would seem to indicate the "real" establishment of the march. The beginning of the clarinet melody, which is accompanied homorhythmically by bass clarinet and violin, derives from elements of the viola's introduction, as I suggest with the brackets and dotted lines in the score. Although the intervals differ, both melodic segments share a downward stepwise motion and a descent by a larger interval, followed by a *sforzando* and a large leap upward.

At measure 9 these elements are put into a full-textured context that has distinctly marchlike features, such as the sturdy bass line, with its paired-fifth motions (D–A, C–G, and so on). The brackets under the cello part, emphasizing the pairings, are Schoenberg's own. But theme and bass line fail to adhere to the metrical grid of 2/2. In fact, Schoenberg sets up a pattern of five beats parsing as 2 + 3, 3 + 2, 2 + 3 (as shown on example 13.3). To my ear, the theme manifests an identity crisis; it can't decide whether to be a march or a waltz. The upward leap of a minor ninth in measure 10 seems a gesture more appropriate to the latter. Indeed, it closely resembles the opening of the waltz in the "Serenade" number of *Pierrot* discussed earlier (see example 13.2).

The special quality of subjectivity and the expressive-formal ambiguities of the March have never been better explored than in the earliest article on Schoenberg written by the young Theodor Adorno, who was a precocious twenty-two years old when it appeared in 1925.[17] (It is a great pity that this article on the Serenade has never been published in English translation.) Adorno immediately frames his discussion of the Serenade in terms of irony and points to *Pierrot* as an antecedent. For Adorno, the irony of the Serenade consists in the kinds of tensions we have already examined, which Adorno explains as a "distance between expression and intention." But for Adorno this irony does not consist of an inappropriateness of content to form; he sees these as existing in the Serenade in a comfortable relationship. To his mind, Schoenberg intentionally made the formal structures "light" and "transparent" to allow the subject—*das Subjekt*—to "shine through."[18]

Adorno captures perfectly the character of the main theme of the March movement, as follows:

Example 13.3. Schoenberg, March from Serenade, Op. 24. Used by permission of Edition Wilhelm Hansen AS, Copenhagen.

Example 13.3. (continued)

> [It] is not one of those Schoenberg melodies which, arching well beyond themselves, help determine the structure of a movement, and which, without consideration for the overall design, open and plantlike, strives to become some unknown organism. . . . It is a closed theme, one that is complete in itself and requires no expansion, one that can be subsumed into a form but does not determine the form.

The theme is dominated by a "terse, seven-measure phrase structure, an economy of motives, and an insistent B♭ that functions to rein in any free motion." For Adorno, the march theme is discreet (*verschwiegen*), because "it does not reveal itself in a stormy manner," because "it does not claim full individuality," and because it is discreet in the "sober and mysterious objectivity of its tone."[19] The march indeed seems to get stuck with its constant landing on the B♭, which eventually causes the theme to grind to a halt in measure 15, much as the introduction seemed to run aground in the triplet figures of measures 7–8. In this movement, the themes have trouble sustaining forward momentum.

Schoenberg's is not any conventional march, but an ironic one on many levels. If we put it another way, in listening to the March we have a sense of being in a hall of mirrors, where things are not what they seem, or where they are put in a process of reflection. This quality extends to, or is perhaps generated by, the most basic formal and tonal aspects of the March, which we should now explore.

The pitch universe of the March is arrayed symmetrically around D. D had been one of Schoenberg's favorite tonic pitches in his large-scale early tonal works, including *Verklärte Nacht*, *Pelleas und Melisande*, and the First String Quartet. In each of them he explored tonal relationships symmetrically around D in ways that sometimes replaced or undermined traditional harmonic functions. D is also the "tonic" of the March, but the treatment now involves what we might call "tonality about tonality," or tonality in the "second degree." D is the first pitch we hear in the viola; it is the first bass note under the march theme. It is even followed by its dominant, A. Furthermore, the final cadence of the march arrives on D (see example 13.4). But D is not supported by any hierarchical harmonic or melodic syntax. And this is where the metaphor of the hall of mirrors seems à propos. In figure 13.1 I reproduce an illustration from David Lewin's classic article about inversional symmetry in Schoenberg, which addresses a range of works from all periods of the composer's career, including the March.[20]

Lewin shows how pitches and, potentially, harmonies are arrayed around a wheel with D and A♭ as the tritone axis. Lewin's wheel offers a useful guide to Schoenberg's March. Beginning in measure 17 of the March (not shown in the example), Schoenberg inverts the entire introduction and first theme around the D axis. Thus the introduction begins again on D, as before, but now the bass line (in the cello) moves down to C♯, G♮, B♭, and so forth. The march theme

Example 13.4. Final cadence of the March from Serenade, Op. 24. Used by permission of Edition Wilhelm Hansen AS, Copenhagen.

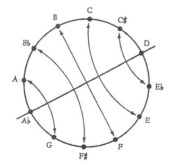

Figure 13.1. Inversional axis around D (from David Lewin 1968).

begins with a D bass in measure 25, now played by the bass clarinet, but the original pattern of fifths is inverted. The melody, in the clarinet, begins on F♮, moves up to F♯, and so forth—the precise inversion of the original melody. What is striking is that Schoenberg moves directly, in measure 33, back to the march tune in its original form and then, at measure 41, again to the inverted form. He is thus compressing and repeating the entire process of the first thirty-one measures.

In the sketches for the Serenade we see Schoenberg exploring the possibilities of inversional symmetry around D.[21] Amid sketches for the March (see figure 13.2) he writes out a D-centered scale and with beams and stems connects notes in a symmetrical relationship on either side. These include C–E and B–F. Beneath the scale are chords which further explore the symmetries. In each of the top chords, the upper three notes remain invariant: B and F exchange places in an inversion, and G♯ remains the same. The A♯ and F♯ become D♯ and F♯, respectively. In fact, these chords do appear in the March, in measures 53–54, where they accompany a statement of one of the "sets" in its original form, and inverted around D (cello, viola).

Elsewhere among the March sketches (figure 13.3), Schoenberg jotted down as a kind of aide-memoire or mental exercise a symmetrical array of notes spanning out from D.

Not only the March, but the Serenade as a whole is a kind of hall of mirrors because it is also symmetrical on the largest scale. As noted earlier, there are seven movements, all instrumental except the fourth, the setting for baritone of the Petrarch sonnet. That movement, which lies at the center of the Serenade, is also the only fully twelve-tone movement in the piece, and one of the three earliest that Schoenberg created. The Petrarch movement, as contemporaries noted, is the most serious and least ironic in tone of all the parts of the Serenade. It is as if Schoenberg momentarily strips away the mood of the first three movements, which evoke traditional forms (march, minuet, variations), to announce his new, very serious musical discovery, the twelve-tone method. Or, we might say, he turns from a light irony to a bitter irony. He does so with a text that communicates pain and anguish:

> O könnt' ich je der Rach' an ihr genesen,
> Die mich durch Blick und Rede gleich zerstöret,
> Und dann zu grösserm Leid sich von mir kehret,
> Die Augen bergend mir, die süssen, bösen!
> So meiner Geister matt bekümmert Wesen
> Sauget mir aus allmählig und verzehret
> Und brüllend, wie ein Leu, an's Herz mir fährt
> Die Nacht, die ich zur Ruhe mir erlesen!
> Die Seele, die sonst nur der Tod verdränget,
> Trennt sich von mir, und, ihrer Haft entkommen,

Figure 13.2. Arnold Schoenberg, sketches for March from Serenade, Op. 24 (w/o number, after 853). Arnold Schönberg Center, Vienna. Used by permission of Belmont Music Publishers.

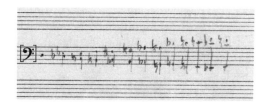

Figure 13.3. Arnold Schoenberg, sketches for March from Serenade, Op. 24 (856). Arnold Schönberg Center, Vienna. Used by permission of Belmont Music Publishers.

Fliegt sie zu ihr, die drohend sie empfänget.
Wohl hat es manchmal Wunder mich genommen,
Wenn die nun spricht und weint und sie umfänget,
Dass fort sie schläft, wenn solches sie vernommen.

[Oh, that I might find relief from that resentment of her, who assails me by glance and speech alike, and then causes still greater suffering by turning away, hiding from me her sweet, evil eyes! Thus night, which I have chosen for my rest, gradually saps and consumes the feeble, distressed essence of my soul, and, roaring like a lion, attacks my heart. The soul, which should be driven out only by death, departs from me, and, escaping its imprisonment, flies off to her, who receives it threateningly. I have often wondered, when it speaks and weeps and embraces her, how she can sleep on, having heard such things.][22]

At the heart of Schoenberg's Serenade lies a vocal serenade that is quite different from the Mozart-Wagner model. What fly up to the window in this case are not sweet, seductive sounds of love, but the feelings of a soul filled with anger and resentment. The poet reasonably wonders how his beloved could sleep though such a toxic serenade. We may in turn wonder whether with this serenade within a serenade Schoenberg is creating an image of his own perceived situation—that of introducing to a world he believes is hostile and uncomprehending a new twelve-tone method of composition.

From the depths of this subjectivity, Schoenberg climbs back into to the lighter ironic world of the Serenade with the *Tanzscene*, which is in a clear, symmetrical ternary form, and like the March has many internal repetitions. Then comes the brief *Lied (ohne Worte)*, leading without pause into the Finale. The work closes as it began: the finale is an exact repetition of the opening March, to which are added an introduction and episodes that quote earlier movements. Thus the March literally frames the entire work in a mirrorlike fashion.

If I seem to be developing a kind of program or narrative for the Serenade, one in which a detached, ironic world view subsumes or encloses a more subjective and personal one, I might actually be in good company—the composer's own. Let me give two pieces of supporting evidence. When Olin Downes reviewed the Donaueschingen Festival for the *New York Times* in August 1924, he wrote as follows about the Serenade:

Apparently Schönberg [*sic*] wished this work to be judged as absolute music. No explanation of its contents, other than a thematic analysis, was given in the program. But a friend of Schönberg, who claimed to understand intimately the composer's intentions, told us that the Serenade was conceived as the expression of a disappointed lover. This lover, in the course of the opening March, the Minuet, &c., approaches his beloved and makes his plea. He is unsuccessful, and the baritone sings Petrarch's poetic expression of love unful-filled. We are then to conceive of the resignation and departure of the lover, as, in the finale, fragments of the march, the minuet, and other preceding movements are heard.[23]

We know that Schoenberg acknowledged and occasionally divulged "secret" programs to some of his instrumental works, from the First String Quartet to the late String Trio.[24] Thus Downes's commentary, although third-hand, or in the "third" degree, does not seem so implausible. It at least opens up the possibility of reading beneath the crisp, neoclassical façade of the Serenade.

My second example brings us back more closely to the topic of irony. In the same year, 1924, Schoenberg's pupil (and a generally reliable source) Erwin Stein reported the composer's telling him that the opening of the finale was like a "Conference of the Instruments on the question of what ought to be played at the end of the *Serenade*." This comment would refer to the introductory portion, in which fragments of earlier movements collide with each other before settling down at measure 44 into an exact repeat of the March. As Stein develops this idea, he notes that the instruments seem not to have recalled the themes cor-rectly, since the melodic shape of one earlier theme is combined with the rhyth-mic profile of another. Or, he observes, "the state of affairs becomes particularly amusing when the guitar is about to intone the minuet ingeniously in two-part texture [m. 13], but instead plays a canon on the inversion and retrograde ver-sion of the variations' theme."[25]

Schoenberg's characterization of the finale, as transmitted by Stein, alludes to a classic kind of irony in which the characters, or in this case the performers, take on a special agency and thus in an important sense break the frame of a work. This is the *Illusionsstörung*, the destruction of illusion, which Friedrich Schlegel saw as the basis of irony.[26] Famous examples include Ludwig Tieck's early plays, in which characters and even the audience step out of their normal roles. If something like that process is going on in Schoenberg's Serenade— whether in the finale alone, or in the story of the disappointed lover that unfolds across the work as a whole—then we can claim for this work a special ironic sta-tus, one that differentiates it from the other neoclassical compositions in its immediate cohort—the Suite for Piano, Op. 25; and the Wind Quintet, Op. 26, both of which also of course use older forms and techniques.

Adorno also hears the finale of the Serenade in terms of irony, not for its *Illusionsstörung*, but for the repetition of the opening March: "After the quidproquo of all themes [in the introduction to the finale], where each one almost disguises itself as another, the beginning returns, the familiar March, as though nothing hap-pened in between. The return to the beginning, which arises with each repetition and almost makes us believe that it is arbitrary what opens and what closes passages in the Serenade, may be the greatest and boldest symbol of its irony."[27]

To return to my metaphor one last time: Schoenberg's Serenade is a hall of mirrors in which musical materials and musical history are reflected back and forth—across the pitch axis of D and A♭; across the piece's own formal frames; and across years, decades, or centuries. The Serenade also occupies a special place near the chronological center of Schoenberg's oeuvre: it is the twenty-fourth of fifty numbered opuses; it was written at about the midpoint of a sixty-year compositional career extending from 1890 to 1950. It embodies and externalizes for all to hear the tensions of a moment when Schoenberg was looking back at the past (his own and that of music); was eyeing the present (the brash young neoclassicists nipping at his heels); and gazing into to the future, hoping to do whatever he could to ensure—in that notorious quotation—the supremacy of German music for a hundred years.[28]

Notes

1. Erich Heller, *The Ironic German: A Study of Thomas Mann* (London: Secker & Warburg, 1958), 23.

2. See, for example, Rey M. Longyear, "Beethoven and Romantic Irony," *Musical Quarterly* 56 (1970): 647–64; Charles S. Brauner, "Irony in the Heine Lieder of Schubert and Schumann," *Musical Quarterly* 67 (1981): 261–81; John Daverio, "Schumann's 'Im Legendenton' and Friedrich Schlegel's 'Arabeske,'" *19th Century Music* 11 (1987): 150–63; and Heinz J. Dill, "Romantic Irony in the Works of Robert Schumann," *Musical Quarterly* 73 (1989): 172–95; Charles Rosen, *The Romantic Generation* (Cambridge: Cambridge University Press, 1995), esp. Chapter 2 ("Fragments").

3. See especially Scott Messing, *Neoclassicism in Music: From the Genesis of the Concept Through the Schoenberg/Stravinsky Polemic* (Ann Arbor: UMI Research Press, 1988); Richard Taruskin, "Back to Whom? Neoclassicism as Ideology," *19th Century Music* 16 (1993): 286–302; and Nils Grosch, *Die Musik der Neuen Sachlichkeit* (Stuttgart and Weimar: Metzler, 1999).

4. Charles Rosen, *Arnold Schoenberg* (Chicago: University of Chicago Press, 1996 [original ed. New York: Viking, 1975]), 78.

5. See the summary of the genesis of *Ariadne auf Naxos* in my *German Modernism: Music and the Arts* (Berkeley and Los Angeles: University of California Press, 2005), 223–27.

6. Gérard Genette, *Palimpsests: Literature in the Second Degree* (Lincoln: University of Nebraska Press, 1977).

7. Stefan Kunze, "Die ästhetische Rekonstruktion der Oper: Anmerkungen zur 'Ariadne auf Naxos,'" in *Hofmannsthal und das Theater*, ed. Wolfram Mauser, 170 (Vienna: Halosar, 1981).

8. Theodor W. Adorno, *Mahler: A Musical Physiognomy*, trans. Edmund Jephcott (Chicago: University of Chicago Press, 1992), 96.

9. Letter of August 31, 1940, to Erika and Fritz Stiedry, cited in Josef Rufer, *The Works of Arnold Schoenberg*, trans. Dika Newlin (New York: Free Press of Glencoe, 1963), 40.

10. See Rudolf Stephan, "Schoenberg and Bach," in *Schoenberg and His World*, ed. Walter Frisch (Princeton, NJ: Princeton University Press, 1999), 126.

11. I draw the chronology of table 13.1 largely from the superb documentary-analytical work of Martina Sichardt, *Die Entstehung der Zwölftonmethode Arnold Schönbergs* (Mainz: Schott, 1990).

12. Bryan Simms, *The Atonal Music of Arnold Schoenberg, 1908–1923* (Oxford: Oxford University Press, 2000), 209.

13. This point is made by Simms (*Atonal Music,* 204).

14. See the impressive documentary-historical study of the Donaueschingen festivals, Josef Häusler, *Spiegel der Neuen Musik: Donaueschingen* (Kassel: Bärenreiter, 1996).

15. Adès 14.078-2.

16. The term *Weltanschauungsmusik* was coined by Rudolf Stephan. See Stephan, "Aussermusikalischer Inhalt; Musikalischer Gehalt: Gedanken zur Musik der Jahrhundertwende," in *Vom musikalischen Denken: Gesammelte Vorträge,* ed. Rainer Damm and Andreas Traub (Mainz: B. Schott's Söhne, 1985), 309–20, esp. 316. See also Hermann Danuser, *Die Musik des 20. Jahrhunderts* (Laaber: Laaber-Verlag, 1984), 13, 427.

17. Theodor W. Adorno, "Schönberg: Serenade, op. 24," in Adorno, *Gesammelte Schriften,* ed. Rolf Tiedemann (*Musikalische Schriften,* vol. 5) (Frankfurt: Suhrkamp, 1997), 18:325–30.

18. Adorno, "Serenade," 327.

19. Adorno, "Serenade," 328. The excerpts come from the following passage: "Der Hauptgedanke des einleitenden Marsches ist keine jener Schönberg-Melodien, die, weithin aus sich herausschwingend, die Struktur eines ganzen Satzes bestimmen, ohne Rücksicht auf die totale Anlage geöffnet und vegetativ einem unbekannten Organismus zustrebend; auch keines jener komplexen Themen der späteren Zeit, die, aus bunt wechselndem Motivmaterial gebildet, unvermutet zur Einheit höherer Ordnung sich fügen. Es ist ein geschlossenes Thema, eines, das in sich fertig keiner Ergänzung bedarf, das in eine Form aufgenommen werden kann, nicht die Form bildet, kurz nach herkömmlichen Begriffen eher ein Rondo—als ein Sonatenthema. Seine Geschlossenheit ist indessen auch nicht einmalig und unwiederholbar wie etwa die der großen Klarinettenmelodie des Orchesterliedes 'Seraphita.' Die knappe, siebentaktige Periodisierung, die Sparsamkeit der Motivik, das festgehaltene, absichtsvoll freie Bewegung hemmende b: all dies läßt in dem selbst doch recht asymmetrischen Melos bereits die Symmetrie vorfühlen, die seine Umkehrung und Wiederholung getreu regelt. Verschwiegen ist das Marschthema: verschwiegen, weil es nicht stürmisch das Ganze bekennt, verschwiegen, weil es nicht als Einzelnes vollen Sinn beansprucht, verschwiegen auch in der unpathetischen und geheimnisvollen Sachlichkeit des Tones. Und ironisch ist seine Verschwiegenheit, das Subjekt verschweigt sich in ihr und die Form haftet so locker am Material, daß sie stets labil dem subjektiven Willen gehorcht, wenn er etwa durchbricht. Sie haftet locker und haftet dennoch." I am grateful to Traute Marshall for suggestions for translation in this and other German passages cited in this essay.

20. David Lewin, "Inversional Balance as an Organizing Force in Schoenberg's Music and Thought," *Perspectives of New Music* 6 (1968): 1–21.

21. The sketches are held at the Arnold Schönberg Center in Vienna. They are viewable online through the center's Web site at: http://www.schoenberg.at/6_archiv/music/works/op/compositions_op24_sources.htm.

22. Translation adapted and modified from Simms, *Atonal Music,* 215.

23. Olin Downes, "A Donaueschingen Chamber Music Festival," *New York Times,* August 17, 1924, p. X5.

24. On the First Quartet, see Christian M. Schmidt, "Schönbergs 'Very Definite— But Private' Programm zum Streichquartett Opus 7," in *Bericht über den 2.Kongreß der Internationalen Schönberg-Gesellschaft*, ed. Rudolf Stephan and Sigrid Wiesmann (Vienna: Elisabeth Lafite), 230–34. Schoenberg's remarks on the autobiographical dimensions of the Trio have been related many times; see Walter B. Bailey, *Programmatic Elements in the Works of Schoenberg* (Ann Arbor: UMI Research Press, 1984), 151–57.

25. Erwin Stein, "New Formal Principles," in *Orpheus in New Guises* (London: Rockliff, 1953), 73. Originally published as "Neue Formprinzipien," in *Arnold Schönberg zum fünfzigsten Geburtstage: 13. September 1924*, special issue of *Musikblätter des Anbruch* (Vienna, 1924), 300.

26. See Ernst Behler, *Ironie und literarische Moderne* (Paderborn: Schöningh, 1997), 98.

27. Adorno, "Serenade," 329: "Nach einem Quidproquo aller Themen, deren jedes fast sich in ein anderes kostümiert, kehrt der Anfang, der sichere March wieder, als wäre inzwischen nichts geschehen. Die Rückläufigkeit in den Beginn, die mit jener Wiederholung anhebt und beinahe glauben macht, es sei gleichgültig, was anfange und was schließe in der Serenade, mag das größte und kühnste Symbol ihrer Ironie sein."

28. See Rufer, *Works of Arnold Schoenberg*, 45.

Chapter Fourteen

Words for the Surface

Boulez, Stockhausen, and "Allover" Painting

David Gable

> . . . there are no words for he surface, that is,
> No words to say what it really is, that it is not
> Superficial but a visible core . . .
> —John Ashbery
> "Self-Portrait in a Convex Mirror"

It is a commonplace to observe that much of the painting of the twentieth century depends on a radically new principle: "that the pictorial illusion takes place on the physical reality of an opaque surface rather than behind the illusion of a transparent plane."[1] One result of such an approach is "allover" painting, painting the structure of which spreads out with approximately equal weight in all directions across the surface of the picture plane rather than exploiting a framework in depth dependent on perspective. An analogous "allover" structure characterizes much of the music of Pierre Boulez and Karlheinz Stockhausen: Jackson Pollock's classic "drip" paintings (1947–50) established the allover, frontal, "single image" conception that emerged in American painting in the late 1940s in its most ambitious and thorough-going form, and there are manifest parallels between Pollock's allover designs and the ambitious works for orchestra that Boulez and Stockhausen completed in the late 1950s and early 1960s, Stockhausen's *Carré* and *Punkte* and Boulez's *Pli selon pli*. This essay is an attempt to illuminate the styles of Boulez and Stockhausen at a crucial point in their evolution by placing them in the context of allover painting.

During his lifetime, Pollock was widely regarded as an "original" who had emerged from nowhere, or at least as a uniquely American phenomenon, a notion Pollock himself explicitly rejected.[2] In fact, Pollock's allover designs were deeply rooted in tradition, not only in André Masson's surrealist canvases but also in the impressionist painting of the 1870s and 1880s, the period when the impressionists were most closely and enthusiastically allied, and Pollock's "drip" paintings coincided with a new interest in the late work of Monet, an interest that Pollock's paintings helped to provoke. Similarly, the large orchestral scores that Boulez and Stockhausen produced in the late 1950s and early 1960s seemed as radically novel in their day as Pollock's drip paintings had a decade earlier, although the styles characteristic of *Carré*, *Punkte*, and *Pli selon pli* actually represented a kind of rapprochement with tradition, and there are striking anticipations of their allover styles in Richard Wagner's programmatic depictions of atmospheric effects, effects that reflect an interest in the action of ephemeral natural phenomena akin to Monet's. The fully realized allover designs of Pollock, Boulez, and Stockhausen were ultimately rooted in later nineteenth-century traditions. In the following, Pollock's drip paintings are placed in the context of Monet and impressionism, Boulez's and Stockhausen's works in the context of Wagner, the master of atmospheric effects.

All of these examples of the allover design emerged in large part as a consequence of a new attitude toward temporal experience that was already fundamental for impressionist painting. Indeed, Boulez's attitudes are deeply rooted in the avant-garde French traditions of the later nineteenth century. As a young man, Boulez had already discovered a "Debussy-Cézanne-Mallarmé reality at the root of all modernity,"[3] and his essays are dotted with references to Charles Baudelaire, Arthur Rimbaud, Édouard Manet, and Monet. As for Stockhausen, his roots may have differed from Boulez's—the history of the "allover" design encompasses more territory than France—but the two composers were in constant contact throughout the 1950s and shared similar concerns.

Monet and Impressionism

For Monet, the one great subject was all-enveloping atmospheric light or simply the *enveloppe*. In their book on Monet, Robert Gordon and Andrew Forge characterize the *enveloppe* as "the total unbroken fabric of experience."[4] For one Ernest Hareux, the author of a manual on oil painting written in the wake of impressionism in 1899, the *enveloppe* was a kind of technique, "the art of drowning the contours of everything without losing the form."[5]

The impressionists frequently chose momentary atmospheric effects for motifs—ephemeral and amorphous effects produced by shifting light, by mist and fog, snow, or wind on water—and their techniques matched their motifs.[6] Rather than disguising the painting's medium and the means of its making, "the impressionists' cultivation of the direct and the immediate in paint handling made the medium the message."[7] Monet labored as long and hard over his paintings as any painter, but his brushstrokes embody a rhetoric of haste. Covering the entire surface of the canvas, the rapid brushstrokes necessary to capture a fleeting motif are visible as such, their irregular shapes the consequence of an action of brush hairs in oil paint over which the painter has declined to assert the last degree of control: the pattern of brushstrokes covering the surface of the canvas takes on a life of its own, rivaling in interest the motif visible through it.[8]

With a traditional oil painting in a "painterly" style—in a painting by Rembrandt or Rubens, for example—layers of impasto were built up as the painter modeled the objects distributed in the space of the painting: tied to the objects modeled, the impasto was a direct result of the shaping and contouring brushwork. In an impressionist painting, the motif is not the object in space but the *enveloppe*. Brushwork is divorced from modeling, and the impasto is distributed more or less evenly across the entire surface of the canvas, resulting in what Meyer Schapiro has characterized as "the autonomous, homogeneous crust of paint."[9]

Because it had come to seem purely conventional, the impressionists rejected the well-established technique of chiaroscuro, the seamless gradation of color used both to represent light filling the volume of space depicted in a traditional painting and to structure that space. Rather than mixing hues on the palette or relying on the seamless gradations of value or intensity characteristic of chiaroscuro, the impressionists famously juxtaposed flecks of pure color within a narrow range of values, producing a flickering or scintillating effect as the colors blend in the viewer's eye. During the 1870s and 1880s, Monet often applied unmixed paints directly to a canvas prepared with a pure white base, enhancing the luminosity of each color, the paintings of the 1870s in particular revealing "a tendency to keep the flickering light averaged out at an approximately even value over the whole surface."[10]

Impressionism was suspended between the two meanings of subjectivity underlying the impression.[11] On the one hand, vision—and therefore the impression made by light on the retina—is always from the unique vantage of a perceiving subject in a given place at a given time. On the other hand, every painter's style is the unique product of a temperament: a painting is his or her impression.[12] Impressionist painting was an attempt to make a record of the "sensation," the sensation made by light in the painter's eye.[13] The flecks of color in the impressionist's allover brushwork were at once an attempt to capture the myriad of sensations produced by light and an attempt to reproduce the conditions under which color is transmitted by atmospheric light before coalescing in the eye.

Jackson Pollock

The possibilities implicit in impressionist brushwork opened the doors for painters of every stripe from Cézanne, Seurat, Signac, and Van Gogh on down to the abstract expressionists and those surrealists who interested Pollock most, including André Masson. In retrospect, it does not seem that far a step from the "scintillating painterly fields of impressionism"[14] to the big scintillating picture of Jackson Pollock. In the most substantial treatment of Pollock's drip paintings to date, William Rubin writes, "Almost as significant in understanding [Pollock's] classic period [as knowing his sources] is to know the styles he did *not* build on, among them expressionism (pace that hard-dying misnomer, 'Abstract Expressionism')."[15] For the minimalist painter Donald Judd, a generation younger than Pollock, "The term 'Abstract Expressionism' was a big mistake. For one thing it implied that Pollock and De Kooning were alike, that both were expressionists. De Kooning's paintings are substantially the same as those of the various expressionist painters from Soutine back to van Gogh [with their] recurrent use of expressive brushwork. [Expressive brushwork] portrays immediate emotions. It doesn't involve immediate sensations," the source of the impressionist motif.[16] Whatever might be said about the awkward "expressionist" of the preceding years, the Pollock of the late 1940s was "an aesthete tuned to the passing nuance."[17] That Pollock carried aspects of the impressionist's art of sensations to new extremes. Pollock's drip paintings are characterized by their allover patterning, scintillating atmospheric effects, a conception of value or intensity ultimately derived from the impressionists, and a dematerializing insubstantiality.[18]

Precisely what struck Clement Greenberg when he first saw Pollock's drip paintings was their allover designs, and other viewers were struck by the same phenomenon.[19] Pollock "cover[ed] an entire field with incidents that were not arranged in hierarchies of size or emphasis."[20] His "line forms a series of looped and arabesqued patterns all roughly similar in character and in approximate size and more or less even in density over the whole surface of the picture," which is the very definition "of an 'all-over' configuration."[21] Pollock's allover designs are instances of the "single image" painting characteristic of many of the American painters of his generation. That is, the allover web of lines in a dripped Pollock coalesces into a single frontal image. In the profusion of Pollock's drip paintings, some spikes and spatters may reach and even spill over the edge of the canvas, but, in a majority of the paintings, the body of the skein of paint—the "single image"—clearly remains within its borders. Unsupported by the edges of the canvas, the allover skeins in Pollock's drip paintings appear to hover before the canvas within a shallow and ambiguous space.

Pollock's conception of space derived directly from his experience of the paintings that Mondrian painted after visiting Paris in 1912, where he saw the fruit of Pablo Picasso's and Georges Braque's analytic cubism firsthand, and from many analogous and somewhat later paintings by a range of painters including Joan Miró and André Masson. All of these paintings depend on the frontal presentation and shallow and ambiguous space already characteristic of analytic cubism.[22] Although detached from the other three sides, the motif in Picasso's and Braque's pictures is rooted in the lower edge of the canvas, and the same is true of the first cathedral façades that Mondrian painted rising up from their foundations. In Mondrian's "Pier and Ocean" series from 1914, the motif is cut loose from the scaffolding provided by the bottom edge of the canvas, floating free from any support, and surrounded by an oval that delimits the frontal image of pier and ocean, this "single image" hovering in shallow relief before the picture plane. Although frontal in design, neither Mondrian's seascapes nor Pollock's skeins appears entirely flat (unlike, for example, Mondrian's late, entirely rectilinear compositions, the last works of Matisse, or the doctrinaire minimalist paintings of the 1960s). Mondrian's floating lattices appear to be made up of elements advancing and receding within a space no thicker than a crêpe, while the lines crisscrossing Pollock's tangled skeins of paint dart in and out of the shallow recesses they define. With Pollock's skeins, cubism had been "subsumed by a kind of Impressionism."[23]

Which brings us to Pollock's "drip" technique.[24] Pollock's dribbling "essentially constituted a technique for *extended drawing with paint*."[25] As Frank O'Hara wrote in a statement often quoted from one of the earliest monographs on Pollock, "There has never been enough said about Pollock's draftsmanship, that amazing ability to quicken a line by thinning it, to slow it up by flooding, to elaborate that simplest of elements, to build up an embarrassment of riches in the mass by drawing alone."[26] Although they often run together, Pollock never used fluid lines like a sheet to cover the surfaces they run across. Endlessly turning back in on themselves, Pollock's skeins exist in a state of dynamic equilibrium. Rather than coalescing into broad patches of solid color, Pollock's lines produce an endless variety of atomized sensations, the juxtapositions of color producing the sort of flickering already familiar from impressionist painting.

The Allover Design in Music

What we routinely refer to as the "surface structure" of traditional music does not literally unfold on the actual surface of the music. Slightly recessed, it unfolds from attack point to attack point along a metric grid lying below the surface, where it is controlled by such deeper structures as cadences. Nevertheless, composers have consistently exploited the actual surface of music, especially when writing in a *sostenuto* style. Unfolding from attack point to attack point, the surface structure of the subject of the fugue that opens Beethoven's String Quartet in C-sharp Minor, Op. 131, is the pattern of pitches and attacks that constitutes the subject, but there is also a more immediate structure unfolding on the actual surface of the music that Beethoven has notated along with his subject (see example 14.1). The first violinist not only attacks notes at appropriate points along a metric grid: he or she supplies a continuous stream of sound, shaping it with a seamlessly applied dynamics, inscribing an allover design. The allover design on the actual surface and the so-called surface structure define the shallow space in which all of the activity unfolds, although we also grasp the harmonic structure underlying the subject.

The continuous features that are projected by a performer's phrasing have always played an important role in music, particularly in music written in a *sostenuto* style. Phrasing music written in a *sostenuto* style entails the projection

Adagio, ma non troppo e molto espressivo

Example 14.1. Beethoven, String Quartet in C-sharp Minor, Op. 131, mvt 1., mm. 1–4.

of the overall shape of a motive, phrase, or other span, not only through carefully weighted attacks and strategic deviations from a strictly metronomic interpretation of the score, but also through the application of a seamless dynamics to the continuous supply of sound enveloping the span.[27] Boulez would refer to the supply of sound as "*l'enveloppe.*"[28] Dynamics are to the envelope what rhythm is to the phrase. In shaping the envelope, the dynamics inscribe an allover design.

The tempo of Beethoven's fugue is *Adagio*, albeit *non troppo*, opening up ample space in time for an allover design. While the seamlessly applied dynamics focus attention on the seamless passage of time, the comparatively slow *tempo* allows ample space in time for an exploitation of the expressive power of dissonance. Consonances are the deeper "structural" phenomena, dissonances "ornamental" surface elements, but dissonances are potentially more expressive. The function of a consonance is discharged the moment it is attacked, but the function of a dissonance is not discharged until it is resolved. The phenomenological impact of a dissonance necessarily extends through time, and the expressive use of dissonance characteristic of so much nineteenth-century music intrinsically depends on this fundamental fact. The expressivity of the tendency tones appearing on the first two downbeats of Beethoven's fugue subject is heightened by strong metric placement, and Beethoven capitalizes on their expressivity by sustaining them, the first for half a measure, the second for three full beats, while the dynamics focus attention on their extension through time (ex. 14.1). The structure of Beethoven's subject depends on the hierarchical subordination of dissonance to consonance basic to tonal syntax, but decorative patterns unfolding on the surface assume extraordinary prominence in our actual experience of the music in time.

As the nineteenth century unfolded, composers took increasing care with the envelope, relying on a *sostenuto* style to ensure that their structures were enveloped by a seamless and smoothly shaped continuum, a *sostenuto* style projected by a *legato* or *spianato* phrasing and shaped by a seamlessly applied and ever more meticulously regulated dynamics. Increasingly apt to linger over the surface, nineteenth-century composers exploited an increasingly chromatic voice leading, slowing down the harmonic rhythm in the process: the fastest *tempi* in the music of Wagner, Bruckner, Brahms, and Mahler tend to be slower than the faster *tempi* in the music of Haydn, Mozart, and Beethoven, opening up space in time for an elaboration of the increasingly refined system of dynamics shaping the envelope. Much of this shaping is consistent with what an eighteenth-century musician would have supplied instinctively, but Wagner and Bruckner wrested a large measure of control from the performer, placing greater emphasis on the dynamics, treating them as quasi-determinants of a more continuous form.

Wagner

The development of a *sostenuto* style characteristic of so many nineteenth-century composers reflected a shift in emphasis from "structure" to "experience," from the articulation of underlying forms to reflection of something like the "unbroken fabric of experience," to borrow Gordon and Forge's gloss on the term "*enveloppe.*"[29] In the famous letter to Mathilde Wesendonck in which he refers to his "deepest and most refined art" as "the art of transition," Wagner explains that "the whole fabric of [his] artistic tissue consists of transitions" because of his own shifting moods: "From the very beginning, it has been a part of my nature for my moods to change rapidly and abruptly from one extreme to another. [. . .] True art essentially has no other object than to show these heightened moods in their extreme relation to one another."[30]

    As Wagner describes it, his subjectivity is directed inward, focused on his inner life, while the subjectivity of the impressionists was directed outward toward sensations found in nature. Nevertheless, Wagner and the impressionists exhibited analogous attitudes toward the nature of experience, focusing on its immediate temporal structure, which in turn provoked similar attitudes toward the proper subject of art. In principle, both were more interested in the immediate continuous experience of processes than in solid or traditional forms, and Wagner's art of transitions embraced the depiction of ephemeral atmospheric effects comparable to those treated by the impressionists. There is a long history of programmatic depictions of nature and weather in music, but Wagner developed atomizing techniques that made possible a more consistently and quasi-naturalistically amorphous depiction of ephemeral processes than ever before, and the depictions of the motion of vaporous substances and similar atmospheric effects in Wagner's operas are among the most striking ever realized.

    Despite his claims, Wagner was very far from abandoning either discrete or quasi-traditional forms, but the formal units in Wagner's operas are smoothly elided by means of seamless transitions, and his continuums are often enveloped by a quasi-seamless surface, allowing us to glimpse how the new approach to form envisioned in his letter might have been realized. Boulez has remarked that "Wagner makes increasing use of the contrast between pure and mixed colors [as the *Ring* unfolds], bringing to a fine point the art of transition from one field of sonority to another."[31] In *Parsifal*, as he told Cosima, Wagner's goal was an orchestration—note the choice of metaphor—"like layers of clouds that separate and reform."[32] In developing new approaches to instrumentation and texture, Wagner created allover patterns that approached the degree of atomization characteristic of the impressionist surface.

In the opening of the transition from scene 2 to scene 3 of Wagner's *Das Rheingold*, the descent into *Nibelheim*, Wagner set himself the task of illustrating an amorphous atmospheric process (example 14.2). Here is his description from the score:

> Der Schwefeldampf verdüstert sich zu ganz schwarzem Gewölk, welches von unten nach oben steigt; dann verwandelt sich dieses in festes, finstres Steingeklüft, das sich immer aufwärts bewegt, so dass es den Anschein hat als sänke die Scene immer tiefer in die Erde hinab.

> [The mist darkens forming a black cloud that rises from below; after which it is transformed into a solid dark wall of craggy stone that rises continuously upward, giving the appearance that the stage is sinking deeper and deeper into the earth.]

In illustrating this process and others like it, Wagner effected a revolution in the handling of texture.

At the first downbeat of example 14.2, there is a cadence to an E-major triad, the sheer duration of which suggests an articulating caesura, but there is no cadence in Fricka's line until the second downbeat. The surface of the triad is covered with a layer of continuous thirty-second-note motion that blurs the contours of the linear processes embedded in it.

The thirty-second-note motion results from the oscillation of semitone-related pitches, but which pitch in any given instance is structural and which ornamental, the upper or the lower, varies from quarter to quarter. The E in the upper voice at measure 1 of example 14.2 is sustained by the oscillation for a measure and a half, but in measure 1 it is ornamented with F naturals, in measure 2 with D sharps. The oscillation flickers from one side of the structural pitch to the other, creating a potential for ambiguity. In the third quarter of measure 2, for example, it is not immediately apparent that E is ornamenting F. We only realize it in retrospect when F is ornamented by G♭ in the final quarter of measure 2. Throughout these five bars, the direction of the underlying lines is clear enough in the long run, but the changes of pitch are embedded within the erratic flickering of the ornamentation, which blurs them precisely where the changes occur.

This passage and others like it mark a turning point in the history of ornamentation. With a conventional series of trills, the ornamentation is applied

Fricka

bald   zur ban - gen-den Frau!

Example 14.2. Wagner, *Das Rheingold*, end of scene 2.

Example 14.2. (continued)

consistently to every pitch in the line, the subordination of ornament to structure is unambiguously clear, and there is no question which elements constitute the structural line. With the oscillating thirty-second notes in example 14.2, the surface patterning is not consistent but varies from bar to bar, from structural pitch to structural pitch.

Here is a summary of the oscillating patterns. The strokes indicate whether the oscillations within any quarter move up from the lower note or down from the higher note:

/ / / /	\ \ / \	/ / \ /	\ / \ /	/ \ / \
m. 1	m. 2	m. 3	m. 4	m. 5

Unlike the ornamenting pattern in a conventional series of trills, the regularities here are deprived of any predictive value because they are abandoned before we can become accustomed to them. It is impossible to predict which element in any oscillating pair will turn out to be the structural element. Although the oscillation is subject to grouping—it is already grouped into groups of eight thirty-seconds at the most immediate level—the underlying linear structure emerges with its contours blurred, like the motif in an impressionist painting. No longer mere decoration, Wagner's oscillating ornamentation begins to take on a life of its own.

Wagner developed many procedures analogous to those used here, and a similar concern with covering the surface is revealed in the sequence found in measures 10–14 (see example 14.2). The sequence unfolds a straightforward chromatic ascent from downbeat to downbeat, but the spaces between the downbeats are filled with rising and falling chromatic lines that saturate the surface with a layer of chromatic activity: neutral and undifferentiated, their interest resides in their contribution to the overall texture. Covering the surface in contrary motion, they serve the same purpose as cross hatching in a painting or drawing: lines hastily sketched in in "contrary motion" to shade patches on the surface. In measures 10–13 (ex. 14.2), the descending lines move in steady eighths, the ascending lines in steady triplets, the lines more nearly resembling a draughtsman's cross hatching because of these cross rhythms. Rather than marching in lock step, they are sketched in with a degree of simulated irregularity. Wagner is constrained by a metric grid, which enforces a greater degree of regularity than might be found in a painting or drawing. Nevertheless, his cross rhythms serve to create the kind of "interference patterns" that are characteristic of cross hatching, the three's in one part blurring the two's in the other and vice versa, covering more of the surface in the process: there are more attacks per quarter in the overall texture than in either of the constituent lines.

The rate of surface motion in this example shifts along with the texture. The trilling quarter notes prevailing from the middle of measure 3 give way to the rising triplet lines in measure 6, which alternate with the descending eighths and skittish sixteenth-note motive in measure 7 until measure 10, where the cross hatching begins. The inconsistent motion and changing surface figuration combine to depict the action of a vaporous substance, the accumulation of detail and unpredictability of the patterning focusing the kind of attention on the surface once reserved for the so-called surface structure.

***

Marked "*Stürmisch*" and surprisingly specific in mimetic detail, the prelude to *Die Walküre* is a programmatic depiction of Siegmund's flight through wind and rain: the first period is given as example 14.3. Siegmund's relentless movement is suggested by a running bass in the lower strings, while second violins and violas supply a tremolo mimetic of sheeting rain: like the countless individual drops that coalesce into a sheet of rain, the individual strokes of the bow that make up the tremolo coalesce into a seamless entity in our perception. Acting on the tremolo as wind on rain, the dynamics fluctuate like lacerating wind, periodically attaining stinging *fortes*, the action of the dynamics on the continuous supply of sound inscribing an allover design. Rather than adhering to the motives and bringing out their shapes, they are leveled off and spread uniformly across the entire surface, turning the usual situation on its head.

Example 14.3. Wagner, *Die Walküre*, Prelude.

As pitch, a pedal may be motionless, but—thanks to the continuous *tremolando* and the steady growth in volume characteristic of the successive *crescendos*—the pedal projected by Wagner's tremolo is not so much motionless as constant, exerting a steady pressure. A tremolo is made up of a series of individual attacks so rapid that they run together rather than being perceived as individual pulsations:

the pattern of attacks gives the impression of being and functions as a textured but unbroken line.

Textured lines of this kind exhibit characteristic rhythms of their own independent of any metric structure. At the circus, for example, the continuous rhythms of a drum roll generate the kind of sustained suspense apt for the interval before some dangerous and bravura feat. Projecting a static tonic pedal against a background of motionless harmony, the tremolo in the opening of *Die Walküre* and the rhythms of the dynamics applied to it are similarly continuous, generating a similarly sustained tension.

In the *Walküre* prelude, the rhythms of the dynamics are out of phase with the metric structure, contributing a degree of rhythmic unrest suggestive of the irregular periodicity of the action of the wind. Unfolding from a second beat, each *crescendo* is sustained through the duration of a first beat, the volume abruptly dropping on a second beat. The shifts are not only abrupt but syncopated, their effect complex: each abrupt drop in volume gives the listener a jolt, but only within a seamless process otherwise generating a sustained tension. There is no precise point in time when the sudden abrupt increase in tension produced by the drop in volume can be released, because the point where the volume drops is precisely the point where the next seamless process of growth begins: the tension fluctuates without ever being definitively released.

Even the harmony is bent to the demands of Wagner's novel conception. In measures 14–15 there is a hint of diminished seventh harmony, allowing for a cadence at the end of the period, but traditional harmonic motion is a long time coming. Up to the cadence, the D minor tonic is a static presence, the root of the tonic triad appearing on the downbeat of each of the first thirteen bars. Spinning their wheels, the lower strings induce a kind of vertigo that has little to do with a traditional use of tonal syntax: the bass line is "motionless and moving at the same time," as Boulez once said of the prelude to *Das Rheingold*.[33] Although the tension engendered by the last long *crescendo* is ultimately released with a cadence, the vertiginous effect it produces is a result of building without moving.

Boulez and Stockhausen

As the 1950s unfolded, Boulez and Stockhausen experienced a progressive disillusionment with "total" or "integral" serialism, and their allegiance quietly shifted from Webern and Messiaen to Debussy and Berg.[34] An integral serialism extrapolated from Webern's conception of serialism and Messiaen's speculations about the organization of rhythm had taken them "*à la limite du pays fertile,*" and both composers longed for the kinds of Baroque forms and textures that Debussy and Berg had realized in their music.[35] As Boulez wrote to Stockhausen in 1957, "I plunge into Berg because he had a fabulous sense of complexity and montage and I would even say of 'collage' that, in the end, is cruelly lacking in Webern, where everything, at least for me now, ends up being too obvious [*évident*]."[36] Debussy's significance for Boulez is well documented, but Stockhausen, too, became especially interested in Debussy during this period, completing a study of the shifting textures in Debussy's *Jeux* as a key to its form while embarking on the composition of *Gruppen*.[37] This profound shift of emphasis from all-generating abstract structural principles to the sounding surface went hand in hand with a progressive transformation of the kinds of pointillist textures that were characteristic of their earlier music, textures that were an inevitable consequence of integral serialism. Already in parts of Stockhausen's *Gruppen* (1955–57) and Boulez's *Doubles* (1957–58) and definitively with Stockhausen's *Carré* (1959–60) and *Punkte* (1962) and Boulez's *Pli selon pli* (1957–62), the two composers realized *sostenuto* styles in which the unmeasured continuum characteristic of their earlier music was realized with a continuous supply of sound. Finally in a position to realize their ambitions more fully than ever before, Boulez and Stockhausen arrived at an allover conception. The ambitious orchestral tapestries that Boulez and Stockhausen produced during this period are analogous to the big scintillating picture of Jackson Pollock, the parallels extending to their spacious and scintillating atmospheric effects.

In a program note written for the first performance, Stockhausen recalls his absorption in certain atmospheric effects during the composition of *Carré*: "The first sketches of *Carré* were made in aeroplanes at the end of 1958 during a six-month tour of America, when I flew several hours a day and—above the clouds—experienced the slowest rates of change and widest spaces."[38] The experience had a palpable effect on the character of *Carré*. Both *Carré* and *Punkte* consistently depend on slowly shifting processes and spacious effects, while *Pli selon pli* is filled with the programmatic depiction of atmospheric effects suggested by the poems that Boulez made use of in his *Portrait de Mallarmé*, of hovering fog and the song of the siren, of waves crashing around the mast of a vessel sinking under a starlit sky, of sea spawn and sea wrack.[39]

Speaking of *Pli selon pli*, Robert Craft once claimed that "No living composer approaches [Boulez] in the invention of beguiling instrumental colors."[40] Charles Rosen has described him as "the master of iridescent sonorities."[41] In the program note for the first performance of *Tombeau* in 1959, the movement that would grow to become the final movement of *Pli selon pli*, Boulez summarized its content with a single word: scintillation [*scintillement*].[42] *Pli selon pli* consists of a kind of chamber music for large orchestra written for an ensemble that includes not only the usual complement of winds, brass, and strings, but also a variegated battery of pitched percussion instruments. The "scintillation" in *Pli selon pli* is largely due to the sounds produced by the percussion instruments—together with the mandolin and guitar they inscribe glinting arabesques in ever changing combinations—and each of the instrumental families is represented in all registers, making possible endless permutations throughout the registral space.

Rather than treating the range of the octave as normative for the motive, in the music of Boulez and Stockhausen the intervallic structure is projected through the available space. As Rosen once put it, "A seventeenth for Boulez is not a transposed third but a projection in space," and the same can be said for Stockhausen.[43] In at least some of Boulez's earlier music, the exploitation of the available space was a function of a kind of automatism, of the interaction of a registral system and a pitch system under a serial regime. As Boulez observed many years later:

> When you don't pay attention to the overall envelope of the pitch [while composing], then you cannot follow anything. [. . .] In my Second Sonata [. . .] the registers were not only a little bit, they *were* anarchic. There was some direction but not enough control for me. Then, when I began to work with total serialism and all the parameters, it was no longer possible to control anything.[44]

In Boulez's *Structures 1a*—admittedly the extreme case—there is an automatic kaleidoscopic shifting from one register to another in the distribution of individual pitches.[45] In *Carré*, *Punkte*, and *Pli selon pli*, the shifting nature of the material determines its registral disposition, and registration is handled with an extraordinary sensitivity. Individual lines may leap wide intervals, but the continuous automatic shifting characteristic of the most extreme pointillist scores is abandoned. Moreover, there are now points of reference if only points based on shifting criteria, whether pitches frozen in register for periods of time or slowly shifting pedal points.

In Beethoven's symphonies, a *tutti* is more or less the norm, but there are also contrasting sections for reduced forces variously scored. In some passages the strings, normally first among equals, accompany a soloist from a different family of instruments. In others, the winds or brass in one register respond antiphonally to the strings in another. Stemming from the traditions of European art music, the music of Boulez and Stockhausen embodies a later refinement of a not entirely dissimilar conception, although Boulez and Stockhausen exploited the broad range of register that was already fundamental for Debussy. Near the end of the "*Dialogue du vent et de la mer*" from *La mer*, five measures after rehearsal number 54, an oasis of calm opens up, and a high A♭ (A♭6) is projected *pianissimo* by the violinists playing harmonics over a *pianissimo* low D♭ (D♭2) supplied by the double basses four octaves and a fifth lower, and much of the effect of this passage depends on this spacious registration.[46] It is just such passages that lie behind *Carré*, *Punkte*, and *Pli selon pli*, and a breath taking sense of space is evident on almost any page from these scores. The space of the *tutti* is the entire available range—a wider range than Beethoven's—and a fluid conception of register and instrumentation is the norm, both gradually shifting and sharply contrasting blocks of material unfolding successively or simultaneously in contrasting registers against the implicit background of the entire field.

There are two distinct approaches to the available range in *Carré*, *Punkte*, and *Pli selon pli*, the first of which is more characteristic of Stockhausen. Stockhausen is more apt to exploit the full expanse of the registral field within any given context than Boulez, the distribution of lines at roughly equal intervals across the entire field creating an allover structure in space, contributing to a sense that everything is in a state of equilibrium. In *Punkte*, activity is strategically distributed across the spectrum for long periods of time, the bass instruments quietly growling at one extreme, the violins playing wispy harmonics *pianissimo in Alt*. The timbre, volume, and extreme register of the harmonics make it difficult or impossible to distinguish their actual pitch: the insubstantiality of the sound and extreme registration are more fundamental than the pitch.

Stockhausen's use of space in *Carré* and *Punkte* is analogous to Pollock's in the drip paintings, the effect of which depends in part on an abandonment (not unique to Pollock) of the intimate scale of traditional easel painting. Similarly, the spacious effects in *Carré* and *Punkte* depend on a range that extends well above and below the more intimate space of the typical four-part vocal setting. "[W]hat happens within [Pollock's paintings] reaches out toward a scale and velocity that [. . .] leaves the world of bodies behind,"[47] and Pollock hoped that the viewer would be engulfed within their comparatively vast expanses. With *Carré* and *Punkte*, we take a vertiginous plunge into the fathomless expanse of a labyrinthine inner or outer space: either metaphor seems appropriate. Moreover, in *Carré*, the listener is submerged in sound, surrounded on four sides by the ensembles performing the score.

In Boulez's music, the bass register is consistently de-emphasized. Floating bass-less in the alto register, the music in *Le marteau sans maître* had already been scored for a contralto soloist and an ensemble consisting entirely of alto and treble instruments when Boulez came to write *Pli selon pli*: suspended in a mid-register cut loose from any bass support, the result was not unlike the floating frontal image of Pollock. Similarly, the bass register evaporates completely from long stretches of *Pli selon pli*. Elsewhere Boulez exploits the wide registration more consistently characteristic of Stockhausen.

Of course, the effect of a spacious distribution depends not only on the registration but also on the intervallic structure that results from it. In the absence of functional relationships, a serial system would seem to treat all intervals as equivalent, but composers of music purported to be atonal, whether serially organized or not, are as sensitive to the various weights and characters of the intervals traditionally classified as perfect consonances, imperfect consonances, and dissonances as composers of tonal music. The tension inherent in intervals traditionally classified as dissonant cannot be conjured away by removing them from the context of functional harmony, in which sense Schoenberg's music, for example, is more dissonant than Wagner's. In the music of Schoenberg's expressionist period, the melodic lines resemble Wagner's in shape and compass, and the total range is still essentially Wagner's, the accumulation of a dissonant post-Wagnerian chromaticism in two dimensions contributing to the almost unbearable intensity of Schoenberg's expressivity.

Boulez and Stockhausen are no more "expressionists" than Pollock: the expressivity characteristic of Boulez's music is the impersonal expressivity of *La mer* with its wide-open spaces and atmospheric effects rather than the intensely personal hyper-expressivity of Schoenberg. Stemming from the German tradition, *Carré* and *Punkte* are characterized by a certain expressive intensity, but their character is better described as meditative than expressive. Both composers rejected the rhetoric and vocabulary of post-tonal gestures that Schoenberg inherited from late nineteenth-century music, making use of at least two techniques for diffusing the tension inherent in the dissonant intervals, one in space and one in time. One of these techniques was a spacious registration.

Although a major seventh and a major thirty-fifth are formed with the same pitch classes, the tension characteristic of the major seventh is palpably reduced with a more spacious registration. In a major seventh chord with the seventh in the outer voices, the seventh is more apt to be represented by a major fourteenth or twenty-first or even a twenty-eighth than by a major seventh, diffusing the tension inherent in the base interval, while—given the structure of a major seventh chord—whatever tension remains is cushioned by the presence of consonant intervals rather than being compounded by the addition of further dissonant ones. At least some of the impact of the dissonance characteristic of the various seventh chords is absorbed by their tertian construction. In that sense, the quality of these sonorities is not purely dissonant, although the presence in the sonority of at least one dissonant interval prevents the total relaxation of tension characteristic of an entirely consonant sonority. Quite apart from its function as a dissonance, the phenomenological impact of a dissonant sonority—our perception of the degree of tension inherent in it—depends on both registration and the tempering role played by whatever consonant intervals are present. These same principles apply to the non-functional harmonies distributed across the registral space in Stockhausen's *Punkte*.

Describing what sounds not unlike the space of Jackson Pollock's allover skeins, Schoenberg once wrote of the available musical space, "In this space, as in Swedenborg's heaven [. . .], there is no absolute down, no right or left, forward or backward."[48] In fact, the language of tonality was rooted in the bass, the functions and rhetoric of tonality imposed a strong sense of direction on the music unfolding through this space, and much of that sense of direction was preserved even in Schoenberg's own more omnidirectional music, whether during his more radical expressionist phase or in the classicizing music of his serial period.[49] Boulez and Stockhausen exploited something more nearly like the uninflected space of Schoenberg's description. Both composers were sensitive to the weights and characters of the various consonant and dissonant intervals in both wide and close registrations, but—rather than depending on the functional opposition of dissonance to consonance that gives tonal music its impulsion or

Schoenberg's recreation of such impulsion by other means—their styles depend on the ongoing maintenance of a state of equilibrium, a state produced in part by the distribution of harmonic tension across the entire registral field. There are varying degrees of tension in their music, the tension shifting through time and from register to register, but the difference in degrees of tension, like the range of values in an impressionist painting, is subtle and seldom extreme. The tension characteristic of the dissonant intervals is subject to diffusion and generally cushioned by the presence of strategically enregistered consonant intervals without ever being definitively released by a functional resolving consonance.

***

The first painting that Monet labeled an impression—*Impression, soleil levant* (1872)—depicts the sun rising over the Thames through the haze suspended over the river. Other pictures that Monet labeled impressions include *Fumées dans la brouillard: Impression* (1874) and *Vétheuil dans la brouillard: Impression* (1879). As Meyer Schapiro remarks:

> The public was not easily convinced. Fog was considered a disagreeable state of nature, an absurd if not perverse subject, like an ugly nude. Three years [after *Vétheuil dans la brouillard*] the public's resistance and mockery were exploited for comic effect in a play by Henri Meilhac, *La cigale*, in which an artist inserted in the foreground of his painting, which featured an impenetrable coat of gray, a clearly rendered knife to indicate his subject: a fog thick enough to slice.[50]

Nevertheless, a whole tradition grew out of the sensibility revealed in the impressionists' depiction of just such motifs. The title of Boulez's portrait of Mallarmé, *Pli selon pli*, is taken from "*Remémoration d'amis belges,*" a sonnet in which Mallarmé describes the fog being stripped *pli selon pli* from the city of Bruges by the rising sun, and Boulez seized the opportunity to depict an amorphous atmospheric effect. In *Don*, the first movement of *Pli selon pli*, fog and the hovering characteristic of fog are suggested by the long soft roll on the suspended cymbals that underlies much of the movement, the sudden motion of denser thickets of fog in a gust of wind by adding other rolls to the suspended cymbal roll.[51]

The fundamental conditions of Boulez's music are already met with the pedal projected by this roll: seamless rhythms covering the surface in depicting an amorphous atmospheric effect. We listen to music continuously in time, but the immediate structural patterns characteristic of most music unfold from one discrete point in time to another, from attack point to attack point. In music with a meter, patterns of attack unfold along a grid implicit in the music itself, and we are generally aware of the position of each attack within a hierarchy embodied in the grid. We are generally aware whether an attack occurs on the beat or subdivides it; on which beat within a measure an attack on the beat has occurred; and on which downbeat within a phrase an attack on the downbeat has occurred. Generally we are even aware of the beats in the absence of attacks to mark them. With the *sostenuto* styles of Boulez and Stockhausen, the attack points are still the most prominent points in the continuum, but a sustained suspense is engendered by withholding the metric framework that would enable us to predict where attacks might occur. We are oriented, not by the progressive unfolding of a metric grid, but by a seamlessly shifting dynamics. The music of Boulez and Stockhausen unfolds within the shallow space defined by the relationship of the literal surface to the points of attack lying deeper within it, but the dynamics continuously focus attention on the immediate rhythms of the surface, and "One is always cresting into one's present"[52]

The *sostenuto* styles of Boulez and Stockhausen entailed a transformation of phrasing and of the role played by dynamics in phrasing. During rehearsals for the first performance of *Le marteau sans maître* in 1955, Boulez encountered an unforeseen obstacle: the ingrained habits of his musicians. As he wrote to Stockhausen, "They always inject a kind of 'pathos' into their dynamics that it will be very difficult, I think, to uproot."[53] As Rosen writes, "Boulez's motifs are neutral agents: the expressive content of his music is conveyed through texture and dynamics. Schoenberg's motifs [. . .] imply direction and movement, tension and resolution. Boulez's are not emotionally charged."[54] The problem Boulez encountered was a tendency to treat the individual motive as an articulating shape in its own right, to supply it with its own individuating envelope. At least until the fairly recent past, musicians raised on music from the tonal tradition brought certain ingrained habits of phrasing to the table, and rightly so, habits that arose in coping with the expressive and formal demands of the repertory they played. The shaping supplied by the performer served to aid in the individuation of shapes at the level of the motive, the smallest possible shape, and at the level of the phrase, the basic formal unit. Subsuming the motive or phrase under the projection of a smooth and seamless whole was neither the immediate nor the primary function of the shaping, and there were audible joints in the continuum: "articulation" is derived from the Latin word for joint. *Carré, Punkte,* and *Pli selon pli* depend on a paradoxically continuous articulation: in projecting their *sostenuto* styles, the performer's immediate responsibility is not the delineation of discrete motives marking the progressive stages in an articulated process but the smooth projection of a seamless continuum.

In a chapter from their study of Monet significantly entitled "Moment and Duration," Gordon and Forge address the gradual shift in attitude characteristic of Monet in the 1880s that would increasingly inform his later paintings:

> There is something contradictory about Monet's increasing insistence on the moment on one hand and his increasingly long-drawn-out and labored procedure on the other. On the face of it there would seem to be an inevitable connection between a short-lived

motif and a rapid and spontaneous style. . . . With Monet, the fleeting moment is everything, yet he arrives at a point where he is no longer trying to capture that fleeting
moment so much as meditating on its passage. . . . In a sense his art had always been
about time. His rejection of the art of the museums in favor of working out of doors
was a polemical declaration and an argument about time: on an ideological level for
the *now* of modern life against the *then* of the museums, and on a practical and psy-
chological level for the simultaneity of motif and painting act and against the layered
reflective judgment implied by working in the studio. As he grew older, he turned
increasingly to "timeless" subjects—or rather to the time of the day and the time of the
seasons, eschewing man's time.[55]

As with any music, the structure of *Carré*, *Punkte*, and *Pli selon pli* depends on the
relationship of part to whole. If these extraordinarily ambitious works no longer
depend on the relationship of motive to phrase or of period to articulated whole
characteristic of eighteenth- and nineteenth-century music, they are sustained
meditations on the relationship of the "moment" to "duration," of the continuous seamless unfolding of patterns in time in the present to the vast and seamless expanse of time itself as directly exploited in these works. *Carré* and *Punkte*
are long slow movements characterized by their leisurely rates of unfolding—
Stravinsky complained that "Stockhausen's time scale is that of *Götterdämmerung*"[56]—
while *Pli selon pli* is a suite of five slow movements: the effect of sheer vastness
they produce is a direct consequence, not only of their spacious registration, but
of the level at which we move through them. As we have already seen with the
subject of the fugue from Beethoven's C-sharp Minor Quartet, the allover
designs characteristic of a *sostenuto* style require space in time. In *Carré*, *Punkte*,
and *Pli selon pli*, the "discourse" is brought to the surface, making the amount of
space available there seem all the more vast. We pursue their allover designs at
closer range than the metric patterns in tonal music, at which level the basic
shape is the sustained sound. With any *sostenuto* style, the continuous projection
of the seamless continuum shifts from one pitch to another with each new
attack, but—with Boulez and Stockhausen—points of attack never line up with
a regular pattern of metrical divisions, the envelope is never used merely to
smooth over points of articulation, and there is a constant recourse to sustained
pedals. In short, it is not only the sustained sounds in their music but the continuum projected by the sustained sounds that exhibits a continuous temporal
structure. There are more rapid patterns of attack, of course, instantaneous
effects, but—given a style so radically dependent on the immediate and continuous experience of the present—the instantaneous effect is only the other side
of the coin from the continuous unfolding of the sustained sound.

And with each sustained sound, the performer is faced with the same situation
as in the prelude to *Walküre*, where the smooth projection of the seamlessly fluc-
tuating dynamics is more fundamental than the shaping of motives. In *Carré*,
Punkte, and *Pli selon pli*, the tension that once fueled the dynamism characteristic of tonal music is subject to diffusion, not only through a spacious registration,

but also through the inexorable unfolding of the continuum itself. Like a drum roll or the tremolo in the *Walküre* prelude, the sustained elements in the continuum exert a steady pressure, the pressure continuously absorbing the tension generated by the intervallic patterns unfolding from attack point to attack point. Rapid patterns of attack aside, every pitch plays a role as a sustained sound before it ever enters into an intervallic relationship with other pitches in the same line, and our attention is constantly diverted from the relationship of attack point to attack point to the unfolding of the sustained sound as such. In other words, pitches are sufficiently widely separated both in space and in time to diffuse the tension inherent in the dissonant intervals.

This orientation goes a long way toward explaining the expressive character of the music of these composers. Techniques of meditation and particularly those taught within the Buddhist tradition generally entail a conscious and continuous focus on the seamless passage of time, on the seamless experience of consciousness in itself as distinct from the specific memories and considerations of future activity that arise in a conscious state, which—for the purposes of the exercise—are viewed as mere contingencies. Some meditation techniques even avail themselves of the drone as a point of focus, and the opening of *Carré* was probably inspired by the sound of Tibetan monks chanting. As Stockhausen was well aware, the listener's relationship to the continuum in *Carré* and *Punkte* is the relationship of the contemplative toward time. As he suggested in program notes for the first performance of *Carré* in 1960, "It is necessary to take time if one wishes to absorb this music; most of the changes take place very gently INSIDE the sound. I wish that this music could impart [. . .] an awareness that we have a lot time, if we take it."[57] Entirely at ease with the loss of faith characteristic of many an educated Westerner of his generation, Boulez is unconcerned with gaining access to the divine, but he was no less preoccupied with the ethical, ritual, and communal aspects of music than Stockhausen: these concerns replaced self-expression narrowly defined at the expressive center of the music of both composers.[58]

***

The evolution of Boulez's and Stockhausen's characteristic *sostenuto* styles was not necessarily accompanied by any return to the kinds of larger gestures characteristic of tonal music. Boulez was always interested in the kind of ornamental cantillation that resurfaces in the rhapsodic vocal writing in *Pli selon pli*—it is already evident in the explosive and ecstatic vocal writing in *Le visage nuptial*, the most fully realized work from Boulez's first period—but Stockhausen's textured and pulsating lines are not necessarily used to inscribe larger motivic shapes. While the lines in metric music unfold attack by attack, in the music of both Boulez and Stockhausen the extension of a sustained note is already a line, and, in *Carré* and *Punkte*, the isolated point characteristic of the pointillist texture is drawn out, covering the surface. Indeed, *Punkte* literally subsumes an early pointillist score from 1952 and was composed in part by extending the points found in it, engulfing the surface in swarms of continuous activity.[59]

In projecting their forms, Boulez and Stockhausen made an unprecedentedly extensive use of the tremolo, the trill, the roll, and lines projected by double or triple tonguing wind or brass instruments, in short, of textured lines, but the textured lines spun out using these instrumental techniques are generally spun out of single consistent patterns. Stockhausen not only made use of such textured lines, he developed analogous lines that change shape as they unfold. Examples include the textured lines for violins, trumpets, and bassoons respectively found at rehearsal number 68 in *Punkte*. The parts for these instruments are extracted from the full score and given as example 14.4.[60]

The line projected by the violins is based on an oscillating figure. Violins 5–8 trill on E♭ and D an octave above high E♭, periodically renewing their trill with accented re-attacks. Violins 3 and 4 project the same alternation with quarter note triplet harmonics. Violins 1 and 2 project the alternation of E♭ and D in two-part counterpoint, connecting E♭ to D with slow *glissandi* that cross at different speeds, each sliding line blurring the other as well as the other violin parts. There is too much activity in a very high register within a narrow band of frequency for us to perceive the continuity projected as counterpoint, and we perceive it as a kind of textured line that changes shape as it unfolds.

The textured lines projected by the bassoons and trumpets depend on elaborate cross rhythms. The three bassoons flutter tongue a rapidly pulsating G♯, the rate of pulsation gradually slowing as the line unfolds. As it slows, the three bassoons separate, and the following cross rhythms occur in succession:

7 against 8
6 against 7 against 8
5 against 6 against 7
4 against 5 against 6
3 against 4 against 5
2 against 3 against 4
1 against 2 against 3

When the bassoons reach 3 against 4 against 5, the trumpets enter flutter tonguing high G with the following accelerating series of cross rhythms:

3 against 4 against 5
4 against 5 against 6
5 against 6 against 8

Nevertheless, the point of this passage is not the projection of a series of complicated cross rhythms: the pulsation is too rapid and the attacks are too dense for the cross rhythms to be perceived as such. The rhythms of these lines unfold, not at the level of the beat in music with a meter, but on the surface. Like the

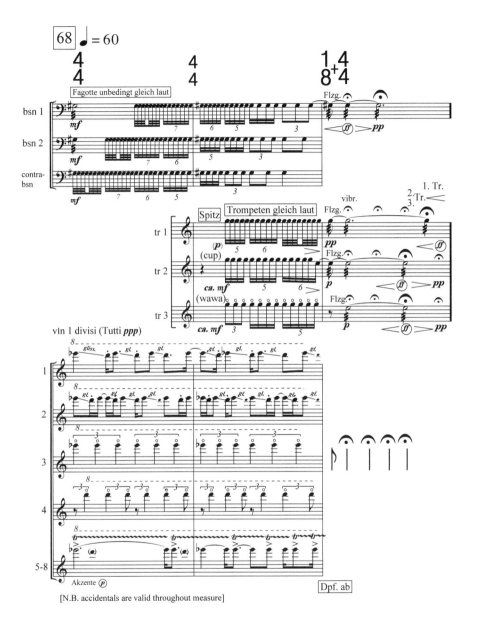

Example 14.4. Stockhausen, *Punkte*, rehearsal no. 68, parts for bassoon, trumpet, and violin only. Used by permission. © Copyright 1963, 1966 by Universal Edition (London) Ltd., London/UE 19474.

two's against three's characteristic of Wagner's cross hatching (which do unfold at the level of the beat), Stockhausen's cross rhythms set up interference patterns that define distinctive textured lines characterized by a dense and irregular accelerating or decelerating pulsation. Stockhausen's textured lines are interesting not so much for their "individual [constituent] forms" as for their "collective density and rhythm," as William Rubin once said of the allover patterning in one of Miró's paintings.[61] Like Monet's or Pollock's, Stockhausen's surfaces are covered with a gradually shifting field of atomized sensations, and the shifting affects the rhythms they project. Stockhausen's shifting textured lines generate the kind of sustained tension characteristic of a drum roll, but— gradually accelerating, decelerating, and changing shape—they are more elastic than a drum roll, and the tension fluctuates accordingly.

***

With the *sostenuto* styles of Boulez and Stockhausen, the relationship of point to span was transformed. As we move through traditional music, the meter provides a fixed series of reference points and other points of reference emerge in time: the first downbeat of the phrase, cadence points, and so forth. These points establish a stable framework much of which pre-exists, as it were, our discovery through listening of the structure ultimately built on it, a framework dependent not only on a metric grid, but also on the expectations of future events that the operations of tonal syntax arouse, events often accurately predictable at the distance of such spans as phrases. With the seamless and unmeasured continuums of Boulez and Stockhausen, the only fixed point of reference is a point "stable within instability," to borrow from John Ashbery again, "a ping-pong ball secure on its jet of water,"[62] our seamlessly shifting vantage from the present moment: the perspective of the impressionist painter. Stockhausen forces the issue with the "stereophonic brass chords" section from *Gruppen*, a passage somewhat anomalous for *Gruppen* itself but entirely representative of Stockhausen's *sostenuto* style.

Gruppen is scored for 109 players divided into three roughly identical orchestral groups, each led by its own conductor. Orchestra I is seated to the left, orchestra II in front, and orchestra III to the right of the audience, an arrangement that irresistibly lent itself to various antiphonal and stereophonic effects. The most immediately spectacular stereophonic effects can be found at one measure after rehearsal number 119 in the printed score, at track 32 of the compact disc reissue of Stockhausen's own recording of the work.[63] In this passage, three groups of brass instruments seated in different locations pass a series of sustained chords back and forth, and the sounds they produce seem to migrate through space, just as a signal will seem to move from one stereo speaker to another if the volume is gradually increased in one speaker while gradually being lowered in the other. What raises this passage above the level of novel sound effects, dazzling as they are, however, is its rhythmic structure.

Example 14.5. Stockhausen, *Gruppen*, from one measure after rehearsal no. 119.
a: Crescendo Patterns

A progression of four chords, a reduced score of this passage is given as example 14.5. The passage is scored for three identical groups of brass instruments made up of pairs of trumpets, horns, and trombones. The initial attacks of the four chords are numbered from 1 to 4. The initial double *sforzando* attack of each chord is reinforced with a sharp attack by the piano and snare drum, which lends it a percussive edge absent from subsequent reattacks. (The parts for piano and snare drum have been omitted from the example.) The progression is transcribed in $\frac{4}{4}$ time, but the notated meter is only a convenience intended to facilitate performance. In fact, the passage is unmeasured, its temporal structure dependent on the dynamics. Stockhausen varies the rates at which the dynamics unfold, pulling time as if it were taffy, and the tension fluctuates accordingly.

The attack at measure 1 sets the stage for all of the effects in the passage (ex. 14.5). Each chord is initially attacked by two of the three groups, one group attacking it double *sforzando* with a short percussive attack reinforced by the piano and snare drum, the other attacking it triple *piano* and sustaining it, gradually swelling to *fortissimo*. The triple *piano* attack is wholly inaudible in the context of the sharper double *sforzando* attack, and the audience perceives a sharp attack in one location prolonged by a swell from triple *piano* in another.

After the initial attack, the pattern inscribed by the *crescendi* applied to chord 1 unfolds, not from attack point to attack point, but from *fortissimo* peak to *fortissimo* peak as summarized at example 14.5a. Once a *fortissimo* peak is reached in one location, the sound stops only to emerge from beneath the peak in another. The periodic cessation of sound divides the continuum into a series of smoothly elided and overlapping shapes, and it is the shapes we pursue. The prominence lent to the peaks is not intrinsic to the peaks but contingent on the cessation of sound that follows them. It is impossible for us as listeners to measure the relationship of *fortissimo* peak to *fortissimo* peak with any precision. The peaks are not marked by attacks, and, unlike beats, the points where they lie are not privileged in advance, while the shapes are subsumed by a continuum we never stop pursuing.

As each of the three groups sustains chord 2, it swells from triple *piano* to *fortissimo* before shrinking back to triple *piano*. As the chord approaches inaudibility in one location, it begins to swell imperceptibly from triple *piano* in another, and the sound seems to migrate through space. As with chord 1, the dynamics unfold a series of shapes defined by their *fortissimo* peaks, but the peaks are now assimilated to seamlessly shifting arcs of volume. At first we are aware that the volume is increasing. Then, as the volume begins to recede, we become aware of the new trend. We can infer the existence of the peaks from our experience of these trends, but we are not aware of the precise points in time when the trends are reversed. We only become aware that a peak was reached after the volume begins to recede.

***

> ... today is uncharted,
> ... reluctant as any landscape
> To yield what are laws of perspective
> After all only to the painter's deep
> Mistrust.
>
> —John Ashbery
> "Self-Portrait in a Convex Mirror"[64]

In discussing Monet's eye, Gordon and Forge remind us that "Only occasionally in ordinary life do we catch glimpses of the world as pure appearance in which identities are, as it were, loosened from their moorings and floating free—as perhaps when we are just rising out of sleep and the room around us drifts into view like a flotilla of nameless patches of color," but that is the aspect of experience that Monet wanted to paint.[65] We find an analogous profusion of detail, a similarly lifelike and quasi-unsystematic jumble of uninterpreted regularities and irregularities in the unbroken fabric of *Carré*, *Punkte*, and *Pli selon pli*. Embodying a similar naturalism, these works depend on a similar shift from "structure" to "experience" at the most immediate level of time and memory.

We can never do more than approximate distances in time or space without the aid of tools for measurement, but that does not prevent us from recognizing similarities and differences in the seamless profusion of information that our ongoing experience throws up as we experience it. Although it is impossible for us as listeners to measure the distance between the *fortissimo* peaks in the "stereophonic brass chords" section from Stockhausen's *Gruppen* with any precision, Stockhausen's music is not predicated on that kind of measurement, and we can readily distinguish similarities and differences within the variation on the surface in Stockhausen's music as we experience them in time.

As Stravinsky once said, "We are located in time constantly in a tonal-system work, but we may only 'go through' a polyphonic work, whether Josquin's *Duke Hercules Mass* or a serially composed non-tonal system work [by Boulez or Stockhausen]."[66] Because of its periodic divisions and the range of its plotting, when we listen to the first movement of the *Eroica* we grasp the whole with a certain clarity, experiencing its overall trajectory as a single dynamic and palpable design. Adrift in an unmeasured time, we are too close to the surface in the music of Boulez and Stockhausen to gain the kind of perspective that the *Eroica* affords, and—to quote Stravinsky again—Boulez and Stockhausen are not "concerned with 'dynamic passage through,' which betrays a dramatic concept, Greek in origin."[67] With Boulez and Stockhausen, the overall framework that once subsumed the local details in a hierarchical arrangement is replaced by a seamless continuum issuing in forms that are monolithic in character: for all of the surface variation in their music, there is a certain monotony at the level of the overall form if only in a literal sense. The ultimate vehicle for through composition, the continuum in their music does not depend on any inherited rhetoric or throw up any traditional formal routines. The potential for the generation of new material is encoded at every point and can be used to create spans of any length, but there is no intrinsic capacity for the articulation of form or the generation of closure: the ongoing articulation of form is replaced by "invention in a perpetual state of becoming."[68]

With its sustained tension and sheer breadth, the form of the final movement of *Pli selon pli* depends on the intrinsic character of its continuum. Most of *Tombeau* is consumed by a vast and monolithic *crescendo* that slowly and steadily gains in textural and contrapuntal complexity as it unfolds before breaking off after some fifteen minutes: it is the monolithic inexorability of its unfolding over so vast an expanse of time that makes the experience of *Tombeau* so gripping.

In this repertory, form is more dependent than ever on the imaginative capacity of the composer, and the generation of closure at the end of Stockhausen's *Punkte*—the development of a convincing means for bringing the piece to an imposing climax at the very end—is a compositional *tour de force* in the context of Stockhausen's style. We can only "go through" *Carré*, which does not end but simply stops.

Stockhausen implicitly acknowledged this aspect of *Carré* in program notes for the first performance in 1960, writing that "each moment [in *Carré*] stands alone," further suggesting that one could listen in and out at will.[69] The implication here that the overall continuity in *Carré* is less fundamental than the continuity in *Gruppen*, *Punkte*, *Don*, or *Tombeau* is not entirely fair to the work itself: tightly through-composed and almost monomaniacally focused, *Carré* is of a piece with *Punkte* and the outer movements of *Pli selon pli*, and no less stern a critic than Stravinsky felt that it represented an advance over *Gruppen*.[70] Nevertheless, Stockhausen's remarks are tacit acknowledgement that the form of *Carré* is open, that we have only a cut from a potentially indefinitely extensible form.[71]

With Boulez, the single closed form is replaced with a series of open works or successive versions of a single work spun out of the same material, an approach analogous to Monet's. For Monet, the motif was inexhaustible, not a definitive form but—depending on the period in his life—a momentary impression of or one of a potentially infinite number of meditations on a form that could never be definitively fixed. This ultimately led to the series paintings of the 1890s: series of paintings of, for example, grain stacks, the façade of the Rouen cathedral, or a row of poplar trees viewed from a single or similar vantage point in changing light.[72]

To the French art-viewing public of the 1870s, Monet's paintings "seemed not to be *of* anything. Neither anecdotal nor heroic, topographical nor inspiring, they seemed to have no purpose except to be looked at."[73] Unmeasured, unarticulated, and eschewing the rhetoric that had been fundamental to Western music at least since the late eighteenth century, the forms of Boulez and Stockhausen are similarly uncommunicative, at least through the traditional channels. Whether in painting or in music, the allover design represents the triumph of the decorative. *Carré, Punkte,* and *Pli selon pli* are not "expressive" in the traditional sense but decorative meditations, although the music of Boulez and Stockhausen can be distinguished in part on the basis of national character. The refined and often scintillating surfaces in *Pli selon pli* betray a fascination with sensory experience as the fundamental vehicle for art characteristic of a significant part of the French modernist tradition, a preoccupation with color, texture, sonority, transparency, and evanescence of a piece with Monet's absorption by the luminous sensation. Boulez exhibits a Frenchman's disinclination to wear his heart on his sleeve, and his music also exhibits the detachment and reticence, the elusiveness and mystery, characteristic of a certain French tradition. Stockhausen made use of a more traditional palette than Boulez—his surfaces are less scintillating than Boulez's—but, if anything, he was more ruthless in his acceptance of the fundamental conditions of his continuum, more consistently monomaniacal in projecting it. Stockhausen's music ultimately stems from a transcendental strain within the German Romantic tradition, and—in diffusing the tensions characteristic of the hyper-expressive chromaticism he inherited from Schoenberg and Berg—Stockhausen's continuums embody a transformed Romantic rhetoric. Exhibiting an explicitly inward quality, *Carré* and *Punkte* are intensely sustained explorations of inner space.

Notes

Epigraph. John Ashbery, "Self-Portrait in a Convex Mirror," in *Self Portrait in a Convex Mirror* (New York: Penguin Books, 1976), 70.

1. Robert Rosenblum, *Cubism and Twentieth-Century Art* (New York: Harry N. Abrams, 1976), 71–72.

2. See Kirk Varnedoe, "Comet: Jackson Pollock's Life and Work," in *Jackson Pollock,* exhibition catalogue, ed. Varnedoe and Pepe Karmel (New York: Museum of Modern Art, 1998), 85, n. 206.

3. Pierre Boulez, "Corruption in the Censers," in *Notes of an Apprenticeship,* trans. Herbert Weinstock (New York: Alfred A. Knopf, 1968), 27.

4. Robert Gordon and Andrew Forge, *Monet* (New York: Harry N. Abrams, 1983), 49. On the *enveloppe* see also Anthea Callen, *The Art of Impressionism: Painting Technique and the Making of Modernity* (New Haven and London: Yale University Press, 2000), 187–90.

5. Callen, *The Art of Impressionism,* 177.

6. Studies specifically addressing the techniques of the impressionist painters include Callen, *The Art of Impressionism*; Richard R. Brettell, *Impression: Painting Quickly in France, 1860–1890* (New Haven and London: Yale University Press, 2000); and John House, *Impressionism: Paint and Politics* (New Haven and London: Yale University Press, 2004).

7. Callen, *The Art of Impressionism,* 156.

8. To a skeptical public an impressionist painting appeared unfinished because the brushwork had not been integrated within a smooth "licked" surface, within the

"*fini*," the glossy surface characteristic of the polished academic artwork as opposed to the oil sketch. See Callen, *The Art of Impressionism*, also Charles Rosen and Henri Zerner, *Romanticism and Realism: The Mythology of Nineteenth-Century Art* (New York: Viking Press, 1984), 205–32.

9. William Rubin, "Jackson Pollock and the Modern Tradition," in *Jackson Pollock: Interviews, Articles, and Reviews*, ed. Pepe Karmel (New York: Museum of Modern Art, 1999), 134.

10. Rubin, "Jackson Pollock," 142.

11. See Richard Schiff, *Cézanne and the End of Impressionism* (Chicago: University of Chicago Press, 1984), 3–13.

12. Every temperament is conditioned by a history, a culture, a tradition, but the impressionists emphasized those innate and irreducible aspects of temperament that could not be taught at the academy, discounting techniques traditionally taught there and even tradition itself. See Joachim Pissarro, *Pioneering Modern Painting: Cézanne and Pissarro* (New York: Museum of Modern Art, 2005), 20–28.

13. See Schapiro, *Impressionism*, 23–24, and the various references to the sensation in Schiff, *Cézanne and the End of Impressionism.*

14. Rubin, "Jackson Pollock," 133.

15. Rubin, "Jackson Pollock," 121. Rubin's study addresses virtually every aspect of Pollock's drip paintings including their relationship to impressionism, analytic cubism, surrealist automatism, and Monet's late style.

16. Donald Judd, "Jackson Pollock," in *Jackson Pollock: Interviews, Articles, and Reviews*, ed. Pepe Karmel (New York: Museum of Modern Art, 1999), 117.

17. Robert Hughes, "Jackson Pollock," in Hughes, *Nothing if not Critical: Selected Essays on Art and Artists* (New York: Alfred A. Knopf, 1990), 219.

18. See Rubin, "Jackson Pollock," 134.

19. See Pepe Karmel, "Pollock at Work: The Films and Photographs of Hans Namuth," in *Jackson Pollock*, exhibition catalogue, ed. Kirk Varnedoe and Karmel (New York: Museum of Modern Art, 1998), 100–101.

20. Hughes, "Jackson Pollock," 218.

21. Rubin, "Jackson Pollock," 127.

22. Rubin, "Jackson Pollock," 150–65, traces Pollock's conception of space and its effect to analytic cubism.

23. Rubin, "Jackson Pollock," 159.

24. "Drip technique" is something of a misnomer. Pollock made use of thinned oil paint and commercial enamels, normally dribbling paint from a loaded brush. The technique did not originate with Pollock: Max Ernst claimed that Pollock had stolen it from him. Ernst's and other precedents are discussed in Rubin, "Jackson Pollock," 163–64, 166–68, and Jeffrey Wechsler, "Abstract Expressionism: Other Dimensions," in *Abstract Expressionism: Other Dimensions. An Introduction to Small-Scale Painterly Abstraction in America, 1940–1965*, exhibition catalogue, ed. Jeffrey Wechsler (New Brunswick, NJ: Jane Vorhees Zimmerli Art Museum, Rutgers University, 1989), 102–4.

25. Rubin, "Jackson Pollock," 127.

26. Frank O'Hara, *Jackson Pollock* (New York: George Braziller, 1959), 26.

27. William Rothstein, *Phrase Rhythm in Tonal Music* (New York: Schirmer Books, 1989), 11–12, despairs of salvaging the term "phrasing" from the vagaries of usage, but interesting insights into the topic are sprinkled throughout his book.

28. See David Gable, "Ramifying Connections: An Interview with Pierre Boulez," *Journal of Musicology* 4 (1985–86): 111–12.

29. Gordon and Forge, *Monet*, 49.

30. Richard Wagner, Letter to Mathilde Wesendonck, October 29, 1859, *Selected Letters of Richard Wagner*, trans. and ed. Stewart Spencer and Barry Millington (New York: W. W. Norton, 1988), 474–75.

31. Pierre Boulez, "The *Ring*: Time Re-Explored," *Orientations* (Cambridge, MA: Harvard University Press, 1986), 273.

32. Cosima Wagner, diary entry for April 27, 1879, *Cosima Wagner's Diaries, Volume II: 1878–1883* (New York: Harcourt Brace Jovanovich, 1980), 297.

33. Pierre Boulez, "Das Rheingold," booklet accompanying the compact disc reissue of Boulez's recording of the opera, Wagner, *Das Rheingold* (Philips Classics 434 421–22, 1992), 14.

34. Stravinsky comments on the relationship of these composers to Berg in a review of Stockhausen's *Carré* anthologized in Igor Stravinsky and Robert Craft, *Themes and Episodes* (New York: Alfred A. Knopf, 1966), 11–13. A remarkable treatment of the evolution of Boulez's style through the composition of *Pli selon pli* drawing on the unpublished Boulez-Stockhausen correspondence is Philippe Albèra, ". . . *l'éruptif multiple sursautement de la claret* . . . ," in *Pli selon pli de Pierre Boulez: Entretiens et etudes*, ed. Philippe Albèra (Geneva: Éditions Contrechamps, 2003), 59–82.

35. À *la limite du pays fertile* is the French translation of the title of a painting by Paul Klee, *An der Grenze des Fruchtlandes*, that Boulez used as the title for an early essay and contemplated using as a title for the *Structures pour deux pianos, premier livre*.

36. Albèra, " . . . *l'éruptif multiple* . . . ," 73, my translation.

37. Karlheinz Stockhausen, "Von Webern zu Debussy: Bemerkungen zur Statistischen Form," in Stockhausen, *Texte zur Instrumentalen und Elektronischen Musik, Band 1, Aufsätze 1952–1962 zur Theorie des Komponierens* (Cologne: M. DuMont-Buchverlag, 1963), 75–85.

38. Karlheinz Stockhausen, *Carré*, program note, in Karl H. Wörner, *Stockhausen: Life and Work*, intr., trans., ed. Bill Hopkins (Berkeley: University of California Press, 1973), 42–44. The translation from which I quote is included with the compact disc reissue of the composer's recording of *Carré* (Kürten: Stockhausen Verlag CD 5, 1992).

39. An early discussion of the programmatic dimension of *Pli selon pli* by a friend of Boulez's who had heard early performances of the work's various movements is Michel Butor, "Mallarmé according to Boulez," in *Inventory, Essays by Michel Butor*, trans. Richard Howard (New York: Simon and Schuster, 1968), 294–304.

40. Robert Craft, "Boulez: Teacher at the Philharmonic," in *Prejudices in Disguise* (New York: Alfred A. Knopf, 1974), 203.

41. Charles Rosen, "From the Troubadours to Sinatra: Part II," review of *The Oxford History of Western Music*, by Richard Taruskin, *New York Review of Books*, March 9, 2006, 48.

42. Robert Piencikowski, "*Tombeau: extrait de Pli selon pli de Pierre Boulez*" in *Pli selon pli de Pierre Boulez: Entretiens et études*, ed. Philippe Albèra (Geneva: Éditions Contrechamps, 2003), 46.

43. Charles Rosen, "The Piano Music," in *Pierre Boulez: A Symposium*, ed. William Glock (London: Eulenburg Books, 1986), 87.

44. David Gable, "Ramifying Connections: An Interview with Pierre Boulez," *Journal of Musicology*, 4 (Winter 1985–86), 111.

45. Boulez's *Structures pour deux pianos, premier livre* (1951–52), is the straw man in my argument. I make no attempt to do justice to such "pointillist" but fully realized scores as Stockhausen's *Kontrapunkte* (1952–53). Stockhausen's evolution from early derivative scores through the early pointillist scores and on to the epochal *Gruppen* resembles the evolution of many a young composer. Boulez's detour through the doctrinaire integral serialism of *Polyphonie X* (1950–51) and *Structures* is more puzzling to this extent: during the same period, Boulez was already capable of a score as ambitious and fully realized as *Le visage nuptial* (1951–52), a work that is finally coming into its own in the revision of 1989.

46. Claude Debussy, *La mer*, reprint of the first edition (New York: Dover Publications, 1983)

47. T. J. Clark, *Farewell to an Idea: Episodes from a History of Modernism* (New Haven and London: Yale University Press, 1999), 310.

48. Arnold Schoenberg, "Composition with Twelve Tones," in *Style and Idea: Selected Writings of Arnold Schoenberg*, ed. Leonard Stein, trans. Leo Black (London: Faber and Faber, 1975), 223. Robert Morgan discusses the fundamental role played by spatial metaphors in the conception of twentieth-century music in "Musical Time/Musical Space," *Critical Inquiry* 6 (1980), 527–38. Rosen addresses the "gift for spatial metaphor" revealed in Boulez's music in "The Piano Music," 94–95.

49. According to Rosen, "The Piano Music," 87–88, "For Schoenberg the series is a quarry for motifs, and it is the motifs that provide the energy for the piece, that have a generating force. They provide the energy by implying sequential motion or—Schoenberg's practice is both complex and occasionally contradictory—by a mimesis of the tonal functions of dissonance and consonance, which therefore push toward resolution."

50. Meyer Schapiro, *Impressionism*, 23.

51. The suspended cymbal roll is first introduced at rehearsal number 6 in the first published edition of *Pli selon pli: Don*, one measure before rehearsal number 6 in the revised edition, just before 2:36 on the compact disc reissue of Boulez's first (1969) recording of *Pli selon pli* (Sony SMK 68 335, 1995).

52. Ashbery, "Self-Portrait in a Convex Mirror," 70.

53. Albèra, ". . . *l'éruptif multiple . . .* ," 81, my translation.

54. Rosen, "The Piano Music," 88.

55. Gordon and Forge, *Monet*, 191.

56. Igor Stravinsky and Robert Craft, *Retrospectives and Conclusions* (New York: Alfred A. Knopf, 1969), 94.

57. Karlheinz Stockhausen, *Carré*, program note.

58. In a fascinating letter to Stockhausen of 1954 published in Albèra, ". . . *l'éruptif multiple . . .* ," 77–78, Boulez seeks to dissuade the younger composer from embarking on the composition of a Mass on the grounds that the era of belief in the Evangelist has passed. Writing under the influence of the metaphysics implicit in Mallarmé's *Igitur* and *Un coup de dès*, he outlines a view of the laic and ritual function of music. Albèra, 76–80, relates Boulez's views to an interest in Artaud's theatre and the ritual aspects of the performance of Balinese music.

59. This process is briefly discussed in a note accompanying the printed score of Karlheinz Stockhausen, *Punkte für Orchester* (1952/62), Werk Nr. 1/2, revised edition (Vienna: Universal Edition, 1995).

60. Stockhausen, *Punkte für Orchester*, 34, rehearsal no. 68.

61. William Rubin, *Miró in the Collection of the Museum of Modern Art* (New York: Museum of Modern Art, 1973), 81, makes this claim about motifs in Miró's "The Beautiful Bird Revealing the Unknown to a Pair of Lovers" (1941).

62. Ashbery, "Self-Portrait in a Convex Mirror," 70.

63. Karlheinz Stockhausen, Nr. 6 *Gruppen für drei Orchester* (London: Universal Edition, 1963); compact disc reissue of the 1965 recording with Stockhausen, Michael Gielen, and Bruno Maderna conducting the West German Radio Symphony (Stockhausen Verlag CD 5, 1993).

64. Ashbery, "Self-Portrait in a Convex Mirror," 72.

65. Gordon and Forge, *Monet*, 56.

66. Igor Stravinsky and Robert Craft, *Conversations with Igor Stravinsky* (Garden City: Doubleday, 1959), 23.

67. Igor Stravinsky and Robert Craft, *Dialogues and a Diary* (Garden City: Doubleday, 1963), 27–28.

68. Pierre Boulez describing Schoenberg's *Erwartung* in *Stocktakings from an Apprenticeship*, trans. Stephen Walsh, with an introduction by Robert Piencikowski (Oxford: Clarendon Press, 1991), 283.

69. Stockhausen, *Carré*, program note. Stockhausen removed the suggestion that one could listen in and out at will when he reprinted his program note in the booklet accompanying the compact disc reissue of the recording of the first performance.

70. Stravinsky and Craft, *Themes and Episodes*, 11.

71. Schoenberg's *Erwartung* is a kind of precedent for this approach. In Pierre Boulez and Michel Fano, "A Conversation," trans. Thomas Repensek, *October* 14 (1980): 102, Boulez remarks that "*Erwartung* really went farther [than *Pierrot lunaire*] in combining all the formal elements in a continuous line that is remarkably long for something as chaotic as this twenty-five-minute work." "*Erwartung . . .* is for me the prototype of a kind of open form whose development is unknown, . . . a sort of rift in time, a scrap of time that ends. Moreover, the end of *Erwartung* always leaves people up in the air, because, in effect, it is an end without conclusion."

72. On the series paintings see Gordon and Forge, *Monet*, 191–217, and Paul Hayes Tucker, *Monet in the 90's: The Series Paintings*, exhibition catalogue (Boston: Museum of Fine Arts, 1989).

73. Gordon and Forge, *Monet*, 223.

Part Seven

Criticism and the Critic

Chapter Fifteen

Rosen's Modernist Haydn

James Webster

Modernism in music emerged roughly between 1890 and 1914, when it was associated primarily with expressionism, the avant-garde, and the rejection of methods of tonal, formal, and rhythmic organization that had long been taken for granted. During the second and third quarters of the twentieth century it enjoyed a dominant position, marked by increasing consolidation of musical techniques (and the necessary accompanying theories) and increasing prestige among critics and scholars. Around 1970 or so, however, new and incompatible trends began to emerge, including a withering away of dogmatic serialism; minimalism, "downtown" style, and non-Western influences; and altogether an increasingly pluralistic scene. For better and worse, these trends were eventually gathered under the sloganeering but apparently inescapable banner of "postmodernism." Today, modernism is no longer regarded as the inevitable goal of progress in music, as was believed by its votaries during its heyday. It has taken its place as no more, but also no less, than one of the major style periods in the *past* history of music, following the Renaissance, the Baroque, and the Romantic, and preceding the postmodern.[1] Notwithstanding the vast literature, there has been as far as I see relatively little acknowledgement that in the arts postmodernism is not merely a sensibility, but a historical period—the one we are living in.[2]

I inflict this potted history on the reader because it is relevant to my topic. Charles Rosen, born in 1927 and coming of age after World War II, is an important modernist figure in his own right. His significance in this respect goes beyond his obvious roles as a performer of contemporary music and collaborator with major composers (for example Pierre Boulez and Elliott Carter) and as an influential writer on twentieth-century music (for example his classic *Arnold Schoenberg*).[3] Indeed his entire sensibility (as far as I see) is modernist, whatever his subject, and exhibits all the virtues—and some of the limitations—of that orientation. I shall explore this topic with respect to his writings on Haydn, in conjunction with other important recent studies of Haydn's music.

During the twentieth century, Haydn's reputation exhibited complex (and therefore interesting) relationships to the sensibility of modernism. From roughly the mid-nineteenth century through the early twentieth, his music had been more or less marginalized, except for only a few late string quartets and symphonies and *The Creation*. Around 1950, however, a notable "Haydn Renaissance" began in musical life, proclaimed by H. C. Robbins Landon and others (in Landon's case justifiably). The same renewal of interest applies to Haydn scholarship. In contrast to the other Germanic "great composers," who were the subjects of thematic catalogues, complete editions, and foundational biographies during the second half of the nineteenth century, the first comprehensive Haydn catalogue ("Hoboken") and the first successful complete edition (*Joseph Haydn: Werke* [Henle], now approximately 85 percent complete) were not begun until after World War II, and we still lack a satisfactory life-and-works biography. In addition, *JHW* has been supplemented by numerous good editions of individual genres, notably Landon's of the complete symphonies. Similarly, not until the pioneering work of Jens Peter Larsen in the 1930s were comprehensive source studies and publications of documents, and the many problems of attribution and chronology, systematically pursued; in the last half century these desiderata have been largely met. Thus the Haydn Renaissance originated and celebrated its first great successes during the flowering of modernism.[4]

To see that this conjunction is more than a coincidence, one need only turn to Rosen's *The Classical Style* (1971). It is not merely that this volume was written by a modernist toward the end of the modernist age and that it decisively influenced an entire generation of readers (including myself); nor merely that it was the first sustained critical study that in principle took Haydn's music as seriously as that of Mozart and Beethoven. (The qualification "in principle" is addressed below.) It is that Rosen understood Haydn's music as *intrinsically* modern:

> This sense that the movement, the development, and the dramatic course of a work all can be found latent in the material, that the material can be made to release its charged force so that the music no longer [merely] unfolds, as in the Baroque, but is literally impelled from within—this sense was Haydn's greatest contribution to the history of music. We may love him for many other things, but this new conception of musical art changed all that followed it.[5]

It would be difficult to imagine a pithier or more forceful statement of the modernist belief in the autonomous character and self-generating procedures of high art (though Rosen does not use the term *modern* itself). Also noteworthy is his explicit historical assertion that Haydn's discovery (or invention) "changed all that followed it." Nor is this empty rhetoric; it lies embedded in a densely argued chapter on Haydn's string quartets, featuring a dozen brilliantly analyzed examples from the decade 1781 to 1790 (Opus 33 through Opus 64), all demonstrating how Haydn's music is indeed "impelled from within." Here as so often Rosen productively takes off from Donald Francis Tovey, who wrote in 1929 (i.e., during an earlier subperiod of modernism), in a sentence that has received far less attention than it deserves, of the String Quartet, Op. 20, no. 2:

> Haydn shows . . . that if composition within the time-scale of the sonata had not absorbed his interest, he could easily have produced a music that moved like a modern symphonic poem. His art of composition is a general power which creates art-forms, not a routine derived from the practice of *a priori* schemes.[6]

Rosen's chapter on Haydn's quartets gains additional force from its position as the first of many on individual genres by Haydn or Mozart, following a long, general, and equally modernist chapter on "the coherence of ["Classical"] musical language."[7] Here again, a plurality of the examples are by Haydn, including the famous demonstration (pp. 83–88) of the structural homology between an Andante theme in the Piano Trio, Hob. XV:19, and a much longer, fast section later in the same movement.[8] In this way too Haydn's late instrumental music is implicitly singled out as a *locus classicus* of musical modernism. One can only agree, although in my case this belief is grounded in the larger intellectual-historical context as well as stylistic aspects, and (in contrast to Rosen) I reject the term and concept *Classical style.*[9]

But if the Haydn Renaissance was thus multifariously linked to modernism, how shall we explain the continuing rise in his prestige during the postmodernist years since 1970, as measured both by performances and popular esteem and by reputation among scholars and critics? The easiest explanation, and not necessarily the worst, is that modernism is not dead at all, but lives on in a state of continual tension with postmodern sensibilities, or as Jürgen Habermas's eternally deferred "unfinished project."[10] I surmise that Rosen believes something of the sort. Another possible explanation is that the vicissitudes of reception and reputation are not bound by crude notions of *Zeitgeist* but, like all artistic phenomena, possess "relative autonomy."[11] There is no necessary contradiction between the continuing increase in Haydn's prestige since 1970 and fundamental changes in the general sensibilities of intellectual-cultural life.

Be that as it may, the question naturally arises: if it made sense in 1970 to view Haydn's music as modern, should it not make equally good sense today to view it as postmodern? A few recent contributions do this, albeit more often implicitly than explicitly. George Edwards has written about the "nonsense" (i.e., lack of closure) of his endings, Daniel K. L. Chua about "chemical experiments" in his instrumental music, Tom Beghin about the rhetoric (not the structure) of his musical forms, Nancy November about vocality in his string quartets.[12] More common have been approaches that, although inspired by postmodern ideas (especially the increasing "contextualization" of music), do not treat his music as intrinsically postmodern. Some writers attempt to deconstruct binary oppositions that under modernism were taken for granted but now seem rigid and counter-productive. Michael Spitzer wishes to explode the distinction between the so-called *Sturm und Drang* period around 1770 and the supposedly shallower music that followed, and I have interrogated (as they say) the supposed distinction between "art" and "entertainment" in Haydn's symphonies of the 1770s.[13] Others emphasize social-political aspects of his music, especially the operas, oratorios, and other public genres.[14]

Arguably the most important development in recent Haydn criticism is the increasing tendency to interpret his music in terms of its intellectual-cultural contexts. An important step (albeit in no obvious way postmodern), because it shattered the traditional image of Haydn as an unreflective or naïve composer, involves research into his library and his literary interests, and his aesthetics.[15] David P. Schroeder interprets him (sensibly enough) as an Enlightenment figure whose intention is seen (more controversially) as the conveying of moral instruction in his music.[16] The most important work of this kind is the recent *Painting the Cannon's Roar* by Thomas Tolley. Tolley argues persuasively that Haydn was not only the first artist of any kind to attain celebrity throughout Europe during his own lifetime, but more than any other individual was responsible for the turn to a new sense of *public* art around 1800, in both music and the visual arts. Tolley's depiction of all this as having taken place in "the age of Haydn" resonates with my own interpretation of the age of Haydn, no longer merely "enlightened" but not yet Romantic, when his late works, especially the oratorios and masses, created the Kantian sublime in music.[17] On another front, Haydn, like Handel, is a canonical composer whose life and career give the lie to the usual modernist prejudices about artists. (In this respect modernism faithfully followed upon Romanticism).[18] He was a worldly figure but one of integrity, what the French called an *honnête homme*; he was successful both financially and in terms of high reputation; his position at court did not inhibit his originality or creativity; his art was not opposed to entertainment (or the reverse) but achieved the best of both worlds, in a way that Mozart, despite his protestations, could only dream of; and so forth. None of this is intrinsically postmodern, of course, but it does seem as if these insights about Haydn and his career could only have developed after romantic-modernist notions of the artist (Mozart, the "unappreciated genius"; Beethoven, "the man who freed music") had been successfully contested.

But to return to Haydn's music: no less important than the contextualizations just mentioned has been the increased attention paid to previously marginalized periods, genres, and tendencies in his oeuvre. Elaine Sisman's magisterial study of the variations has been praised by Rosen himself.[19] Her argument—this is the postmodern aspect—implicitly lays the foundation for a rhetorical and paratactic musical aesthetics, fundamentally different from the traditional teleology of sonata form, although she does not explicitly pursue this aspect of her topic.

Sisman has also attempted to develop an aesthetics of Haydn's baryton trios, without marginalizing them in comparison with other genres.[20] (Following her oral presentation of the study in question in 1982, one of the world's most distinguished Haydn scholars complained to me that it was perverse, in that it did not acknowledge the inferiority of the baryton trios to the "great"—and contemporaneous—String Quartets, Op. 20. That the latter are demonstratively great and the baryton trios outwardly modest, nobody will deny; but the comment exhibited all too clearly the limitations of the traditional modernist view of Haydn's music, according to which, say, his early string quartets are also insignificant.) Richard Will has contributed several outstanding studies of Haydn's (and others') programmatic music, and we have several excellent recent studies of the piano trios.[21]

I could go on, but the point is clear enough. An astonishing proportion of Haydn's oeuvre was long ignored; no other composer of his stature has traditionally been understood in so partial a manner. Indeed (for what it is worth) the majority of my own writings on Haydn have been motivated in part by the desire to persuade readers to "take seriously" periods and genres that have traditionally been marginalized. The crucial recognition is that Haydn was not merely a great genius, but a nearly universal one, throughout his career and in all genres; today, only the operas still remain contested. But this is not a matter of genre and chronology alone, but of style and content as well. Haydn was a composer not merely of "symmetrical" sonata forms, but of freely developing, through-composed works (as Tovey understood); a master not only of "absolute" instrumental music and motivic development, but of rhetorically persuasive programmatic and vocal works; a man whose musical persona conveys not only great wit, but deep feeling.

It is in its traditional (modernist) limitation to the partial view of Haydn just described that Rosen's treatment in *The Classical Style* is lacking. His account is by and large restricted to the late symphonies and quartets, with a nod toward the piano trios and late sacred vocal music; he mentions many genres and most of Haydn's music before 1780 not at all or only in passing. In and of itself this would be no defect; his volume is not a survey but a work of criticism, which legitimately focuses on those genres that best represent the author's subject and with which he identifies most closely. But Rosen does not merely ignore Haydn's pre-1780 music; he subjects it to a negative, at times astonishingly harsh, critique. I have argued elsewhere that this blind spot resulted primarily from untenable notions of the overall development of musical style toward "Classicism" and of Haydn's supposed "immaturity" before 1780; I will not repeat those arguments here.[22] But even his late music is not immune: the piano trios, despite their (lovingly described) compositional qualities, are "doomed" (p. 354), owing to the subordinate nature of the string parts; the late masses are "uncomfortable compromises" (p. 369), and the only example offered is the "trivial" solo soprano melody in the Kyrie of the *Mass in Time of War*, and so on. With but occasional revisions (for example, of the "Creation" Mass and the *Harmoniemesse*), Rosen has maintained these opinions ever since;[23] he has scarcely addressed the recent perspectives adumbrated above.

Indeed, skepticism about postmodern ideas and sensibilities is characteristic of all of Rosen's writings on music, including recent ones.[24] (Of course, this skepticism is often well founded; many of the writers whom he skewers "had it coming.") He also continues to defend classic modernist writings by others; he once criticized me for asserting that Joseph Kerman's "new-critical" *Opera as Drama* (1956) seemed "dated" in the postmodern "critical climate" of 1990, before proceeding to his real topic, an elaborate defense of "tonal planning" in Mozart's operas.[25] But opera studies had dramatically changed in the intervening years, and indeed had played the largest role in the general "turn" toward postmodernist musicology in the 1980s; the comment still seems to me justified. So let me conclude by affirming that the best parts of *The Classical Style* are *not* dated. On the contrary: if (as implied above) the best criticism shares some characteristics of art, it likewise enjoys some measure of art's "relative autonomy," including the potential to outlive its own time, to remain capable of surprising and enlightening later readers as well.

In the final sentence of his wonderful essay on tonality in Schubert, Tovey wrote of the retransition towards the recapitulation in the composer's last sonata:

> I have often been grateful to a dull description that faithfully guides me to the places where great artistic experiences await me, and with this hope I leave the reader poised on Schubert's dominant of B flat.[26]

But of course Tovey's own descriptions are never dull, and although it once pleased certain theorists who believed themselves "advanced" to criticize him as superficial (and worse), those days are thankfully past: today he is everything but dated. The same applies to Charles Rosen, who has often been praised as Tovey's peer. Rosen's descriptions too are never dull. They do not merely lead the reader to "places of great artistic experience" but penetrate deeply into his chosen works. "The first movement of [Haydn's] Quartet in B flat, Op. 50, no. 1, is built from nothing at all," he writes, "an opening ostinato pedal, a strange, soft chord, and a little six-note figure."[27] What follows, in six closely argued pages, is no less astonishing as critical exegesis than is Haydn's music as composition. The conclusion (p. 125) may be a familiar modernist riff—"[Haydn's] imaginative understanding of the dynamic impulse [these elements] contain shapes the form the material itself seems to create"—but Rosen's analysis is not to be gainsaid by any later sensibility, not even a postmodern one.

Notes

1. On this sense of modernism as a period in the past, see James Webster, "Between Enlightenment and Romanticism in Music History: 'First Viennese Modernism' and the Delayed Nineteenth Century," *19th Century Music*, 25 (2001–2), 118–20, and the references given there; *Music and the Aesthetics of Modernity*, ed. Karol Berger and Anthony Newcomb (Cambridge, MA: Harvard University Press, 2005).

2. One writer who does understand this is Fredric Jameson; see his *Postmodernism; or, the Cultural Logic of Late Capitalism* (Durham, NC: Duke University Press, 1991), 35–36, 59–61.

3. Princeton, NJ: Princeton University Press, 1975.

4. In this it was perhaps typical of such intersections between musical life and musicology; on these see Joseph Kerman, *Contemplating Music* (Cambridge, MA: Harvard University Press, 1985).

5. New York: Norton, 1971, 120; numerous later reprints and updatings. Rosen's contemporary Joseph Kerman (b. 1924) offers a sustained appreciation of *The Classical Style* in *Contemplating Music*, 150–54.

6. Donald Francis Tovey, "Haydn's Chamber Music" (1929), reprinted in *Essays and Lectures on Music* (Oxford University Press, 1949), 43.

7. An intervening general chapter, "Structure and Ornament," is briefer and less compelling.

8. Elaine Sisman, following up this hint, demonstrated the importance of such relations in late-eighteenth-century theory and practice generally: "Small and Expanded Forms: Koch's Model and Haydn's Music," *Musical Quarterly* 68 (1982): 444–75.

9. Webster, "Between Enlightenment and Romanticism," 120–24. The case against "classical" is argued in Webster, *Haydn's "Farewell" Symphony and the Idea of Classical Style . . .* (Cambridge: Cambridge University Press, 1991), 341–66.

10. Jürgen Habermas, "Die Moderne—Ein unvollendetes Projekt," in *Kleine politische Schriften* (Frankfurt am Main: Suhrkamp, 1981), 444–64; an English version is "Modernism vs. Postmodernism," *New German Critique* 22 (1981): 3–14. A more general treatment in English is *The Philosophical Discourse of Modernity* (Cambridge, MA: MIT Press, 1990).

11. On this concept see Carl Dahlhaus, *Foundations of Music History*, trans. J. B. Robinson (Cambridge: Cambridge University Press, 1983), ch. 8.

12. Edwards, "The Nonsense of an Ending: Closure in Haydn's String Quartets," *Musical Quarterly*: 75 (1991): 227–54; Chua, "Haydn as Romantic: A Chemical Experiment with Instrumental Music," in *Haydn Studies*, ed. W. Dean Sutcliffe (Cambridge: Cambridge University Press, 1988), 125–51; Beghin, "Haydn as Orator: A Rhetorical Analysis of his Keyboard Sonata in D Major, Hob. XVI:42," in *Haydn and His World*, ed. Elaine Sisman (Princeton, NJ: Princeton University Press, 1997), 201–54; November, "Haydn's Vocality and the Ideal of 'True' String Quartets" (PhD diss., Cornell University, 2003).

13. Michael Spitzer, "Haydn's Reversals: Style Change, Gesture and the Implication-Realization Model," in *Haydn Studies*, 177–217; Webster, "Haydn's Symphonies between *Sturm und Drang* and 'Classical Style': Art and Entertainment," in *Haydn Studies*, 218–45.

14. On the operas see Rebecca Green, "Representing the Aristocracy: The Operatic Haydn and *Le pescatrici*," in *Haydn and His World*, 154–200; Patricia Debly,

"Social Commentary in the Music of Haydn's Goldoni Operas," in *Metaphor: A Musical Dimension*, ed. Jamie Croy Kassler (Sydney: Currency Press, 1991), 51–68; Pierpaolo Polzonetti, "Opera Buffa and the American Revolution" (PhD diss., Cornell University, 2003), chap. 4, "America as the Moon" (on *Il mondo della luna*).

15. On literature: *Haydn und die Literatur seiner Zeit*, ed. Herbert Zeman (Eisenstadt 1976); Maria Hörwarthner, "Joseph Haydn's Library: An Attempt at a Literary-Historical Reconstruction," in *Haydn and His World*, 395–462. On aesthetics: Sisman, "Haydn, Shakespeare, and the Rules of Originality," in *Haydn and His World*, 3–56; Webster, "Haydn's Aesthetics," in *The Cambridge Companion to Haydn*, ed. Caryl Clark (Cambridge: Cambridge University Press, 2005), 30–44.

16. Schroeder, *Haydn and the Enlightenment: The Late Symphonies and Their Audience* (Oxford: Oxford University Press, 1990).

17. Thomas Tolley, *Painting the Cannon's Roar: Music, the Visual Arts and the Rise of an Attentive Public in the Age of Haydn, c.1750 to c.1810* (Aldershot: Ashgate, 2001); Webster, "The *Creation*, Haydn's Late Vocal Music, and the Musical Sublime," in *Haydn and His World*, 57–102.

18. Webster, "The Century of Handel and Haydn," in *The Century of Bach and Handel*, ed. Thomas Forrest Kelly et al. (Cambridge, MA: Harvard University Department of Music, 2008), 299–317.

19. *Haydn and the Classical Variation* (Cambridge, MA: Harvard University Press, 1993); cf. Rosen, *Critical Entertainments* (Cambridge, MA: Harvard University Press, 2000), 256.

20. Sisman, "Haydn's Baryton Pieces and His Serious Genres," in *Joseph Haydn: Bericht über den Internationalen . . . Kongress Wien . . . 1982*, ed. Eva Badura-Skoda (Munich: Henle, 1986), 426–35.

21. Richard Will, "When God Met the Sinner, and Other Dramatic Confrontations in Eighteenth-Century Instrumental Music," *Music and Letters* 78 (1997): 175–209; Will, *The Characteristic Symphony in the Age of Haydn and Beethoven* (Cambridge: Cambridge University Press, 2001); Jürgen Brauner, *Studien zu den Klaviertrios von Joseph Haydn* (Tutzing: Hans Schneider, 1995); Katalin Komlós, "The Viennese Piano Trio in the 1780s" (PhD diss., Cornell University, 1986); W. Dean Sutcliffe, "The Piano Trios of Haydn," (PhD diss., University of Cambridge, 1989).

22. Webster, *Haydn's "Farewell" Symphony*, 335–41, 353–55.

23. See "The Rediscovering of Haydn" (1979), reprinted in *Critical Entertainments*; and the new preface to *The Classical Style*, expanded ed. (New York: Norton, 1997). I should however acknowledge that Rosen graciously accepts portions of my critique in the former volume, p. 256, and the latter volume, pp. xiv–xv.

24. See Rosen, "The New Musicology" (1994), and Rosen, "Beethoven's Career" (1996), both reprinted in *Critical Entertainments*.

25. Rosen, *The Classical Style*, expanded ed., xxi, n. 13; for the larger argument, xxi–xxvi. My comment was in "Mozart's Operas and the Myth of Musical Unity," *Cambridge Opera Journal* 2 (1990): 200n. I invite readers to compare my argument in this article with Rosen's just cited; I would only note (not that any defense is needed) that I indeed cite the "great" Hermann Abert, whom Rosen seems to believe I ignore.

26. Tovey, "Tonality in Schubert" (1928), reprinted in *Essays and Lectures*, 159.

27. Rosen, *The Classical Style*, 120, 125; my quotation shamelessly (as Charles likes to say when confessing "sharp practice" with citations) conflates two comparable but slightly different formulations.

Chapter Sixteen

Facile Metaphors, Hidden Gaps, Short Circuits

Should *We Adore Adorno?*

Leo Treitler

Europeans began writing down music in the ninth century as an aspect of the powerful orientation toward scripturality that characterized the Carolingian culture. Whether as a matter of chance coincidence or not (I think not), medieval writing *about* music began, as far as we know, in the same century and under the same cultural and political circumstances. To get a sense of what the musically curious and informed thought should and could be described and explained, we can consult the oldest comprehensive—and most widely transmitted—didactic manual about music that has come down to us from the Middle Ages, the *Musica enchiriadis* ("Handbook of Music"), written about 900 C.E. by an anonymous author.

> [W]e can judge whether the construction of a melody is proper, and distinguish the qualities of tones and modes and the other things of this art. Likewise we can adduce, on the basis of numbers, musical intervals or the sounding together of pitches and give some explanations of consonance and dissonance.

For a hint of what the author might have meant by "qualities," in reference to music we can read a bit further:

> [It] is necessary that the *affects* of the subjects that are sung correspond to the *effect* of the song, so that melodies are peaceful in tranquil subjects, joyful in happy matters, somber in sad [ones], and harsh things are said or made to be expressed by harsh melodies [my emphases].[1]

Regarding the association of "qualities" with "tones and modes," we can consult a manual written about two centuries later, the *Micrologus* by Guido of Arezzo. Guido writes that, for the cognoscenti, recognizing the "characters and individual features" of the modal patterns is like distinguishing people of Greek, Spanish, Latin, German, and French origin from each other. Thus, the "broken leaps" of the authentic deuterus mode, the "voluptuousness" of the plagal tritus, the "garrulousness" of the authentic tetrardus, and the "suavity" of the plagal tetrardus are distinctly recognizable. Guido also writes that this diversity of characters matches the diverse mental dispositions among different people, so that one prefers this mode, whereas another prefers that one. Further, Guido compares this diversity of musical qualities and tastes with the diversity of phenomena that enter the "recess of the heart" through the other senses, the "windows of the body"—colors, odors, tastes. Finally, Guido reaches beyond this matter of affects and tastes to the effects or powers of music, reporting by way of examples on a madman cured of his madness by music and another man brought to the point of rape by one kind of music and then made to back off at the last moment by another kind.

Guido's is a particularly colorful and replete spelling out of this medieval music concept, but in its core aspect it is an elaboration of the ancient concept according to which the cosmos, the human soul, and music are bound together through their regulation by the same proportions. This was familiarly expressed by Boethius: "When we hear what is properly and harmoniously united in sound in conjunction with what is harmoniously coupled and joined together within us and are attracted to it then we recognize that we ourselves are put together in its likeness."[2] The certainty of this notion was beyond question or need for argument to the author of the *Musica enchiriadis* even though it he could not fully eliminate it. He wrote, "[I]n what way music has so great an affinity and union with our souls— for we know we are bound to it by a certain likeness ["we know" this through the inherited doctrine that is expressed by Boethius in the passage I've just quoted]— we cannot express easily in words." I interpret that as a way of saying that "we" cannot step outside ourselves to gain an objective view of this affinity.

This music concept was only one aspect of a medieval way of experiencing the self in relation to the world. Owen Barfield has written of "the organic universe of the Middle Ages" that had "beaten with the same heart as the human being."[3] To the people of the Middle Ages, "the world was more like a garment they wore about them than a stage on which they moved." (Associated with this observation is Barfield's suggestive interpretation of the lack of interest in visual perspective in medieval painting). Compared with us, they "felt themselves and the objects around them and the words [we can add the music] that expressed these objects immersed together in a clear lake of meaning." They viewed the human being as "a microcosm within a macrocosm." In his relation to the world around him, "the man of the Middle Ages was less like an island, more like an embryo, than we are."

This is to say that properties and associations of music that we today would differentiate as technical, aesthetic, affective, rhetorical (effective), cultural, or sociological were all experienced at once as music, and in description folded into a continuous, unified music concept. How different, then, is the modern—or modernist—conception that Charles Rosen accurately characterized in the opening of his review "Should We Adore Adorno?": "No art appears as remote as music from the life and the society that produce it. . . . The sounds of music . . . are artificial and set apart." By contrast, he writes, "Painting and sculpture reflect some aspects of the figures and objects or at least the forms and colors that we encounter; novels and poems convey experiences and aspirations that recall, however distantly, the world that we know" (p. 59).

If we compare the two conditions—medieval and modern—it must be evident that the second is the result of a kind of parturition, a rending of the self from the world, the mind from the body, the senses from the intellect, such as has been influential since the promulgation of the dualism that Descartes preached. This dualism makes impossible Guido's image of the sweetness of sensual things entering the recesses of the heart through the windows of the body. Barfield refers to this parturition as the foundation of the scientific revolution. (See the introduction to my book *Music and the Historical Imagination*).[4]

Diderot provides Rosen an opening for the suggestion of an alternative with the former's observation that "even though the signs of music are more ephemeral and less easily definable than those of painting or literature, their emotional impact upon our senses is even greater" (p. 59). Whether knowingly or not, Diderot revives here the ancient doctrine that lay behind the medieval conception. As it was expressed by Aristotle in the *Politics*, "rhythms and mele contain representations of anger and mildness, and also of courage and temperance and all their opposites and the other ethical qualities . . . whereas the other objects of sensations contain no representation of ethoses . . . though the objects of sight do so slightly, for there are forms that represent character, but only to a small extent."[5]

Insofar as music's emotional impact trumps its ineffability, Rosen implies, it must reveal something significant about the musicians who created it and the age, the culture, and the society in which it was made. This is Rosen's occasion for introducing Adorno as the writer on music who "devoted more energy" to the challenge of understanding "the significance of music for the musicians who created it and the society in which it was produced" than any other.

There may be a presumption that Adorno showed the way to the healing of the breach that has been upon us in his conception of the world that is the locus of his studies as an integrated totality of culture and society whose manifestations are reflective of one another by virtue of underlying relations that bear on them all. That outlook enabled Adorno, like a man of the Middle Ages or a contemporary of Aristotle, to explicate musical processes or structures in the light of human comportment, as when he posed "the musical dialectics which in sonata form mediate between harmony (the general) and thematism (the particular) as a reflection of the conflict between society as a whole and a 'particular interest.'"[6] Music's enactment of the conflict between the individual and the society in post-Enlightenment Europe is perhaps the leading thread in Adorno's narrative of the history of central European music from Beethoven to Schoenberg that is the backdrop for the 50 percent or so of his prolix output that is concerned with music.

Adorno larded his writing with such exegesis throughout his life. In the late *Minima moralia*, he wrote:

> Beethoven's music, which works within the forms transmitted by society and is ascetic towards the expression of private feelings, resounds with the guided echo of social conflict, drawing precisely from the asceticism the whole fullness and power of individuality. That of Richard Strauss, wholly at the service of individual claims and dedicated to the glorification of the self-sufficient individual, thereby reduces the latter to a mere receptive organ of the market, an imitator of arbitrarily chosen ideas and styles.[7]

These portrayals are issued with ease and without the slightest hint of doubt or clue to Adorno's grounds for them, as if reported by an uninvolved observer from a platform above the fray.

Rosen characterizes such bridges as "Adorno's attempt to unite art and society with a facile metaphor."He cites Carl Dahlhaus's similar characterization: "The verbal analogies perform the function of hiding a gap which the argument could not close."[8] But it is worth citing the rest of the passage in which this sentence occurs:

> [Adorno] provokes the impatient objection that these are merely verbal analogies which have no basis in fact but owe their origin and a semblance of plausibility to a generously ambivalent use of words like 'integration', 'subject and object,' or 'general and particular.' . . . Yet the blind spots are not simply an accidental defect. Rather, the contrast between the methods—between the formal-analytically individualizing and the sociologically generalizing procedure—returns as a flaw in the individual analysis. . . .[9]

There is yet another type of flaw created by this disequilibrium.

> [A] detailed analysis of motivic technique in the first of Schoenberg's Five Orchestral Pieces culminates in the observation that 'the growth in complexity, as if according to the fundamental tenets of the contemporary sociology of Herbert Spencer goes together with growing integration as its correlative.'[10] It remains unclear whether the digression into the sociological realm is meant to be merely an illustration of the connection between complexity and integration, or an allusion . . . to a sociological exegesis of Schoenberg's motivic technique. But in any case the 'correlation' to which the sociological commentary refers is not peculiar to Op. 16. Rather, it is a feature common to all of Schoenberg's works since the time of the transition from tonality to atonality.

This is to say that the excursion into the sociological realm contributes virtually nothing to the elucidation of the particular work that is its target; the excursion is virtually meaningless. The flaw is unavoidable in this type of many-to-one relationship between the specific musical and general sociological members of this sort of analogy.

Later in the same passage, Dahlhaus explicitly raises the question of meaning:

> An assertion like the one that the musical dialectic between the rationality of compositional technique and the irrationality of expression represents a reflection and consequence of the social conflict between the rationality of the technical means and the irrationality of the 'indigenous' ends, which are at cross purposes,[11] is simply impossible to understand. For even the most daring of psycho-analytical theories would find it hard to establish a link between the irrationality of the emotions and that of economic liberalism.

It is a comfort to be offered an alternative to the peculiar bit of "Polyansh" (a neologism I learned during a conversation with Saul Steinberg) that is frequently offered, according to which Adorno's "difficult prose . . . is an attraction; it forces one to pay attention," as Rosen puts it.[12]

From "impatient objection" to outrage. Milan Kundera, in his essay "Improvisation in Homage to Stravinsky," cites Adorno's interpretation of the dissonances in Stravinsky's adaptations of works of Gesualdo, Pergolesi, and Tchaikovsky:

> These notes become the marks of the *violence* the composer wreaks against the idiom, and it is that *violence* we relish about them, that *battering, that violation, so to speak of musical life.* Though dissonance may originally have been the expression of *subjective suffering*, its harshness shifts in value and becomes the sign of a *social constraint.* . . . It may be that the widespread effect of these works of Stravinsky's is due in large part to the fact that inadvertently, and under color of aestheticism, *they in their own way trained men to something that was soon methodically inflicted on them at the political level* [Kundera's emphases].

Kundera comments:

> Let us recapitulate: a dissonance is justified if it expresses "subjective suffering," but in Stravinsky . . . that very dissonance is the sign of brutality: a parallel is drawn (by a brilliant short circuit of Adorno's thought) with political brutality: . . . the coming political oppression (which in this particular historical context can mean only one thing: fascism).[13]

Adorno's practice in the sociological interpretation of music might be thought to pursue the lead that Max Weber took in his book *The Rational and Social Foundations of Music* (written in 1911 and published ten years later).[14] This is an analysis of the historical development of music in terms of the increasing rationality of its technical basis (the tonal system, the system of meters, the regulation of multivoice composition) and of its social organization as an institution.

Weber conducts this analysis in parallel with an analysis of the development of capitalism in terms of its rationalization. What Adorno did not observe, however, is Weber's caveat that the empirical history of music must analyze these factors without involving itself in the aesthetic evaluation of musical works of art.

Although he is one of many critics who have blown the whistle on this practice of Adorno's, Rosen chooses generously to sidestep the issue. After all, the available responses to it are limited. Confronted with such exegesis, one can adopt Adorno's practice under the illusion that one has somehow "historicalized" the music, or one can throw up one's hands and say, "I don't get it." The practice does not lend itself to confirmation or disconfirmation—a charge that would not have upset Adorno. (As Rosen observes, Adorno shared with Oswald Spengler not only the thesis of the "Decline of the West," but a "preference of intuition to empirical research and theory.") Whether the claims under such a practice even have heuristic value is questionable.

Instead, Rosen writes, "Perhaps the fundamental insight of Adorno was a recognition that works do not passively reflect the society in which they arise, but act within it, influencing it and criticizing it." His language makes clear that he endorses this axiom—as well he might, for it would constitute a basis for a historiography in which things happen because of what people do (and fail to do). Adorno espouses such a historiography. But he seems not to have been able to desist from issuing such seemingly playful and essentially meaningless characterizations as this, which Rosen cites: "The functional interconnections present throughout Haydn's music give an impression of competence, active life and suchlike categories, which ominously call to mind the rising bourgeoisie." But Adorno was dead serious, as he made clear in this introductory instruction, which he published in 1932 in the *Zeitschrift für Sozialforschung* (under the title "Zur gesellschaftlichen Lage der Musik") and reaffirmed in his *Introduction to the Sociology of Music.*

> Here and now, music can do nothing but *represent*, in its own structure, the social antimonies, which also bear the guilt of its isolation. It will be the better the more deeply it can make its forms lend shape to the power of those contradictions, and to the need to overcome them socially—the more purely the antimonies of its own formal language will *express* the calamities of the social condition and call for change in the cipher script of suffering. It does not behoove music to stare at society in helpless horror; its *social function* will be more exactly fulfilled if the social problems contained in it *in the inmost cells of its technique*, are *represented* in its own material and according to its own formal laws [my emphases].[15]

This question—passive reflection or interaction—compares two incommensurables. The decoding of "passive reflection" in Adorno's writing is generally performed from the standpoint of the present-day exegete, without much concern whether the proposed meanings would have been picked up by the composer's contemporaries. The analyses of interactions between music and society have at least the potential of generating a history, potentially subject to degrees of justification, as the meanings Adorno read out of scores, or more often oeuvres, are not.

This is to say that Adorno's interpretations are not either one or the other. Readings (translations) of musical detail and historical interpretation are mutually interdependent, something that is about as plain as can be in the passage that Kundera cites about the meaning of dissonance in Stravinsky's arrangements of music by Gesualdo, Pergolesi, and Tchaikovsky. That passage, with its focus on the approach of authoritarianism that is played out in Stravinsky's music, links that music with the "12-tone constructivism," or (in Rosen's citation, p. 60), "the rigid apparatus of the twelve tone system"[16] of Schoenberg, in Adorno's disapproving view. Adorno's sociological reading of the twelve-tone system forced him into characterizations of the compositional procedure and its music that are as arbitrary and distorted as are the flawed interpretations of the music of the late Beethoven under the influence of his historical readings, as Rosen has demonstrated. But the top-down nature of his interpretation here is perhaps more striking, considering his closeness to Schoenberg and his disciples.

We read in the section "The Concept of Twelve-Tone Technique" of *Philosophy of Modern Music* (pp. 6off.) the following characterizations:

> The twelve-tone technique demands that every composition be *derived from* such a "fundamental structure" or "row." This refers to an *arbitrarily* designated ordering of the twelve tones available to the composer in the tempered half-tone system. . . . Every tone of the composition is *determined* by this row: there is no longer a single "*free*" note.

The emphases are mine, and they are intended to denote the fallaciousness of the respective terms. To say that every twelve-tone composition is derived from a row is as if we would say that every tonal piece is derived from a key, without implying that the row is the exact counterpart of a key. But like a key, a row sets certain sonic constraints in one sense, and potentials in another. That the ordering of tones in a row is arbitrary is to imply that it might equally well be determined by a throw of the dice or a sequence of letters randomly chosen from a telephone directory. The implication is confirmed in a footnote: "The twelve-tone composer resembles the gambler; he waits and sees what number appears and is happy if it is one offering musical meaning" (n. 30). In another footnote he writes, "It is hardly a coincidence that the *mathematical* techniques of music originated in Vienna, the home of logical positivism [which Adorno despised]. The inclination towards numerical games is as unique to the Viennese intellect as is the game of chess in the coffee house." (One wonders whether Adorno played chess.) And then, sure enough, this is explained by means of a kind of vulgar Marxism: "While productive intellectual forces in Austria developed to the highest level of capitalist technique, material forces did not keep pace. For this very reason controlling calculation became the dream image of the Viennese intellectual . . . " (n. 24).

On July 27, 1932, Schoenberg wrote to Rudolf Kolisch: "I tried to convince Wiesengrund, and I can't say it often enough: my works are twelve note *composi-tions*, not *twelve note* compositions." On February 5, 1951, Schoenberg wrote to Joseph Rufer, "The first conception of a series always takes place in the form of a thematic character." We can read how he meant these remarks in Rosen's book *Arnold Schoenberg.*[17] "The series was, for Schoenberg, both a group of motifs and an organization of the tonal spectrum" (p. 81). "The series is . . . not a melody but a pre-melodic idea" (p. 78). Rosen writes of another twelve-note composer, "So intense was Webern's concentration on the motif that one may say that his motifs are not really derived from the series, they generate it" (p. 113). This understanding of the place of the series in the ontology of the work has been borne out by numerous analyses, including my own of Berg's *Lulu.*[18] Whether a series is abstracted from a concrete musical idea (or a complex of such ideas), or is constructed to produce properties that a composer means at the outset to impose on a work, is moot. What is important is that Adorno's characterization of the ordering of the series as "arbitrary" is wrong; his insinuation that the process of twelve-tone composition is some sort of Viennese mathematical game is wrong; and his claim that the composition is determined by the series (impli-cation: rather than by the artistic design of the composer) is wrong. It is all, shockingly, like the sort of banal journalistic polemic against twelve-tone com-position that one could read regularly not so many years ago in various organs of the popular press.

Rosen writes: "For his view of the history of music and society, [Adorno] needed [the *Missa solemnis*] to be a failure" (p. 64). Adorno also needed to pres-ent a distorted portrayal of twelve-tone composition even though he surely must have known better. It allowed him to depict twelve-tone composition as the tri-umph of the form or the method over the material, of the object over the sub-ject, of the system over the creator, of the triumph of order. "The new ordering of twelve-tone technique virtually extinguishes the subject. . . . [M]usic becomes capable of restraining itself coldly and inexorably, and this is the only fitting position for music following its decline."[19] Thus is completed a process that was immanent in music history "since the beginning of the bourgeois era," a "long-ing . . . to 'grasp' and to place all sounds into an order, and to reduce the magic essence of music to human logic."

In a rare swerve outside the confines of the Beethoven-to-Schoenberg frame-work for his history, he continued, "Luther calls Josquin des Pres, who died in 1521, 'the master of notes who compelled the notes to his will, in contrast to other composers, who bent the will to the notes.' "[20] And here is where the Stravinsky and Schoenberg lines converge in Adorno's story of the decline of music in an authoritarian society.

A personal note: whatever I may think of Adorno's thesis of a tendency in Western society toward a state of authoritarianism, I do not hear it in the late music of Beethoven; in Stravinsky's transformations of music by Gesualdo,

Pergolesi, and Tchaikovsky; or in Schoenberg's twelve-tone music. And I resist as a piece of authoritarianism in itself the dogma that this tendency is *in* that music.

It is a matter of some dispute whether Adorno was influenced by Oswald Spengler. (Rosen claims Spengler's influence as an instance of Adorno's "derivative intelligence.")[21] But I don't know that we have to attribute Adorno's extreme pessimism directly to Spengler's influence. For one thing, the idea of the decline of the West, which is writ large across Adorno's work, was in the air.[22] But more specifically, reading *Dialectic of Enlightenment*[23] and *Minima moralia*, one can get an impression of how the Nazi years had turned Adorno's criticism of capitalism into a vision of the decline of Western civilization over a much longer span of time. And given his lifelong consuming engagement with music and his totalizing view of society and culture, one can well ask how could he *not* see that vision reflected in music history, regardless of whether that outcome is defensible on the evidence of hearing or on the logic of reason.

At the conclusion of his review, Rosen reflects on Adorno's historical view against the background of his biography. "His view of modern culture arises from the natural despair of one who lived through the terrible inflation in Germany of the 1920s, which ruined so many upper middle-class families. His attack on commercial interests betrayed him into an idealization of the past." Rosen asks "What was this world whose disappearance could inspire in Adorno such profound and ironic nostalgia?" By way of answer he closes with a paragraph from *Minima moralia* which he introduces with these words: "[A]t one point his prose rises to a truly poetic evocation of the Golden Age, a world whose disappearance is a cause of poignant regret." I repeat it here because reading it does truly contribute to an understanding of the very enigmatic, and contradictory, character of Adorno's work—and also because Adorno deserves to be represented here by a specimen of his finest writing, beside the writing that I have cited with less enthusiasm:

> Rampant technology eliminates luxury, but not by declaring privilege a human right; rather, it does so by both raising the general standard of living and cutting off the possibility of fulfillment. The express train that in three nights and two days hurtles across the continent is a miracle, but traveling in it has nothing of the faded splendor of the *train bleu*. What made up the voluptuousness of travel, beginning with the goodbye-waving through the open window, the solicitude of amiable accepters of tips, the ceremonial of mealtimes, the constant feeling of receiving favors that take nothing from anyone else, has passed away, together with the elegant people who were wont to promenade along the platforms before the departure, and who will by now be sought in vain even in the foyers of the most prestigious hotels. That the steps of railway carriages have to be retracted intimates to the passenger of even the most expensive express that he must obey the company's terse regulations like a prisoner. Certainly, the company gives him the exactly calculated value of his fare, but this includes nothing that research has not proved an average demand. Who, aware of such conditions, could depart on impulse on a voyage with his mistress as once from Paris to Nice?

With a wider understanding of Adorno's pessimism about the course of music's history, in the context of his personal history's engagement with world history, and of the way that doleful overview forced his interpretations of individual musical works or *oeuvres* into congruence with it, there might have been less enthusiasm for extracting from his work and, on his authority, an autonomous practice of deciphering music on the strength of sheer intuition, a practice with the bravado of tightrope walking without a net.

I began by asking whether Adorno's holistic view of culture and society constitutes the basis for a healing of the parturition that accompanied the age of Enlightenment. Considering the unconvincing way in which, in his practice, he transposed phenomena of one domain (art) as phenomena of another (commerce), I would have to say, hardly. It is a kind of artificial, counterfeit holism, required for the story that Adorno had to tell. It falls too far short of portraying our experience of music in the world as the alternative we seek to the tradition of approaching music as an autonomous phenomenon—a tradition that in fact Adorno himself explicitly embraced as a grounding principle of his complex views.[24]

Rosen never comes back around to answer the question of his title. I believe most readers would conclude that, on balance, his review implies a negative answer. It is all too true that "unfortunately Adorno's admirers often treasure [I would add "and imitate"] the worst aspects of his work," as Rosen writes. But it is unfortunate, too, that, with the exception of that striking passage from *Minima moralia*, Rosen makes no mention of any work of Adorno that can inspire the admiration of even those of us who share Rosen's distaste for the worst aspects.

In his essay "Homage to Adorno's 'Homage to Zerlina,' "[25] Berthold Hoeckner writes, "Adorno's 'Homage' may be no more than a sketch, but it claims for itself no less than the quality of a master painting." He reproduces this "bagatelle," as he calls it, so that we can see for ourselves, and stresses its character as a late work. But he mentions in the same breath the breathtaking essay "Schubert," which Adorno wrote in 1928, during his twenty-fifth year. Thirty-six years later, Adorno judged this essay to be his "first somewhat comprehensive . . . work touching on the meaning of music."[26] I read with the same pleasure the omnibus essay he published two years later in the Viennese journal *Anbruch* under the title "Hermeneutik," comprising a brief theoretical statement and a number of exemplary critical sketches. Probably the best-known extended critical work in this "high-flying style" (Hoeckner) is Adorno's *Mahler: A Musical Physiognomy.*[27]

We might consider it another casualty of the Nazi era that Adorno on the whole had higher priorities when it came to writing about music. Or perhaps we might better say that work of this uniquely inspired character and eloquence of style, to which Hoeckner likes to refer with the expression "aesthetics of the moment," had to compete for Adorno's attention with his high-flying (in a different sense) oracular ambitions in work that he could well have left to others—and lament the critical writing that he might otherwise have produced and inspired in his followers. In an indirect sense Adorno's work was a casualty of the very conditions that he diagnosed. At the same time we can be consoled by the fact that not all escapees from the Nazi horrors who took refuge amidst the commercialism of America allowed their work to be so embittered by the experience of both.

Notes

This essay is a sort of trope—in the medieval sense—of Charles Rosen's review "Should We Adore Adorno?" *New York Review of Books*, October 24, 2002, 59–66. Reference to that review, if possible, is recommended.

1. *Musica enchiriadis and Scholica enchiriadis*, trans. Raymond Erickson, ed. Claude V. Palisca (New Haven: Yale University Press, 1995), 31–32. *Hucbald, Guido, and John on Music: Three Medieval Treatises on Music*, trans. Warren Babb, ed. Claude V. Palisca (New Haven: Yale University Press, 1978), 69–70.

2. *Fundamentals of Music: Anicius Manlius Severinus Boethius*, trans., and intro. Calvin M. Bower, ed. Claude V. Palisca (New Haven: Yale University Press, 1989), 9–10.

3. Owen Barfield, *Saving the Appearances: A Study in Idolatry* (Middletown, CT: Wesleyan University Press, 1965, 1988).

4. Leo Treitler, *Music and the Historical Imagination* (Cambridge, MA: Harvard University Press, 1985).

5. Oliver Strunk, ed. *Source Readings in Music History*, rev. ed., general ed. Leo Treitler (New York: W. W. Norton, 1998), 29.

6. Theodor W. Adorno, *Klangfiguren* (Frankfurt am Main: Suhrkamp Verlag, 1959), 24. My translation.

7. Adorno, *Minima moralia: Reflections from a Damaged Life* (Frankfurt am Main: Suhrkamp Verlag, 1951; New York, 1974), 149.

8. Rosen, "Should We Adore Adorno?," 63.

9. Carl Dahlhaus, "The Musical Work of Art as a Subject of Sociology," in *Schoenberg and the New Music: Essays by Carl Dahlhaus* (Cambridge: Cambridge University Press, 1987), 243.

10. "Zur Vorgeschichte der Reihenkomponisten" in *Klangfiguren*, 113.

11. *Klangfiguren*, 16.

12. Rosen, p. 59. I have seen this peculiar idea attributed to George Lichtheim in his writing about Adorno but have not been able to confirm that.

13. Milan Kundera, "Improvisation in Homage to Stravinsky" in *Testaments Betrayed* (New York: Harper Collins, 1995), 78–79.

14. Max Weber, *The Rational and Social Foundations of Music* (Carbondale, IL: Southern Illinois University Press, 1958, 1969).

15. Adorno, *Introduction to the Sociology of Music* (New York: Continuum, 1988), 70.

16. Adorno, *Philosophy of Modern Music* (New York: Continuum, 1985).

17. Rosen, *Arnold Schoenberg* (New York: Viking Press, 1975).

18. Treitler, "The Lulu Character and the Character of *Lulu*," in *Music and the Historical Imagination*, chap. 10.

19. Adorno, *Philosophy of Modern Music*, 69.

20. Adorno, *Philosophy of Modern Music*, 64–65. Adorno culled this bit of early music history from Richard Batka, *Allgemeine Geschichte der Musik* (Stuttgart: C. Grüninger, Klett & Hartmann, 1909–15). Altogether, what he mentions here is a well-worn cliché of flimsy music history popularizations. Pertinent to the present subject is a judgment of the music of Ockeghem in Cecil Gray, *The History of Music* (London: K. Paul, Trench, Kubner & Co. Ltd., 1928): According to Gray, Ockeghem was "a pure cerebralist, almost exclusively preoccupied with intellectual problems. . . . Expression was for him a secondary consideration, if indeed it existed for him at all. He seems to have had something of the mentality of Arnold Schoenberg today: the same ruthless disregard of merely sensuous beauty, the same unwearying and relentless pursuit of new technical means for their own sake. He is the schoolmaster, the drill sergeant of music." This passage was brought to my attention by Lawrence Bernstein's excellent study of zealous and creative music historiography, "'Singende Seele' or 'unsingbar'? Forkel, Ambros, and the Forces behind the Ockeghem Reception during the Late 18th and 19th Centuries," *Journal of Musicology* 23/1 (2006): 2–61.

21. Rosen writes that Spengler's "influence on Adorno is not mentioned by his admirers because [Spengler] is no longer intellectually respectable." Another influence about which one can say the same is that of Alfred Lorenz, the author of *Das Geheimnis der Form bei Richard Wagner*. See Carl Dahlhaus, "Soziologische Dechiffrierung von Musik—zu Th. W. Adornos Wagnerkritik," *International Review of the Aesthetics and Sociology of Music* 1 (1970): 137–48. Regarding the disagreement about Spengler's influence, see Rosen's reply to correspondence in the *New York Review of Books*, February 13, 2003.

22. See Arthur Herman, *The Idea of Decline in Western History* (New York: Free Press, 1997), with numerous references to Adorno.

23. Adorno (with Max Horkheimer), *Dialectic of Enlightenment* (New York: Continuum, 1972).

24. See, for example, his lecture, "On the Problem of Musical Analysis," intr. and trans. Max Paddison, *Music Analysis* 1 (1982): 2.

25. Hoeckner, "Homage to Adorno's 'Homage to Zerlina,'" *Musical Quarterly* 87 (2004): 510–22; also published in *The Don Giovanni Moment: Essays on the Legacy of an Opera*, ed. Lydia Goehr and Danny Herwitz (New York: Columbia University Press, 2006).

26. Theodor W. Adorno, "Schubert (1928)," trans. Jonathan Dunsby and Beate Perrey, *19th Century Music* 29 (2005): 3–14.

27. Adorno, *Mahler: A Musical Physiognomy*, trans. Edmund Jephcott (Chicago: University of Chicago Press, 1992).

Chapter Seventeen

The Music of a Classical Style

Scott Burnham

Memorable criticism merges style and idea. Few writers on music have attained this elusive desideratum to anywhere near the same degree as Charles Rosen. This is why his 1971 book *The Classical Style* remains among the preeminent accounts of any artistic style in any age. Critical sensibility seems to map onto the subject matter; both seem to speak with the same transparency and the same stylistic authority. Rosen's prose style is worth drawing out, for its most telling effects are never on parade; it is neither baroque nor purple. Moreover, an appreciation of the poetic ethos of Rosen's style can lead to an enhanced understanding of his critical *modus intellegendi*.

The general tone and heft of Rosen's style? Sturdy rather than precious, yet buoyant rather than ponderous; relaxed rather than strained, yet commanding and assertive. In short, his prose breathes with easy authority. This assuredness is established before we can become aware of it, for Rosen often opens a paragraph or section with a sweeping evaluation that turns our attention toward the feeling that we are in for something special. In such instances, he deploys superlatives unencumbered by enervating qualifications. Take the opening sentence of the chapter "String Quintets" from *The Classical Style*:

> By general consent, Mozart's greatest achievement in chamber music is the group of string quintets with two violas.[1]

The only qualification to this assertion is the clause "by general consent," which minimizes Rosen's direct role in the claim while strengthening the claim's plausibility. (Note the difference in tone if the initial clause is removed.) The word "consent" subliminally prompts the reader's own consent, and the superlative gains authority without automatically raising the suspicion that it may be a presumption of the critic.

The assignment of a superlative can also come in the form of litotes, through which the speaker states something by denying its negative:

[T]here is no more beautiful nuance in all of Schumann.[2]

This sentence goes down like water, but we can learn much from it. The level of specificity captured in the word *nuance* marks the experience as one of rarified particularity. ("There is no more beautiful *movement* in all of Schumann" says something decidedly less singular.) To isolate and value a nuance: here is a precious token of the joy of connoisseurship. The reader feels in the presence of something unutterably special. And Rosen's use of litotes takes the measure of "all of Schumann" more searchingly than would the simple assertion "This is one of the most beautiful nuances in all of Schumann." To assert that no more beautiful nuance exists implies a census taken (while subtly allowing that nuances just as beautiful may exist) and thus gives a more tangible sense of the allness of Schumann's music. Moreover, "there is" carries a broader, more inclusive force of assertion than "This is." General assertion plus litotes plus hyperbolic metonymy ("all of Schumann") results in a powerfully compelling assessment—all the more powerful for seeming to be understated! And what is the musical nuance thus placed on velvet? Rosen refers here to measure 12 of the piano piece "Des Abends" from the Op. 12 *Fantasiestücke*, in which an inner-voice C♭ catches momentarily on a B♭ at the expressive high point of the line, like an emotion-laden voice catching on a fraught word.

Rosen also offers general assertions about the nature of music that enjoy aphoristic cogency:

> The two principal sources of musical energy are dissonance and sequence—the first because it demands resolution, the second because it implies continuation. (*CS*, 120)

The choice of verbs after the dash greatly assists the thought. Notice how they work with the Latinate nouns—resolution is "demanded," continuation only "implied." Thus the demand increases the force of resolution, whereas the urge to continue is folded into the looser weave of future possibility. This pronouncement enjoys greater authority because the careful choice of words helps it ring true.

Rosen's projections of authority resort at times to an almost comic exaggeration in order to profile the requisite level of connoisseurship:

> Op. 64, no. 3, in B-flat Major is one of the great comic masterpieces: the listener who can hear the last movement without laughing aloud knows nothing of Haydn. (*CS*, 140)

Here the assertion of greatness pulls up to a colon, often in Rosen the upbeat to a statement whose significance will move beyond what the first clause would lead the reader to expect. And the statement that follows this colon throws down the gauntlet with a hyperbolic claim about Haydn's comedy that is itself comedic.

But note the almost stringent poetics of this clause: the liquid alliterations that culminate in "laughing aloud"; the way "knows nothing" echoes the *th* in "without" as well as the gerundive end of "laughing"; the rhyming assonance of "without" and "aloud," "nothing" and "of"; the way the name *Haydn* backstops the entire thought, reaching back to the *h* in "hear" and offering a final *n*. Though the clause hardly draws attention to itself as being marked poetically, change any word and the effect is diminished.

Other pronouncements employ the common figure of speech known as isocolon (repeated grammatical structure with different words), as in this assessment of Mendelssohn's *Songs Without Words*:

> The *Songs Without Words* have a Mozartean grace without Mozart's dramatic power, a Schubertian lyricism without Schubert's intensity. (*RG*, 589)

Rosen echoes the word *without* in Mendelssohn's title, making it into a critical rallying point. Thus the work itself seems to hand him the means with which to critique it.

Here is another use of isocolon, in a paradoxical pronouncement about Liszt:

> The early works are vulgar and great; the late works are admirable and minor. (*RG*, 474)

Rosen pulls the word "great" out of "vulgar" and "minor" out of "admirable." This alliterative music sharpens the paradox, as does the trailing rhythm of "admirable and minor" after the bracing accents of "vulgar and great."

Rosen seems more given to paradox when writing about the Romantic generation; here is another paradoxical formulation from the same book:

> We must admire an economy of means which results in such extravagance. (*RG*, 293)

In this culminating judgment about "the greatest military passage in Chopin's Polonaises" (*RG*, 288), the striking final word of the sentence gains impact through the way it is set up. Unlike the word pairs in the immediately previous example, "extravagance" is not forecast through directly adjoining alliteration. This circumstance profiles its sonic extravagance, allowing the word to be what the word denotes, an extravagance in the sentence. (The effect is also abetted by the rhythm of mostly one-syllable words issuing into a four-syllable extravagance.) But at the same time, "extravagance" lightly echoes the beginning and end of the phrase "economy of means" (*ex*-travaga-*nce*). The word thus gathers into a cogent unit the phrase "economy of means"—and here we are made to hear how extravagance can indeed be the result of an economy of means!

Sometimes Rosen's sentences take on the form of a musical structure. Again discussing Schumann's "Des Abends," Rosen notes an inversion in the usual procedure of melody and accompaniment:

> Melody is integrated into the general texture, accompaniment becomes intensely expressive. (*RG*, 35)

This is a periodic sentence, in the musical sense: elements in the antecedent clause are answered in the consequent clause. Note the heavy, closural downbeat on ex-PRESS-ive, and how "intensely expressive" answers "general texture." The sentence in fact becomes more expressive as it continues, because the sibilants and the *x* sound culminate an alliterative process that started back with "integrated": integrated-texture-intensely-expressive. Rosen's verbs support this process, as the second clause answers the static verb "is" with the more fluid "becomes."

Much of the authority of Rosen's writing—the feeling that he is on target when he describes musical style—is due to this musical quality of his prose. In fact, his poetic effects often seem to map directly onto the music he is discussing.

As a first example of such mapping, consider his account of some inner-voice accents in the last movement of Schumann's *Kreisleriana*. Listen to how the anaphoric iterations of the word *they* replicate the musical effect of these accents:

> In terms of voice leading, they come from nowhere, and they lead to nothing. They disturb the regular surface of the melody; they hint at forces that will not discover themselves, an ironic interference with the course of the music. (*RG*, 683)

Or take this passage, about the end of a Schumann song from the Heine *Liederkreis*:

> As the final chord arrives, the tonic note in the bass is removed, leaving the B-major chord suspended in a $^6_4$ inversion. . . . It makes a closure at once complete and incomplete, leaving the harmony of a final tonic chord but taking away the bass root, as if only the overtones of the tonic note were sustained. The resolution is not questioned, but only left open to question. (*RG*, 655)

Rosen's last sentence makes a subtle distinction that works on the mind, and thus has the same effect as Schumann's ending. Also, note the rhythm and the vowel music of this sentence, as heard in the following reduction: resolution . . . questioned/only . . . open . . . question. The second clause has the effect of opening up and unclenching the first clause, as the long *o* sound of "resolution" is dispersed into "only" and "open." The entire sentence is a fine example of a point that lingers suggestively, both in its thought and its poetic content—thus it is very like a Romantic fragment.

Rosen's prose is also capable of musical effects on a larger scale. After several dense pages detailing complexities of phrase rhythm in Chopin's A-flat-Major Ballade, Rosen reaches a resolution that matches Chopin's own:

> The extraordinary tranquility of the return of A-flat major in bar 116, its sense of breadth, comes from the sudden disappearance of all this elaborate dovetailing. Treble and bass are now in phase; the four-bar period is untroubled. (*RG*, 314)

Note how Rosen's final sentence is not only periodic but almost consistently iambic, and how the word "untroubled" reaches back to the beginning of the sentence (to gather in the word *treble*) and caps the thought. Like the musical phrase it describes, this sentence resolves the tensions of the previous pages.

There are obvious classical precedents for poetic effects that seem to enact the very thing being described. Greek and Roman authors could exploit such sonic effects because of the freedom of word order they enjoyed. (With inflected languages, syntax is determined by word endings and is not dependent on word order, as it is in English, for example.)

Here's a famous example from the opening of Virgil's first Eclogue:

> Tityre, tu patulae   recubans sub tegmine fagi
> Silvestrem tenui   musam meditaris avena.
> Nos patriae finis   et dulcia linquimus arva,
> Nos patriam fugimus;   tu, Tityre, lentus in umbra
> Formosam resonare doces Amaryllida silvas.

> (You, Tityrus, lie under your spreading beech's covert, wooing the woodland Muse on slender reed, but we are leaving our country's bounds and sweet fields. We are outcasts from our country; you, Tityrus, at ease beneath the shade, teach the woods to re-echo "fair Amaryllis.")[3]

Within the conventions of dactylic hexameter, the meter of Virgil's last line is unusual: it rolls right through the normative caesura within the third foot, a place usually marked by a word boundary (see the spaces in the Latin version above). And the word that overrides the caesura is *resonare*, to resonate. So already in a semantic and metrical sense the line seems to enact the resonance it describes. But the best effect is yet to come. The word order of the Latin is as follows: beautiful/to echo/you teach/Amaryllis/the woods. Freedom of word order allows Virgil to place *formosam* with *resonare* and *Amaryllida* with *silvas*. Whereas the word for "beauty" is thus subtly reflected in the word for "resonate," a stronger, more literal-sounding echo caps the line: *Amaryllida silvas*. Thus the word for "woods" is made to echo the word *Amaryllida*, just as the woods are said to resonate with her name.

By enacting musical effects in his descriptive prose, Rosen appears to speak from inside the music. This is in large part his modus operandi as a critic: speaking for and within the music. Whereas the denotative function of his words imparts his matchless knowledge of musical repertoire and musical conventions, their music reinforces this sense in a way at once more subtle and more forceful.

The art of Rosen's style is not unlike that of his revered Viennese Classical style. We hear clarity and resolution, rhetorical power without an overmastering show of force. And also like that style, part of the buoyancy of Rosen's critical writing is due to an ever-available sense of humor. Sometimes this takes the form of a provocative tongue-in-cheek assertion, as in this sentence from the preface to the revised edition of *Sonata Forms*:

> Sonatas are like chimpanzees.[4]

This remark is doubly funny in that it comments as briefly as possible on a rather longer citation from Stephen Jay Gould, drawing a succinct moral from Gould's emphasis on zoological individuality over any sort of zoological essence. It also constitutes a paragraph unto itself, as well as the last word of the preface (before some acknowledgments). Thus it comes off as a parting one-liner, making a fundamental point—nothing less than the conceptual justification of the title "Sonata Forms"—with an irreverent *bon mot*.

Few things bring out a critic's flair for humor more than hoary wrongheadedness:

> Other prejudices take even longer to disappear, but now there are only a few miserably isolated diehards who claim that Chopin could not handle large forms, that Beethoven was a poor melodist, or that Schoenberg's music is inexpressive. (*RG*, 473)

"Miserably isolated diehards" is wonderfully funny in its double qualification, its fussing to get the quality of mediocrity just right: not just *diehards*, and not just *isolated* diehards, but *miserably* isolated diehards (and indeed, "only a few" such diehards).

Rosen's polemics often find expression in smiling sallies, and were they not almost always at the expense of other living scholars I would cite more examples here (for some of these, see the aptly named *Critical Entertainments*, a collection of his reviews). But here's a characteristically humorous swipe at Theodor Adorno. After chipping away at Adorno's view that Beethoven's *Missa Solemnis* "remains enigmatically incomprehensible," Rosen gets to this series of moves:

> No other essay of Adorno is so riddled with unsupportable assertions. He writes: "Who after all can sing a passage from [the *Missa solemnis*] the way one can sing a passage from any of the symphonies or from *Fidelio*?" I can.[5]

Rhetorical questions rarely expect an actual answer. Thus the effect of Rosen's brief, matter-of-fact reply is a sudden, deflating puncture. We could easily imagine Adorno's assured query launching a countering catalogue of singable passages in Beethoven's mass. But Rosen's simple utterance is memorably funny: never was a rhetorical question brought up so short with so little.

At the opposite end of the spectrum stands a piece of comedy whose full force is not immediately apparent but that seems to grow funnier the more one considers it. Rosen prefaces *The Classical Style* with an epigraph from Nestroy's 1842 farce *Einen Jux will er sich machen*:

> Zangler: Was hat Er denn immer mit dem dummen Wort "klassisch"?
> Melchior: Ah, das Wort is nit dumm, es wird nur oft dumm angewend't.

> (Zangler: Why do you keep repeating that idiotic word "classic"?
> (Melchior: Oh the word isn't idiotic; it's just often used idiotically.)

At first blush, the epigraph seems to want to instruct us about loaded terms such as *classic*: they are often bandied about uncritically. This is a useful reminder to take on board before settling into a book premised on the name and concept of the classic. And the pronounced Viennese dialect of the epigraph perhaps makes another kind of point, somewhat less serious but still potent, reminding us that the Classical style has a regional home in Vienna. Finally, it is funny to make the point about "classic" through the patently comic patter of a pair of characters out of Nestroy.

But this is only the beginning of the humor embedded in this epigraph. When we recover the original context of the exchange between Zangler and Melchior (act 1, scene 6), an irony arises. In Nestroy's farce, "klassisch" is a term of approbation and/or astonishment from the private argot of a wise-guy servant, Melchior. Melchior uses the term indiscriminately to describe anything he approves of or is taken aback by (it has roughly the force of the word *outrageous* in present-day American usage). After several repetitions of the word "klassisch" in very short order, Melchior's new boss Zangler finally calls him on it, and the above exchange ensues. The humor in the original context resides in the irony of the servant's defending the word he overuses by putting the blame on "idiotic" usage—precisely the sort of usage he has just amply demonstrated by his own practice. It is funny for Rosen to deploy the words of a clownish character in this way, to let Melchior's unintentionally hilarious irony seem to set a serious point about the use of freighted words such as *classic*. Moreover, Melchior's usage reenacts a linguistic commonplace: the conversion of terms of august approbation into terms of automatic approbation. In the Western tradition, "classic" resonates as one such term. Melchior comically misappropriates it, much as the present generation misuses "awesome": a term once reserved for the overwhelming appearance of the sublime is now used to describe anything from a cup of coffee to the ratification of a social plan ("See you at the Rat?" "Awesome, dude.") Who could ask for more from an epigraph? Rosen's citation from Nestroy launches broadening ripples of significance, like an ever-widening smile.

The ready humor, easy authority, and elegant music of Charles Rosen's critical prose together constitute a style whose prevailing ethos is generosity. Above all, we hear a reassuring confidence in the communicability of the musical experience: rather than cast hopeful or anxious words into a mysterious void, Rosen's voice expects and receives a solid echo. In this sense, his is a classic rather than a romantic style. It is premised on the general assumption that things are knowable; that music stands in the light of day; and that its effects (however subtle and elusive) are felt and shared and identifiable.[6] Rosen's style is also classic in its impact, rising above the contemporaneous landscape to join ranks with the great voices of modern British and American criticism of the last several centuries. But why keep repeating that idiotic word *classic*? Much better to open any of Rosen's books to any page and hear him yet again let music speak.

Notes

1. Charles Rosen, *The Classical Style: Haydn, Mozart, Beethoven*, expanded ed. (New York: Norton, 1997), 264. Subsequent references to this work are cited in the text using the abbreviation *CS* and page number.

2. Charles Rosen, *The Romantic Generation* (Cambridge, MA: Harvard University Press, 1995), 35. Subsequent references to this work are cited in the text using the abbreviation *RG* and page number.

3. Virgil, *Eclogues, Georgics, Aeneid I–VI*, trans. H. Rushton Fairclough, Loeb Classical Library (Cambridge, MA: Harvard University Press, 1935), 3.

4. Charles Rosen, *Sonata Forms*, rev. ed. (New York: Norton, 1998), viii.

5. Charles Rosen, "Should We Adore Adorno?" *New York Review of Books*, October 24, 2002.

6. I have borrowed this notion of classic and romantic prose styles from Francis-Noël Thomas and Mark Turner, *Clear and Simple as the Truth: Writing Classic Prose* (Princeton, NJ: Princeton University Press, 1994).

Chapter Eighteen

Montaigne hors de son propos

Charles Rosen

For Yves Bonnefoy

In his "Consideration sur Ciceron" (livre I, chapitre 40), Montaigne remarks that when someone dwells on the language, the style, of his essays, "j'aimerois mieus qu'il s'en teust."[1] It was, above all, the objective content of which he was proud, more material and denser, he says, than in other writers. But, as he observes at once, this matter is not always straightforward:

> Ny elles [mes histoires], ny mes allegations ne servent pas tousjours simplement d'example, d'authorite ou d'ornement. Je ne les regarde pas seulement par l'usage que j'en tire. Elles portent souvant, hors de mon propos, la semance d'une matiere plus riche et plus hardie, et sonent a gauche un ton plus delicat, et pour moi qui n'en veus exprimer davantage, et pour ceus qui recontreront mon air.[2]

This open invitation to read between the lines is followed by a condemnation of style for style's sake (a subject to which we may return briefly), reinforced by a quotation from Seneca: "Elegance is not a masculine ornament." (All these considerations were added in the margins of the 1588 edition.)

Hors de propos, we might remark (thinking of the present academic fashion of imposing a Montaigne *bien pensant* and impeccably orthodox Catholic) that an author who is unwilling to express himself completely and who expects the happy few (the readers who understand his "*air*") to guess at oblique resonances *à gauche* is not likely to hold the most respectable opinions or positions. Sainte-Beuve's summary observation that Montaigne would have been a very good Catholic if he had only been a Christian still seems to me the most cogent formula, although still unsatisfactory. It also explains his importance for Pascal: it is through Montaigne that Pascal found within himself the realization that incredulity has an attraction as powerful as faith—an orthodox Montaigne would have been of little use to him. The power and the intelligibility of the *Pensées* rest on recognizing the seduction of disbelief and indifference.

The matter that Montaigne derived from his reading has an ambiguous status. He mocks writers who quote frequently from the classics, although this was certainly his own practice. But he boasts of deforming his citations:

> Je desrobe mes larrecins, et les desguise. Ceux-cy [les auteurs] les mettent en parade et en compte; aussi ont-ils plus de crédit avec les loix que moy. Comme ceux qui desrobent les chevaux, je leur peins le crin et la queuë, et parfois je les esborgne; si le premier maistre s'en servoit a bestes d'emble, je les mets au trot, et au bast, s'ils servoient à la selle.[3]

In this passage of 1588 from "De la phisionomie" (livre III, chapitre 12), he later canceled from his own copy (the so-called "Exemplaire de Bordeaux"), the picturesque reference to horse thieves. However, he boasts elsewhere of concealing his borrowings from the classics, since it amused him to be attacked by those who did not realize when he was citing some famous authority, so that, as he says, the critics who mock him are really thumbing their noses at Plutarch or Seneca without knowing it. "Je veus qu'ils donnent une nasarde a Plutarque sur mon nez" (livre II, chapitre 10, "Des livres").[4]

At his most characteristic, Montaigne does not use his quotations or his anecdotes as final authority but only as steps in a movement of thought that leads somewhere else—and the conclusion itself is not a final step, a place of rest. In livre III, chapitre 11, "Des boyteux," he takes up the antique belief that sexual intercourse is most enjoyable with a cripple:

> A propos ou hors de propos, il n'importe, on dict en Italie, en commun proverbe, que celuy-là ne cognoit pas Venus en sa parfaicte douceur qui n'a couché avec la boiteuse. La fortune, ou quelque particulier accident, ont mis il y a longtemps ce mot en la bouche du peuple; et se dict des masles comme des femelles.[5]

Montaigne speculates on the reason for this belief: perhaps the eccentric movements of the lame give a new taste or pleasure to the action, he suggests, but quickly adds that he has just learned that ancient philosophy gives a different reason (he got this from the pseudo-Aristotle of *The Problems*): since the thighs and the calves of the lame do not get enough nourishment, the genital parts are fuller and more vigorous. Or else the lame get so little exercise that they give themselves more completely to the games of Venus, and that is why the Greeks claimed that female weavers were so much warmer about sex than other women because of their sedentary occupation.

This leads Montaigne to the first of his double conclusions:

> Dequoy ne pouvons nous raisonner à ce pris là? De celles icy [les tisserandes] je pourrois ausi dire que ce tremoussement que leur ouvrage leur donne ainsi assises les esveille et sollicite, comme faict les dames le crolement et tremblement de leurs coches. Ces exemples servent-ils pas à ce que je disois au commencement:

que nos raisons anticipent souvent l'effect, et ont l'estendue de leur jurisdiction si infinie, qu'elles jugent et s'exercent en l'inanité mesme et au non estre?[6]

The second conclusion, however, turns around and goes full circle:

> Car, par la seule authorité de l'usage ancien et publique de ce mot, je me suis autresfois faict à croire avoir receu plus de plaisir d'une femme de ce qu'elle n'estoit pas droicte, et mis cela au compte de ses graces (1588 text).[7]

It is evident that neither the proverb nor the various steps of reasoning or even the conclusions have a permanent value for Montaigne. It is the voyage that counts; it leads from ancient authority though empty speculation to the ironic and basically worthless rehabilitation of the traditional view.

This aspect of Montaigne's thinking was essential to him. It is the process of thought that concerns him. Shortly after the opening of "De la ressemblance des enfants aux peres" (livre II, chapitre 37), he remarks:

> Au demeurant, je ne corrige point mes premieres imaginations par les secondes; oui, a l'avanture quelque mot, mais pour diversifier, non pour oster. Je veux representer le progrez de mes humeurs, et qu'on voye chaque piece en sa naissance.[8]

It is, indeed, true that the variant readings are far more often additions than corrections, but the interest of Montaigne's "progress of humors" means that the study of even his simple revisions is more illuminating than those of most other writers. That he liked the "commerce des belles et honnestes femmes,"[9] for example, gains in interest when we know that he originally wrote simply "honnestes femmes et bien nees"[10] and that "belles" was added somewhat later.

Fundamental to Montaigne is the mistrust of conclusions. The refusal to conclude properly, in fact, can reveal him at his most profound. In the opening chapter of the third book, he launches into a catalogue of vice that foreshadows the preface to *Les fleurs du mal*:

> Nostre estre est simenté de qualitez maladives; l'ambition, la jalousie, l'envie, la vengeance, la superstition, le desespoir, logent en nous d'une si naturelle possession que l'image s'en reconnoist aux bestes; voire et la cruauté vice si desnaturé: car, au milieu de la compassion, nous sentons au dedans je ne scay quelle aigre-douce poincte de volupté maligne à voir souffrir autruy; et les enfants la sentent.[11]

The description of cruelty, one of the poetic triumphs of sixteenth-century literature, immediately precedes some political reflections inspired by an age torn apart by religious strife:

> . . . desquelles qualitez qui osteroit les semences en l'homme, destruiroit les fondamentalles conditions de nostre vie. De mesme, en toute police, il y a des offices

necessaires, non seulement abjects, mais encore vitieux:. . . . S'ils deviennent excus-
ables, d'autant qu'ils nous font besoing et que la necessité commune efface leur vrai
qualité, il faut laisser jouer cette partie aux citoyens plus vigoureux et moins craintifs qui sacrifient leur honneur et leur conscience, comme ces autres antiens sacri-
fierent leur vie pour le salut de leur pays; nous autres, plus foibles, prenons des
rolles et plus aisez et moins hazardeux. Le bien public requiert qu'on trahisse et
qu'on mente et qu'on massacre; resignons cette commission à gens plus obeissons
et plus souples.[12]

"Et qu'on massacre" was added later after 1588 as the political situation wors-
ened. The last words, "plus souples," strike with greater force if we reflect that
it is difficult to be more supple than Montaigne, but the coarseness of the irony
reaffirms the contempt that is naked in the previous clauses. The comparison of
those heroes of the past who sacrificed their lives for their country with their
modern counterparts who sacrifice their honor and their conscience may, I sus-
pect, have been remembered by Edward Gibbon in one of the most extraordinary works of English polemics, *A Vindication of Some Passages in the Fifteenth and
Sixteenth Chapters of the History of the Decline and Fall of the Roman Empire*, where he
attacked the claim that an ecclesiastical historian had the right to cover up the
defects of the early Christian church. He wrote: "The historian must indeed be
generous, who will conceal, by his own disgrace, that of his country, or of his reli-
gion." The irony and the contempt are similar. In Montaigne, however, the irony
is also directed against virtue and honesty: "craintifs," "aisez," and "obeissons"
undermine the position of decency. Montaigne clearly intends his attempt to
balance the utility of treason, murder, and vice with the feeble and cowardly sup-
pleness of virtue to be deeply unsatisfactory and inconclusive.

To return briefly to the "Consideration sur Ciceron," we can see that the popular controversy on style current in sixteenth-century France and, indeed,
throughout Europe clearly found Montaigne in the anti-Ciceronian camp on
the side of Seneca, or—to put it another way—on the side of Erasmus as
opposed to Etienne Dolet. In his praise of Seneca's letters in this essay, however,
Montaigne makes a sudden and unexpected allusion in Cicero's favor, a reversal
that is left undeveloped and is all the more striking for that. It follows only two
paragraphs after the passage quoted at the opening of this chapter. He expresses
his appreciation of Seneca's letters:

[E]ncore ne sont ce pas letteres vuides et descharnées, qui ne se soutiennent que par
un delicat chois de mots, entassez et rangez à une juste cadence, ains farcies et pleines
de beaux discourse de sapience, par lesquelles on se rend non plus eloquent, mais plus
sage, et qui nous aprennent non à bien dire, mais à bien faire. Fy de l'eloquence qui
nous laisse envie de soy, non des choses; si ce n'est qu'on die que celle de Ciceron,
estant en si extreme perfection, se donne corps elle mesme.[13]

The last clause is Dolet's argument in favor of Cicero, his claim that the beauty of style does not depend on its relation to the subject matter as Erasmus insisted, but that at its greatest perfection, it becomes matter, provides its own "body," its own justification.

Elsewhere, Montaigne is brutal in his treatment of Cicero. In "Des livres," he writes:

> Mais, à confesser hardiment la verité (car, puis qu'on a franchi les barrieres de l'impudence, il n'y a plus de bride), sa façon d'escrire me semble ennuyeuse, et toute autre pareille façon. . . . Si j'ay employé une heure à le lire, qui est beaucoup pour moy, et que je r'amentoive ce que j'en ay tiré de suc et de substance, la plus part du temps je n'y treuve que du vent.[14]

At the time, the positions of both sides of the contemporary argument on style, Senecan and Ciceronian, were equally commonplace. Montaigne gives them greater force by his surprisingly reasonable juxtaposition of them and greater depth by presenting them as part of his autobiography. Historically he was on the side that eventually won, partly due to the originality with which he exemplified the Senecan tradition.

He knew how to give force to the wisdom embodied by the commonplace, the moral saws of tradition. "Sur les vers de Virgile" (livre III, chapitre 5) is not simply a discussion of sex but for most of its length a catalogue of misogynist anecdotes, banalities of the medieval and classical literature. But when, on the last page, he writes:

> Je dis que les masles et femelles sont jettez en mesme moule: sauf l'institution et l'usage, la difference n'y est pas grande[,][15]

This derives its power from the mass of the preceding misogyny. And the effect is reinforced by further commonplaces:

> Il est bien plus aisé d'accuser l'un sexe, que d'excuser l'autre. C'est ce qu'on dict: Le fourgon se moque de la poele.[16]

This declaration is more persuasive than the fashionable and generally insipid feminism of many of Montaigne's contemporaries precisely because of its following from the medieval realistic tradition and by its evasion of the idealistic current.

Notes

The French-language portions of this essay were translated by Kevin Byrnes.

1. "I would prefer that he keep quiet."

2. "Neither they [my stories] nor my citations always serve simply as example, authority, or ornament. I don't consider them just for the use I draw from them.

They often carry, apart from my purpose, the seed of richer and bolder material, and obliquely sound a more delicate note, both for me, who wish to express nothing more of it, and for those who might share my sensibility."

3. "I hide my thefts, and disguise them. These other authors put them on parade and on account; thus they have better credit with the law than I. Like those who steal horses, I paint them mane and tail, and sometimes poke out an eye; if their first master used them as amblers, I put them to trot, and to the pack saddle if they served for the riding saddle."

4. "I want them to give a fillip to Plutarch, on my nose."

5. "On this subject it doesn't matter; there is a common proverb in Italy that he knows not Venus in her perfect sweetness who has not lain with a cripple. Fortune, or some particular incident, long ago put this saying into the mouth of the people; and it is said of males as well as of females."

6. "What can we not reason about at this rate? Of these [the weavers] I could also say that the jiggling that their task causes them, thus seated, arouses and stirs them, as the rocking and shaking of their coaches does to our ladies.

"Do not these examples serve to what I said at the beginning: that our reasonings about causes often anticipate the effect and are so infinite in the extent of their jurisdiction that they judge and act in inanity and in non-being?"

7. "For solely by the authority of the ancient and public use of that saying, I once made myself believe that I had received more pleasure from a woman who was not straight, and attributed that to her charms."

8. "Besides, I do not correct my first fantasies by my second; yes, sometimes a word, but to diversify, not to take away. I wish to display the progress of my humors, and that each piece be seen at its birth."

9. "Commerce [company] of beautiful and respectable women"

10. "honest and well-born women"

11. "Our being is cemented with sickly qualities; ambition, jealousy, envy, vengeance, superstition, and despair lodge in us with such natural possession that their image is recognized among the beasts; even cruelty, so unnatural a vice: for, in the midst of compassion, we sense within an indefinable bittersweet prick of malignant pleasure in seeing someone else suffer, even children feel it."

12. ". . . . which qualities, whoever would remove their seeds from man, would destroy the fundamental conditions of our life. Similarly, in every government, there are necessary offices, not only abject but also vicious. If they become excusable, to the degree that we need them and that common necessity erases their true quality, we must leave the playing of this part to the more vigorous and less timid citizens who sacrifice their honor and their conscience, as the ancients [classical Greeks and Romans] sacrificed their lives, for the salvation of their country; we, the weaker, let us take roles that are both easier and less hazardous. Public welfare requires that one betray, and that one lie and that one massacre; let us resign this commission to those who are more obedient and more supple."

13. "Still, these are not void, fleshless letters, sustained only by a delicate choice of words, piled up and arranged into a proper cadence; but rather are stuffed and filled with fine discourses of wisdom, by which we become not more eloquent, but wiser, and which teach us not to speak well but to act well. Fie on the eloquence that leaves us wanting itself, and not things; unless, as one says of Cicero's that, being of such extreme perfection, it gives itself its own body."

1 4. "But, to boldly confess the truth (for, once we have broken through the barriers to impudence, there is nothing to hold us back), his way of writing strikes me as boring, and every similar style as well. . . . . If I have given one hour to read him, which is much for me, and should I recall the sap and substance that I have drawn from it, most of the time I find nothing there but wind."

1 5. "I say that male and female are cast in the same mold: but for education and custom the difference is not great."

1 6. "It is much easier to accuse the one sex than to excuse the other. It is as they say: the poker makes fun of the shovel [Translator's note: the pot calls the kettle black]."

Three Tributes

Une culture vraiment intimidante

Pierre Boulez

Charles Rosen possède une culture vraiment intimidante. Non seulement en musique, d'ailleurs. Mais dans le domaine musical, il a écrit des ouvrages qui font date aussi bien sur l'univers contemporain que celui de la musique dite, avec plus ou moins d'exiguïté, de répertoire. Mais justement il la sort de cette notion étriquée de répertoire, de même qu'il extirpe la musique contemporaine d'où l'on veut la confiner pour la replacer dans une perspective plus large et entièrement justifiée. De même que ses qualités d'interprète sont irriguées par l'étendue de ses connaissances et l'acuité de sa réflexion, de même sa vaste culture donne à ses interprétations une intensité et une validité qui montrent que la culture, loin de la tuer, enrichit la spontanéité. Cette combinaison de culture et d'approche pragmatique donnent un relief exceptionnel à sa personnalité; ce qui fait de lui, au demeurant, un excellent pédagogue au sens le plus large et le moins pédant du terme.

Charles Rosen exhibits a degree of culture that is genuinely intimidating. And not just in the field of music. Not only has he contributed works that are landmarks in their field on the subject of what is still referred to—not entirely satisfactorily—as the standard repertory: he has made fundamental contributions to our understanding of the world of contemporary music. Leaving behind more narrow conceptions of repertory, he has uprooted contemporary music from the corner where it has all too often been confined and placed it in the broader perspective it deserves. His qualities as an interpreter are nourished by the range of his knowledge and the acuity of his reflections, his vast culture lending his interpretations an intensity and validity that prove that, far from killing spontaneity, culture enriches it. It is precisely this combination of culture and a pragmatic approach that lends his personality its exceptional profile. In the end, it is also what makes him an ideal pedagogue in the broadest and least pedantic sense of the term.

Paris, décembre 2005

Charles Rosen for
His Eightieth Birthday

Elliott Carter

I believe I first met Charles Rosen after the war in 1949 at an ISCM concert in New York, where Aaron Copland introduced us. A few years later I was fascinated by remarks he made at Milton Babbitt's apartment in New York City. It must have been when I was in Paris around 1951 that the American Consul told me of a performance of my Piano Sonata in Brussels; arriving there I was amazed at how wonderfully in command of my work Charles was, both technically and expressively. This performance was certainly the best I had heard up to that time.

Since then I have frequently enjoyed his company and consider him one of my best friends. Early on we usually talked about French literature—his PhD at Princeton on the seventeenth-century poet La Fontaine had made him extremely well informed on the subject—but our conversations over the years have covered an extraordinary range: music, literature, art, and many other topics including gastronomy. (We have had long and penetrating discussions of wine, French cheese, and cooking!) Always apparent has been his awareness of people and their special characteristics and the sources of some of their remarkable contributions.

As for his invaluable devotion to music, I must say that piano recitals of most other performers leave me disturbed by their lack of understanding of phrasing, of character or expressivity, and even of form; but when I hear a recital by Charles I am completely convinced and carried away. He not only has a complete command of technique but also of color, which is rare; and he puts this all to use in bringing out not only a vision of the period in which the music was composed but in making it a present, vivid experience. It is astonishing how he plays Mozart as compared to Beethoven or each of these as compared to Chopin or Schumann or Stravinsky or Schoenberg: this highly imaginative awareness of the distinctions among styles makes him one of the most engaging performers I have ever heard; and his many recordings from Haydn to Schoenberg and of my own Piano Sonata, Double Concerto, and *Night Fantasies* bear witness to this.

His memory astonishes. Once he was invited to play my *Night Fantasies* as part of a festival of my work in Turin, Italy. When he arrived, the presenters of the festival asked him if he could play my Piano Sonata as well. He explained that he did not have the music with him and had not performed the work in over two years; so a musician in New York was contacted, the score was faxed two days before the intended performance, and, to everyone's delight, Charles came forth with a brilliant captivating performance.

Another remarkable side of Charles, of course, is his writing, beginning with *The Classical Style*—which means so much to me, since it is dedicated to my wife and me—and then a series of books, including especially *The Romantic Generation* and the little one on Schoenberg. His essays in the *New York Review of Books*, covering not only the German philosopher Walter Benjamin but many diverse subjects, are well worth reading, as is his charming interview in French, "Plaisir de jouer, plaisir de penser." In this interview he says that, viewed from the perspective of musical history, the so-called modernist movement is being carried on in a way that makes "neo-romanticism" and repetitive music seem like a step backward—which seems a very reasonable point of view to me.

In writing this I feel I cannot express how grateful I am for all that Charles has done, not only for my work and for my imagination, but for music in general. Many more wonderful birthdays!

November 29, 2006

Charles Rosen: A Personal Appreciation by a Contemporary

Charles Mackerras

It was some time during the 1970s that I first had the pleasure of meeting Charles Rosen. At the time, we shared the same manager, Basil Douglas, who had been the General Manager of Benjamin Britten's English Opera Group. Basil had become an agent with quite a short list of a rather specialized kind of artist. When visiting London, many of Basil's artists used to stay in his beautiful Regency house on Primrose Hill, which is where I met Charles. Charles must have been playing in London while I was making one of my lightning visits from Hamburg, where I was permanently employed at the time.

I was busy promoting my then somewhat revolutionary ideas about Mozartean ornamentation and appoggiaturas, and, of course, I found a sympathetic ally in Charles Rosen. I had always known of him as a tremendous intellectual and as a stylist as a pianist. I had not expected that he would have an encyclopedic knowledge, not only of Mozart's and Handel's operas, but of the *bel canto ottocento* operatic style typified by Donizetti, Bellini, and Verdi. I was soon to discover that Charles Rosen is a specialist in just about everything, as indeed the title of this *Festschrift* suggests, "from Bach to Boulez" and even beyond.

I think Charles was a pioneer in the notion that you could combine analytical academic music research (now called "musicology") with the colossal technique of an international virtuoso. This type of combination has become much more prevalent in recent years, but I think that Charles was the first and noble example. I remember that he expatiated fascinatingly on the performance practice of the Baroque and Classical periods; that he was a mine of information on Beethoven and Schubert, and their entire oeuvres—not just the piano works; and that Chopin, too, was one of his many specialities. In fact, it was in Chopin that we first collaborated, because we recorded his two piano concertos for the BBC. Despite his tremendous intellectual grasp of Chopin's idiom and his formidable technique, we found him not all that easy to follow. He played with such a tremendous sense of fantasy that the concertos sounded as if Charles were actually composing and improvising as he went along. Given his improvisatory style, whenever we did a new take in the recording process, he would play the same passage completely differently, with new emphases and accents and rhythmic freedoms, rather as I imagine Chopin himself must have played. As is well known, Chopin's orchestral accompaniments are not the most interesting or inspiring features of his concertos, but Charles soon showed the players that they could not just sit back and play a lot of boring long notes in strict tempo: they had to be alert to every nuance of his rubato.

Although conducting the Chopin concertos with Charles was indeed a revelatory experience, for me, the greatest revelation of all was when we did the Elliott Carter Piano Concerto together in 1978. At that time I was Principal Guest Conductor of the BBC Symphony Orchestra. Although one of the main functions of that orchestra is to play contemporary music, at that time my experience of twentieth-century music was limited to the styles of such composers as Britten, Shostakovich, Bartók, and Schoenberg. Thus, the immense complications of Carter's Piano Concerto were for me rather daunting. However, Charles had already played the concerto several times in America and was able to steer us successfully through the very grueling rehearsals, and especially rehearsals with the *concertino*, which plays such a crucial part in this work. When it came to rehearsals with the full complement of solo piano, *concertino*, and large symphony orchestra, I was quite nervous when Carter himself appeared. But Charles had as intimate an understanding of that charming man as he did of his cerebral but passionate music, and the composer seemed delighted with our efforts. The concert in the Festival Hall also included the Stravinsky Symphony in Three Movements and the Bartók Concerto for Orchestra, but it was the virtuosity and intellectual power that Charles Rosen brought to the Carter Piano Concerto that transformed it into the hit of the evening.

Later in the year we repeated that memorable concerto at a Prom. The number of rehearsals for the Proms is always fairly severely limited because of the huge number of concerts that the BBC Symphony Orchestra has to perform during that period. But with his extremely sympathetic attitude toward his *concertino* and the orchestra, Charles got us through the Prom, despite the fact that we had less than a quarter of the rehearsal time that we had originally had. Afterward, I remember the Prommers stamping their feet with the same enthusiasm as if it had been a concerto by Tchaikovsky.

Charles and I are approximately the same age, and I regard it as a privilege to have known and worked with him and, in fact, to have learned so much from his prolific writings and his charming conversations. Charles Rosen is one of the truly great musical minds of our time and a great virtuoso to boot.

Appendices

Appendix 1

A Discography of the Recordings of Charles Rosen

David Gable

Shortly after the introduction of the "long-play" record, or LP, by Columbia Records in 1948, Charles Rosen made his first recordings for two of the numerous small labels that proliferated during this period: EMS (for Elaine Music Shop) and REB (for Robert E. Blake) Editions. EMS was founded by Jack Skurnick, a co-owner of the Elaine Music Shop, located at 9 East 44 Street in New York City: the shop was named after the co-owner Harry Lew's wife, Elaine. Nothing if not ambitious, Skurnick undertook a series of recordings of early music under the general title Anthology of Twelfth- to Seventeenth-Century Music with the Brussels-based ensemble Pro Cantione Antiqua under the leadership of Stafford Cape; but the single most celebrated release on the EMS label was *The Complete Works of Edgard Varèse*, volume 1, which was recorded under the composer's supervision and made famous long after the fact when rock'n'roll musician (and closet composer of serious music) Frank Zappa wrote about it in *Stereo Review* in 1971. A forthcoming second volume never materialized because of Skurnick's death on September 6, 1952. Rosen made his first recording for EMS Records in the summer of 1950 while still a graduate student at Princeton University. Robert E. Blake was the engineer for at least some of the recordings on the EMS label, including Rosen's, and the founder of his own label, REB Editions.[1]

In 1960, Rosen made his first recording for Epic Records, and through the early 1970s, his recordings appeared on Epic and various other labels owned by CBS Records. Among the more ambitious undertakings from this period were recordings of the last keyboard works of Bach and a recording of the last six Beethoven sonatas, a perennial bestseller that remained in the Columbia catalogue until the demise of the LP. During this period Rosen was enlisted to participate in the first recording of Stravinsky's *Movements* for Piano and Orchestra with the composer conducting. Boulez invited Rosen to record his complete piano music, of which the first sonata and the extant movements of the third were recorded. Boulez also invited him to participate in a complete recording of the music of Anton Webern. Most of Rosen's CBS recordings were produced by Jane Friedmann or Thomas Z. Shepard. A number of them have been reissued on compact disc.

Rosen's later recordings include an anthology of the music of Robert Schumann, music of Chopin, and Elliott Carter's *Night Fantasies*, a work that was written for and dedicated to Rosen along with three other pianists who have championed Carter's music. During this period, Rosen worked with such well-known producers of digital recordings as Klaas Posthuma and Max Wilcox.

Something of Rosen's attitude toward the role of the performer is revealed in notes he wrote to accompany the Columbia set of the last six Beethoven piano sonatas, which included his second recording of the *Hammerklavier* sonata:

> When I started to record this set of the last six piano sonatas of Beethoven, it was with the intention of re-issuing the recording of the *Hammerklavier* that I had made some six years ago. We quickly decided to record it again. . . . The quality of sound was too different to put the new together with the old without a shock as one passed from Opus 90 to 106, made in a different city on a different piano. And by a different pianist, one might say. The old recording no longer represented what I thought about the *Hammerklavier*.
>
> Not that it ever did; a recording, like a performance, represents not what we think but what we can do. A record is always provisional, and each one is a wager—with the music—which the performer is honor bound to lose if he wishes to keep his self-respect. The so-called definitive performance is the death of music; it substitutes itself for the work, and by so doing, destroys it.
>
> A second recording would seem at first sight to bring one at least a little closer to a representative version—representative in my terms, of course, not Beethoven's—but, if that were true, it would be like hedging one's bets. Luckily this second recording is even more provisional. It has served to open up new possibilities for me, some of which I have only partially realized and not all of which could ever be realized in any one performance.[2]

In general, Rosen has written the liner notes for his own recordings. When he has written his own notes, it is indicated in the following.

I. The Early Recordings

Recordings in this section are listed in chronological order.

Franz Joseph Haydn:
Sonata in D Major, Hob. XVI:51
Sonata in A-flat Major, Hob. XVI:46 (mislabeled 43 on record jacket)

(Coupled with Partita in F Major [arrangement of Notturno, No. 4], Hob. II:28. EMS Chamber Orchestra [members of the N.B.C. Symphony Orchestra], cond. Edvard Fendler.)

"Charles Rosen, New York born pianist, is making his record debut here. His distinguished performance of these Haydn sonatas has won him an exclusive contract with EMS. (He will be heard in REB and other Record Affiliates Recordings). He is a pupil of Moriz Rosenthal, Hedwig Kanner-Rosenthal, and Robert Casadesus."

"Recorded during summer 1950," presumably in Rowayton, Connecticut. Engineer: Robert E. Blake. Notes on sonatas by "C. Welles Rosen." [EMS Series 1950] EMS No. 3 (monaural LP), (P) 1950.

Bohuslav Martinů:
    Étude in F
    Polka in A
    Étude in F
    Polka in E
    Étude in C
    Les ritournelles
(Coupled with the Sonata for Flute and Piano [René le Roy, flute, and George Reeves, piano])

Rosen was invited to participate in this recording by the composer, who was on the faculty at Princeton University when Rosen was a doctoral student there.

"Complete and Authentic Editions Recorded in Fall 1950 by Robert Blake, Recording Engineer," presumably in Rowayton, Connecticut. [EMS Recordings, Series 1950] EMS 2 (monaural LP), (P) 1950.

Wolfgang Amadeus Mozart:
    Rondo in A Minor, K. 511
    Suite in the Style of Handel, K. 399/385i (identified as K. 385 on jacket)
    Gigue, K. 574
    Sonata in F Major, K. 533/494
Recorded in Rowayton, Connecticut, December 1950. REB Editions REB 5 (monaural LP), (P) 1951.

Claude Debussy:
    Douze études
Recorded in Rowayton, Connecticut, December 1950. Notes by Charles Rosen. R.E.B. Editions 6 (monaural LP), (P) 1951.

Francis Poulenc:
    Sextet for Piano and Winds
    Trio for Piano, Oboe, and Bassoon

Sonata for Clarinet and Bassoon
The Fairfield Chamber Group: Harry Shulman, oboe; Leonard Sharrow, bassoon; Fred Klein, horn; David Weber, clarinet; Harold Bennett, flute; Charles Rosen, piano
Presumably recorded 1950 or 1951, in Rowayton, Connecticut. R.E.B. Editions 7 (monaural LP), (P) 1951.

Wolfgang Amadeus Mozart:
   Sonata No. 32 in B-flat Major for Violin and Piano, K. 454
   Sonata No. 33 in E-flat Major for Violin and Piano, K. 481
Reinhard Peters, violin
London LL 674 (monaural LP), (P) April 1953; [French] Decca FST 153.035 (monaural LP), (P) 1953. (Place and date unknown.)

Johannes Brahms:
   Variations on a Theme of Paganini, Op. 35, Books 1 and 2
Recorded December 18, 1953. [British] Decca LW 5092 (10-inch monaural LP), (P) 1954; London LD 9104 (10-inch monaural LP), (P) 1954.

The Siena Pianoforte
"The legend is that this piano was made of wood from Jerusalem, from the very pillars of Solomon's Temple. . . . Hear for yourself the 'divine sounds' that Liszt heard from its depths."
Domenico Scarlatti:
   Sonata in C-sharp Minor, L. 256 (K. 247)
   Sonata in E Major, L. 221 (K. 134)
   Sonata in C Major, L. 202 (K. 242)
   Sonata in F Major, L. 432 (K. 44)
   Sonata in D Major, L. 107 (K. 140)
   Sonata in G Major, L. 487 (K. 125)
Wolfgang Amadeus Mozart:
   Sonata in B-flat Major, K. 333
Esoteric Records ESP-3000 (monaural LP), (P) 1955; Counterpoint CPT 3000 (monaural LP), (P) 1958.
Compact-disc reissue: First release in stereo (coupled with Mozart, Sonata in A Major, K. 331 [Kathryn Déguire]).[3] Boston Skyline BSD 131, (P) 1995 by Everest Records, © 1995 Boston Skyline records.

II. Recordings for Various CBS Labels

Recordings in this section are listed in alphabetical order by composer or, in the case of the anthology *Virtuoso!*, by album title.

Johann Sebastian Bach: *The Last Keyboard Works of Bach*
  Goldberg Variations, BWV 988
  The Art of Fugue, BWV 1080
  A Musical Offering, BWV 1079: Ricercar in three voices, Ricercar in six voices
Recorded in the 30th Street Studio, New York City, June 1, 2, 7, and 8 (*Goldberg Variations*), January 16–19 and March 16–22 (*The Art of Fugue*), 1967. Ricercars presumably recorded during these sessions. Producers: Thomas Z. Shepard (*The Art of Fugue, Goldberg Variations*) and Andrew Kazdin (Ricercars). Engineers: Fred Plaut, Arthur Kendy, Ed Michalski, Raymond Moore. Notes by Charles Rosen. Columbia Odyssey 32 36 0020 (three stereo LPs), (P) 1969.
Compact-disc reissues: (1) *Goldberg Variations*. Producer, digital remastering: Bejun Mehta. Engineer, digital remastering: Christopher Herles. Sony Essential Classics SBK48173, (P) 1992;
(2) *The Art of the Fugue*, in *Bach: The Keyboard Album*. Producer, digital remastering: Arthur M. Fierro. Engineer, digital remastering: Robert Wolff. Sony Essential Classics SB2K 63231;
(3) *Musical Offering*, Ricercar in Six Voices; *The Art of the Fugue, Contrapunctus I, Contrapunctus IX*, in *Greatest Hits: Baroque Piano*. Sony MLK68455, (P) 1995.

Béla Bartók:
  Improvisations on Hungarian Peasant Songs, Op. 20, Sz. 74
  Études, Op. 18, Sz. 72
(See Franz Liszt, *Réminiscences de Don Juan*, below.)

Ludwig van Beethoven: *Charles Rosen Plays Beethoven*
  Sonata No. 29 in B-flat Major, Op. 106
  Sonata No. 31 in A-flat Major, Op. 110
Producer: Thomas Z. Shepard. Notes by Charles Rosen. Epic LC 3900 (Monaural LP)/Epic BC 1300 (Stereo LP), (P) 1965.

Ludwig van Beethoven: *The Late Piano Sonatas*
  Sonata No. 27 in E Minor, Op. 90
  Sonata No. 28 in A Major, Op. 101
  Sonata No. 29 in B-flat Major, Op. 106
  Sonata No. 30 in E Major, Op. 109
  Sonata No. 31 in A-flat Major, Op. 110
  Sonata no. 32 in C Minor, Op. 111

Recorded at EMI Studios, London, November 4–5, 1968; May 13–14, 1969; November 6–7, 1969; June 23–25 and July 3, 1970. Producers: Paul Myers and Bill Newman. Engineers: Christopher Parker, Robert Gooch, Roy Emerson. Notes by Charles Rosen.
Sonatas 28 and 32, [British] CBS 61127, (P) 1970; Sonatas 30 and 31, [British] CBS 61172, (P) 1970 Sonatas 27 and 29, [British] CBS 61173, (P) 1970. Columbia Masterworks M3X 30938 (three stereo LPs), later D3M 30938, (P) 1971.
Compact-disc reissue, digitally remastered by Kevin Boutote: Sony Essential Classics SB2K 53531, (P) 1994.

Georges Bizet–Sergei Rachmaninoff:
    Minuet from *L'Arlésienne* Suite No. 1
(See anthology *Virtuoso!*, below)

Pierre Boulez: *Boulez Piano Music*, vol. 1 [British title only]
    Piano Sonata No. 1
    Piano Sonata No. 3, *Trope* and *Constellation/Miroir*
"Pierre Boulez was so generous with his time as to be present at the recording sessions of these works, and I am grateful for his kindness and suggestions."
Producer: Thomas Z. Shepard. Engineers: Fred Plaut, John Guerriere. Notes by Charles Rosen. [British] CBS S 72871 (stereo LP), (P) 1972. Columbia Records M 32161 (stereo LP), (P) 1973.

Elliott Carter:
    Piano Sonata
(Coupled with *Pocahontas* [suite from the ballet]. Zürich Radio Orchestra, cond. Jacques Monod.)
Recorded April 25, 1961. Notes by Charles Rosen. Epic LC 3850 (monaural LP)/ Epic BC 1250 (stereo LP), (P) 1962. With Double Concerto (see next listing): [British] EMI ALP 2052 (monaural LP)/[British] EMI ASD 601 (stereo LP), (P) 1965.

Elliott Carter:
    Double Concerto
Ralph Kirkpatrick, harpsichord; unidentified ensemble, cond. Gustav Meier.
(Coupled with Leon Kirchner, Concerto for Violin, Cello, Ten Winds and Percussion.)
This recording directly followed the premiere performance at a concert sponsored by the Fromm Music Foundation, during the eighth congress of the International Society for Musicology, at the Grace Rainey Rogers Auditorium, New York City, September 6, 1961. Rosen writes about the experience of learning this piece for the première in "One Easy Piece" (Bibliography, 1973a).
Recorded September 7–8, 1961. Producer: Jane Friedmann. Epic LC 3830 (monaural LP)/Epic BC 1157 (stereo), (P) 1962. With Piano Sonata (see previous listing): [British] EMI ALP 2052 (monaural)/[British] EMI ASD 601 (stereo), (P) 1965.

Elliott Carter:
Double Concerto
Paul Jacobs, harpsichord; English Chamber Orchestra; cond. Frederick
Prausnitz. (Coupled with Variations for Orchestra. New Philharmonia Orchestra
cond. Frederick Prausnitz.)
Recorded January 4, 1968. Producer: Andrew Kazdin. Engineers: Edward Kramer
and Murray Zimney. Notes by Elliott Carter. Columbia MS 7191 (stereo LP) (P) 1968.

Frédéric Chopin: *Chopin Recital*
    Ballade No. 4 in F Minor, Op. 52
    Scherzo No. 3 in C-sharp Minor, Op. 39
    Polonaise No. 6 in A-flat Major, Op. 53
    Mazurka No. 2 in C-sharp Minor, Op. 6, no. 2
    Mazurka No. 31 in A-flat Major, Op. 50, no. 2
    Mazurka No. 32 in C-sharp Minor, Op. 50, no. 3
    Nocturne No. 8 in D-flat Major, Op. 27, no. 2
    Nocturne No. 5 in F-sharp Major, Op. 15, no. 2
    Nocturne No. 17 in B Major, Op. 62, no. 1
Epic LC 3709 (monaural LP)/Epic BC 1090 (stereo LP), (P) 1960.

Frédéric Chopin, Franz Liszt: *Two Great Romantic Concertos*
Frédéric Chopin:
    Concerto for Piano and Orchestra No. 2 in F Minor
Franz Liszt:
    Concerto for Piano and Orchestra No. 1 in E-flat Major
New Philharmonia Orchestra, cond. John Pritchard.
Recorded at Watford Town Hall, London, 1966. Producer: Thomas Z. Shepard.
Notes by Charles Rosen. Epic LC 3920 (monaural LP)/Epic BC Epic BC 1320
(stereo LP), (P) 1969. Columbia Odyssey Y 31529 (stereo LP), (P) 1972.
Compact-disc reissues: (1) Chopin, Concerto No. 2, with Concerto No. 1 (Gilels,
Philadelphia Orchestra, cond. Eugene Ormandy). [French] Sony Maestro SBK
64047, (P) 1995; (2) Liszt, Concerto No. 1, with Chopin, Concerto No. 1
(Gilels, Philadelphia Orchestra, cond. Ormandy). CBS Great Performances
MYK 37804, (P) 1983.

Frédéric Chopin–Moriz Rosenthal:
    "Minute" Waltz in Thirds
(See anthology *Virtuoso!*, below)

Claude Debussy:
    Douze études
Producer: Jane Friedmann. Notes by Charles Rosen. Epic LC 3842 (monaural
LP)/Epic BC 1242 (stereo LP), (P) 1962.

Claude Debussy: *Piano Music of Debussy*
  Images, Livre I
  Images, Livre II
  Estampes
  La plus que lente
  Hommage à Haydn
  Berceuse héroique
  L'isle joyeuse
Producer: Thomas Z. Shepard. Notes by Charles Rosen. Epic BC 1345 (stereo LP)/Epic LC 3945 (monaural LP), (P) 1967.

Franz Josef Haydn: *Charles Rosen Plays Haydn: Three Piano Sonatas* [American title only]
  Sonata in C Minor, Hob. XVI: 20
  Sonata in A-flat Major, Hob. XVI: 46
  Sonata in G Minor, Hob. XVI:44
Producer: Paul Myers. Notes by Charles Rosen. [British] CBS 61112 (stereo LP), (P) 1969.
Vanguard Cardinal VCS 10131 (stereo LP), (P) 1978.

Fritz Kreisler–Sergei Rachmaninoff:
  Liebesleid
(See anthology *Virtuoso!*, below.)

Franz Liszt:
  Concerto for Piano and Orchestra No. 1 in E-flat Major
(See Frédéric Chopin, Franz Liszt: *Two Great Romantic Concertos*, above)

Franz Liszt:
  Réminiscences de Don Juan, S. 418
  Années de pèlerinage, deuxième année, S. 161, "Italie": No. 5, *Sonetto 104 del Petrarca*
  Hungarian Rhapsody no. 10 in E major, S. 244
Béla Bartók:
  Improvisations on Hungarian Peasant Songs, Op. 20, Sz. 74
  Études, Op. 18, Sz. 72
Recorded at 30th Street Studio, New York City, December 12–16 (Bartók), 16 and 18 (Rhapsody), 18 and 23 (*Réminiscences*), 1963. *Années* presumably recorded during these sessions. Producer: Thomas Z. Shepard. Notes by Charles Rosen. Epic LC 3878 (monaural LP)/Epic BC 1278 (stereo LP), (P) 1964.
Compact-disc reissues: (1) Liszt, *Réminiscences*, Hungarian Rhapsody (coupled with Piano Sonata in B Minor, and *Grandes Études de Paganini*, 1851 version [André Watts]). Producer, digital remastering: Thomas Z. Shepard. Engineer, digital remastering: Robert Wolff. Sony Essential Classics SBK 62 664, (P) 1996; (2) Bartók, *Improvisations* (coupled with Concerto for Orchestra [Philadelphia

Orchestra, cond. Eugene Ormandy] and Sonata for Two Pianos and Percussion [Robert and Gaby Casadesus, pianos; Jean-Claude Casadesus and Jean-Pierre Drouet, percussion]). Reissue producer and engineer: Richard King. Sony Classic Library SK 94726, (P) 2005.

Felix Mendelssohn–Sergei Rachmaninoff:
   Scherzo from *A Midsummer Night's Dream*
(See anthology *Virtuoso!*, below)

Wolfgang Amadeus Mozart:
   Rondo in A Minor, K. 511
(See Schubert, Sonata in A Major, D. 959, below)

Maurice Ravel:
   Gaspard de la Nuit
   Le Tombeau de Couperin
Notes by Charles Rosen. Epic LC 3589 (monaural LP). (P) 1960.

Arnold Schoenberg:
   Two Piano Pieces, Op. 33a and Op. 33b
   Suite for Piano, Op. 25
(See Igor Stravinsky, Serenade in A, below)

Franz Schubert:
   Sonata in A Major, D. 959
Wolfgang Amadeus Mozart:
   Rondo in A Minor, K. 511
Producer: Jane Friedmann. Notes by Charles Rosen. Epic LC 3855 (monaural LP)/Epic BC 1255 (stereo LP), (P) 1963.

Franz Schubert–Franz Liszt:
   Soireés de Vienne, No. 6
(See anthology *Virtuoso!*, below)

Robert Schumann:
   Carnaval, Op. 9
   Davidsbündlertänze, Op. 6
Recorded at 30th Street Studio, New York City, March 4–6 and 8, 1963. Producer: Jane Friedmann. Notes by Charles Rosen. Epic LC 3869 (monaural LP)/Epic BC 1269 (stereo LP), (P) 1963.
Compact-disc reissue (coupled with Schumann, *Papillons*, Op. 2 [Robert Casadesus]): Producer, digital remastering: Louise de la Fuente. Engineer, digital remastering: Ellen Fitton. Sony Essential Classics SBK 68345, (P) 1995.

Johann Strauss–Leopold Godowsky:
  Wine, Women and Song
Johann Strauss–Carl Tausig:
  You Only Live Once
Johann Strauss–Moriz Rosenthal:
  Carnaval de Vienne:
(See anthology *Virtuoso!*, below)

Igor Stravinsky:
  Serenade in A
  Sonata for Piano
Arnold Schoenberg:
  Two Piano Pieces, Op. 33a and Op. 33b
  Suite for Piano, Op. 25
Recorded New York City, December 28–30, 1960. Producer: John McClure. Notes by
Charles Rosen. Epic LC 3792 (monaural LP)/Epic BC 1140 (stereo LP), (P) 1961.
Compact-disc reissue: Stravinsky, Sonata for Piano (within Igor Stravinsky
Edition, vol. 7: *Chamber Music and Historical Recordings*). Remix producer: John
McClure. Remix engineer: Larry Keyes. Sony SM2K 46 297 (two CDs), (P)
1991.

Igor Stravinsky:
  Movements for Piano and Orchestra
Columbia Symphony Orchestra; cond. Igor Stravinsky
Stravinsky was not satisfied with the pianist who had commissioned and played
the first performance of the *Movements*, and she generously bowed out of the
recording. Rosen was asked a week before the recording session if he would
learn the piece for the recording.
Recorded Hollywood, California, February 12, 1961. Producer: John McClure.
(1) In *Igor Stravinsky Conducts, 1961.* Columbia ML 5672 (monaural
LP)/Columbia MS 6272 (stereo LP), (P) 1961; (2) In *The Recent Stravinsky.*
Columbia MS 7054 (stereo LP), (P) 1967.
Compact-disc reissues:[4] (1) *Igor Stravinsky Edition: Concertos.* Remix producer:
John McClure. Remix engineer: Larry Keyes. Sony Classical 46295, (P) 1991;
(2) In *The Original Jackets Collection: Stravinsky Conducts Stravinsky.* Remix pro-
ducer: John McClure. Remix engineer: Larry Keyes. Sony SX9K 64136 (nine
CDs), (P) 1999.

Virtuoso!
Frédéric Chopin–Moriz Rosenthal:
  "Minute" Waltz in Thirds

Johann Strauss–Leopold Godowsky:
  Wine, Women and Song
Felix Mendelssohn–Sergei Rachmaninoff:
  Scherzo from *A Midsummer Night's Dream*
Franz Schubert–Franz Liszt:
  Soireés de Vienne, no. 6
Johann Strauss–Carl Tausig:
  You Only Live Once
Fritz Kreisler–Sergei Rachmaninoff:
  Liebesleid
Georges Bizet–Sergei Rachmaninoff:
  Minuet from *L'Arlésienne*, Suite No. 1
Johann Strauss–Moriz Rosenthal:
  Carnaval de Vienne
Producer: Thomas Z. Shepard. Notes by Charles Rosen. Epic LC 3912 (monaural LP)/Epic BC 1312 (stereo LP), (P) 1966.

Anton Webern: *Complete Works, Opp. 1–31*
  Fünf Lieder, Op. 3, aus *Der siebente Ring* von Stefan George
  Fünf Lieder, Op. 4, nach Gedichten von Stefan George
  Vier Stücke für Geige und Klavier, Op. 7
  Drei Kleine Stücke für Violoncello und Klavier, Op. 11
  Vier Lieder für Singstimme und Klavier, Op. 12
  Quartett für Geige, Klarinette, Tenorsaxophon und Klavier, Op. 22
  Drei Gesänge, Op. 23, aus *Viae inviae* von Hildegard Jone
  Drei Lieder für Singstimme und Klavier, Op. 25, nach Gedichten von Hildegard Jone
  Variationen für Klavier, Op. 27
Opp. 3, 4, 12: Recorded EMI Studios, London, April 20–21, 1970 with Heather Harper, soprano. Op. 7: Recorded in New York, May 7, 1971 with Isaac Stern, violinist. Op. 11: Recorded at Gregor Piatigorsky's home in Hollywood, California, March 29, 1972 with Gregor Piatgorsky, cellist. Op. 22: Recorded in Cleveland, April 4, 1970 with Daniel Majeske, violin; Robert Marcellus, clarinet; Abraham Weinstein, saxophone. Opp. 23, 25: Recorded EMI Studios, London, September 5, 1970 with Halina Łukomska, soprano. Op. 27: Recorded EMI Studios, London, June 13, 1969.
Producers: Paul Myers and Roy Emerson. Producer and engineer, Op. 11: Charles Rosen. [British] CBS Masterworks 79402/Columbia M 35732 (four CDs), (P) 1978.[5]
Compact-disc reissues: (1) Sony SM3K 45845 (three CDs), (P) 1991; (2) *Vier Stücke für Geige und Klavier*, Op. 7 (coupled with Bartók, Violin Sonatas nos. 1 and 2 [Isaac Stern, violin; Alexander Zakin, piano]). Sony Classical SMK 64535, (P) 1996.

III. Later Recordings

Recordings in this section are listed in alphabetical order by composer or, in the case of the anthology *The Romantic Generation*, by album title.

Ludwig van Beethoven:
  Variations on a Waltz by Diabelli, Op. 120
Producer: Isabella Wallich. Engineer: Michael Sheady. Notes by Charles Rosen.
Symphonica SYM 09 (stereo LP), (P) 1977 (UK). Peters International PLE 042 (stereo LP), (P) 1977.
Compact-disc reissue (including notes): IMP Carlton Classics 30367 00112, (P) 1995.

Ludwig van Beethoven:
  Piano Concerto No. 2 in B-flat Major, Op. 19
Symphonica of London, cond. Wyn Morris.
Recorded by 1978 in sessions for Concertos 4&5. See next two listings.
Carlton Classics 30367 00162 (CD), (P) 1996.

Ludwig van Beethoven:
  Piano Concerto No. 4 in G Major, Op. 58
Symphonica of London, cond. Wyn Morris.
Notes by Charles Rosen. Peters International Stereo PLE 110, (P) 1978, Symphonica SYM 12, (P) 1986, UK.
Compact-disc reissue: see previous listing.

Ludwig van Beethoven:
  Piano Concerto no. 5 in E-flat major, Op. 73
Symphonica of London, cond. Wyn Morris.
Producer: Isabella Wallich. Engineer: Michael Sheady. Notes by Charles Rosen.
Symphonica SYM 10 (stereo LP), (P) 1977, UK. Peters International Stereo PLE 024 (stereo LP), (P) 1977.

Ludwig van Beethoven: *The Great Middle Period Sonatas*
  Piano Sonata No. 16 in G Major, Op. 31, no. 1
  Piano Sonata No. 17 in D Minor, Op. 31, no. 2 ("Tempest")
  Piano Sonata No. 18 in E-flat Major, Op. 31, no. 3
  Piano Sonata No. 21 in C Major, Op. 53 ("Waldstein")
  Piano Sonata No. 23 in F Minor, Op. 57 ("Appassionata")
  Piano Sonata No. 24 in F-sharp Minor, Op. 78 ("À Thérèse")
  Piano Sonata No. 26 in E-flat Major, Op. 81a (*Les adieux*)
Producer: Klaas Posthuma. Notes by Charles Rosen. Nonesuch NC 78010 (three stereo LPs), (P) 1981. Compact disc reissue: Globe GLO 2-5018 (two CDs), (P) 1989.

Ludwig van Beethoven: *Beethoven Piano Sonatas*
    Piano Sonata No. 12 in A-flat Major, Op. 26 ("Funeral March")
    Piano Sonata No. 13 in E-flat Major, Op. 27, no. 1
    Piano Sonata No. 14 in C-sharp Minor, Op. 27, no. 2 ("Moonlight")
    Bagatelles, Op. 119
Recorded at the American Academy and Institute of Arts and Letters, New York City, April 3 and June 14, 1985. Producer and engineer: Max Wilcox. Digital engineer: Kevin Boutote. Mastering: Jim Shelton. Notes by Charles Rosen. Nonesuch Digital 9 79122-1 F (stereo LP), (P) 1985.

Ludwig van Beethoven: *Beethoven: Piano Sonatas*
    Piano Sonata in A-flat Major, Op. 110
    Piano Sonata in B-flat Major, Op. 106
Recorded at the American Academy of Arts and Letters, New York City, March 23–25, 1996. Producer and engineer: Max Wilcox. Digital engineering by Nelson Wong, SoundByte Productions, Inc., New York. Hamburg Steinway piano provided and serviced by Mary Schwendeman. Notes by Charles Rosen. Music Masters 67183-2 (CD), (P) 1997.[6]

Elliott Carter: *Elliott Carter: Piano Works*
    Night Fantasies (1980)[7]
    Piano Sonata (1945–46)
Recorded Amsterdam, 1982. Producer and engineer: Klaas A. Posthuma. Notes by Charles Rosen. ETCETERA 1008 (Stereo LP), (P) 1983. Compact disc reissue: 1988.

Elliott Carter: *The Complete Music for Piano*
    90+ (1994) Sonata (1945–46)
    Night Fantasies (1980)
Includes Elliott Carter and Charles Rosen recorded in conversation. Recordings of the Sonata and *Night Fantasies* reissue of ETCETERA recordings (see previous listing); *90+* recorded by Mastersound, Astoria, New York, December 1996. Notes by Charles Rosen. Bridge Records BRIDGE 9090 (CD), (P) 1997.

Elliott Carter: *The Music of Elliott Carter*, vol. 5: *Nine Compositions (1994–2002)*
    Two Diversions (1999)
    Retrouvailles (2000)
(Only these two performances involve Charles Rosen.)
Recorded at KAS Studio, Astoria, New York, 2001, 2002. Producer: David Starobin. Engineer: David Merrill. Recording editor: Silas Brown. Mastering engineer: Adam Abeshouse. Bridge Records BRIDGE 9128 (CD), (P) 2003.

Frédéric Chopin: *Works for Solo Piano*
   Polonaise-Fantaisie in A-flat Major, Op. 61
   Sonata No. 2 in B-flat Minor, Op. 35
   Ballade No. 1 in G Minor, Op. 23
   Ballade No. 3 in A-flat Major, Op. 47
   Barcarolle in F-sharp Major, Op. 60
Recorded at the School of Music, State University of New York, Purchase. Producer and engineer: Judith Sherman. Editing and postproduction: Lowell Cross. Notes by Charles Rosen. Music & Arts CD-609 (CD), (P) 1990.

Frédéric Chopin: *Charles Rosen plays Chopin*
   Four Mazurkas, Op. 6
   Mazurka in F Minor, Op. 7, no. 3
   Mazurka in A Minor, Op. 17, no. 4
   Four Mazurkas, Op. 24
   Mazurka in D Major, Op. 33, no. 2
   Four Mazurkas, Op. 41
   Three Mazurkas, Op. 50
   Three Mazurkas, Op. 56
   Three Mazurkas, Op. 63
Recorded Amsterdam, July 1989. Producer: Klaas Posthuma. Notes by Charles Rosen. Globe GLO 5028 (CD), (P) 1990.

Frédéric Chopin: *Charles Rosen plays Chopin with David James, Cello*
   Sonata for Piano in B Minor, Op. 58
   Sonata for Cello and Piano in G Minor, Op. 65
   Largo from the Sonata for Cello and Piano, original manuscript version
Recorded Amsterdam, December 1989. Producer: Klaas Posthuma. Notes by Charles Rosen. Globe GLO 5026 (CD), (P) 1990.

Wolfgang Amadeus Mozart: *Piano Music*
   Sonata in A Minor, K. 310/300d
   Unfinished Suite, K. 399/385i: Allemande, Courante
   Sonata in A Major, K. 331/300i
   Sonata in D Major, K. 576
   Rondo in A Minor, K. 511
Piano: C. Bechstein Op. n. 15664, Berlin, 1884.
Recorded at the Sala Musica "Caetani," Villa di Ninfa, Giardini di Ninfa, Latina, Italy, October 28–30, 2001. Notes by Charles Rosen. CD Fonè 2015 (CD), (P) 2001, Guilio Cesare Ricci Editore.

The Romantic Generation
Frédéric Chopin:
 Nocturne in B Major, Op. 62, no. 1
Franz Liszt:
 **Réminiscences de Don Juan*
 Die Loreley
Frédéric Chopin:
 *Nocturne in D-flat Major, Op. 27, no. 2
Chopin–Liszt:
 *My Joys
Robert Schumann:
 Davidsbündlertänze, Op. 6
Recorded at the American Academy of Arts and Letters, New York City, June, July, and October 1993. Producer and engineer: Max Wilcox. Digital engineer: Nelson Wong, Soundbyte Productions. Notes by Charles Rosen. MusicMasters Classics 01612-67154-2 (CD), (P) 1995.

Robert Schumann:
 Davidsbündlertänze, Op. 6
(See anthology *The Romantic Generation*, above)

Robert Schumann: *The Revolutionary Masterpieces*
 Impromptus on a Theme of Clara Wieck, Op. 5, first edition
 Davidsbündlertänze, Op. 6, first edition
 Carnaval, Op. 9
 Sonata in F-sharp Minor, Op. 11
 Kreisleriana, Op. 16, first edition
 Dichtungen für das Pianoforte: first version of the *Fantasy* in C Major, Op. 17
Producer: Klaas Posthuma. Notes by Charles Rosen. Nonesuch 79062-1 (Stereo), (P) 1984. ETCETERA 3001 (CD), (P) 1986.
Compact-disc reissues: (1) *The Revolutionary Masterpieces*, vol. I: *Impromptus on a Theme of Clara Wieck*; *Davidsbündlertänze*. Globe GLO 5001, (P) 1988; (2) *The Revolutionary Masterpieces*, vol. II: *Carnaval*; Sonata in F-sharp Minor. Globe GLO 5009, (P) 1988; (3) *The Revolutionary Masterpieces*, vol. III: *Kreisleriana*; *Dichtungen für das Pianoforte*. Globe GLO 5012, (P) 1988.

* These recordings are identical to those included in the book of the same title. See Section IV.

IV. Recordings on Compact Discs Included with Books by Charles Rosen

1995a   *The Romantic Generation*
CD includes Franz Liszt: *Réminiscences de Don Juan;* Chopin–Liszt: *My Joys;* Frédéric Chopin: Nocturne in D-flat Major, Op. 27, no. 2. These three recordings are identical to those included in the recorded anthology *The Romantic Generation* (see above). In addition:
Robert Schumann:
> From *Carnaval,* Op. 9: "Eusebius," "Florestan"
> From Phantasie in C Major, Op. 17: mvts. 1, 2, opening; mvt. 3, conclusion
> From Impromptus on a Theme of Clara Wieck: theme, var. 1, conclusion
> From *Kreisleriana,* Op. 16: nos. 1, 4, 5, and 8

Franz Liszt:
> *Sonetto 104 del Petrarca*

Recorded at the American Academy of Arts and Letters, New York City, June, July, and October 1993. Producer and engineer: Max Wilcox. Digital engineer: Nelson Wong, Soundbyte Productions.

1997a *The Classical Style: Haydn, Mozart and Beethoven,* expanded edition with compact disc
The recording of Beethoven's Piano Sonatas, Opp. 106 and 110, listed in section III above, was also included with the first hardcover edition of this book.

2002a *Beethoven's Piano Sonatas: A Short Companion*
CD consists of excerpts from works by Haydn, Mozart, and Beethoven that illustrate issues of phrasing and articulation, the consistency of tempo indications during the period, and points made in the book. Excerpts are introduced by the pianist. A detailed track listing is included in the book. Recorded at the Villa Caetani, Ninfa, Italy, 2001. Recorded by Giulio Cesare Ricci. CD (P) 2002, Yale University Press.

V. Library of Congress Concerts and Lectures

The Library of Congress has recordings of the following concerts and lectures presented there, the catalogue numbers for which are given.

Elliott Carter:
> Piano Sonata

Lecture and performance. Library of Congress, October 7, 1978. (Revision of lecture later published as "The Musical Languages of Elliott Carter," in *The Musical Languages of Elliott Carter.* See bibliography, 1985a.) LWO 12474.

"Brahms the Subversive"
Lecture. Library of Congress Symposium: International Brahms Conference, May 5, 1983. (Revision of lecture later published as "Brahms the Subversive" in *Brahms Studies: Analytical and Historical Perspectives.* See bibliography, 1990b.) RWA 5595-5599.

Johannes Brahms:
    Trio in E-flat Major for Violin, Horn and Piano, Op. 40
    Vier Klavierstücke, Op. 119
    Serenade in A Major, Op. 16
Robert Gerle, violin; Richard Todd, horn; Concerto Soloists of Philadelphia, cond. Robert Gerle.
Concert. Library of Congress, May 7, 1983. RWA 5615-5616.

Notes

1. I am indebted to Maynard Solomon for his recollections of Jack Skurnick and EMS Records. For further information on Safford Cape in relationship to the EMS label, see http://www.medieval.org/emfaq/performers/cape.html. For discussion of *The Complete Works of Edgard Varèse*, vol. 1, see Frank Zappa, "Edgard Varèse: The Idol of My Youth," *Stereo Review* 26/6 (June 1971): 62–63, and Frank Zappa, *The Real Frank Zappa Book* (New York: Poseidon Press, 1989).

2. Charles Rosen, liner notes accompanying *The Late Beethoven Sonatas* (see section II of the discography).

3. "The original Stereo masters . . . are not extant. We have used the best available safety copies for this reissue."

4. There is an editing error in the transfer to CD: the first movement and its first ending are directly followed by the second ending without a repeat of the movement.

5. In addition to the works listed here, Rosen recorded virtually all of the early songs without opus numbers with Heather Harper for a projected second volume that was never forthcoming, in part because these recordings were lost.

6. This recording also accompanies the expanded edition of *The Classical Style*, CD (P) 1997 (New York: W. W. Norton).

7. The *Night Fantasies* were written for and dedicated to Rosen, Ursula Oppens (who gave the first performance), Paul Jacobs, and Gilbert Kalish. Kalish is the only pianist who has not recorded them to date.

Appendix 2

A Bibliography of the Writings of Charles Rosen

Robert Curry

Key to Abbreviations

NYRB   *The New York Review of Books*
TLS   *The* [London] *Times Literary Supplement*

Books

1951   "Style and Morality in La Fontaine," PhD diss., Princeton University.

1971a   *The Classical Style: Haydn, Mozart and Beethoven.* London: Faber; New York: Viking Press.
Corrected edition with expanded chapters on *opera seria* and Beethoven. New York: Norton Library Edition, 1972.
2nd rev., expanded ed. with CD, New York: W. W. Norton, 1997.
Hungarian: Zeneműkiadó, 1977; French: Gallimard, 1978; Serbo-Croatian: Nolit, 1979; German: Bärenreiter, 1983; Spanish: Alianza, 1986, 1994.

1975a   *Arnold Schoenberg.* New York: Viking Press.
Rev. ed., Princeton, NJ: Princeton University Press, 1985.
French: Editions de Minuit, 1979; Spanish: A. Bosch, 1983; Italian: Mondadori, 1984; Japanese: Iwanami gendi sensho, 1984; Croatian: Matica hrvatska, 2003.

1980a   *Sonata Forms.* New York: W. W. Norton.
2nd rev., expanded ed., New York: W. W. Norton, 1988.
French: Actes Sud, 1993; Japanese: Akademiamyujikku, 1997;
Spanish: Editorial Labor, 1987, Cornellà de Llobregat, 2004.

1984a   [with Henri Zerner] *Romanticism and Realism: The Mythology of Nineteenth-Century Art.* New York: Viking Press.
French: Albin Michel, 1986.

1985a   *The Musical Languages of Elliott Carter.* Guide to Elliott Carter Research Materials at the Library of Congress, Music Division. Washington, DC: Library of Congress.

1993a   *Plaisir de jouer, plaisir de penser: Conversation avec Catherine Temerson.* Paris: Georg Eshel.

1994a   *The Frontiers of Meaning: Three Informal Lectures on Music.* Annual *New York Review of Books* and Hill and Wang Lecture Series, 1. New York: Hill and Wang.
French: Seul, 1995; Italian: Garzanti, 1998.

1995a   *The Romantic Generation.* Cambridge, MA: Harvard University Press (includes CD). Based on the Charles Eliot Norton Lectures, 1980–81.
Italian: Adelphi Edizioni, 1997; French: Gallimard, 2002; German: Residenz, 2000; Portuguese: Editora Universidade de São Paulo, 2000.

1998a   *Romantic Poets, Critics, and Other Madmen.* Cambridge, MA: Harvard University Press.
Portuguese: Atelie Editorial, 2004.

2000a   *Critical Entertainments: Music Old and New.* Cambridge, MA: Harvard University Press.

2002a   *Beethoven's Piano Sonatas: A Short Companion.* New Haven: Yale University Press (includes CD).
Spanish: Alianza Editorial, 2005; French: Gallimard, 2007.

2002b   *Piano Notes: The World of the Pianist.* New York: Free Press.
Korean: Samho Music, 2004; Portuguese: Jorge Zahar Editions, 2004;
Spanish: Alianza Editorial, 2005.

Editions

1975b   *Bach: The Fugue.* Oxford Keyboard Classics. Edited and annotated by CR. London and New York: Oxford University Press.
Early Romantic Opera [ERO]. Introductions to facsimile photo reprints. New York: Garland Press, 1978–81.

1978a   Meyerbeer, *Le Prophète* (1849 edition), ERO, 21.

1978b   Cherubini, *Démophoön* (1788 edition), ERO, 32.

1978c   Cherubini, *Lodoïska* (1791 edition), ERO, 33.

1978d   Méhul, *Ariodant*, ERO, 39.

1979a   Cherubini, *Eliza, ou le voyage aux glacier du Mont St. Bernard*, ERO, 34.

1979b   Le Seuer, *Ossian, ou les bardes* (1804 edition), ERO, 37.

1979c   Méhul, *Joseph*, ERO, 41.

1979d   Spontini, *La vestale*, ERO, 42.

1980b   Meyerbeer, *Robert le diable* (1831 edition), ERO, 19.

1980c   Meyerbeer, *Les Huguenots* (1836 edition), ERO, 20.

1980d   Meyerbeer, *L'étoile du nord*, ERO, 22.

1980e   Meyerbeer, *L'africaine* (1865 edition), ERO, 24.

1980f   Auber, *La muette de Portici* (1828 edition), ERO, 30.

1980g   Auber, *Gustave, ou le bal masqué* (1833 edition), ERO, 31.

1980h   Cherubini, *Les deux journées* (1800 edition), ERO, 35.

1980i   Halévy, *La juive* (1835 edition), ERO, 36.

1980j   Méhul, *Euphrosine, ou le tyran corrigé*, ERO, 38.

1980k   Méhul, *Uthal* (1806 edition), ERO, 40.

1980l   Spontini, *Olimpie*, ERO, 44.

1981a   Meyerbeer, *Le pardon de Ploërmel* (1859 edition), ERO, 23.

2000i   Preface to *NYRB* reprint of Lorenzo Da Ponte's *Memoirs*, translated by Elizabeth Abbott (1959), edited and annotated with an introduction by Arthur Livingston, ix–xiv. New York: New York Review of Books.

Articles and Chapters

1955   "M.I.T. Teaches History of Ideas in French." *French Review* 4 (Feb. 28): 345–50.

1959   "Where Ravel Ends and Debussy Begins." *High Fidelity* 9 (May): 42–44. Reprinted in *Clavier* 6/9 (1967): 14–17 and in *Cahiers Debussy* 3 (1979): 31–38.

1962   "The Proper Study of Music." *Perspectives of New Music* 1/1 (Autumn): 80–88.
Kerman's reply and CR's answer, *PNM* (Autumn–Winter 1963): 151–60.

1970a   "Ornament and Structure in Beethoven." *Musical Times* 111, no. 1534 (Dec.): 1198–99, 1201.

1970b   "The Piano as the Key to 'Late' Beethoven." *Stereo Review* (June): 69–71.

1971b   "Should Music be Played 'Wrong'?" *High Fidelity* 21 (May): 54–58.

1972a   "The Aesthetics of Stage Fright." *Prose* 5 (Fall): 115–23.
Revised and reprinted as ch. 1 in 2000a.

1972b   "The Keyboard Music of Bach and Handel." In *Keyboard Music*, edited by Denis Matthews, 68–107. London: David and Charles.
Reprinted as ch. 3 in 2000a.

1972c   "Do We Need a New Way to Play the Classics?" *New York Times* (Mar. 19), D28.

1974a   "Controversial Schoenberg." *High Fidelity* 24 (Sept.): 52–54.
Reprinted as ch. 1 in 1975a.

1974b   "Private Property." *NYRB* 21/20 (Dec. 12): 29–30
Reprinted in 1975e.

1975c   "Schoenberg and Atonality." *Georgia Review* 29/2: 298–327.
Reprinted as ch. 2 in 1975a.

1975d   "Théories de la forme." *Musique en Jeu* 19 (June): 7–19.

1975e   "Public and Private." In *W. H. Auden: A Tribute*, edited by Stephen Spender, 218–19. London: Weidenfeld and Nicolson.

1976a   "Homage to Milton: Sounds and Words; A Critical Celebration of Milton Babbitt at 60." *Perspectives of New Music* 14/2 (Summer): 37–40.

1976b "Should Music Be Played 'Wrong'?" In *High Fidelity's Silver Anniversary Treasury*, edited by Robert S. Clark, 151–58. Barrington, MA: Wyeth Press.

1980m "The Performance of Contemporary Music: Elliott Carter's Double Concerto; One Easy Piece." *Composer* 69: 1–8.

1981b "The Romantic Pedal." In *The Book of the Piano*, edited by Dominic Gill, 106–13. Oxford: Oxford University Press. Rev. and partially incorporated in 1995.

1981c [Remarks on "influence"]. In *Haydn Studies: Proceedings of the International Haydn Conference, Washington, DC., 1975*, edited by Jens Peter Larsen, Howard Serwer, and James Webster, 412–14. New York: W. W. Norton.

1981d "Influence: Plagiarism and Inspiration." In *On Criticizing Music: Five Philosophical Perspectives*, edited by Kingsley Price, 16–37. Baltimore and London: Johns Hopkins University Press. Originally delivered in the 1978–79 Thalheimer Lecture Series in Philosophy.
Reprinted as ch. 9 in 2000a.
An abridged version first appeared in *19th Century Music* 4/2 (Fall 1980): 87–100.

1982a "The Quandary of the Writing Pianist." *New York Times* (Jan. 17), D24.
Reprinted in *Clavier* 23/3 (1984): 34.

1982e "The Original Schumann." *Keynotes* (Jan.): 6–10.

1986a "The Piano Music." In *Pierre Boulez: A Symposium*, edited by William Glock, 85–97. London: Eulenburg Books; New York: Da Capo Press.

1987a "Quelques aspects du temps musical chez Beethoven." *L'Analyse Musicale* 6 (Jan.): 23–27.

1988a "Happy Birthday, Elliott Carter," *NYRB* 35/19 (Dec. 8), 24–25.

1990a "Language, Music and the Classical Style." In *La musica come linguaggio universale: genesi e storia di un'idea*, edited by Raffaele Pozzi, 77–88 (papers given at an international conference). Florence: Leo S. Olschki.

1990b "Brahms the Subversive." In *Brahms Studies: Analytical and Historical Perspectives* edited by George Bozarth, 105–22. Oxford: Oxford University Press.
Reprinted as ch. 10 in 2000a.

1990c   "The First Movement of Chopin's Sonata in B♭ Minor, Op. 35." *19th Century Music* 14/1 (July): 60–67.
Rev. and incorporated in part in 1995a.

1990d   "Chopin, poésie et métier: A propos de la sonate op. 35 en si bémol mineur," translated by N. Hussein. *L'Analyse Musicale* 21 (Nov.): 96–101.

1992a   "The Necessity of Being a Musician." *American Record Guide* 55/6: 6–9.

1992b   "*Ritmi di tre battute* in Schubert's Sonata in C Minor, D. 958." In *Convention in Eighteenth and Nineteenth Century Music: Essays in Honor of Leonard G. Ratner*, edited by Janet M. Levy, Wye Jamison Allanbrook, Leonard G. Ratner, and William P. Mahrt, 113–21. Stuyvesant, NY: Pendragon.

1992c   "Variations sur le principe de la carrure: Périodicité rythmique et accentuation à l'époque romantique." *L'Analyse Musicale* 29 (Nov.): 96–106.

1993b   "Charles Rosen." In *Rembering Horowitz: 125 Pianists Recall a Legend*, compiled and edited by David Dubal, 248–50. New York: Schirmer.

1995b   "*Sturm und Drang* et lumières en literature et en musique (Propos recueilles par Catherine Temerson)." *Revue germanique internationale* 3: 117–25.

1997d   "Schubert's Inflections of Classical Form." In *The Cambridge Companion to Schubert*, edited by Christopher H. Gibbs, 72–98. Cambridge: Cambridge University Press.

1997h   "Master Class: The Riddle of Beethoven's Pedal." *Piano Today* 17/2 (Spring): 8, 53–54, 64.

1998b   "Who's Afraid of the Avant-Garde?" *NYRB* 45/8 (May 14): 20–25. Conflated with 1998d and reprinted as ch. 18 in 2000a.

        Ivan Hewett, Jessica Krash and CR, "Who's Afraid of the Avant-Garde?: An Exchange," *NYRB* 45/11 (June 25): 65.

1998c   "Freedom of Interpretation in Twentieth-Century Music." In *Composition-Performance-Reception: Studies in the Creative Process in Music*, edited by Wyndham Thomas, 66–73. Aldershot: Ashgate.

1999a   "On Playing the Piano," *NYRB* 46/16 (Oct. 21), 49. Lecture given at the New York Public Library.

Rev. and reprinted in part in 2002b.

Replies from Marc Ryser and Kenneth Wolf and CR's answer, "Playing the Piano." *NYRB* 46/20 (Dec. 16): 100–101.

Response to "Playing the Piano" from Carolyn Kumin and David W. Ross, and CR's reply, *NYRB* 47/3 (Feb. 24, 2000): 49.

1999b   "Influences: Fryderyk Chopin; A Wonderful Complexity of Voices." *BBC Music Magazine* 8/2 (Oct.): 35–37.

1999c   "Six Parts Genius: Writing for the Newfangled Piano, Bach Nailed It." *New York Times Magazine* (Apr. 18): 6, 132:1.

2000b   "Piano physiology: The playing technique of great classical pianists, according to their morphologies." *Nouvelle Revue française* 555 (Oct.): 168–81.

2000c   "A Private Lesson." *BBC Music Magazine* 8/12 (Aug.): 28–31.

2000d   "Genius in Private." *NYRB* 47/20 (Dec. 21), 36–37.

2001c   "The Future of Music." *NYRB* 48/20 (Dec. 20), 60–65. Reprinted in *Sinn und Form* 54/4 (Sept.–Oct. 2002): 581–98.

2001d   "The Aesthetics of Stage Fright." *Piano Today* 21/1 (Winter): 16–17, 59, 62.

2001e   "Col Basso?" In *'Mirakel wirken: Mozarts Klavierkonzerte; ein Lesebuch zu Mozarts Klavierkonzerten*, edited by Andreas Wernli, 119–30. Bern: Peter Lang.

2001f   "Tradition Without Convention: The Impossible Nineteenth-Century Project." In *The Tanner Lecture on Human Values*, Vol. 22, edited by Grethe B. Peterson, 351–88. Salt Lake City: University of Utah Press.

Originally given as the annual Isaiah Berlin Lecture, Wolfson College, Oxford, May 20, 1999.

2002f   "Beethoven's 'Moonlight'." *Piano Today* 22/2 (Spring): 8–9, 52.

2002g   [with Henri Zerner] "L'union des arts, un idéal romantique." In *L'invention du sentiment: aux sources du romanticism* [n.e.], 40–42. Paris: Musée de la Musique.

2003a   "Schubert and the Example of Mozart." In *Schubert the Progressive: History, Performance Practice and Analysis*, edited by Brian Newbold, 1–20. Aldershot: Ashgate.

2003b "Culture on the Market." *NYRB* 50/17 (Nov. 6): 70–73.

Reply from Benjamin Moser and CR's answer, "Culture and the Market." *NYRB* 51/1 (Jan. 15, 2004): 49.

2006 Preface to *Moriz Rosenthal in Word and Music: A Legacy of the Nineteenth Century*, edited by Mark Mitchell and Allan Evans, ix–xiv. Bloomington: Indiana University Press.

2007 "An Old Master Still in Development." *New York Times*, Arts and Leisure Sect. 2, Dec. 9.

2008 "*Montaigne hors de son propos.*" In *Variations on the Canon: Essays in Musical Interpretation from Bach to Boulez*, edited by Robert Curry, David Gable, and Robert L. Marshall, 311–17. Rochester, NY: University of Rochester Press.

Reviews and Replies

1970c "A Tone-Deaf Musical Dictionary." *NYRB* 14/4 (Feb. 26): 11–14.
Reprinted as ch. 13 in 2000.
Re: *Harvard Dictionary of Music*, 2nd ed., rev. and enl. Willi Apel

1970d "TV Guide." *NYRB* 14/9 (May 7): 27–29.
Re: Kenneth Clark, *Civilisation*

1971b "Art Has its Reasons." *NYRB* 16/11 (June 17): 32–38.
Reprinted as ch. 8 in 1998a.
Re: Heinrich Schenker, *Five Graphic Music Analyses*, with a new introduction and glossary by Felix Salzer
La Poétique, la Mémoire, Change, no. 6 (Editions du Seuil, 1970)
Roman Jakobson and Lawrence G. Jones, *Shakespeare's Verbal Art in the Experience of Spirit*
CR corrects minor factual error: "There Are Twelve." *NYRB* 17/1 (22 July 1971): 37.

1972d "Music to Compose By." *NYRB* 18/2 (Feb. 10): 31–32.
Re: Pierre Boulez, *Boulez on Music Today*, translated by Susan Bradshaw and Richard Rodney Bennett

1972e "Love That Mozart." *NYRB* 18/9 (May 18): 15–17
Reprinted as ch. 5 in 2000a.
Re: Michael Levy, *Life and Death of Mozart*

1972f   "Berg, Schoenberg." *New York Times Book Review* (2 Jan.): 3–4.
         Re: *Alban Berg: Letters to His Wife*, edited, translated, and annotated
         by Bernard Grun
         Willi Reich, *Schoenberg: A Critical Biography*, translated by Leo Black

1973a   "One Easy Piece." *NYRB* 20/2 (Feb. 22): 25–29.
         Reprinted in *Composer* (Spring 1980), in 1985a, and as ch. 17 in
         2000a.
             On the following works by Elliott Carter:
             Quartet No. 1
             Eight Etudes and a Fantasy
             Sonata for Flute, Oboe, Cello and Harpsichord
             Variations for Orchestra
             Quartet no. 2
             Double Concerto for Harpsichord, Piano and Two Chamber
             Orchestras
             Piano Concerto
             Concerto for Orchestra; Quartet No. 3

1973b   "Isn't It Romantic." *NYRB* 20/10 (June 14): 12–18.
         Reprinted as ch. 2 in 1998a.
             Re: M. H. Abrams, *Natural Supernaturalism: Tradition and Revolution
             in Romantic Literature*
             William Empson and David Pirie, eds., *Coleridge's Verse: A Selection*

1973c   "What Did the Romantics Mean?" *NYRB* 20/17 (Nov. 1): 12–17.
         Reprinted as ch. 5 in 1998a.
             Re: William Vaughan, Helmut Boersch-Supan and Hans Joachim
             Neidhardt, *Caspar David Friedrich, 1774–1840: Romantic Landscape
             Painting in Dresden*
             Alan Walker, ed., *Robert Schumann: The Man and His Music*
         Reply from Helmut Boersch-Supan and CR's answer, "Medium and
         Message," *NYRB* 21/2 (Feb. 21).

1975f   "A Master Musicologist." *NYRB* 22/1 (Feb. 6): 32–34.
         Reprinted as ch. 2 in 2000a.
             Re: Oliver Strunk, *Essays on Music in the Western World*
         Reply from Eric Werner and CR's answer, "Grateful to Strunk." *NYRB*
         22/6 (Apr. 17).

1975g   "Romantic Documents." *NYRB* 22/8 (May 15): 15–20.
         Reprinted as ch. 3 in 1998a.
             Re: Jean Bruneau, ed., *Flaubert: Correspondence Tome I, 1830–1851*

Leslie A. Marchand, ed., *Byron's Letters and Journals*, vol. 1: *"In my hot youth," 1798–1810*; vol. 2: *"Famous in my time," 1810–1812*; vol. 3: *"Alas! the love of Women!" 1813–1814*
Reply from Donal H. Reiman and CR's answer, "Did Wordsworth Kill Lucy?" *NYRB* 22/11 (June 26): 38.

1975h   "Schoenberg: The Possibilities of Disquiet." *TLS* 3843 (Nov. 7): 1335–36.
Reprinted as ch. 16 in 2000a.
Re: Arnold Schoenberg, *Style and Idea* and *Berliner Tagebuch*

1976b   "The Revival of Official Art." *NYRB* 23/4 (Mar. 18): 32–39.
Re: Geneviève Lacambre with Jacqueline de Rohan-Chabot, *Le Musée du Luxembourg en 1874: Peintures Novembre 18, 1974* (catalog of the exhibition at the Grand Palais, Paris, May 31–November 18, 1974).
Albert Boime, *Academy and French Painting in the Nineteenth Century French Painting 1774–1830, The Age of Revolution: Grand Palais, Paris, November 16, 1974–February 3, 1975; the Detroit Institute of Arts, March 5–May 4, 1975; the Metropolitan Museum of Art, New York, June 12–September 7, 1975. Exhibition sponsored by Founders society, the Detroit Institute of Arts, the Metropolitan Museum of Art, and the Réunion des Musées Nationaux, Paris* (catalog of the exhibition "French Painting from David to Delacroix").
Robert Isaacson, *William-Adolphe Bouguereau* (catalogue of the exhibition at the New York Cultural Center, Dec. 13, 1974–Feb. 2, 1975)
T. J. Clark, *Image of the People: Gustave Courbet and the Second French Republic, 1848–1851*
T. J. Clark, *The Absolute Bourgeois: Artists and Politics in France, 1848–1851*
This article is a revision and abridgement of Paul Auster's translation of Rosen and Zerner, "L'antichambre du Louvre, ou l'idéologie du fini." *Critique* 329 (Oct. 1974).

1977a   "The Ruins of Walter Benjamin." *NYRB* 24/17 (Oct. 27): 31–40.

1977b   "The Origins of Walter Benjamin." *NYRB* 24/18 (Nov. 10): 30–38.
Reprinted together as ch. 7 in 1998a.
Reprinted as ch. 6 in Gary Smith, ed., *On Walter Benjamin: Critical Essays and Recollections*, 129–75. Cambridge, MA: MIT Press, 1991.
Re: Walter Benjamin, *The Origin of German Tragic Drama*, trans. John Osborne

1979e   "Too Much Opera." *NYRB* 26/9 (May 31): 14, 16–20.

        Re: Donald Jay Grout, ed., *The Operas of Alessandro Scarlatti*, vol. 1: *Eraclea*

        Donald Jay Grout and Joscelyn Godwin, eds., *The Operas of Alessandro Scarlatti*, vol. 2: *Marco Attilio Regolo*

        Donald Jay Grout, ed., *The Operas of Alessandro Scarlatti*, vol. 3: *Griselda*

        Donald Jay Grout, ed., *The Operas of Alessandro Scarlatti*, vol. 4: *The Faithful Princess*

        Donald Jay Grout and H. Colin Slim, eds., *The Operas of Alessandro Scarlatti*, vol. 5: *Massimo Puppieno*

        Howard M. Brown, ed., *Italian Opera 1640–1770*.

1979f   "Rediscovering Haydn." *NYRB* 26/10 (Jun. 14): 8, 10–14.

        Reprinted as ch. 4 in 2000a.

        Re: H. C. Robbins Landon, *Haydn: Chronicle and Works*, vol. 2: *Haydn at Eszterháza, 1766–1790*

        H. C. Robbins Landon, *Haydn: Chronicle and Works*, vol. 3: *Haydn in England, 1791–1795*

        H. C. Robbins Landon, *Haydn: Chronicle and Works*, vol. 4: *Haydn: The Years of "The Creation," 1796–1800*

        H. C. Robbins Landon, *Haydn: Chronicle and Works*, vol. 5: *Haydn: The Late Years, 1801–1809*

1979g   "The Permanent Revolution." *NYRB* 26/18 (Nov. 22): 23–30.

        Parts reworked and incorporated in 1984a.

        Re: Hugh Honour, *Romanticism*

1981e   "The Real Business of the Critic." *TLS* 4108 (Dec. 25): 1379–81.

        Reprinted as ch. 10 in 1998a.

        Re: Dan H. Laurence, ed., *Shaw's Music: The Complete Music Criticism in Three Volumes*

1981f   "The Musicological Marvel." *NYRB* 28/9 (May 28): 26–27, 30–38.

        Reprinted as ch. 14 in 2000a.

        Re: *The New Grove Dictionary of Music and Musicians* edited by Stanley Sadie

        Replies from Bea Frieland, Roger Scruton, and Stanley Sadie, and CR's answers, *NYRB* 28/12 (July 16): 53; 28/13 (Aug. 13): 52–53; 28/19 (Dec. 3): 53–54.

1981g   "Proto-Photo." *NYRB* 28/19 (Dec. 3): 31–32.

        Parts reworked and incorporated in 1984a.

        Re: Peter Galassi, *Before Photography: Painting and the Invention of Photography*

Before Photography: Painting and the Invention of Photography, an exhibition at the Museum of Modern Art, New York; the Joslyn Art Museum, Omaha; the Frederick S. Wright Art Gallery, University of California, Los Angeles; the Art Institute of Chicago (May 1981–May 1982)

1982b "What Is, and Is Not, Realism?" *NYRB* 29/2 (Feb. 18): 21–26.
Parts reworked and incorporated in 1984a.
> Re: *The Realist Tradition: French Painting and Drawing 1830–1900*, an exhibition at the Cleveland Museum of Art, the Brooklyn Museum, the St. Louis Art Museum, and the Glasgow Art Gallery and Museum, November 1980–January 1982
> Gabriel P. Weisberg, *The Realist Tradition: French Painting and Drawing 1830–1900*

1982c "Enemies of Realism." *NYRB* 29/3 (Mar. 4): 29–33.
> Re. exhibition and catalogue cited in 1982b.
Reply from Robert Rosenblum and CR's answer, "Neo-Con Art." *NYRB* 29/14 (Sept. 23): 61

1982d "The Unhappy Medium." *NYRB* 29/9 (May 27): 49–54.
Parts reworked and incorporated in 1984a.
> Re: Albert Boime, *Thomas Couture and the Eclectic Vision*

1983a "Verdi Victorious." *NYRB* 30/16 (Oct. 27): 33–34, 36, 38, 40–41.
> Re: Philip Gossett, ed., *The Works of Giuseppe Verdi*
> Francesco Maria Piave, *Rigoletto: Melodrama in Three Acts* edited by Martin Chusid

1984b "The New Sound of Liszt." *NYRB* 31/6 (Apr. 12): 17–20.
Revised and incorporated in part in 1995a.
> Re: Alan Walker, *Franz Liszt*, vol. 1: *The Virtuoso Years, 1811–1847*

1984c "Battle Over Berlioz." *NYRB* 31/7 (Apr. 26): 40–43.
Revised and incorporated in part in 1995a.
> Re: Julian Rushton, *The Musical Language of Berlioz*

1985b "And Thou Beside Me Boiling a Pig's Head." *New York Times Book Review* (July 14): A3.
Reprinted as ch. 4 in 1998a.
> Re: Elizabeth David, *An Omelette and a Glass of Wine*

1986b "Now, Voyager." *NYRB* 33/17 (Nov. 6): 55–60.
Revised and incorporated in part in 1995a.
> Re: Barbara Maria Stafford, *Voyage into Substance: Art, Science, Nature, and the Illustrated Travel Account, 1760–1840*

1987b   "The Judgment of Paris." *NYRB* 34/3 (Feb. 26): 21–25.

         Parts reworked and incorporated in 1984a.

            Re: *Le Musée d'Orsay* 1, rue de Bellechasse, Paris

            Le Triomphe des mairies, an exhibition at the Musée du Petit Palais, Paris (November 8, 1986–January 8, 1987), catalogue by Thérèse Burollet, Daniel Imbert, and Frank Folliot

            Les Concours d'esquisses peintes, 1816–1863, an exhibition at the Ecole Nationale Supérieure des Beaux-Arts, Paris (October 8, 1986–December 14, 1986), and the National Academy of Design, New York (January 13, 1987–March 15, 1987), catalogue by Philippe Grunchec

1987c   "The Chopin Touch." *NYRB* 34/9 (May 28): 9–11.

         Revised and incorporated in part in 1995a

            Re: William G. Atwood, *Fryderyk Chopin: Pianist from Warsaw*

            Jean-Jacques Eigeldinger, *Chopin: Pianist and Teacher as Seen by his Pupils*, edited by Roy Howat, translated by Naomi Shohet, with Krysia Osostowicz, and Roy Howat

1987d   "Romantic Originals." *NYRB* 34/20 (Dec. 17): 22–31.

         Reprinted as ch. 1 in 1998a

            Re: Honoré de Balzac, *La Comédie humaine*, published under the direction of Pierre-Georges Castex

            Lord Byron: The Complete Poetical Works edited by Jerome J. McGann

            The Cornell Wordsworth edited by Stephen M. Parrish

            William Wordsworth and the Age of English Romanticism, an exhibition at the New York Public Library through January 2, 1988

            William Wordsworth and the Age of English Romanticism, catalog of the exhibition by Jonathan Wordsworth, Michael C. Jaye, and Robert Woof

         Reply from Albert Boime and answer from CR and Henri Zerner, "The Avant-Garde and the Academy: An Exchange." *NYRB* 34/12 (July 16): 48–49.

         Correction by Brooks Mumkelt, acknowledged by CR, "Obnoxious." *NYRB* 35/4 (Mar. 17): 45

         Reply from Hugh Amory and CR's answer, *NYRB* 35/6 (Apr. 14): 43.

1988b   "Inventor of Modern Opera." *NYRB*, 35/16 (Oct. 27): 8–10.

         Reprinted as ch. 6 in 2000a.

            Re: Caron de Beaumarchais, *Oeuvres*.

         Reply from Howard Stein and CR's answer, "Vulcan's Net." *NYRB* 35/21–22 (Jan. 19, 1989): 61

1990e   "The Shock of the Old." *NYRB* 37/12 (July 19): 46–52.
Reprinted as ch. 12 in 2000a.
     Re: Nicholas Kenyon, ed., *Authenticity and Early Music: A Symposium*
Reply from Malcolm Bilson and CR's answer, "Early Music: An Exchange." *NYRB* 37/17 (Nov. 8): 60–61.
Reply from Neal Zaslaw and CR's answer, "The Shock of the Old." *NYRB* 38/4 (Feb. 14, 1991): 50.

1991a   "Radical, Conventional Mozart." *NYRB* 38/21 (Dec. 19): 51–58.
Reprinted as ch. 7 in 2000a.
     Re: *Mozart Speaks: Views on Music, Musicians, and the World*, selected and with a commentary by Robert L. Marshall
     Ivan Nagel, *Autonomy and Mercy: Reflections on Mozart's Operas*
     Daniel Heartz, *Mozart's Operas*
CR's letter to the editor noting receipt of various corrections to 1991, *inter alia* from John Yohalem and A. D. Roberts, "Friendly Corrections." *NYRB* 39/3 (Jan. 30, 1992): 46
Leo Teitler and CR, "Radical, Conventional Mozart: An Exchange." *NYRB* 39/7 (Apr. 9, 1992): 54.

1992d   "The Mad Poets." *NYRB* 39/17 (Oct. 22): 33–39.
Reprinted as ch. 6 in 1998a.
     Re: James King and Charles Ryskamp, eds., *The Letters and Prose Writings of William Cowper*, vol. 1: *"Adelphi" and Letters 1750–1781*; vol. 2: *Letters 1782–1786*; vol. 3: *Letters 1787–1791*; vol. 4: *Letters 1792–1799*; vol. 5: *Prose 1756–c. 1799 and Cumulative Index*
     James King and Charles Ryskamp, eds., *William Cowper: Selected Letters*
     Karina Williamson, ed., *The Poetical Works of Christopher Smart*, vol. 1: *Jubilate Agno*
     Marcus Walsh and Karina Williamson, eds., *The Poetical Works of Christopher Smart*, vol. 2: *Religious Poetry*
     Marcus Walsh, ed., *The Poetical Works of Christopher Smart*, vol. 3: *A Translation of the Psalms of David*
     Karina Williamson, ed., *The Poetical Works of Christopher Smart*, vol. 4: *Miscellaneous Poems, English and Latin*

1993c   "The Ridiculous and Sublime." *NYRB* 40/8 (Apr. 22): 10–15.
     Re: *The New Grove Dictionary of Opera* edited by Stanley Sadie
     Wayne Koestenbaum, *The Queen's Throat: Opera, Homosexuality, and the Mystery of Desire*
Reply from Barry Millington and CR's answer, "Wagner's Anti-Semitism." *NYRB* 40/11 (June 10): 59–60.

1993d   "The Miraculous Mandarin." *NYRB* 40/17 (Oct. 21): 72–77.

Reprinted as ch. 9 in 1998a.
Re: John Haffenden, ed., *William Empson: Essays on Renaissance Literature*, vol. 1: *Donne and the New Philosophy*
John Haffenden, ed., *William Empson: Argufying, Essays on Literature and Culture*

1994b   "Music à la Mode." *NYRB* 41/12 (June 23): 55–62.
Reprinted as ch. 15 in 2000a.
Re: Lewis Lockwood, *Beethoven: Studies in the Creative Process*
Susan McClary, *Feminine Endings: Music, Gender and Sexuality*
Richard Leppert and Susan McClary, eds., *Music and Society: The Politics of Composition, Performance, and Reception*
Ruth A. Solie, ed., *Musicology and Difference: Gender and Sexuality in Music Scholarship*
Philip Brett, Elizabeth Wood, and Gary C. Thomas, eds., *Queering the Pitch: The New Gay and Lesbian Musicology*
James Webster, *Haydn's "Farewell" Symphony and the Idea of the Classical Style*
Elaine R. Sisman, *Haydn and the Classical Variation*
Replies from Lawrence Kramer, Warren Keith Wright, and Robert P. Morgan and CR's answer, "Music à la Mode" *NYRB* 41/15 (Sept. 22): 75–76.
Reply from Rita Steblin and CR's answer, "Schubert à la Mode." *NYRB* 41/17 (Oct. 20): 72–73.

1995c   "Beethoven's Triumph." *NYRB* 42/14 (Sept. 21): 52–56.
Re: James H. Johnson, *Listening in Paris: A Cultural History*
William Kinderman, *Beethoven*
Replies from Alfred Brendel and CR's answers, "Beethoven's Triumph." *NYRB* 42/18 (Nov. 16): 64; and "Getting Back to Life." *NYRB* 43/2 (Dec. 1): 42.

1996a   "The Scandal of the Classics." *NYRB* 43/8 (May 9): 27–31.
Re: Jean-Jacques Rousseau, *Oeuvres Complètes*, vol. 5: *Ecrits sur la musique, la langue et le théâtre*
Robert Burton, *The Anatomy of Melancholy*, vols. 1–3
Marquis de Sade, *Oeuvres*, vol. 2
Johann Wolfgang von Goethe, *Sämtliche Werke*, Band 7/I and 7/II
Bettina von Arnim, *Werke*, Band 3: *Politische Schriften*

1996b   "Did Beethoven Have All the Luck?" *NYRB*, 43/18 (Nov. 14): 57–63.
Reprinted as ch. 8 in 2000a.
Re: Tia DeNora, *Beethoven and the Construction of Genius: Musical Politics in Vienna, 1792–1803*

Tia DeNora and CR, "Beethoven's Genius: An Exchange." *NYRB* 44/6 (Apr. 10, 1997): 67.
Reply from Stephen Basson and CR's answer, "The Missing Bassoon." *NYRB* 44/7 (Apr. 24, 1997), 65.

1997a   [review of] John Rink and Jim Samson, eds., *Chopin Studies 2. Music Analysis* 16/3: 392–99.

1997b   "The Great Inventor." *NYRB* 44/15 (Oct. 9): 51–55.
       Re: Laurence Dreyfus, *Bach and the Patterns of Invention*

1997c   "The Fabulous La Fontaine," *NYRB* 44/20 (Dec. 18): 38–46.
       Re: Marc Fumaroli, *Le Poète et le Roi: Jean de La Fontaine en son siècle*
CR corrects mistake, "The Other Perrault," *NYRB* 45/3 (Feb. 19, 1998): 46.

1998d   "Variations on a Descending Theme, II: Classical Music in Twilight." *Harper's Magazine*, 296/1774 (Mar.): 42–58.
       Re: Norman Lebrecht, *Who Killed Classical Music?*
       Hilton Kramer and Roger Kimball, eds., *The Future of the European Past*
Conflated with 1998b and reprinted as ch. 18 in 2000a.

1998e   "Aimez-vous Brahms?" *NYRB* 45/16 (Oct. 22): 64–68.
Reprinted in part as ch. 11 in 2000a.
       Re: Jan Swafford, *Johannes Brahms: A Biography*;
       Johannes Brahms: Life and Letters;
       Brahms Studies 2;
       Brahms: The Four Symphonies
Jan Swafford and CR, "Aimez-vous Brahms? An Exchange." *NYRB* 46/5 (Mar. 18, 1999): 57.

1998f   [review of] Neal Zaslaw, *Mozart's Piano Concertos: Text, Context, Interpretation*. *JAMS* 51/2 (Summer): 373–84.

1999d   "Mallarmé the Magnificent." *NYRB* 46/9 (May 20), 42–46.
       Re: Stéphane Mallarmé, *Oeuvres complètes*, vol. 1, edited by Bertrand Marchal
Reply from Michael Comenetz and CR's answer, "Rhymes with 'IX'." *NYRB* 46/11 (June 24): 82.

2000e   [review of] Marshall Brown, *Turning Points: Essays in the History of Cultural Expressions. Modern Philology* 98/1 (Aug.): 97–100.

2000f   The Drama Inside the Concerto." *NYRB* 47/1 (Jan. 20): 49–52.
       Re: Joseph Kerman, *Concerto Conversations*

2000g "Fleeting moments," *TLS* (Feb. 18): 27
Re: J. A. Hiddleston, *Baudelaire and the Art of Memory*

2000h "Scenes from the American Dream." *NYRB* 47/13 (Aug. 10): 16–20.
Re: *Norman Rockwell: Pictures for the American People 17–September 24, 2000*, an exhibition at the Corcoran Gallery of Art, Washington, D.C., catalogue of the exhibition edited by Maureen Hart Hennessey and Anne Knutson

2001a "Within a Budding Grove." *NYRB* 48/10 (June 21), 29–32.
Re*: The New Grove Dictionary of Music and Musicians*, 2nd ed., edited by Stanley Sadie
Reply from Ralph Locke and CR's reply, "Multicultural Correctness." *NYRB* 50/1 (Jan. 16, 2003): 60–61.

2001b "Seeing the Stars Again." *TLS* (Nov. 23): 3–4
Re: *The New Grove Dictionary of Music and Musicians*, 29 vols., 2nd ed., edited by Stanley Sadie

2002c "Real Affinities." *TLS* 5155 (Jan. 18): 25–26.
Re: Donald Francis Tovey, *Classics of Music: Talks, Essays and Other Writings*

2002d "Steak and Potatoes." *NYRB* 49/4 (June 21): 19–20.
Reprinted as introduction to 2002a.

2002e "Should We Adore Adorno?" *NYRB* 49/16 (Oct. 24): 59–66.
Re*: Theodor W. Adorno, *Philosophy of Modern Music*, translated by Anne G. Mitchell and Wesley V. Blomster
Theodor W. Adorno, *Essays on Music*, selected and with an introduction, commentary, and notes by Richard Leppert, and new translations by Susan H. Gillespie
Theodor W. Adorno, *Beethoven: The Philosophy of Music*, edited by Rolf Tiedemann, translated by Edmond Jephcott
Replies from Thomas Baumeister, Larson Powell and CR's answer, "Adoring Adorno." *NYRB* 50/2 (Feb. 13, 2003): 49–50.

2004a "Prodigy without Peer: A Composer Who Fell from Grace by Sticking to the World of Ease." *TLS* 5268 (Mar. 19): 3–4.
Re: R. Larry Todd, *Mendelssohn: A Life in Music*

2005a "Red-Hot MoMA." *NYRB* 52/1 (Jan. 13): 18–21.
Re: Yoshio Taniguchi, architect, Museum of Modern Art, New York
John Elderfield, ed., *Modern Painting and Sculpture: 1880 to the Present at the Museum of Modern Art*

2005b   "The Anatomy Lesson." *NYRB* 52/10 (June 9): 55–59.
         Re: Robert Burton, *The Anatomy of Melancholy*, with introduction by William Gass
         Robert Burton, *The Anatomy of Melancholy*, text in three volumes edited by Thomas C. Faulkner, Nicolas K. Kiessling, and Rhonda L. Blair, with an introduction by J. B. Bamborough; commentary in three vols. edited by J. B. Bamborough and Martin Dodsworth

2005c   "Playing Music: The Lost Freedom." *NYRB* 52/17 (Nov. 3): 47–50.
         Re: Robert Philip, *Performing Music in the Age of Recording*

2006b   "From the Troubadours to Frank Sinatra," part I. *NYRB* 53/3 (Feb. 23): 41–45; part II. *NYRB* 53/4 (Mar. 9): 44–48.
         Re: Richard Taruskin, *The Oxford History of Western Music*

2006c   "Paul Henry Láng—Reply." *NYRB* 53/5 (Mar. 23): 45.

2006d   "Mozart at 250." *NYRB* 53/9 (May 25): 20–23.
         Re: Julian Rushton, *Mozart*
         David Cairns, *Mozart and His Operas*
         The Cambridge Mozart Encyclopedia edited by Cliff Eisen and Simon P. Keefe
         Nicholas Kenyon, *The Faber Pocket Guide to Mozart*

2006e   "Opera: Follow the Music." *NYRB* 53/15 (Oct. 5): 36–38.
         Re: Philip Gossett, *Divas and Scholars: Performing Italian Opera*

2007a   "The Best Book on Mozart." *NYRB* 54/16 (Oct. 25): 25–27.
         RE: Hermann Abert, *W.A. Mozart*, edited by Cliff Eisen, translated by Stewart Spencer.

2007b   "What Mozart Meant: An Exchange." *NYRB* 54/19 (Dec. 6): 76–77.
         Robert L. Marshall and CR re 2007a.

2008   "The Genius of Montaigne." *NYRB* 55/2 (Feb. 14): 48–53.
         Re: *Les Essais de Michel de Montaigne* edited by Jean Balsamo, Michel Magnien, and Catherine Magnin Simon.

Contributors

PIERRE BOULEZ has been a leading figure in musical modernism for over sixty years. Internationally acclaimed as a pioneering composer, conductor, and writer, he helped found the Institut de Recherche et Coordination Acoustique/ Musiqe (IRCAM).

SCOTT BURNHAM, Chair and Professor of Music at Princeton University, is an authority on the history of tonal theory, problems of analysis and criticism, and eighteenth- and nineteenth-century music and culture. He is the author of *Beethoven Hero* (1995). His recent projects include essays on Haydn, Mozart, Schubert, and Schumann.

ELLIOTT CARTER, one of America's preeminent composers, is noted for the aesthetic integrity, drama, and intellectual rigor of his work, particularly with respect to the organization of rhythm and musical time.

ROBERT CURRY is an Australian musicologist and pianist. A medievalist, he has focused his research on eastern and central Europe and the musicoliturgical traditions of women's religious orders. He is currently Principal of the Conservatorium High School and Honorary Senior Lecturer at the Centre for Medieval Studies, University of Sydney. He is the author of *Ars antiqua Fragments and the Evolution of the Clarist Order in East Central Europe* (Krakow, forthcoming).

WALTER FRISCH is the H. Harold Gumm/Harry and Albert von Tilzer Professor of Music at Columbia University, where he has taught since 1982. He has published widely on Austro-German music of the nineteenth and twentieth centuries, including Schubert, Brahms, and Schoenberg, and on the topic of modernism.

DAVID GABLE is Professor of Music at Clark Atlanta University. He is the author of articles on the music of Giuseppe Verdi and Pierre Boulez and the coeditor of *A Life for New Music: Selected Papers of Paul Fromm; Fromm Music Foundation 1952–1987* (with Christoph Wolff, 1989) and *Alban Berg: Historical and Analytical Perspectives* (with Robert P. Morgan, 1991).

PHILIP GOSSETT, the Robert W. Reneker Distinguished Service Professor at the University of Chicago, is general editor of *The Works of Giuseppe Verdi* (The University of Chicago Press and Casa Ricordi) and *Works of Gioachino Rossini* (Bärenreiter-Verlag). His *Divas and Scholars: Performing Italian Opera* was published in 2006 by the University of Chicago Press.

JEFFREY KALLBERG is Professor of Music at the University of Pennsylvania. He has written extensively on the music and cultural contexts of Chopin.

JOSEPH KERMAN has written several times about Charles Rosen's work in the *New York Review of Books*. He has recently published on Bach and the fugue: several essays on single fugues, and *The Art of Fugue: Bach Fugues for Keyboard, 1715–1750* (University of California Press, 2003; paperback 2008).

RICHARD KRAMER, Distinguished Professor at the Graduate Center of the City University of New York, is the author of *Distant Cycles: Schubert and the Conceiving of Song* (1994), *Unfinished Music* (2008), and essays on the work of C. P. E. Bach, Mozart, Beethoven, and Schubert. Kramer is a Fellow of the American Academy of Arts and Sciences.

WILLIAM KINDERMAN has written many studies of music from Mozart to Mahler, including several books on Beethoven. As a pianist he has recorded Beethoven's last sonatas and the "Diabelli" Variations. He is Professor of Music at the University of Illinois at Urbana-Champaign.

LEWIS LOCKWOOD, the Fanny Peabody Research Professor of Music at Harvard University, has written extensively on Renaissance music and on Beethoven. His *Beethoven: The Music and the Life* (2003) was a finalist for the Pulitzer Prize in biography. He has recently published a book on selected Beethoven quartets coauthored by the Juilliard String Quartet (Harvard University Press, 2008).

SIR CHARLES MACKERRAS, a noted Australian conductor and the director of the English National Opera, is acclaimed above all for his interpretations of Mozart, Janáček, and Gilbert and Sullivan. He is currently Principal Guest Conductor of the Czech Philharmonic and Conductor Laureate of the Scottish Chamber Orchestra.

ROBERT L. MARSHALL, Sachar Professor of Music Emeritus at Brandeis University, is the author of *The Compositional Process of J. S. Bach* (1972) and *The Music of Johann Sebastian Bach: The Sources, the Style, the Significance* (1989). His *Mozart Speaks: Views on Music, Musicians, and the World* (1991) was described by the dedicatee of this volume as "one of the few useful contributions to the Mozart bicentenary."

ROBERT P. MORGAN, Professor of Music Emeritus at Yale University, is currently completing a book on the development of Heinrich Schenker and the relationship between his theoretical and aesthetic beliefs.

CHARLES ROSEN has a PhD from Princeton University (1951) in Romance languages.

JULIAN RUSHTON, Professor Emeritus at the University of Leeds, has published mainly on Gluck, Mozart, Berlioz, and Elgar. He is the author of the Mozart entries for *The New Grove Dictionary of Opera*. His *Mozart: An Extraordinary Life,* appeared in 2005, and he published a volume on Mozart for the well-known *The Master Musicians* series in 2006. He was president of the Royal Musical Association, 1994–99, and has been chairman of the editorial committee of *Musica Britannica* since 1993.

DAVID SCHULENBERG, a music historian and performer on historical keyboard instruments, is Professor and Chair of the Music Department at Wagner College (Staten Island, New York). His publications include *The Keyboard Music of J. S. Bach* and *Music of the Baroque*, critical editions of sonatas and concertos by C. P. E. Bach, and recordings (with the Baroque flutist Mary Oleskiewicz) of chamber music by Quantz.

LÁSZLÓ SOMFAI is Professor Emeritus at the Liszt Academy of Music in Budapest and the former director (1972–2005) of the Bartók Archives of the Hungarian Academy of Sciences. His books include *Joseph Haydn's Keyboard Sonatas* (1995) and *Béla Bartók: Composition, Concepts, and Autograph Sources* (1996). He is the editor in chief of the forthcoming *Béla Bartók Complete Critical Edition* and is currently working on the Bartók thematic catalogue.

LEO TREITLER is Distinguished Professor of Music Emeritus at the Graduate Center of the City University of New York. He is working on a book provisionally entitled *Speaking of Music.*

JAMES WEBSTER is the Goldwin Smith Professor of Music at Cornell University. He is the author of *Haydn's "Farewell" Symphony and the Idea of Classical Style* (Cambridge, 1991) and the Haydn article in the revised edition of the *New Grove Dictionary of Music and Musicians.* He has published widely on all aspects of Haydn's music, as well as Mozart's operas, Beethoven, Schubert, Brahms, analysis, editorial and performance practice, and the historiography of music.

ROBERT WINTER holds the Presidential Chair in Music and Interactive Arts at UCLA. He was a coauthor (with Douglas Johnson and Alan Tyson) of the award-winning *The Beethoven Sketchbooks: History and Reconstruction* (1985). Since that time his seven multimedia titles on a wide range of topics have pioneered in the application of digital media to research and teaching about music.

Index

Compiled by Kevin A. Byrnes

Page numbers displayed in bold type include musical examples.

Eastman Studies in Music

Charles Rosen, the pianist and man of letters, is perhaps the single most influential writer on music of the past half-century. While Rosen's vast range as a writer and performer is encyclopedic, it has focused particularly on the living "canonical" repertory extending from Bach to Boulez. Inspired in its liveliness and variety of critical approaches by Charles Rosen's challenging work, *Variations on the Canon* offers original essays by some of the world's most eminent musical scholars. Contributors address such issues as style and compositional technique, genre, influence and modeling, and reception history; develop insights afforded by close examination of compositional sketches; and consider what language and metaphors might most meaningfully convey insights into music. However diverse the modes of inquiry, each essay sheds new light on the works of those composers posterity has deemed central to the modern Western musical tradition.

Contributors: Pierre Boulez, Scott Burnham, Elliott Carter, Robert Curry, Walter Frisch, David Gable, Philip Gossett, Jeffrey Kallberg, Joseph Kerman, Richard Kramer, William Kinderman, Lewis Lockwood, Sir Charles Mackerras, Robert L. Marshall, Robert P. Morgan, Charles Rosen, Julian Rushton, David Schulenberg, László Somfai, Leo Treitler, James Webster, and Robert Winter.

Robert Curry is Principal of the Conservatorium High School and Honorary Senior Lecturer in the Centre for Medieval Studies, University of Sydney. David Gable is Professor of Music at Clark Atlanta University. Robert L. Marshall is Louis, Frances, and Jeffrey Sachar Professor Emeritus of Music at Brandeis University.

"*Variations on the Canon* is written in honor of Charles Rosen, whose life—as pianist, writer, critic, music historian—has been devoted to the furtherance and appreciation of music. In Mozart's time, such achievement might have been marked by an instrumental serenade, including an assembly of musicians, a grand walk, a performance in the open air or in an auditorium. Nowadays we celebrate with words and music—or with words about music. *Variations on the Canon* is one of the great collections of musical essays, bringing together a brilliant phalanx of contributors offering their best work in as fine a collection of writings on music as has been created in our time."

—Maynard Solomon, author of *Mozart: A Life,* and
Late Beethoven: Music, Thought, Imagination

"It is hard to imagine a more vivid testimony to the far-reaching and enduring impact of Charles Rosen's musical thoughts, words, and deeds over the last half century than the extraordinary line-up of scholars assembled in these pages. The copious new insights these essays offer shows how much we can learn through encounters with Rosen's provocative, inspiring, and energizing writings and performances, all usefully cataloged in the extensive discography and bibliography."

—Joseph Auner, Tufts University, author of
A Schoenberg Reader: Documents of a Life